# TANGIBLE ANGELS

For Michelle
Always

# Contents

# PART 1

# TAKE
# EVERYTHING

# A Common Disaster

When Jeannie Ivory first come to work for me, I took her interpersonal skills as just another layer of make-up, like *Bruised Passion Fruit* or *Glitter of Ashes*. But no. The more time I spent in her company, the more you could drive a big rig through the gap in that girl's soul. We are all damaged goods, let me be quick to admit. I don't mean to call her evil. I truly never thought of her that way for more than a minute at a time. More like, they ever come to Keening looking to shoot a remake of Zombie the Thirteenth and needed to cast a few extras? I'd have made damn sure she got to the auditions.

Her eye color, just as a for-instance. You know how a fountain Coke looks after somebody's sucked most of it down with a straw? Brown, but an icy brown. Now, picture the cup tossed out by the side of the highway and you got the way she moved, the way she talked, the way she rung up an order or did most anything—neither fast nor slow but just whichever speed and direction the wind happened to pick her up that day. She was as apt to show up for work in a leotard and tutu as fishnets, gym shorts, and a motorcycle jacket with a unicorn patch, but whatever else she wore, she come ready for combat. Same pair of beat up jump boots day-in, day-out.

Way too much like I was at her age. Like a lot of kids, you could say. Only not really.

You might not know me, do you? My name is Vanessa Cavendish. I own and operate what begun as a nursery-turned-tourist attraction out south of town. Tangible Angels, if that rings a bell? I used to call it Repurpose Farm. I probably should've gone with my gut and named it Recluse Farm, but my luck, it might've only compounded the mystique of it all and give me what they call a paradoxical result. I built my house, my shop with the attached greenhouse, and most of my outbuildings out of cob and straw bale and whatever else I could lay my hands on because that's what I could afford at the time. Nowadays folks show up by the bus load, Sundays included, and as flabbergasted as I am by it all I do not have the heart to turn them away.

One thing else real quick before we get started: I like big words and I

2

keep a ten gauge close to hand. I shoot from the hip and I write the way a certain blind friend of mine plays piano: partly by ear and the rest by heart. So don't even think about correcting my grammar.

Did I say that with enough sugar on it?

Business slowed down some when I took Jeannie on and put her in charge of customer relations. That's what we called standing behind the register, chewing the yarn ends of a pair of fingerless gloves and staring at people with eel-like affection until they either bought something or didn't and got the hell out of Dodge. She didn't say boo to nobody that didn't speak to her first, and I had to teach myself to stop coming to the rescue when they did.

One time she asked me — right to the face of a woman I thought was showing genuine interest in one of my welded cutlery wind chimes — she said, "Why are you being so nice to her, Vanessa? She's not buying, she's just waiting to take a shit."

The woman turned her walker right around and hauled ass back out to her son-in-law's RV in the parking lot. It took her three tries to slam the door behind her.

I turned to Jeannie. I said, "You're not right."

She'd already gone back to reading her paperback. *The Sunlight Dialogues*, said the cover. "I decommissioned my sense of compassion a long time ago, Ms. Cavendish." She flipped a page.

"Jeannie," I contradicted her, "a short time ago, you weren't born yet. How'd you get so jaded so quick?"

"You should probably fire me."

I lost track of how many times she told me the same thing. "You ought to fire me. I have no qualifications, I don't particularly give a shit, and I'm certainly not good for business."

I couldn't argue, but nor did I get a lot of Rhodes scholars applying for part-time. At least with her around I managed to get a few things done in the greenhouse. Plus, the one thing I could say about Jeannie Ivory, she was reliable. ("That," she told me when I tried to pay her the compliment, "is because I have no life.") She rode her bike out every day in the beginning, rain or shine. My odometer tells me it's seven miles to the Keening City Limits and another two point four to the door of her mother's house on Fair Meadow Lane, the time or two she let me

3

throw her child-size Schwinn in the back of my pickup truck and drive her. One of those times, the rain blew so hard it felt and sounded like machine-gun fire against my side of the cab, while the passenger-side window stayed bone dry. I stopped under the Highway 60 overpass and waited out the worst of the hail.

"I might not have made it home in this weather," she admitted.

"You think?"

She peeled her sleeve back and picked at a scab on the inside of her wrist. When she caught me looking, she quick, pulled her long sleeve back down over the cuff of the glove. This was August, in Oklahoma, where the wind comes right out of a blast furnace.

"You never do take those things off, do you?" I said. "Is that why?"

"What?"

"Your gloves."

She didn't answer.

"You use a razor blade or what?"

She creased her brow and folded her arms with both of her hands shoved up deep in her armpits.

"I been there," I confided. "Done the same damn thing."

"So I've noticed."

If you know how to look, if you get the angle of the light just right, you can still make out a scar like a drunk snail left his sheen up the inside of my forearm. I have considered getting a tattoo, but who knows if it'd do much to disguise my history. Might make matters worse.

"You did it the right way," she said.

That struck me funny. "Oh? Like there's a right way and a wrong way!"

"The more proficient way, if you prefer. You meant it. I don't."

"I meant something different, maybe, from what you mean."

She wagged her head, tucked the corner of her lips inside her mouth. "I don't *mean* anything."

We had time to kill. The storm showed no sign of letting up, so I cut the engine and kicked off my right sandal, pulled that foot up on the seat between us and leaned against my door so I could look at the side of her face. She had fine, dark hair, lately faded from the blue-black shimmer of a crow's wing, the kind of hair that likes to lay close to the scalp. It flowed in front and back of an ear that stuck straight out from her head, small and frail as a fairy's wing. "Blue's almost gone," I said.

4

"We could color it again, if you want."

She flinched ever so slightly, then she rolled her eyes. "Why are you being so nice to me? I'm not a good person, Ms. Cavendish. I don't exactly invite human kindness. You ought to have realized that by now."

"That don't give you the right to stop me from being human. Or offering kindness when I feel like it."

I took her sigh for a lack of argument.

"We could pick any color you choose. I like the blue — I do — but maybe you're tired of it and want to go — I don't know, magenta or something. Or is that too overdone?"

"Actually," she furrowed her brow, kept her lap in focus. "I was thinking I might want to try white. Like an albino."

"Ooh!" I wondered if they made pink contacts. I had to check my enthusiasm, though. I didn't know how she'd take it if I was to come out with something like that.

She slid her eyes in my direction. "Do you think it would look stupid?"

I laughed. "You're asking the wrong person. Most people around here think pretty much everything I do looks stupid."

"Maybe that's why I asked you. Maybe I don't want to do it if it doesn't look stupid."

"Thanks a lot!" I gave her a slap on the shoulder. "I know what you mean, though." (Actually, I didn't. Did stupid mean the same as dope?)

"Well, Ms. Cavendish, you are an artist. That makes it different."

I had to think about that one. *Artist* is one of those words, like *genius* or *special*. It might sound one way if I said it about myself and altogether different if somebody else said it to me. Or about me. When I tried to explain that to her, she just wagged her head, like you do with someone you give up on.

"It wasn't intended as an insult."

"I didn't say it was."

She considered that. "Okay. But it might have been, depending on your interpretation."

"Name one thing that couldn't."

She took her sweet time. I could almost hear her mentally flipping backwards and forwards through the pages of the dictionary:

> television
> incense

yellow
courageous
macadamia
elopement

"Good point," she said finally, and in the instant she said it, I fell in love with her.

Yes, I said that. And I do not use the term lightly.

And I certainly don't use it to mean the first thing that comes to mind. Let's get clear about that, because I do have a reputation and I have been accused of corrupting an impressionable, wayward young girl. Or her, me, depending on how you look at it. Not that either she or I could give a rat's ass. She was old enough to consent, and I'm not in the nursing home yet, but — and I want you to get this, because — that is not the way this particular story goes. Sorry to disappoint you, but if your mind's already in the toilet, you can just flush it. I like men, and I can vouch for Jeannie Ivory; she does, too.

Here's what I'm saying:

I felt validated in a way I hadn't in a good long while because I knew, young as she was, that she had taken the time to think through what I said, not just rubber stamp it with the Good Housekeeping Seal of What Folks Think Other Folks Will Approve Or at Least Not Say Is Retarded. What she give me back was her own quick recognition of an idea subjected to a swift and rigorous calculation that come up, for her at least, in the affirmative.

"Yes," she said, still testing it. "Anything."

"It's just a matter of who you are when you say it, and where your head is."

She smirked. Or maybe just grinned. "You may have discovered the cure for irony."

"See? Now, I might could take that as an insult."

She looked at me for the first time ever in a way that allowed me to see the true color of her eyes — as warm and timid as two field mice, with centers softer and darker than the beat of a screech owl's wing at midnight.

The hailstorm rattled out a final flourish along the wet-dry border of the asphalt and headed off across Keening Canyon, towing its cloud-shadow behind it. I turned the key and stepped on the starter button, pulled the stick into first, let out the clutch, and off we sailed — me with one foot bare and my sense of optimism restored to working condition, while Jeannie slumped in the seat with her combat boots propped on Jiminy's dashboard. Jiminy Cricket, by the way, that's the name I give my mid-century two-toned, rust-and-primer GMC pickup truck. If Jiminy had a radio that worked half the time, not a doubt in my mind, Cowboy Junkies would've serenaded us the rest of the way with that song of theirs. You know the one I mean?

# NAKED AS A PORCUPINE

Come Monday when she showed up for work again, she had the color stripped out of her hair. I don't mean she went platinum. Not even bleach-blonde. We're talking the color of splintered bone, her entire head frayed out like one big nerve-ending. She kept her usual eggplant eye-shadow and wore her lips chapped and frosted like the way you can antique-finish a chair with that crackle glaze.

I said, "You don't hold back, do you?"

She rewarded me with maybe a millimeter's worth of a smile. Just a quick crease in the dimple at the corner of her mouth. Blink and you missed it.

Something about the dye job, or maybe it was the way she dressed that day, in jeans stitched so tight to her skin they looked to be the work of a tattoo artist. Or scrimshaw is more like it. Her tank top left nothing to guess-work, either, from her collar bones down to the precise number of her ribs. I thought, Girl, I could play you like a marimba, but I didn't say that because I couldn't make it come out sounding the right way in my head. It made her seem tough, though, that look. And at the same time, frail. Like if you brushed too hard against her, something—a leg or, if you were lucky, just a finger—might snap off. Or else just disintegrate, sift to the floor in a fine dust. And like, if it did, she wouldn't give two shits about it. She'd still just as soon bite your head off as catch you staring.

She kept a pair of fingerless gloves on all day, as usual. We didn't talk any more about her razor tricks. I had the very clear sense that topic was off-limits unless she brought it up. Which she didn't.

"Business slows down in the wintertime, I presume?" That was the way she talked sometimes, like she had an English degree stuck up her ass, though she was barely out of high school.

"Not till after Christmas. People like their poinsettias." I worked the soil around the trunk of a potted fig tree to aerate it. "Why?"

"Nothing. I was just wondering if I need to look for another job."

"Not if I have anything to say about it."

She give me a nod, once, as if that cleared the matter up sufficiently for her liking.

8

I'll never know for sure, but let me hazard a guess. She got her hair done in the city that weekend just the way she wanted it. Not because I might screw it up (always a possibility) but because there was maybe something too intimate in the idea of her boss washing and dyeing and rinsing her hair. I get that, but it wasn't anything I could ask her about. She had already opened up about as much as she was liable to that day under the underpass. Now it seemed like she was either testing how anorexic sexy can get or vice versa.

To me she looked every bit as naked as a porcupine.

Things went on that way for the rest of the year. By virtue of working side by side day after day, we developed an understanding of one another's rhythm and blues, I like to call it, but not until after Christmas and before Easter, when business dwindled to a trickle and we could get some work done — not until that dead time of the year — did I discover just how deep the troubled waters in her run.

I will tell you this: I was not prepared. Not for that winter and not for what it brought out in her.

Along about February is typically when Spider McCormick, photographer in town who handles freelance work for *The Highlander Pride*, will run out of material and come sniffing around my greenhouse to shoot some local color. He always brings two or three students with him, usually just a boy and a girl for a tender memory photo spread to contrast with the carnage of the football stadium. If you're not from here, "Highlanders" is the nickname or mascot or what-have-you of Keening High School, and *The Pride* is their senior yearbook. Spider's served as an adjunct fixture for the school system since before I dropped out of eighth grade, which, we're talking more decades ago than we need to get into right here, right now. He gets his name from the little pooch of a middle he's got, about the size of a bowling ball, and the reach and angularity of his limbs. He does not, to my knowledge, shoot cables of silk from his wrist-veins, but I have seen him climb vertical walls with no discernible hand- or foothold and dangle from the scaffolding at a construction site by two fingers and a prayer, with his sockless ankle hooked around a pipe to stabilize his camera hand. I would be remiss in my description if I failed to mention, one, that his wife died young and, two, that Spider had the shiniest, blackest skin in Keening County. So you can work out for yourself what kind of spider they called him and why he always brought at least one male student along on his photo-excursions—two if the first one had any thickness to his lips or too broad a nose or went by the name of Jamal or Porter or even Ortiz.

That particular year, he brought two girls along to pose with my hot-house flowers—both of them with faces and minds as pure as marshmallow—and a smallish, polished-looking boy I half-recognized.

"Hey, Spider," I said. "Who's this you got with you today?"

"We have here Ms. Patricia Andrews and Ms. Angela Dunhof."

The taller of the two blonde girls revealed a stunning array of hardware when she smiled. More than most satellites deploy. "I love your shop!" she gleamed.

I told her she hadn't seen anything yet. I wasn't bragging; she just hadn't bothered to look around before she gushed, so she must have been coached to play up to me.

Ms. Patricia Andrews, a shorter, more robust version of blonde-headedness, strode up to me and stuck out her hand at an unusual angle. I shook it and we smiled at one another. She didn't have much else to add.

The whole time they stayed, neither one of them wandered very far from the boy.

"I'm Eugene Lamb," he informed me.

I'd been trying to come up with his name. "I seem to remember you from somewhere," I said. "Or you remind me from someone on TV."

"Do you watch Two Point Perspective?" the taller girl asked me, the one with braces.

I didn't think I had ever seen that program. "No. No," I said to the boy. "If you're who I think you are, you were just about this high." I put my hand out flat, estimating.

"Oh. Yeah, my folks had a show."

"All about home-schooling, wasn't it?"

"School at Home with Gay and Todd." He also had a full set of braces, though they made less of an impact than Angela's. What you noticed more was the Buddy Holly eye wear and that stylish kind of bedhead that kids do. He kept his hands in the pockets of his letter jacket. *KHS.*

"They must've had a change of heart."

"My dad decided to run for School Board and work to change things from within the system."

"I see."

10

I turned to introduce my assistant, Jeannie Ivory, but she must have slipped out, either the back way or through the door to the greenhouse. Her winter jacket was still on the hook.

"Tulips are looking good," I told Spider. "Lots of color. You have anything in mind you want to see?"

"Nothing in particular, Ms. Cavendish. I always know I'll find something pleasing to the eye when I come out here." He was like that, always playing it down the middle. He might not have been flirting with me, but in such a way that I couldn't outright accuse him of it.

So I said, just to throw him off guard, "You know your way around my place by now, Spider? Cause if you do, you can have at it."

He didn't bite.

Jeannie and I each had a cup of tea going by the wood stove. Hers was getting cold. Several years back, I raised an entire field of Echinacea across the road, which, it was kind of a fad for a while. That's a relative of the daisy family called a purple coneflower. The petals look to be blown straight back from the center so they bring to mind a badminton birdie in flight. What makes me think of that now is, Spider was the first to point it out to me. Only, the way he put it, he called it a gamecock.

He has got a face as straight as a Kansas blacktop, that man, so I dropped his serve. Seems I been trying to pick it up and bat it back to him ever since, to no avail.

Where was I?

Nice thing about Echinacea is what you grow that don't sell, you can dry it out and grind it up for tea. It don't fly off the shelves like it once did, but I get a few die-hards that still come looking for it during flu season. I got to be honest, it don't do a damn thing for a cold, but if you take it with local honey, it's supposed to help with allergies and headaches and like that.

The wood stove was burning low, so I went out back to bring in an armload of firewood, and there sat Jeannie under the shed in her shirt-sleeves, hunched against the wind, smoking a butt. I never rode her about smoking. It didn't exactly mesh with the whole earthy-crunchy vibe Repurpose Farm supposedly embraced, but she said, "I don't inflict my second-hand smoke on anyone," and that was good enough for me.

I said, "Grab a couple logs when you come back in," and stooped to

11

pick up a few myself.

"After they go, I will."

I straightened and looked at her. Her roots had grown back in by this time, color of wet chestnut. The way the wind caught, they stood out around her head like dark blazes, her eyes two pits of cold iron. I had no idea what I might have said or done or if it was me or Spider or what. "They're gonna be here most of the afternoon."

I saw the panic hit like a clanger in a bell. "No way!"

"I'm afraid so. You know who Spider is, don't you?"

She looked away, biting her lip and shivering. "Yeah."

"He comes out once a year to do a shoot for the yearbook."

"And it takes all day?"

"Depends," I said. "But yeah." I hoped so.

"I gotta go."

"Where? Home?"

"I'm sorry, Ms. Cavendish."

I wouldn't let her pedal her bicycle out here in the wintertime, and I couldn't pay her enough that she could afford to buy a car, so on a day that she couldn't find a ride—which wasn't that often—she didn't work. On days when she did work, I drove her home. That way, if I had any errands in town, I could run them at the end of the day. The situation was far from ideal, but that was how we worked it out. She knew I couldn't take off in the middle of the day.

"I can't take you," I said. "Not now."

Her smoke stammered and shifted on the cold wind. "I'll walk."

"You out of your mind?"

She pulled on her cigarette so hard it glowed like a warning sign, then threw it down and ground it out. "I might be." The words trickled out of her in a thin stream, the way we used to talk back in the day when we were holding a toke.

I looked at her. "Something ain't right. You want to tell me what it is?"

She expelled the last of her smoke in one long blast. "Nope."

I hated to ask it. It just seemed to feed the wrong line of reasoning, a way of looking at things that I resisted on principle. But what was I supposed to do? Let something go because I didn't want to be proven wrong about a person? I had to ask. "Have you had some kind of problem with him before?"

12

I meant Spider.

I watched her clench her jaw. Her whole face seemed to close up. Darts appeared between her brows and around her mouth like maybe she'd cinched her panties too tight. She had never said anything that struck me as remotely racist, but you grow up south of the Mason-Dixon, you catch on pretty quick that camouflage is more than a fashion statement, it is also a sly form of preaching to the choir.

"You can tell me," I said.

Her head vibrated. The wind pushed her hair across her face like a ghost-white veil. I reached to pull it back from her cheek in order to see her better, but she turned her head away and hitched one shoulder to ward against me. When my fingers didn't stop, she grabbed me by the wrist and stopped them for me. "Don't!" she said.

"All right," I decided. "I'm gonna get you your jacket, at least, and you can sit out here and freeze your ass off if you want to or you can tell me what the problem is, and if it's Spider, I'll tell him he don't need to be here."

She looked at the ground and refused to say anything, so I went and got her jacket and brought it to her. I picked up a few extra logs and asked her to stack another one on top of what I had. She didn't say boo or howdy or thank you until I turned to go back in. Then she said, "Vanessa?"

I think that might have been the first time she ever called me by my first name. I turned and looked at her, and something about the sound of my name and the way the wind tickled my hair across my face made me feel ghostly, too. I waited.

"It's not Spider."

"Okay..."

When she didn't say anything else, I said, "That's a relief," and I turned around again.

Soon as I had my back to her, she said, "It's Eugene."

This time, I didn't turn to look at her, in case she had more to say. She didn't, so I said, "Don't go anywhere. I'll be right back."

I dropped the wood in the cradle by the stove and dug in my pocket for my keys. I keep the house locked up even when I'm on the premises, because you would not believe how often I get people thinking it's no problem whatsoever to just go traipsing through my living room without an invitation, because it's "so unique!" My house, I think I

13

told you, is built of cob. That's mud, in plain English. I've got a book in mind all about how it got built, but I haven't written it yet. I'm not sure I want to draw more attention to where and how I live.

When I give Jeannie the keys and told her to take some wood and go get a fire started in the rocket stove in the house, she tried to pretend she hadn't been crying. The day had turned bitter cold, though. The wind by itself can cause your eyes to tear up and give you the sniffles. She said, "Thank you."

And I said, "We're gonna talk, Jeannie, in a little while. But I need to know right now what he did to you."

"Nothing."

"Has he ever touched you…" I rummaged through my old support-group vocabulary for the right turn of phrase, but all I could come up with was, "…you know? Inappropriately?"

She wiped her cheeks with the backs of her gloves. They were wearing out, unraveling around her knuckles. "He sucks the life out of me, if you want the truth."

Whatever that meant. I decided not to pursue it. "You know where everything is. Make yourself comfortable. They might be a while."

If she'd just given me something to go on, I might could've taken Spider aside and said God-knows-what, but for all I knew, Jeannie just had a crush on the Lamb boy and was too shy to admit it or to know how to act around him. Maybe she felt on the outs, seeing him on a field trip with those other two in constant orbit around him. Or it might have been something worse. He might have verbally abused her at some point. Or physically. Or you name it.

Or nothing whatsoever. Maybe he talked too much to suit her. *Sucks the life out of me.*

Whatever.

Spider McCormick had always treated me right. If I'd asked him to leave and come back later, without that particular boy in tow, I believe he would've done it for me. But I had no leg to stand on. Part of what I got out of his annual visit to Repurpose Farm was a selection of photographs I could use any way I wanted. One of them always ended up in the yearbook for free, anyway, plus I always bought advertising space in the back, because I didn't have to pay to use his photos, and *The Pride* always brought in a little extra come prom season and then graduation. I couldn't afford to be rude if I didn't have to.

14

I don't relish the thought, but I do have to tell you one thing. When, for just a split second, I thought it was Spider that made her so uncomfortable, like he'd flirted with her? Or worse, like something had actually passed between the two of them? I wanted to smack her. And I don't mean to wake her up, either. I mean, I wanted to rip the tight, young skin off her face. That scrawny, haughty, seductive, I-know-you-want-to-hurt-me look.

As it turned out, they didn't stay long.

"You get some nice shots, Spider?"

"Oh, yes, Ms. Cavendish! Some beauties!" He scrolled back through them on his camera, some with and some without his young models. "I'll get the best ones printed out, so you can see them blown up. I think you'll be very pleased with what I got to show you!"

They were halfway out the door when Eugene said. "This is a fascinating place, Miss Cavendish. All the different stuff you do! I'm in the Journalism Club at school and I— "

"He's the President," the tall girl interrupted. Angela. She beamed her signals at him.

Eugene showed just the right smidgen of embarrassment. "I'd like to do a story about Recluse Farm. It could go in the issue of *The Swirl* that comes out right before the prom."

"It goes online, too," Angela put in. "It's like a blog this year and everything. Eugene set it up on Typepad."

"No kidding?" I said. I had not a clue what she was talking about.

"I'd like to come out another time—at your convenience—and do an interview with you."

"Let me think about that. How can I get in touch with you?" I was already thinking I might schedule it for a day when I didn't need Jeannie to work in the morning, so she wouldn't freak out. Assuming the problem was all in her head, naturally.

Eugene patted his jacket pocket and come up with a pen. I handed him a notepad, and he wrote down his name and number. "Call me anytime," he said. "I took one of your cards. I'll email you with a link to the blog."

I studied him. He returned my gaze, direct and confident, his lips stretched across his braces in a grin that reassured me. "It'll be great press."

I wrinkled my nose at Spider. "Where'd you find this one?"

"Oh, he's a mover and a shaker, all right. What he hasn't told you is, half the time his stories get picked up by *The Klarion*, too. Heck, he gets me business!" *The Keening Klarion*, he was talking about. Local paper. I advertised there, too. *The Pictish Swirl*, that Eugene had mentioned, was the student paper for Keening High. You grow up around here, it's second nature to know this stuff.

"All right, Eugene." I stuffed his number in my pocket. "You send me that email, and we'll see about getting together."

Eugene back-pumped his fist at his hip to show me he considered me a score, and they all took off together, his dark head flanked by the two blondes, one a little higher than his, one a little lower. In the back of my mind, I wondered, *Sucks the life out of you, huh?* Because me, I felt pretty inflated.

"We need to talk, Jeannie," I said, busting through the front door with my mouth already running. "No, I take that back. You need to talk. Last thing on earth I need is to come across as some kind of hard-ass boss to you, but I do have a business to run, and if you're the one that's gonna be helping me out around here, I need to know I can rely on you to ke—"

She sat in my old rocking chair, one of the ones my grandma left me, her feet planted on the floor, wearing nothing but her jeans, a wife-beater and a set of goose-bumps, shivering and clutching her arms across her chest with one palm facing up and her face turned away.

"To what?" she said.

I held my breath, my train of thought derailed by a trickle of blood down her left bicep.

"Rely on me to what?"

"I don't know," I said carefully. "I don't know where I was headed with that."

She swung her head around slow and give me a look, her eyes sunk in her head like two small animals backed into a cave. "It's not about you!" she growled. "It has nothing to do with you!"

I said, "Even still," and left it at that. I knew better than to approach her. "How deep did you go?"

"Not deep."

I hadn't taken my coat off yet. I'd known other girls besides just her and me who'd done things like this, and I'm no expert—I know you're supposed to always take it seriously—but forgive me if you have to, I

16

also did not want—I could not afford—to get caught up in her drama. I suppose that sounds cold, don't it? I could spend all day justifying it, but I won't. I said, "I'm gonna go close up the shop and bring the sign in. Please don't get blood on anything that's liable to stain."

I needed to think.

Clearly, something was going on or had gone on—even if it was just in Jeannie's head—between her and that boy, Eugene. How much did I want to know? How much of it was my business to know? I counted out the bank, locked up the register and made a drop in the safe. Not but a few dollars. I wrote down what it was and figured I'd enter it in Quicken in the morning. I flipped the sign around in the front window, made sure the stove wouldn't burn the joint down and the door to the greenhouse, which had its own propane heater, was sealed tight, then I took the dolly and headed down the driveway to fetch the sandwich board that said—

And that's when it hit me.

("I'd like to do a story about Recluse Farm, Ms. Cavendish.")

Recluse. Not Repurpose, Recluse. How could he have known that? Eugene, I mean. I had never told a soul about my first choice of a name. The name I discarded.

I don't want to make too much of a thing of it. It was a "Huh?" kind of moment, that's all. I had a lot else on my mind, so I tucked that question away for future reference. Filed it under "shit I've evidently told people that I don't remember saying" and cross-referenced it with "shit I think I heard but I could be mistaken" and went back to thinking about Jeannie Ivory.

Because here's the thing: I felt played and I felt guilty. I don't do well with people cutting up in my living room, do you? You'd have to know a little bit about my grandma, I suppose, to understand just how on edge that kind of shit could put me. Or maybe not. It's a long story.

On the other hand, I did have a business, and this Lamb kid wanted to write it up in the newspaper. *You can't afford to say no to free advertising,* I told myself. I knew that boy. I mean, it felt like I did, in a small-town celebrity kind of way. I knew of him and his parents and how well-regarded they were in town.

Curious thing about Todd Lamb. Here he's got his own show, him and his wife, on local access TV. All about home-schooling. And then he up and runs for School Board.

*And wins!* I reminded myself. *And wins!*

If you can't beat 'em, join 'em, I guess.

I felt guilty because I wanted that kid to interview me. I wanted him to rave about my little farm slash consignment shop slash floral emporium slash tourist attraction because—now, here's the thing—I wanted revenge on his mother.

Revenge is too strong a word. I didn't need to get back at her for anything specific she ever did to me. I just didn't like the way she looked at me. Or didn't look at me. Like she couldn't be bothered. No, that's not it, either. More like, she knew perfectly well who I was, but second-hand, because she didn't even grow up around here. She just took it for granted that what people said about me must be true. I always imagined I represented a class of people the good Lord required her to tolerate—her and a host of others like her. Like they knew I could never be prosecuted to the full extent of their satisfaction. Nobody ever said anything, of course. It wouldn't be Christian.

My baggage, I know. I don't mean to burden you with it.

Where in the hell did I put my happy place?

I bounced the sandwich board along back to the shed and locked it away, thinking how wouldn't it be a fine thing if her son wrote up my shop in the school paper? Wouldn't it? Not to mention if an article of his, about me, found its way into *The Klarion*. One day I intended to sew a flag and stick a pole in the ground out by the road to let people know I was open for business. Be a lot easier to put up and take down than that heavy two-by-four-and-plywood contraption.

I felt guilty, though, because wanting that interview with Eugene Lamb meant:

a) asking Jeannie not to come to work one day, when she needed the money and I needed the help,

b) having to go behind her back when I could see how much Eugene upset her, and

c) she'd find out about it sooner or later, anyway, when he put it in the paper.

Not necessarily.

*Well, now, that's true. She probably don't read the paper. What teenager does?*

She goes online, though. Didn't that tall girl with the braces say something about Eugene's stories going online?

18

*So what? Are you going to let an employee dictate your advertising policy, Vanessa?*

That was a laugh. Like I even had an advertising policy!

*Well, then, don't you think it's time you better get one?*

So by the time I got back to the house, I had worked myself up about it, when I'd meant to do the exact opposite and calm my nerves.

"Jeannie?" I said. I heard her running water.

"In here."

I went and stood in the bathroom door. "There's Band-Aids in the cabinet and some kind of antibiotic."

"I'm sorry." She didn't sound it. "It really isn't about you, and it really isn't a plea for help."

"Okay," I said. "But I think I might need some help." I opened the cabinet, handed her the tube of antibiotic and got the box of Band-Aids. I saw right away that the strips I had were too small. "Shit."

I made her stand back while I looked under the bathroom sink. While I was down there searching for a roll of sterile gauze I knew I had, I asked myself (since she didn't), "What kind of help do you need, Vanessa?"

"Oh," I answered myself, "I need help deciding whether to take this girl I know to the Emergency Room or not, that's what I need help deciding."

"I don't need the Emergency Room."

"You don't need stitches, maybe." I rifled through the plastic tub of medical shit I keep under the sink, not finding anything useful. I said, "Not physical stitches."

"What? Mental stitches?" In her voice, the way she said it, I almost detected a grin.

I stood up. She had smeared antibiotic all around on her right wrist, getting blood mixed up in it and making a mess.

"Jesus!" I said.

"What? It stanches the flow."

"Yeah, okay. Whatever. I got some gauze somewhere. Maybe it's in the kitchen." I took the tube from her and run it under the hot water before I screwed the cap back on, wondering if it made any sense to worry about antibiotic ointment getting contaminated?

"I don't need it." She took and unrolled a long strip of toilet paper and wrapped it several times around her wrist. "I really didn't go that deep."

"What did you use, one of my razors?"

She dug in her right pocket with her left hand and pulled out a little miniature switchblade. "I was a Girl Scout."

I thought, *duh!* I'd seen her use it a hundred times before, pruning in the greenhouse.

"I'm sorry to put you through this."

"Last thing I want is an apology from you. Ever. That goes for if you screw up or you deliberately go out of your way to do whatever. Apologies don't mean shit to me."

She nodded. "I'll keep that in mind."

"I don't mean to be hard on you. That's just the way I feel."

"I hear you. Copy. No apologies."

"What works a whole lot better, in my humble opinion, is a simple explanation of what you think you're doing and why."

"You say that."

Something in the tone of her voice, the way she hitched her eyebrow maybe. I stood back. Then I got in her face. "Oh? What is this, Jeannie? An episode of Vanessa Can't Handle the Truth? The tough girl act just went out the fucking window, in case you missed the memo. And don't tell me it's none of my business, because you brought it to me, and you own it, and you owe me some kind of a way of making sense of it, because let me tell you something, okay? That boy wants to come out here and interview me about the shop and write up an article for the school newspaper. Now, that might not mean much, but it's free advertising, and before I turn my nose up at it, I need to know why."

"Ah."

"Ah?"

"Yes, ah. As in, putting two and two together."

"Good for you! Because I'm still waiting for clue number one."

"It's just—look, it's how he operates. And it's my fault. Mine. I created him, he's my monster, and I'll deal with it." She rolled her eyes and chuckled, low and easy, but there wasn't any humor in it. "He's going to win you over, and I'm out of luck. Again. It's what he does. It's not your problem, Ms. Cavendish. In fact, it'll probably be good for you. It invariably is."

I looked at her. I watched her lips moving and the words shuffling out of her mouth and I waited until I made sure she was done before I spoke. I said, "I feel so played, Jeannie Ivory. You have no earthly idea. Played out like a deck of cards. But guess what? They're all face down."

I took her by the arm—I didn't care if it was the good one or the one she'd carved on—and I set her down on the sofa in the living room. I took my grandma's rocker and scooted it up close to her, facing her straight on. "Now, I'm gonna take those cards out one by one and turn them over, and we're gonna look at them together like you're my telling my fortune or some goddamn thing, okay? And you're gonna tell me what each one means. You got it?"

"Be careful what you ask for, Vanessa."

"Perfect," I said. "That's just what I want to hear. Let's start with, he's your monster and you created him. What does that mean?"

"That goes back a few years. Quite a few."

"So take me there, why don't you?"

She patted her toilet paper bandage and, all with her left hand, unlaced her Doc Martens and kicked them off to sit cross-legged, her right arm resting on her knee, palm facing up.

She launched into her story, which if you're interested, I will tell you.

In fact, that's the real reason I started this book: one, to get it off my chest, and two, because if I told anyone around here about it, one way or another, they'd see to it I get locked up again.

So you sit tight, and I'll get to the good parts.

# Earthworm Soup

Jeannie sat on my sofa cross-legged, studying the blotch design her blood made as it soaked through her toilet paper cuff, like one of those psychology tests where they see what they want to see and disregard the rest. "You know in town where Bruce Street crosses over the creek?" she asked me. "Up past Fair Meadow?"

I said I did.

"That's where it started. I was nine or ten." She looked up, not at me but off to one side. "The summer before fourth grade, anyway. We used to play down in the creek bed all the time. By we, I mean all the kids in the neighborhood. It was like community property back there, where the creek winds between all the back yards in the neighborhood. The City takes care of it, mows the banks and everything. We had the run of it."

She went on.

On a particular day in the summer of Y2K, she and a boy named Jarrod Frye followed the creek upstream in search of a fabled cable swing that Jarrod had heard about but no one had ever seen. Ordinarily, such a thing would have called for Jarrod to rally the neighborhood and form a grand expedition. Unfortunately, owing to an incident pertaining to a certain tree house construction project gone wrong, his step-dad had grounded Jarrod from playing with any of the other kids. Jeannie was exempt from the general ban for some reason, either because Mr. McEarland considered her a positive influence on Jarrod or he just didn't think to include her. Be that as it may, she and Jarrod took off together down the creek, just the two of them. They got as far as Bruce Street at the east end of town, where it widens to become divided highway and eventually merges with Highway 60. At that point, the creek runs underground for several hundred feet. A few steps into the tunnel, Jeannie stopped dead in her tracks. She remembered the day in great detail, down to the pair of pink-and-purple plaid Converse sneakers she wore. She didn't mind them getting wet, but the light dwindled so she could hardly make them out. Something about the conditions under the highway didn't sit right with her. She could smell the stink of old muck and stagnant water in the dark, and when she pointed out to Jarrod that no one had ever come this far upstream before, she heard the quiver in her voice bounce off the concrete ceiling. None of the kids from the neighborhood, she meant. Not to her knowledge. The tunnel under Bruce Street was not just longer and darker than any tunnel under any of the bridges in their neighborhood, it led into unknown territory.

Jarrod Frye was a born leader, though, a grassroots organizer kind of kid. Anytime the whole neighborhood got in trouble, one way or another it turned out to be his responsibility. Even if it wasn't. He never meant any harm, he just held a lot of sway over the rest of them. Jeannie, especially. From what I gathered, his looks didn't hurt, nor the fact that he was a year older and a head taller than most of the other boys. She heard his big feet slapping against the wet, silt-on-concrete floor up ahead, ignoring her concern.

The tunnel stretched on forever. Neither one of them had thought to bring a flashlight. When she caught up to him in the darkness, she dug her fingers into his arm and pulled him up short. "How much further is it? Do you even know?"

"Not for sure. That's what we're going to find out. But here's what I do know: It hangs from a prodigious oak tree and swings out over the creek."

She thought she heard something behind her. When she turned around and looked, she saw everything familiar about her world looking back at her, shrunken to the size of a single round eye. "What's a prodigious oak tree?" she asked. Whatever kind it was, it didn't sound good.

"It means it's about as tall as a goddamn skyscraper. If you was to climb to the top of it you probably could touch the clouds. Low ones, anyway.'

"Yeah, low ones," Jeannie murmured. "Like fog."

"Point being, it's high enough you can swing out over the creek and dive in. There's a—kinda like a noose at the bottom. Like a stirrup, I mean. You stand in it and swing out. You only dive if there's water deep enough."

"There isn't," she pointed out.

"We can still check it out. Do some recon."

His step-father collected old black-and-white movies and played them sometimes for Jarrod and Dieter and their friends. Jeannie pictured Jarrod hanging onto the cable swing one-handed, riding out into space, his free hand cupping his mouth and him yodeling like Johnny Weismuller in *Tarzan of the Apes*.

Turning to study a round black shape in the side of the tunnel, he pried her fingers loose from his arm. "This looks inviting," he said. "Maybe it's a shortcut."

Jeannie squinted. All she could make out of him was his silhouette, but she recognized the familiar pose of Jarrod the Adventurer: hands on his hips, chin angled in the direction he meant to proceed. There before him, a couple of feet off the tunnel floor, gaped the hole of a storm drain, big enough for a kid her size to stand up in, almost. Ancient runoff from the streets of Keening dribbled and glopped from the lower lip of it.

"How many miles into the belly of the earth do you suppose this goes? Must be an entire labyrinth in there! Imagine? Every gutter of every street in town empties into the creek, and it's all connected, the whole system! It's got to be. Can you just picture the extent of it?"

What Jeannie pictured, for some reason, was a little boy—younger than her but not by much—wandering naked, cold and alone, under the streets of Keening. She saw him peering up into the wan light of one grated shaft after another, wading hip-deep in cold earthworm soup, whimpering to the empty curbs above. No one ever heard him, of course. He went lost and alone forever.

Just then a truck grumbled over the Bruce Street bridge, clearing its throat as it shifted gears.

Jarrod braced his hands on either side of the drain pipe. As he leaned in, his head and shoulders disappeared into another dimension. His voice dropped about thirteen octaves. "Hellowrrrats!" His echo rasped along the galvanized conduit, went slithering through all eternity before it banked and bounded back again, booming and hissing. *Lowrrrats-atts-tzzzz!* Jeannie trained her ear for the skitter of little toes clawing their way forward inch by inch, for little, high-pitched twitterings, whiskers twitching, taking notice.

Jarrod cackled in a general kind of way, not at Jeannie but at her fear, maybe. His laughter overrode that fear momentarily, but as the sound of it died away down the length of the pipe, she could hear the rats again—or she thought she did: each tentative scrabble, as they crept

24

forward a little bit and waited, crept forward again and waited, then on they would come, an endless horde of them, over the spongy muck in the bottom of the pipe. She heard each liquid swivel of an eyeball in its furry socket, each moist little nose that twitched and sniffed at the tunnel air, detecting the threat of human confidence in Jarrod and, on her, the sweat of human fear.

His head rematerialized from the void of the drain pipe's mouth to the lesser darkness of the tunnel. "The vermin approach," he announced. "About a million strong, in my estimation. Time to go." His big feet slapped the skim of water left standing since the last rain, a week ago. He went walking fast away.

Jeannie bolted after him, arms pumping, eyes fixed on the hope of green grass and sunlight up ahead, ears yearning for the sound of birdsong at the far end of the tunnel.

Older, taller, stronger, braver than the rest of them, and better looking, Jarrod knew just how to get other kids to do his bidding: to build a tree house, for one thing, in a cottonwood situated directly behind his house, where Keening Creek ran between the back yards of all the houses on Fair Meadow on one side and Charlene Street on the other. Jeannie's back gate opened onto a steep slope to the bottom, but Jarrod's house — where he lived at the time with his mom and his step-dad and Dieter — sat lower down, closer to flood levels. That was where the tree house tree stood. Still does, though the tree house has long since been dismantled. No prodigious oak, but big, even for a cottonwood. For three days, earlier in the summer, he and Jeannie and all the other kids in the neighborhood climbed up and down that cottonwood like a tribe of ants, carrying sections of two-by-four, passing a hammer up and nailing the steps in place until they reached the perfect three-way fork to support a floor of longer two-by-fours and scraps of plywood that they hauled up by rope, hand-over-hand. When the first stage of construction was completed, the tree house perched some fifty thousand feet straight up, with a hole in the floor they climbed through, a half-wall on one side and two-by-four railings on two other sides — so high up they could feel the floor sway underfoot in a stiff breeze. So high that Logan Reynolds got seasick and hurled over the railing. His breakfast spattered the leaves and sprayed all over one side of the trunk. That inspired the Heinecke's black-and-white cat to come investigate, but Logan and Jarrod chased it off for its own good with broken-off twigs and left-over nails. Jeannie climbed down and ran to her house to get the bottle of Pepto-Bismol from the medicine cabinet and climbed back up to pour Logan a dose. They took a vote and decided to keep the bottle there to have on hand.

Along the fourth side of the platform, the one without a railing, Jarrod had sawed off a pair of upright branches and stretched a giant rubber band between them. He gave a tutorial in making arrows from the half- and quarter-inch dowels he had requisitioned from his mother's crafting supplies. He notched one end of each arrow with a knife (provided by Jeannie) and fixed bits of broken glass to the other end with airplane glue, wire, twine, whatever it took. Then he dumped a pile of birdseed out of his pocket in a corner of the floor. He meant to attract a robin, he said, whose feathers they could pluck and use to fletch the arrows. "We have to bring feed every day," he instructed, "so they get used to us. Then we can catch them. Only two feathers per bird, though—one from each wing. That's a rule. Otherwise, they might go off-balance and not be able to fly straight and crash into things." He laid a half-inch dowel in the crooks of the two sawed-off branches to complete the crossbow. "One other thing. This weapon's to be used for defensive purposes only. In case we're attacked by rival factions. And for target practice."

"What will our target be?" Jeannie wanted to know.

"Dieter. He's the smallest. Hardest to hit."

Dieter looked alarmed. He was Jarrod's little brother. Step-brother, technically. "Unh-uh!" he said.

"Just kidding, Deets! Jeez-Marie!"

The tree house lasted three weeks to the day, or until Dieter stepped backwards through the access hole. Had he not been lucky enough to hit the next branch down square-on and had he not possessed reflexes quick enough to latch onto it and wrap himself around it, then, as Jarrod later pointed out, "He would've hit terminal velocity. He'd be nothing but a splat at the base of the tree."

Jarrod climbed down to collect his brother in one arm and carry him down to safety, but Dieter told on them, anyway. After that, Jarrod vowed never to let Dieter in on another secret operation of his for as long as he lived.

Mr. McEarland marched down to investigate. Dieter came slinking along behind him, crying, wiping snot across the back of his arm. His

26

dad conducted an on-the-spot appraisal of the construction methods employed by the Keening Creek Tree House Consortium, and his determination was not entirely favorable. He climbed down again with four homemade arrows in his fist.

"Shit!" Jarrod whispered. "Shit, shit, shit!"

"You kids out of your minds? Where'd you get all this lumber?"

"Just laying around," Jarrod volunteered.

"Layin' around, my ass! Layin' around whose yard, I wonder?"

"Nobody's."

"I don't even want to know. You understand what I'm sayin'? There better not be a tree house next time I come down here. I'm givin' you two days. I don't want to see stick one of it left in that tree or anywhere near here. You do that for me, Jarrod? You make it go away, and I'll do my best to see that your mother doesn't have a friggin' heart attack. Kee-rist!" He looked at the arrows in his fist, then back at Jarrod. "We got a deal?"

"Yes, sir."

"And what in the hell—" (Standing on my sofa, having forgotten all about her self-inflicted wound, her bloody toilet-paper bracelet coming uncoiled, Jeannie looked me in the eye.) "What in the hell were you huntin' from up there? Rhi-fuckin'-noceroses?"

Just the way she said it, I snorted. That got her going, then we both about busted a gut. "Rhi-fucking-noceroses!" I howled and got her started all over again. Then she said it and I tried several more times to say it but couldn't get past "Rhi-rhi-rhi—!" because I couldn't catch my breath, and then she said it one last time and I lost it so bad I like to died.

I guess you had to be there.

When she got herself under control and situated back on the sofa with my crocheted throw around her feet, she continued her story. "So when he said that, I giggled, right? I couldn't help myself."

I kept a straight face and listened.

Mr. McEarland looked at Jeannie and said, "What are you even doin' here, little girl? You surely could find better company to hang with than these knuckleheads, couldn't you?"

She shook her head. She was so scared, it was like she had an electric motor in her skull that got stuck on stutter. She couldn't stop shaking her head.

"Ya'll kids get on home and don't you dare forget what I said! I never want to see anything like this again."

They scattered. Jeannie turned around at the gate to her back yard and looked. Jarrod and Dieter and Mr. McEarland stood talking for a long time under the tree house tree. Jarrod pointed up at the limb that had broken Dieter's fall. The three of them stood looking at it for a long time before Mr. McEarland raised his knee and cracked the arrows over it one by one and tossed them into the creek.

That was all there was to it. "Consortium's been disbanded," Jarrod told Jeannie on the way to the cable swing. "Nobody else's parents'll let them hang out with me. My dad made me go around to everybody's houses and rat myself out. I'm never telling Dieter anything ever again, and don't you, either."

"I won't," she said. Dieter wasn't Jarrod's real brother.

"Don't tell him about the cable swing."

"I won't." After a minute, she said, "Your dad didn't make you go to my mom and dad. They never said anything. That means I can still hang around with you."

"I don't know," Jarrod answered, as if she'd posed a question. "You're a girl, I guess."

She didn't say anything.

"So it's you and me, huh? You're my primary running buddy. For now, at least."

"All right," she said. She liked the sound of it. She knew she was on probationary status with him, since they weren't the same age, but he was Jarrod Frye, and she was the only one on any kind of status with him. For now, at least. She felt bigger, being his primary running buddy.

"I can't stop thinking about that little kid, though," she said, feeling older.

"What little kid?"

"That kid." She forgot she hadn't mentioned the lost boy wandering the drainage system. She knew he was imaginary. She knew that perfectly well. But imaginary things could take on a certain intangible durability—even more so than actual beings sometimes—so much so that you couldn't get them out of your mind, because they had no other place to go. So she said, "You know. Down in the storm drain."

"When was that?"

Jeannie shrugged. "Still down there, I guess."

"Why? What's he look like?"

"He doesn't get much sun, that's for sure!" Jeannie had a smooth, even tan as a kid. Not a freckle on her.

But Jarrod was serious. "He lives down there?"

So she got serious. "Yes. Naked."

"I don't get it. Why?"

"Lost. Can't find his way out."

"Kee-rist!" Jarrod said. He sounded just like his step-dad.

"I know, huh?"

"What's he live on?"

"Rats. He catches and eats them."

"That makes sense. You can live on rat meat."

"He can't cook them, though. He doesn't have matches or lighter fluid or anything or any firewood down there, so he has to eat them raw."

"Jarrod nodded, as if he had been thinking along the same lines. "Plenty water."

"I don't know what he does in the wintertime to keep warm. He must freeze half to death."

"Unless it goes deep enough. Like down in a cave you can keep warm, because it's closer to the center of the Earth, where it's molten lava. Or a mine shaft."

"Probably," Jeannie agreed.

"How'd he get down there, I wonder?"

"I suppose he was abandoned. His parents put him out by the curb as a baby, and he just rolled over and fell down in."

"No. The rats would've eaten him. If he didn't drown first. He had to be older than a baby."

"Yeah."

"We're almost there," he said.

Jeannie looked up. She had all but forgotten about the cable swing.

"Dead ahead."

Jarrod went first. He wanted to conduct a test to make sure the swing was in safe condition before he let her go on it. What he called the "stirrup" was a loop of cable held in place by a clamp with two little bolts.

He made a show of jumping up and down in it as he swung out over the creek bed and back.

"I can't afford any more accidents," he explained. He stepped off onto the slope and held the stirrup for Jeannie to step into.

She held on with both hands, pressing her cheek against the steel cable, while he gave her a push in the small of the back. The wind rushed through her hair going forward, then swirled it in her face on the way back. Jarrod caught her by the waist, carried her backwards up the slope and ran forward, pushing faster and faster, so she had to catch her breath and close her eyes, afraid that if she opened them, she'd look down and see no water in the creek, just rocks and broken beer bottles and busted up concrete, and if her foot slipped out of the stirrup—

She looked down. The ground blurred past going one direction, then hung still, and blurred again going backwards. Jarrod caught her and ran with her. This time she screamed, but a laughing kind of scream, and when she came to ground again and stepped out of the stirrup, she stumbled backwards and laid laughing and panting in the grass and let it be his turn.

"Aiyah-yaiyah!" he Tarzan-bellowed, swinging.

When they'd each swung twenty times, plus one for extra measure—Jarrod kept track with a stick in a patch of dirt—they called it quits and walked back above ground, stopping traffic to cross Bruce Street on a "Walk" signal.

"I wish it would rain!" Jarrod said. "I wish it'd rain for about a week solid and swell the creek, so we could come back and dive. I'd do a jack-knife and slice clean through the water. No splash at all!"

"I'll do a jack-knife, too!" Jeannie offered.

"Like a whisper."

"Yeah. Like a whisper."

"I'll swim right down and touch the bottom."

"Me, too," Jeannie said, even though all she could think about was broken glass and twisted rebar.

"I can hold my breath for ten minutes," Jarrod said. "My dad's got a stopwatch."

They stopped at the corner of Vine Street and stood looking down through the grate of the storm drain. He kicked at the leaves that had backed up in the gutter and watched them sift down into the dark. She knew he was thinking about the sewer boy, because so was she.

"I wonder if you could call down to him and tell him which way to go? We could lead him from one drain to the next until he got to the creek. Then he could just walk out into the fresh air and be like normal again."

"We could try," Jeannie said skeptically.

"Good idea. Who even knows what part of town he's in, though? He could be anywhere."

"It would probably take a whole year just to locate him," she agreed. She did not want to encourage the idea.

"Not if we got everybody to help. We could split up in teams of two and cover a lot of —"

A siren interrupted him. It sounded close, then it got closer. They saw the lights flashing all the way down at Mulberry.

"It's coming this way," Jarrod said. "It's an ambulance."

"I wonder where it's going? I don't see any accident."

"Could be a heart attack or something, though. That's what it looks like."

"How can you tell?"

"Look how slow it's going," he said. "They always slow down when they know the person's already dead."

# ABNORMAL GROWTH

Mr. McEarland rounded the corner of their house on the garage side. Jarrod called, "Hey, Dad!" Jeannie waved. Jarrod had only recently started referring to him as his dad instead of his step-dad. Maybe they had bonded over the tree house incident or something, but it still sounded weird to Jeannie. Mr. McEarland stood in the driveway and waved his arms over his head, not at them. The ambulance pulled over to the curb and stopped. The siren wound down as if it suddenly ran out of juice, but the lights kept pulsing.

"Why's it stopping at our house?" Jarrod wanted to know. "Hey! Why's it stopping at our house?" Then he started running. Jeannie ran, too, but Jarrod ran fast.

EMTs climbed out of the ambulance and opened the doors in the back. They pulled out the gurney and let its landing gear snap into position, then wheeled it up the driveway toward Jarrod's house. Mr. McEarland directed them around the side of the garage. When he saw Jarrod he grabbed him and held him and wouldn't let him go. Another siren wailed from far off, coming closer, and then another one, and soon the yard was full of firemen in their bulky pants and jackets and boots and a pair of cops who stood back at first with their thumbs hooked on their belts and conferred with the firemen.

Jeannie stayed across the street, not sure what to do. After a long time, she watched the EMTs come back around the corner of the garage with Jarrod's mom strapped to the gurney. They loaded her into the ambulance. Jarrod bawled out to her in a voice like a terrified calf. "Ma!" he cried, then more shrilly, "Ma!'" But his step-dad wouldn't let him go to her. Jarrod kept saying, "Let me go!" but he wouldn't.

Mr. McEarland stayed calm, though he spoke in an unnaturally loud voice. "We're gonna get in the car. You, me and Dieter are gonna get in the car and follow. We'll stay right behind the ambulance all the way. We are not gonna let her out of our sight. You got it?" He led Jarrod into the house and came back out with him and Dieter, who looked bewildered. The ambulance left. They all got in their car and drove off after it.

The two policemen and one of the firemen went around the garage and came back after a few minutes. When they saw Jeannie, they wanted to talk to her, but after she told them she hadn't seen what happened, they lost interest.

She went home—she lived two doors down from Jarrod—and told her mom about the whole ordeal. Mrs. Ivory made some phone calls but could not find out what had gone wrong with Mrs. McEarland until later that evening. Over the next few days the story kept changing, getting revised and refined and swapped back and forth until it was pretty well established that Mrs. McEarland—or Amy Frye, as everyone still knew her—had been standing on the ground holding an extension ladder steady for her husband, while he cleaned the gutters in the back of the house. Then, without warning, one leg of the ladder started to sink into the ground. Amy tried to support the ladder with Harlan's full weight on it, to keep him from getting injured, which she managed to do. But instead of him falling and getting hurt, the ladder twisted around on her, and him with it, and flattened her into the ground. The way it caught her, it broke her neck. Not all the way through, they said at first. Everyone kept saying it was fortunate that Amy Frye did not completely sever her spinal cord. That was the good thing about it, they said. That was a blessing, because she died on the operating table, not in the back yard where the two boys might have seen. Jeannie's mom reported that Evie Franklin figured God had made a point of it, not to scar them like that.

Jeannie fell silent and dug in her jacket for cigarettes. She slapped one out of the pack and fiddled with it a minute, then said, "Be right back."

"Through the kitchen," I said.

While she smoked out back, I tidied up in the bathroom, put away the antibiotic and the Band-aids and rinsed her blood down the drain. It occurred to me what I must have done with the gauze and the medical tape, so when she came back in, I said, "Let me put a proper bandage on that wrist of yours." While I had her like that, standing close but not looking at her, focusing on the task at hand, I said, "Sounds like you had something special, you and that boy."

33

"Who, Jarrod?" She gave a little hitch of her shoulder. "I didn't see much of him for the rest of the summer. My stint as primary running buddy expired after less than a day. The other kids' parents allowed them to play with him again, if they wanted to, but he wasn't all that interested in organizing anything anymore. He started fifth grade that year. I went into fourth. We walked home together, since we lived so close, but he had less and less to say. He reverted to calling Mr. McEarland his step-father. Then, less than two months into the school year, a For Sale sign went up in their yard. They moved to Kirkland District."

Exactly when it started, she couldn't say, maybe late November or sometime after Christmas break, but word got around school about the kid who lived in the storm sewer. She dismissed it the first time she heard it. Logan Reynolds told her. He sat directly behind her in Miss Vernier's class.

"Oh, yeah, right!" Jeannie turned her pencil over to erase a stray mark on her math sheet. "I know all about it."

But Logan wasn't the only one talking about it. Anna Sylvester brought it up at lunch the same day. Her and her crowd of followers. From the way Jeannie described them, they were the very same girls I went to school with back in the eighties, only now they wore skinny jeans instead of parachute pants. They still navigated the halls as a unit, like a school of fish, and they did not know how to let go of a story. Jeannie had heard enough and tried to tell them it was made up. She knew because she'd made it up herself.

Deanna Kilpatrick contradicted her. "No, really, Jean. It's true."

"It's not! You can ask Jarrod. I told him about it as a joke. Last summer."

"Who?"

"Jarrod."

"Oh, Jarrod Frye? Sure! He doesn't even go to school here anymore." Coming from Deanna, that was enough to discredit Jeannie Ivory on the subject of the sewer boy forever. Even Samantha Corwin, who'd been friendlier than just about any other girl in school up to that point, gave her a pained expression, and next day, sure enough, Logan passed a note to her, folded the way she and Sam always folded their notes to each other. Inside it said, "You allways think you now everything. You dont." Underline, underline, underline.

Jeannie marched straight through the back yard after school, out the back gate to the creek, and kept on until she reached the bridge at Mulberry Street. It had started to sprinkle, but the creek was dry yet. The bridge sheltered her from the cold and wet, and she didn't care about rats, either. Even they were a figment of her imagination. Although they were at least possible. She did not stick her head inside the drain pipe, the way Jarrod did under Bruce Street, but she stood there with her arms crossed over her chest and yelled at the top of her lungs. "Hey! Sewer Boy! I don't believe in you, just so you know! And I don't care who does! You don't exist! You got that? You don't exist, Sewer Boy!"

Satisfied when she didn't get an answer back, she turned and climbed the creek bank back to her house.

She skipped out of school after lunch the next day. She had to know where Jarrod lived, and the only way she could think of to find him was to wait outside his school. She had ridden past Kirkland in the car before, so she knew if she got to the cable swing and kept walking up Washington Street, she would come to it eventually. What she failed to realize was that Kirkland had exits on three sides of the main building, plus two modular units. She picked the doors facing Beech Street and hoped for the best. When the bell finally rang, she kept her distance and watched in every direction she could. Kids poured out everywhichway, paying her no mind. The teachers came outside and stood at the doors to monitor the exodus, but none of them noticed that Jeannie was not a Kirkland student. Finally, she caught sight of Dieter in a new red jacket. He looked older but still the same. She ran up to him.

"You go to school here now?" he asked, looking confused.

"No. I have to see Jarrod."

"He already left."

"Did he go to your house?"

"Yeah, he has to. In case Dad needs him."

"Oh. How's your dad?" she thought to ask.

Dieter shrugged.

"I need to see Jarrod. It's important."

"What about?" Dieter asked, but she didn't want to tell him. He wanted to stop at a store called Major Mart so he could buy some candy. The lady behind the register knew him by name.

Their house was a yellow bungalow on Cortland Street, next to a used car lot. Dieter sat on the porch to eat his candy. "Go on in," he said.

Jeannie knocked first. Dieter acted put out, but he got up and opened the door for her, calling in a sing-song voice, "Hey Jarrod! A girrul is here to seeeeee you!"

If Jarrod was either surprised or happy about her visit, he masked it. He led her through the house. On the way past the hallway, he called out, "I'll just be out back, Harlan. Deetz's home."

Mr. McEarland did not respond. Jeannie never even saw him.

She and Jarrod sat with their backs against the wall in a little space between the garage and the chain link fence that separated his yard from a bank of late-model fenders. The garage's concrete foundation warmed their backs. Jarrod rolled the sleeves of his tee-shirt up on his shoulders.

"Did you tell everybody about the sewer boy?" Jeannie asked him point-blank.

"What?"

"Are you the one that started it?"

He looked at her like she had three heads.

"It's spread to Murrow. Everyone's talking about it, and I know it didn't come from me."

Jarrod leaned his head back against the garage and puffed his cheeks. "Not just here and Murrow. It's all over town."

"Great."

"It's kinda taken on a life of its own, if you ask me."

"Tell me about it! I can't convince a single person it's not real. They don't believe we made it up."

"What do you mean?"

"People think the sewer boy is real. They go around listening for him and calling down through the grates."

"That was your idea."

"He's not real, though, and people think he is."

"You know that for sure?"

"Yes, I do, Jarrod. We made him up! Remember?"

Jarrod extended one arm out straight, holding up his index finger. "First Rule of Evidence," he said. "It is impossible to prove a negative.

People have known that since ancient times."

"Well, I want you to stop telling people about the sewer boy, Jarrod. It gives me the creeps. He's not good, you know? He's not normal and he isn't going to return to normal because he isn't ever going to get out because he can't. Because he's not real!"

"I'm not the one who told everybody. For your information, it was probably Deetz."

"Dieter? You told Dieter?"

Jarrod shrugged. "He's my brother."

"I thought you were never going to let him in on another secret. After the tree house catastrophe? Seriously?"

Jarrod held up both palms as if to ward her off. "Sorry!" He didn't sound it. "I didn't know it was such a secret."

"Well, it was! It was between you and me. We were supposed to be running buddies, remember?"

She wished she hadn't mentioned that. As soon as the words rolled off her tongue, she knew for a fact he wouldn't remember having said it. No more than she remembered it being her idea to go looking for the sewer boy. Her eyes stung. She got up and left. She wasn't going to let him see her cry over not being his first choice of a running buddy. If he even had one. Needed one. Whatever.

It was a long walk home. She avoided walking past the cable swing.

Every curb in town had its own sewer drain. She stopped at each and every corner to hock and spit. If there was a sewer boy, she wished he'd be there peering up at the cold blue sky, so she could get him smack in the eye.

That night she started awake to find Jarrod crawling out of a mine shaft, sweating profusely. He had a flashlight implanted in his forehead. "Abnormal growth," he remarked, posing as an old-time doctor with a mirror disk. "Say, 'Ah!' ' He studied the inside of her mouth. "Shit!" he said. "Shit, shit, shit! He's got your DNA. We need to excavate." Then she woke up for real.

She looked at me hard then, Jeannie did, with a squint in her eye. Sizing me up. "This is the part where it gets weird, Vanessa," she said. "I hope you're up for it. Can you keep an open mind?"

"Go on," I said.

She nodded, picked something off her lip, and continued.

The school year was almost over by the second time a horde of EMTs, cops, firefighters and onlookers swarmed the street in front of what used to be Jarrod Frye's house, two doors down from hers. Everybody concentrated their attention on the middle of the street this time, where a manhole cover had been flipped over like a big iron coin, crusty side up. Jeannie edged in as close as she could get. Something in her knew what was coming. There was a part of her that didn't need to think things through for the knowledge to function, to flow through her with lightning recognition and then go dark again. *Poof!* Gone. But still there, like you could turn the switch off all you want, but the light bulb is still going to exist.

A fireman's helmet appeared out of the middle of the street, then his face. His eyes looked worried, the set of his lips grim. Then another head emerged, a child's head with a pronounced whorl pattern, bobbing against the fireman's shoulder. The kid's hair hung lank and greasy-black, matted, dripping wet. The fireman's gloved hand cradled two thin naked buttocks. He passed the kid to another firefighter. As the second one scooped the kid up in his arms and carried him to the gurney where they wrapped a sheet around him, Jeannie could tell it was a boy. She saw his penis waggling, the sheathed kind. The boy kept his eyes squeezed tight against the bright sun. The cut and wrinkled skin of his face gleamed as pale and puffy as a grub worm, though his body had a kind of stringy muscularity to it. His ribs worked in and out like the teeth of a trap or a hair clasp. A network of scratches, some old and some new, decorated his arms and legs, his back and all over his abdomen.

"What's your name?" asked the firefighter. He pushed the sewer boy's hair back from his face with a bare hand.

The boy slit his eyes. Jeannie saw the two black centers, wide as gaping drainpipes. Then they closed up. If she'd been thinking straight, she might have realized he'd be blinded in broad day, he probably couldn't make out anything more than shapes hovering. Just the same, when he spoke, he might as well have been pointing his finger right at her.

"I'm you, Jean!" he said.

That was how she heard it.

Then he coughed up a wad of something half-digested, with remnants of fur in it, chewed-up stems of grass and leaves. The firefighter put a glove back on to pluck the gob of vomit from the sheet and toss it to the pavement.

"You been down there for a while, haven't you, Eugene?"

The boy tilted his head at the sound of the voice and scrunched up his face. His mouth opened wide, not in a grin but in a slit from ear to ear. His teeth were little and legion, with spaces of pink gum between them, riddled with specks of grit and vegetation. "I dunno," he croaked. "Ever since they put me there."

The firefighter glanced at a police woman who stepped up close enough to hear. The police woman's hips were extra wide, owing to the equipment she carried on her duty belt. She blocked Jeannie's view. "Who put you there?"

"Them two kids," he said. "Them running buddies. But I got out now."

"That's right," said the cop in a sweet, comforting voice. "You're out now. You're out now, safe and sound." She allowed the EMTs in close to examine him. "We're gonna get you dressed and fed and get you where you'll be safe, okay?" She followed alongside the gurney and climbed into the back of the ambulance after they loaded him in.

With the exception of Jeannie Ivory, the last to leave the scene were two men in coveralls who stayed to flip the cover back over the manhole. It gave a loud, iron ring in the empty street. They climbed in their Department of Engineering truck and took off.

"And that expression on your face right now, Vanessa?" she said in my living room, pointing her finger at me. "That was me. I stood there in the middle of my street, wondering what in the hell had just happened?"

# Mississippi Mud

I studied Jeannie for a country minute. "Eugene?" I said. "As in Eugene Lamb? The boy that was here today with Spider McCormick? That Eugene? Is that what you're telling me?"

She closed her eyes. "You don't have to believe me, Vanessa. Why would you?"

"There ought to be record of it. If it happened."

"Nobody has ever disputed it actually happened. Go Google it if you want to. I don't think you lived here at the time, but it was all over the news."

We migrated to my study off the kitchen, where I keep my laptop. While I waited for it to boot up, I thought back. "You're how old? Nineteen?" That made her story nine or ten years old. I would have been back living in Oklahoma by then, my house finished, more or less, but still working sunup to sundown building my shop, trying like hell to construct a life for myself out of the scraps of a past I don't discuss if I can avoid it. I lost track of what Jeannie was talking about until she got to the part about the couple who bought the McEarlands' house and how they didn't move right in.

They had work done first, she said. A company came in with a machine called a Ditch Witch to dig a trench around the foundation, then they came behind it to lay a bed of gravel and install section after section of clay pipe. Jeannie's dad pointed out to her the line of upturned earth leading from the house to the curb. "It's called a French drain. Looks like they're tying it into the street. I'm not entirely sure that's legal."

The couple who bought the house were Gay and Todd Lamb from Mississippi somewhere. They did not move in right away. The ditches had to be filled in and replacement shrubs planted, roof shingles stripped and new ones laid, vinyl gutters and replacement windows installed and the siding painted white, with a slate blue called "Thunderstorm" for the trim. Jeannie knew because she snooped around of a weekend and read the can lids. And still the house stood empty for weeks on end. Jarrod's house. To her it would always be Jarrod's house.

After the first of the year, a new phase of construction took shape. She had to go down by way of the creek and back up and look through the chain link fence to see what was going on in the back part of the house. Plastic drain pipes and copper pipes wrapped in black foam stuck out of a slab of concrete. After two weeks, a cage of two-by-fours stood two stories tall, and soon they boxed all that in with plywood and covered it in Tyvek until, by and by, it became just more house, with a roof to match the existing one and windows and a big sliding glass door. A brick patio soon appeared and white gravel flower beds and more instant shrubbery. But still no people.

Nobody made the connection—at least, Jeannie didn't, not at first— but it had to be within two or three days after an Allied Moving truck delivered a houseful of furniture and appliances and a steady stream of hand trucks stacked with identical cardboard boxes labeled this, that, and the other thing, when the sewer boy emerged. The story made the headlines of The Keening Klarion and The Oklahoma Times and appeared on WKOK-TV.

I typed in a search for "keening boy found storm sewer" and hit Enter.

The story apparently went viral for a time, because there on YouTube stood the house, just as Jeannie described it, behind a reporter with a microphone and wind-tossed hair.

Jeannie stood over my shoulder at the computer. "Notice how she stumbles over the story, she's so excited to be telling everybody about it, pointing me out as a liar to the entire school."

"Authorities are saying very little about the case at this point. No one seems to have any clues to the identity of the little boy or his parents or how he ended up under, uh, in the underground storah—ah, storm drainage, uh, system in this quiet community. All we know so far is that he appears to be healthy, apart from some minor scratches and bruises, and that he is, uh, indeed, uh, a very lucky little boy even to be alive. This is Karen Overstreet reporting for WKOKTV live from Keening."

Meanwhile, back in the newsroom, the anchor couple went on and on, chit-chatting about the story, saying how the Oklahoma State Bureau of Investigation had been called in and that Bass Memorial Hospital in Enid, where the boy had been taken, reported he had "a good appetite."

It was all anybody talked about at school the next day. Mrs. Charles brought it up. "I know a lot of you consider the creek to be your playground, but it's a dangerous place. You don't have any business down there. A flash flood can come up at a moment's notice. And you kids should not go near or play anywhere near those drains that empty into the creek. The City ought to put grates over those openings."

Everybody had questions and stories of their own about the dangers of playing in Keening Creek and about the bad kids who did it. Mrs. Charles never did get back to social studies that day.

Once the Lambs physically moved in and started living in the house on Fair Meadow, they invited Jeannie and her parents over to Sunday dinner. Jeannie had an older brother, but Billy had his license and a girlfriend and the use of the car on weekends. Jeannie had no choice but to go where her parents went.

Not that she had no curiosity about the Lambs. From the moment Mr. Lamb answered the door and let them in, she could not stop trying to work out what they had done with Jarrod's house, where they had hidden it. Not only was nothing the same color or the same pattern, but none of the rooms were in the same places. Most of the walls had gone AWOL, and what was left of them had been shifted around to such an extent she couldn't help but think that living there had to be like an experiment involving lab rats, where everything changed from one day to the next to see how smart they were under different kinds of stress. All the houses in the neighborhood had been built by the same developer and were laid out according to the same basic plan. Some had the garage to the right instead of the left, but either way, the kitchen would be tucked behind it so you could bring the groceries directly in from the car, while the bedrooms occupied the opposite end of the house, off the hallway across from the combination living/dining room. It all made perfect sense. A person knew where to find the bathroom, the back porch, the fold-down ladder to the attic, everything.

Nothing was the same any longer in Jarrod's house—nothing—no matter how sleek and pretty.

Jeannie knew, of course, that houses existed with different floor plans in other parts of town and that, even in her neighborhood, some of the more expensive ones — the houses built on corner lots, usually — varied to an extent. Some of them had two-car garages and an upstairs on one side or the other. That was to be expected. Not every detail had to be identical. But the variations always followed a similar kind of logic.

Not so in Lamb World.

"First of all," she complained, "the kitchen had been picked up and turned sideways, levitated over to the side of the house where Jarrod's room used to be. It hovered about three feet off the ground floor, to 'distinguish' it from the 'great room'. One wall of solid cabinets, floor to ceiling. That and a bar with a stainless steel top. I couldn't decide if it looked more like a stage or an operating room. And there stood Mrs. Lamb beaming down at us in high heels and a navy blue sheath under a spotless white apron, as if she were the head chef in a four-star restaurant. Her fingernails looked like blue pearls. Her hands, arms and throat were like porcelain."

Where the kitchen should have been, the Lambs had installed a den and lined the walls with expensive paneling and glass bookshelves that lit up from the inside when Mr. Lamb waved his hand in front of them like a magician. Jeannie's mother gasped when she saw that. Her dad, the original man of few words, said, "That's neat, Todd! That's real neat!" and meant it. Mr. Lamb's desk was teak — a wood Jeannie knew about from a film at school that featured elephants capable of wrapping their trunks around whole trees and carrying them out of the jungle. The books on the shelves were all Bibles and Bible study books, Bible concordances and Bible geography books and Bible devotionals.

"Are you a preacher?" she asked.

Todd Lamb laughed in a good-natured way, as if she'd said something adorable but wrong. "No, no. No, merely a student of the Scriptures. And a Gideon."

"What's that?" It sounded like an internal organ, one that not everyone probably had.

"The Gideons are a lay men's group dedicated to the work of the Lord. We provide copies of the Word to servicemen, hospitals, hotels and motels, wherever it's needed. Would you like one, Jeannie?" He reached in a drawer of his desk and slid out a New Testament the size of a deck of cards.

"Oh," she said.

When Mr. Lamb showed them the addition at the back of the house, where the bedrooms had gone, two upstairs and one down, to make room for the new kitchen, Jeannie's mom asked whether they might be planning a family.

"We've left that in the Lord's hands," Gay Lamb answered from behind them. She had a voice as sweet as a Diet Pepsi.

Mr. Lamb gave Jeannie's dad a wink. "We're doing our part."

Mrs. Lamb pursed her lips in a way that caused her cheeks to dimple. "Young ears, Todd!"

"You don't have to worry," Jeannie said. "I know about sex."

"Oh! You do, do you?" Mrs. Lamb looked not at Jeannie but at her mom, smiling in earnest disbelief. "Why, wherever did you get so smart?"

"They teach us all about it in school. It's called biology."

Mrs. Lamb nodded. She and her husband exchanged a look. "That's the problem with public education, isn't it?" She turned back to Jeannie's mom. "Anyway, when we had the addition put in, we thought we—well, we were expecting, but—"

"Oh!" Jeannie's mom touched the porcelain woman on the arm.

"No! No, it's okay!" Mrs. Lamb smiled, so brightly-shining in every aspect of her person, that her eyes, her teeth, her fingernails and even her skin began to glimmer with the optimism of her outlook. "The Lord works things out as He sees fit. He really does! If we follow His guidance, He will not lead us astray."

"There's a reason for everything," Jeannie's mom agreed.

"Why don't you all come and sit down, and I'll get dinner on the table."

Mr. Lamb brought up the tragedy associated with their property and asked, "Were you friendly with the McEarlands?"

Jeannie's mom leaned over her plate. She had anticipated the question. ("There is a certain way my mother gets when she intends to speak from the heart," Jeannie said. I knew her mom, so I had to smile. I could see the targeted look in her eye, feel the intensity of her expression. When she wants to connect with you about something important, she tends to stand one little hair too close. Most people don't seem to notice.) "Amy was a dear!" she told Mrs. Lamb. "And you're right, it was a tragedy, to happen the way it did. I'm sure he torments himself over it every single day. How could he not? But we're glad to see you make something of this place again. If it sat empty another minute, it would — well, it just reminded us all the time. But you've done such a wonderful job with it! This house needed you! It really did!"

"How sweet of you to say that!" Mrs. Lamb looked genuinely moved and confused at the same time. Her eyes pleaded for something. It wasn't clear what. Maybe just friendship. She squeezed Mrs. Ivory's hand.

The conversation turned to the story of the boy found under the street directly in front of the Lamb's new house. Less than a month had passed, and not many questions had been answered: how he got there, who he belonged to, where he came from.

"You mean, they still don't know?" Mrs. Lamb looked shocked.

"I haven't heard anything. Have you, Don?"

Jeannie's dad said no, he hadn't, and Gay Lamb turned to her husband and said, "The Lord has directed us to this place for a reason, Todd. I know He did." She did not take her eyes off him.

They studied one another for a minute that stretched out to a mile. At last Mr. Lamb said, "Let's pray on it, Honey."

"You were there at the time, weren't you, Jean?" (Her mother never called her that.) "Did you hear anything or see anything? Did he look familiar to you?"

Jeannie raised her eyebrows, but her eyes refused to look up from her plate. "He was gross!"

"But he didn't say anything? Who his folks were or anything?"

Her mother knew the answer. Jeannie had told her everything already. The grilling was strictly for the Lambs' benefit. When Jeannie gave her a look to let her know she was onto her, her mother turned away and said, "All he'd give was his first name. Eugene."

"No last name?"

"That's not what he said," Jeannie interrupted. "He said, 'I'm you, Jean.'"

"*Eugene*," Gay Lamb repeated, like someone learning a new language.

Jeannie gave up trying. She wasn't going to convince anyone that what they had read in the newspaper and seen on TV and what she herself had seen in person was anything but the truth, just because she knew it was made up. "Can we go home now?" she said. "I don't feel good."

"Oh, you won't want to miss dessert, Honey! Haven't you ever had Mississippi mud?"

Jeannie tried not to look appalled. "Did you say 'mud'?"

"It's the living end, if I do say so. You just have to try it."

"Can I be excused, Mom? Really. I don't feel good."

She cut across the lawn between the Lambs' house and hers with her fists clenched, not watching where she was going. "People don't invent other people!" she scolded herself. "Not flesh and blood people! When will you learn to keep your mouth shut? Because let me tell you something: he is not me. That sewer boy is not me! There's no way he said, 'I'm you, Jean!' because, one, he's not. Duh! And two, there is no way that he could possibly have known my name!"

But he had said, "Them two running buddies."

Who could that have meant but her and Jarrod?

"That's ridiculous!" she fumed.

Her doubts chased her across the yard and onto the front porch.

Jarrod must have called him out, she decided. Jarrod must have called the sewer boy up from the sewer. Not that he meant to, but Jeannie remembered the bounce of his voice under the Bruce Street bridge. "The vermin approach!"

Her feet ran faster, though she tried to make them not. She found the front door locked and had to scoot between the garage door and the front bumper of the car — it was parked that close — in order to get around the house and let herself in the back way. By that time she was only two percent as creeped out by the turn the conversation had taken between her folks and the Lambs and ninety-eight percent pure pissed off. She slammed the kitchen door so hard it shook the cabinets and rattled the glasses. They never locked the front door — ever — not when they only went to the neighbors' down the street.

Then it occurred to her.

Billy had the car. But there it sat in the driveway. She went to his bedroom door and gave it a kick. "You're home early, Dork Face!" She pushed open his door and stuck her head in to say, "What's the matter, your date with Bimbo Sprague not go as planned?" when she heard a squeal and saw the covers fly up over his bed and two heads duck under, quick. The words she'd meant to say never made it past her lips.

She stared at the frantic shapes under the bedspread. She had already seen more than she wanted to, even though she hadn't actually seen anything. She closed the door and left the house by the back door.

When Billy came outdoors in his boxers and no shirt, she was already halfway up the mimosa tree in the back yard, swaying in the evening breeze. A pale moon rode a jagged horizon of rooftops.

"Get down here!" Billy bossed her. "I want to talk to you."

"You can talk just fine. Your lips aren't broken." If she came down, she knew she was in for it.

"He started climbing after her, barefoot. She climbed higher, up where she hoped the branches would not support his weight.

He came on up, anyway. "I just want to talk, Jeannie. Jesus!"

"You had better get some pants on. And tell her to, too. Mom and Dad are right behind me."

"You little bitch!" Standing on a bigger branch, lower down, he reached up and shook the one Jeannie was on, causing it to dip and bounce. She hung on for dear life.

"Billy!" screamed Lori Sprague as she came zipping her cutoffs and pulling on her sandals. "Billy! Stop it!"

"You little freak!" he growled, but he stopped shaking the tree limb.

"That's how you treat your own sister? You could kill her, doing that! What if she was to fall?"

"She ain't gonna fall."

"If you have one ounce of common sense, you will get down out of that tree and go put your clothes on before I call my dad and tell him to come get me."

"And unlock the front door, moron!" Jeannie yelled after him. "That's a dead giveaway."

Lori Sprague looked up at her from the ground. "You okay? Why don't you come on down?"

"No way. I think I'll just enjoy the peace and quiet from up here."

"He won't hurt you. Come on down. I'll see to it."

"You turned out nicer than I expected. Are you sure you can't do better than my brother?"

Lori took her sweet time answering. "Billy can be a decent guy when he puts his mind to it. He just—he was thinking one way and, well, you surprised him is all. I'm glad you did, if you want the truth."

"Looked to me like you were thinking the same way he was."

"Nothing happened, though. You're not gonna say anything to your folks, are you?"

"Why, if nothing happened?"

Lori smiled up at her. "Because nothing did." She sounded genuine, even if she was lying.

"I don't want to get you in trouble. But I would also prefer not to get chased up a tree like a cat."

"He won't. I'll talk to him."

"Can I tell you something?"

"Sure."

"It wasn't the smartest idea, having sex in our house."

"We weren't, though."

Jeannie just looked at her, like, *Seriously? How stupid do you think I am?*

"I know, I know. Can I tell you something?"

"Go ahead."

"You probably should knock and be invited in before you open your brother's door, don't you think? I know. I have a brother, too."

"Okay. Touche`."

Billy came back out in his jeans and shirt. "Let's get out of here." He stood three heads taller than Lori Sprague and pointed his finger up at Jeannie in the tree. "One word," he threatened.

"Go start the car, Billy."

"One word," he repeated.

"I'm capable of it," Jeannie warned him. "You know I am, so why don't you keep threatening me?"

"You won't be capable of much else."

Lori Sprague turned back to the house. "I'm calling my dad to come get me."

"Wait a minute! No, you're not!" Billy caught up to her, but she slapped his hand away. "Come on, Lori! Now, don't be like that!"

"I'm not playing referee between two children. You go apologize to your sister and take me home, or I'm calling my dad. You don't have but those two choices."

"Why? What're you gonna tell your dad? Nothing."

Lori stood with one hand on her hip and the other one on Billy's chest, reaching up and patting him the way she might a horse, to ease its mind about the saddle. "Remember one thing for me, will you? I'm not afraid of my dad. You are."

Billy towered over her and listened to her. Jeannie did not need to see his face, she saw it in the way his shirt settled onto his back. He took one small shuffle sideways and relaxed into a whole new attitude. It was a miracle the way Lori Leigh handled him.

"Now, go apologize to your sister. That's step one."

# Roman Candle

I planned my house so the window in my study would have the best view of the canyon. When I went to shut my computer off, I noticed it had begun to snow and the wind had picked up. I needed to get Jeannie home or else take her myself to get her cuts looked at. "Let me go get Jiminy started," I said.

"Do I dare to ask why you named your truck after a cartoon cricket?"

"She's a GMC," I said. "GMC, Jiminy. It rhymes."

"No, not really."

"You know what I mean." My grandma, who to my knowledge never drove a day in her life, had left Grandpa's truck to rot in the barn. When I come home to roost and rebuild, among the first of the projects I took on was I brought Jiminy back from the brink of ruination. She has yet to forgive me for it. "Come on back out to the front room," I told Jeannie. "It's chilly back here."

I grabbed my coat and patted the pockets to make sure I had my keys and my cell phone. "Be right back."

I sat behind the wheel and pressed the number to Jeannie's house. Her mom didn't pick up, so I left a message to let her know Jeannie'd had an accident, was the way I put it. I didn't say how, just that I was taking her to the Emergency Room but not to worry. I didn't think she needed stitches, just—I wanted someone to look at it, make sure it didn't get infected, blah, blah, blah. I ended the call and commenced pounding my head on the steering wheel. "Shit, Vanessa! You idiot!" I knew perfectly well what would happen if I took Jeannie to the E.R. (assuming I could even cajole her into going there in the first place). They'd find a reason to keep her, one way or another. Probably have to strap her down and put her on an eyeball watch, because she was bound to go off the hook. Any normal person would. But that's the way I seem to make a decision: open my mouth and start talking. Whatever comes out, that's what I figure I have to do, since I said I would.

Like I'm my own private Oracle of Delphi or some damn thing, right?

I turned the key in the switch and stepped on the ignition, which in a '49 GMC is a push-button on the floor. I'd had the battery on the charger just the day before, so the starter spun like hell, but the motor didn't catch. I tried her again. She coughed once, sputtered and whined. I sat a minute longer, wondering how I intended to talk Jeannie into going peacefully to the E. R. with me before I tried the starter again. No go. I patted Jiminy on the dashboard and said, "You looking out for me, Girl? Trying to cover my ass?"

My ring tone went off, the one I used for people-in-general. I looked, and it was the number I had just called. Jeannie's mom.

"Maureen?" I said. "Hi."

We went through the whole rigmarole—how are you and I'm fine and how are you and is it snowing in town like it is here?—before she finally asked me how bad cut Jeannie was.

I backpedaled. "Not that bad. I might have over-reacted. She's insisting she don't need to go." Which was not a complete lie.

"Is it just a surface cut?"

I said, "Yes, it really is."

"On her wrist?"

I said, "Yes," and nodded my head as if she could see me.

On a cell phone, a sigh can come across like a hurricane. Finally, she said, "What set her off? Any idea?"

"I think it had something to do with a boy she knows."

"Eugene. I know."

I skipped a beat, then: "He come out here today on a field trip from the high school. She wanted nothing to do with him and then—"

Maureen cut me off. "I wish I knew what to tell you. We've tried everything we know to do. I don't mean we've given up, but I'm at my wit's end with her. She won't talk to anybody about it, you know. A professional or anything. Is she there with you?"

"She's in the house. She don't know I called you. I come out to get my truck started and thought I'd give you a holler first to let you know why she's late getting home."

Maureen didn't say anything right away. I told her to hold on while I tried Jiminy again. A whir and a whine and then nothing. "I might have to call Triple A," I said. I thought I smelled electrical smoke.

"I better let you go, then. Or do you need me to come get her?"

"No, that's all right. Let me see what I can do. But could you tell me one thing first?"

"If I can."

"Did Eugene Lamb—" I couldn't think of a way to ask what I really wanted to know, so I switched course. "Was he adopted?"

"Oh, yes. Did she tell you about him?" I could feel her quicken—I don't know how else to put it—the way she would have stepped up closer to me if we stood talking in person. Just a little too close. I felt myself literally leaning backwards, my shoulder blades pushing into the seat back, to give myself room to think.

All I said was Jeannie had told me he was abandoned as a child.

"And they took him in. That's right. They have done wonders with that boy!" I could feel her breath on my face right through the phone. "I don't know what her problem is."

"Where was he—I mean, how was he found? Jeannie says—"

"What did she tell you?"

"That he was wandering around under the street, in the storm drain."

"That part's true."

"All right," I said. "What part isn't true?"

"That depends on what she told you. If she's saying she helped Jarrod Frye put him down there, then that might give you a clue to what we're up against."

When I didn't say anything, she clarified. "That part's not true."

"Put him down there how?"

She sighed so hard into the phone again I had to pull it away from my ear. "With their minds. By mental telepathy. It varies. Some days she says they made him up, that he's not even real. You can't reason with her about it, so don't even try. You'll just set her off again. She'll do worse to herself if she thinks you don't believe her."

I told her we were on the same page, then, and that I'd give her a call back as soon as we were on our way. I sat and watched the windshield pile up with snow till I sat in a white cocoon, and Jiminy Cricket did nothing but click. I had to go in the house to get my Triple A card and make the call, but I felt overwhelmed suddenly. When I pushed the door open, the wind pushed back, and a sudden small flurry powdered the bench seat. A good two inches had fallen in the course of a five-minute conversation, seemed like, but I really had no idea how long I sat there, blanking out.

When I come to, I fetched a few logs from the woodshed to load into the rocket stove, since Jeannie hadn't. Then I went in the house and figured out which purse I'd left all my cards in. I told the guy on the line from Triple A, I said, "Every tow truck in town knows where I live. Just tell them it's Vanessa out at Repurpose Farm." Of course he tried to upsell me on the Gold Card. "Y'all are so good to me," I said. "Next year maybe I will."

Once I got a fire going in the rocket stove, I positioned myself where I could watch out the window. "Where were you?" I said to Jeannie. I wanted to keep her talking. We had a good forty-five minutes to kill.

"I was telling you about my brother and Lori Leigh Sprague."

"Oh, right," I said, watching it snow. "That's Jordan Sprague's daughter, isn't it, from his first wife?"

Jordan Sprague married Leigh Ann Bittle the second time around. I always found that a funny coincidence–Leigh Ann and Lori Leigh, not blood related–until I found out Lori Leigh was in fact named after Leigh Ann, who was a good ten years younger than Jordan's first wife and ended up taking him away from her, when they were all supposed to be the best of friends.

"Leigh Ann's mother," I said, "Lori Leigh's step-grandma, taught me seventh grade English."

Don't laugh. She did the best she could.

Two days after he chased Jeannie up the mimosa tree, Billy came and stood leaning in the door to her room. She had her headphones on and didn't hear him the first time. She pulled one side away from her ear. "What?"

He had his fingers in his pockets, his thumbs through his belt loops. He looked like he hadn't slept in a week. It made him seem fragile.

He said, "Thanks a lot!"

Jeannie wasn't sure what she'd done. She just looked at him.

"Lori Leigh broke up with me. I figured you ought to be the first to know, since you're the one that put her up to it."

Jeannie pulled her headphones all the way off and let them hang around her neck. "I did not."

Billy studied the ceiling as if Lori Leigh's words were printed there. "'Even your own sister thinks you got issues.'"

"I never said you had issues. I never said anything like that."

"Tell you what. You stay out of my room from now on, you understand? You stay out of my life!"

"Fine with me." She put her headphones back on. "Your loser life is not my problem and it's not my fault, either."

He was on her before she could scramble to her feet. He jerked her headphones off and twisted them so the cord tightened around her throat. Then he slapped her across the top of her head three or four times and pushed her flat against the wall. She felt the headphones snap between her shoulder blades. On the way out of the room, he took a swipe at her shelf and knocked her collection of Matchbox cars to the floor.

I rolled my eyes and looked out the window. Her story made me glad I never had a brother. "You collected Matchbox cars?" I liked that about her.

She may have nodded, I don't know. The snow fell fatter, thicker than before.

Billy hung out with Tommy Isabel and his one other friend in the world, Jeannie said, whose real name was Ben Abercrombie III, better known as Crumb Number Three, or just Crumb, or sometimes Three. That summer the loose affiliation of losers solidified around the fact that Three had bought himself a bass guitar in order to back up Iz on lead. They needed a drummer, so Billy took to beating on anything that made noise, including his little sister, but more often a section of pipe or a piece of angle iron. For a cymbal, he had a hub cap that he either found or stole, plus a hollowed-out section of wood, some plastic tubs and pvc pipe that he cut to different lengths. He experimented with luggage, too, which he stuffed with his dirty clothes in order to muffle his thumping. They called themselves The Triumvirate and they practiced at all hours, usually in a Quonset hut across the alley behind the John Deere dealership but sometimes at one another's houses.

Iz and Crumb smoked anything they could get their hands on. Billy liked to exaggerate that there wasn't a substance on Earth that one or the other of them had not inhaled, ingested or injected. "This is information," he imparted to Jeannie, pointing all four fingers at her chin, his eyes crackle-glazed with broken capillaries. "You are not to divulge under any circumstance, you value your life."

Jeannie had cards tacked all over her bulletin board and balloons tied to the four corners of her bed since yesterday morning. Billy had yet to wish her a happy birthday. "I'm ten years old, in case you haven't noticed. And I'm not a rat."

"Good thing."

Later in the week, at night, as she lay asleep with her window open, a commotion erupted across the creek. It woke her up. She couldn't see anything from her window, so she unlatched the screen and climbed out, dropped to the ground and crept across the back yard to the gate. Huge yellow flames jumped between the cracks in the stockade fence around the Pendergrafts' yard on the other side of the creek. Someone must have poured something on the fire, because the flames suddenly leaped higher. She heard the scraping sound of Iz on his guitar, the way he played. He switched to a chirping beat that also sounded familiar, from the intro to a song they had made up, and sure enough, she heard Billy keeping time on his suitcase and Crumb thumping away at his bass. They only had the one song to play and they were done—their entire repertoire used up in seven minutes and fourteen seconds. (Jeannie had timed it for them.)

The flames sank back to normal size. Voices carried across the divide, laughter, whistles and loud calls. Jeannie pushed open the gate and sat high up on the creek bank on her side, concealed among the shadows of a row of cypress trees that screened off the next-door neighbors' back yard in lieu of a fence. From there, she could just make out the tops of people's heads, their shadows thrown against the back of Karyn Pendergraft's house.

She sat watching and wondering what would happen if she went over there, if she hopped across the creek and marched up the opposite bank, opened up that high wooden gate and marched in. Billy wouldn't be happy about it, but what could he do? In front of everybody? Probably nothing.

It surprised her that he had so many friends, outside of Izzy and Crumb, the other two corners of the Loser Triangle, "where IQ points vanish like blips on a radar screen." (She'd heard that one from Anna Sylvester. It mortified her that the other kids at school had found out about The Triumvirate and knew how bad they sucked and that her brother was part of it.)

Suddenly a loud crack split the night sky and showered the creek with sparks. Jeannie jumped to her feet. She didn't know at first what it was but she soon saw the sizzle of a second bottle rocket climbing like a meteor going the wrong direction. She followed its trajectory, and when it flashed, the bang that followed still made her jump. A few minutes later, a whole string of Black Cats rattled and popped from inside the Pendergrafts' fence. She'd forgotten how close it was to Fourth of July. More and more fireworks went off, including the quiet beauty of a Roman candle. She loved Roman candles. One soft blossom of color after another. Just whump…whump…whump! So beautiful it hushed the voices at the party for a minute or two, so that when she first picked up on the rhythm of lights beating against the houses to either side of the Pendergrafts', she assumed it was more fireworks.

Then the back gate flew open. Out spilled a dozen teenagers down the creek fanning out everywhichway, five or six in the direction of Palmer Street and two going the other way, toward Mulberry, while one doubled back and climbed over the chain link fence into the Peerlesses' yard. Jeannie recognized her brother's long-legged lope across the creek and up the near bank in her direction. She scrambled and hid in the deep shadow between two cypress trees. If he saw her, he didn't stop to ask what she was doing out there, he just bolted to the back door.

A spotlight froze the gang of kids running toward Palmer, and a voice over a loudspeaker told them to lie face down and spread their arms and legs. When they didn't move, the voice yelled, "Get down now!" and they all fell flat and stayed there.

A flashlight beam circumnavigated the Pendergrafts' back yard. Another one exited the gate and pointed out the two kids fleeing in the other direction to a third cruiser parked on the bridge at Mulberry with its lights out. It looked to Jeannie as if Billy and the kid who jumped the fence into the Peerlesses' yard were the only two to get away. She waited until everything went quiet again before she slipped back to the house and climbed through the window and back to bed, no one ever the wiser.

It was still dark when the police knocked on the door and asked for her dad by name. "Do you have a gold Ford Escort registered to you, Mr. Ivory?" The cop's voice rattled off the plate number.

She didn't hear what her dad said, but the correct answer, of course, was yes. That was their car.

The cop responded in cop talk to a burst of static from his radio, then: "Mr. Ivory, I wonder, can you tell me the current location of that vehicle?"

# ROUNDABOUT ANGEL

I hadn't planned on company. But the snow fell so thick and stuck so to the glass, I couldn't see much of anything out the living room window. Even standing with the door open, I couldn't make out the shapes of things more than twenty, thirty yards from the house — not the shop, the barn, nothing. "I might as well call and cancel that tow truck," I said. "Even if I do get Jiminy started, we ain't gonna make it into town in this, not in one piece, unless it lets up here in the next few minutes."

Jeannie shivered and rubbed her bare arms. "Whatever you think, Vanessa."

"Oh! Sorry!" I shut the front door.

I found her something in my closet to put on over her wife beater. Her own shirt had blood all on the front of it. On my way by the bathroom I picked it off the floor to throw in the wash, saying, "I wish I knew which garage they called." As I handed her a sweatshirt, a white one with an angel and the words "It's Around Me Not About Me" embroidered on the front of it, a movement in the front window caught my eye, a blur passing by like a ghost in the snow. "Never mind," I said. "Here they are." I beat the guy to the door and had it open before he could knock.

Now, how do I say this? Because I don't want to give you the wrong impression; I am no longer the most sought after thing in tight jeans, nor do I swing like a wrecking ball at a home show. Yet there is not a man in Keening County, eligible or not, whose head at one time or another (as I have passed him by or passed him over) has not pivoted at least enough to allow me to get a good look at him. This boy had a face that, had I been able to place it, I might have started with: on a pedestal, while I thought about where else it might look — oh, I don't know, let's just say — less appropriate. Fat flakes of snow clung to his hair and melted, percolating through it dark and wet as strong coffee before the run-off plunged down his forehead, beads of it getting hung up in his brow. He took a swipe at it with a gloved finger. A pair of eyes the color and scent, I swear, of cinnamon baking searched my face as his lips shaped my name in the form of a question.

"You're new!" I informed him.

"Beg pardon?"

"I haven't had you before." I didn't mean it to come out that way—I didn't—but somebody must've hit the pause button on my brain and deactivated what few verbal filters I have left. I failed to catch a single word that dribbled from my own tongue until my mental replay pointed out to me, much too much later, what an ever-loving fool I'd made of myself. In the moment, all I could think out loud was, "Who sent you?"

He looked confused, like maybe he'd taken a wrong turn somewhere. "Did you call about needing a jump, Ms. Cavendish?"

"I sure do. Why don't you come on in?" I still blush to think what kind of psycho music must have been playing in his head, because there has got to be a statute on the books against the way my eyes trespassed on his facial property. The rest of him, thank Jesus, was bundled up to the neck in insulated coveralls. I stepped back—not very far, I'm sure—to let him by when I caught sight of Jeannie with my angel sweatshirt pulled halfway down over her head, nothing showing of her face except her Coca Cola-colored eyes, supersized, gulping at him over the crew collar.

He looked from one of us to the other and did not step through that door. "My boots are all mud," he apologized.

When the timer function in my head begun to blink again, it struck me with the forlorn realization that, in all the years, tears and recriminations it had recorded since long before this boy learned to shave, I had built both a house and a reputation out of mud, and before I could smear that thought from the instrument panel by which I piloted my life, both before and since I touched down in Oklahoma for the second time, I had to know one thing: "What's your daddy's name?"

He looked at me hard for a second, then his eyes veered, looking behind me, following something from left to right. I didn't register what they saw. (I later realized he'd been watching Jeannie pass behind me—still hiding her face, most likely—but I was oblivious to her at that particular moment in time.) When his eyes come back to rest on me, they had softened some. "My dad's passed on," he said. He looked confused.

"Oh. I'm sorry. Recently?"

"Going on six years. I doubt you knew him. Why?"

Which was all I really wanted to hear, but the mere fact that I needed to ask had banked my flaps, if you take my meaning. I laughed and told him not to mind me, I was being silly, then I lied and said he looked like someone I once knew.

"I was fixing to call Triple A back and say never mind." I turned to Jeannie, but she wasn't where I'd left her. "Where'd she get to now?" I wondered out loud. "Thing is, I need to drop her off in town, but this storm come up so sudden. I just don't think I want to take Jiminy out in this and get her stuck."

Cinnamon Buns just looked at me. He struck me as a young man who minded his manners, and I felt like I needed to correct something about myself, so I said, "So sudden*ly*, I mean," and laughed.

I had to explain who Jiminy was, so of course he wanted to see her. We trudged out to the barn together, and I popped the hood.

"Wow!" he said. I got jealous, the way he leaned up against her and run his eyes over her motor mounts.

"Something, ain't she?"

"She still runs?"

"When she wants to."

He went and got his portable charger and come back, clamped his cables to Jiminy's battery posts and climbed in the cab. I gave him the keys and explained about the ignition switch on the floor. He shook his head and grinned at her antiquity.

Jiminy didn't so much as click. He hit the wipers (which, I could've told him they run on vacuum, not juice) then the headlights for good measure. "You're not going anywhere today, Ms. Cavendish."

"That's what I figured. Darrel says I need a new voltage regulator?" Darrel's Eight Ball Motors was the name on the side of the tow truck. Jiminy had paid him a visit a time or two.

"I think you need a starter, too. I'll have to bring her in, but it might take a couple days to get parts. I'll have to go online to find out who still makes them."

I'd known this was coming and that I'd have to bite the bullet sooner or later, but I still argued. "She's all I got for transportation."

He laughed. "Then you don't have any transportation. If your daughter needs a ride into town, I don't mind taking her, I just can't promise to get her back out here. At least not tonight." I tried not to let his assumption get to me (my daughter, indeed!) while I thought about his

59

offer. I don't know what he read in my face, but he looked sheepish. "Probably not what a mother wants to hear, is it?"

"It'll be her call, I guess." I pointed my trigger finger right between his spice cabinet eyes and said, "You just be gentle with my girl!"

I meant Jiminy.

Right at that moment, I had too much on my mind to worry about what was going through his. Underage goddamn son of a prick! I wrapped my coat around my sorry chest and tramped back in the house.

Jeannie had climbed in my bed crosswise, on her knees, with just the toes of her socks sticking out from under the covers.

"Excuse me?" I said.

She burrowed in deeper and started rocking forward and backward. Her toes disappeared. Whatever she said come out too muffled for me to make sense of it. I explained to her that she had the offer of a ride home if she wanted it, and she froze. Then she resumed rocking and begun to chant, it sounded like, mumbling the same thing over and over.

I walked around the bed, peeled the covers back and lifted the pillow from her head. She kept rocking and repeating. "I can't handle this, I can't handle this, I can't handle this..."

"I'll take that as a no thank you."

I didn't mean to be such a bitch, though. I sat beside her and rested my hand on her back, between her shoulder blades. She felt hot to me. The movement of my hand to and fro with her, as she rocked, soothed me if it did nothing for her. I said, "Honey, you don't have to go anywhere right now, with anyone, if you don't want to."

*You stupid, stupid girl! Can I go in your place?*

In the dimming light of a skyless winter afternoon, Jiminy, with her front end hiked up on the skids of the tow truck, looked like a beagle trying to mount a rottweiler. "I guess we're just gonna stay put for now," I told Adonis-in-coveralls. "I don't have any idea how I'm gonna collect my pickup truck, though, if you take her."

"I don't mind coming back out to get you," he said. "Or Darrel will, if I can't. We'll give you a call with the estimate, one way or the other.

60

If I was you, though, I'd sell this old truck to me for the right price and get you something more reliable."

"You're not the first to say that."

He smiled. "Maybe not the first, but I bet I'm the most sincere. I'd take good care of her for you, fix her up right."

It's a wonder I didn't burn a hole through the paper and scorch his clipboard when I signed my name. "Vanessa Cavendish," I said out loud. "You have my number?" (I just wanted to make sure.)

It occurred to me I hadn't got his name yet. I opened my mouth to ask him as he turned and flipped up his collar. I didn't think he heard me over the wind in his face and the sound of his motor, but he turned and waved before he climbed in his truck, and shouted something. It sounded like "Cherry Pie!" It might have been his name or "You must be high!" or who knew what?

I stood there longer than it took him and Jiminy to disappear through the slantwise veil of falling snow, still holding Jeannie's bloody shirt balled up under my arm and half-covered in snow, because I had never made it to the washing machine. God knows what kind of insane asylum he figured he'd managed to escaped from!

"Is he gone?" Jeannie asked the minute I stuck my head back in the bedroom.

"Yes," I said and let it hang in the air like a question.

She peered out at me from under the covers. She still hadn't pulled my sweatshirt down over the lower half of her face. "You sure?"

I had put up with enough. I said, "Jeannie—" but that was as far as I got in my attempt to find out what her problem was now.

As the collar of my angel sweatshirt fell from her face, she seized up, mouth open, fingers splayed across her face as it contorted in a scream that would not come. She purpled, the veins stood out from her neck, from the backs of her hands. She shook all over like an earthquake had struck. A low, shuddering moan started somewhere so far down, I swear I felt it come rumbling up from under the bedroom floor, building and building, until it clawed its way up her belly to her chest and shredded a hole through her vocal chords. Her back arched, her chest heaved, she hung suspended as if by the ragged shriek torn from her throat. When the scream released her, she collapsed and lay sobbing, her jaw sprung on its hinges as she tried to breathe, tears puddling, fingers clutching at the sheets.

I wrapped her up in my arms the best way I could, and this time I did the rocking, while she blubbered and hitched and tried to speak and couldn't. I made shushing noises to the beat of her caterwauling and tried not to think about Jiminy and the smell of cinnamon. Eventually she calmed down enough to swallow and take deep breaths. Then she told me.

"That wah — wah — was Jarrod Frye!"

I think I said, "Oh."

"*You don't understand!*"

I told her she was right about that. I did not tell her that somewhere around about the time she crawled up under my blankets, I had given up trying. "So that was your running buddy?"

"I haven't seen him since tenth grade."

I remained unenlightened. "So I guess you don't really know what kind of driving record he has."

She give me a blank look. After a minute, though, the light dawned, and she said, "Very funny!" and pushed me away, but then luckily she snorted and started laughing, and so did I. Out of relief, probably, because, as jokes go, I hope I've told better.

"I think I slobbered on your shoulder," she confessed.

"Nice." She had. I took my shirt off and wadded it up with hers and took them both to the back porch to drop them in the wash. She followed and informed me that I had freckles even on my back. I said, "Yep," and she hugged me from behind. Laid her cheek against my shoulder, wrapped her arms around me tight and just held me for a long minute.

"Thank you, Vanessa!"

I said, "You're welcome." Then I said, "It's kinda chilly back here," and she let me go. I made a bee line for my closet and put on a flannel shirt.

"I meant, for not making me explain."

"No problem," I said.

I had a chicken breast I'd baked the day before and a little broth left over, so we cut up some vegetables and boiled water for noodles, while she picked up her story where she'd left off, saying the cop that came to their door that night long ago never actually charged her brother with anything, although he did handcuff Billy and make him sit in the back of the cruiser, behind the plexiglass, while he and Mr. Ivory sat up front and talked the situation over. Billy still had on his jeans and a tee-shirt. He was the only member of the family that was dressed.

Her dad had on a robe, at least. Jeannie and her mom stood on the front porch in their pee jays, watching. After a while, her dad rolled down the window of the cruiser and called up to her mom that the cop was taking him and Billy to get the car. Then the cruiser pulled away from the curb.

A long time later, her dad pulled into the driveway by himself, got out, locked all four doors by hand and checked each one individually before he came in the house. "Where's the flashlight?" he said. He was not happy.

"Where's the flashlight?" her mom said. "Where is my son?"

"I need the flashlight."

"You don't need the flashlight right this minute."

"Yes, I do, too."

"No, you need to sit down and tell me what the hell is going on!"

"If he's got drugs in the car, I need to find them. They were very goddamn lenient. Very goddamn lenient. Now, I need that flashlight, Maureen. I need that flashlight now."

"Why don't you just sit down and calm down and tell me what's happened to my son first, and then I'll help you find the flashlight. Will you do that much for me?"

"They took him down to the station." He spoke with his eyes closed, waving his hands in the air and touching his chest. Jeannie had never seen him in such a state. "I'm going to go get him and bring him home in a minute, but first, before I can do that, I need to make sure that there are no drugs in the car, so that when I do go get him and bring him home, I can know whether to beat him within an inch of his life or a half-inch of his life."

"I am telling you one more time to sit down!" Jeannie's mom commanded him. "I will get you the flashlight! Jeannie, Honey, you go on back to bed."

Her dad did not sit down, Jeannie did not go back to bed, and nobody found the flashlight. They all three searched the car in their pajamas, using the overhead lights. They couldn't see in the trunk very well, until Jeannie came up with the idea to park the car in the street, under the street lamp.

They never did find any drugs.

"I can tell you this," her dad said. "They're not gonna believe we didn't find anything."

"Why do you have to say it like that? Aren't you the least bit relieved?"

"They were going to impound the car. They still could. Yes, I'm relieved, but what are we gonna do if they don't believe me?" He shoved his hand into the crease between the passenger seat and the cushion and fished around in there for the umpteenth time.

"They'll have to. So what if they don't? We'll deal with that in the morning."

Searching the car had been something to do, at least, while her dad let off steam. He spoke more calmly after that, more rationally. "I guess maybe we ought to get dressed before we drive downtown. What do you think, Jeannie?"

She said, "I think we ought to go like this."

That made him laugh. Then he looked sad and worried again and hugged her. "I hope you don't turn out like your brother."

"I hope I don't, either."

I stood with the chicken breast cut up in the cup of my hands and looked at her. "What did you turn out like?" I wondered.

She cocked her eyebrows at me. They were the same color as her roots, just a shade lighter than the mascara streaked across her cheekbone. "Come here," I said. I dumped the chicken in the broth with the vegetables and scrubbed my hands in the sink. Then I wiped her face with my wet thumb. She caught my hand and turned my wrist so she could study my scar. The tip of her middle finger felt like velvet, tracing the faint but still ugly squiggle up to the crease of my elbow. I wanted to pull back, but she gripped me, bowed her head and kissed the most prominent gnarl on the inside of my forearm, right where it always felt the numbest.

When she looked at me again, she smiled only barely and spoke in a voice so soft I had to strain to catch it, a whisper as faint as glass. "What you get is what you see, Vanessa."

Her eyes on me were as wet as two wide worlds, showing me nothing whatsoever but my curved reflections.

# THE TREEHOUSE EXEMPTION

Over supper I said, "So he didn't have anything in the car, your brother? Any drugs, I mean?"

Jeannie tore off a hunk of bread with a chuckle. "Next day, he invited me into his room and told me he was in a lot of trouble. I said, 'Um, yeah!'"

Billy waited for her to make another smart remark, but she kept still.

He said, "I need a huge favor, Jeannie. I need you to get my suitcase back."

"Your suitcase."

"My clothes are in it."

"Why do you carry all your clothes around like that? It doesn't make sense."

He had no answer. "I need to get it back and I can't go over there. I can't even leave the house. You can."

"That's because I didn't get myself arrested."

He looked miserable. "I thought I was going away for good."

Jeannie wondered what it would be like with Billy gone away for good. It would be an improvement, of course, but she didn't need to say so to his face.

"Will you get it for me, Jeannie? Please? I'll get you a new set of headphones."

He already owed her that much.

"What do you want, then?"

She looked him in the eye. "In addition?" she said.

"Yeah. Sure. Why not?"

"What I want is to be left alone by you. To be treated like I'm your sister, like you care whether I live or die. Like, what if it was the other way around? Would you even consider going and getting something back for me from one of my friends' houses, if I needed you to?"

"You don't have any friends."

Jeannie closed her eyes and opened her mouth, reliving the conversation for me there in my kitchen. She let out a little burst of exasperation and told Billy, as if he sat there having soup with us, "You're not helping your case much."

"I would," he said. "I would if you needed me to."

She hated his pleading. Hated the way it made her feel—not sorry for him, but cold inside. She soon learned, though, that inside that coldness—deep down in the pinprick center of it—reigned a powerful little bitch. She scrutinized him. Pointing her butter knife at me as if I, Vanessa, had been drafted to play the part of Billy, she negotiated. "If I need something from you—whatever it is—and nobody else on Earth can do it, you will?"

"Yes?" That was me, speaking his part, agreeing to God knows what. Although, I need you to understand, it wasn't quite that simple. What I thought I was saying was nothing but, "Yes? Go on. What happened next?" Yet she took it as me saying Billy's line. As if I could channel him for her.

"And you will never, ever, under any circumstances, raise your hand to me or kick me or do anything to me ever again?"

I wagged my head. And again, on the one hand, I only meant to express my dismay at the way a teenage boy had treated his little sister, at the predicament that gave rise to her need to wring such a promise out of him. At least, I tell myself that, because I have such a hard time admitting that I felt—I don't know what, exactly, but not in control of my own body—as if some—

But see? If I say it outright like that, it sounds ridiculous. Nothing and nobody took possession of me. I just got caught up in her story and went on automatic for a split-second. Of course I would never raise a hand to her! What need had I ever given her to extract a promise like that from me?

She eyed me, spooned her soup and held it level. " 'Well, okay,' he said me. 'But let me ask you this: What if you deserve it?'

"I told him, 'I don't. I don't ever do anything like that to you.'

"Because you can't."

Now, I swear to God, I have played this over and over in my mind, trying to get it straight—the way it actually played out there at my table—and to this day I cannot be one hundred percent sure who made that particular statement—whether she did or I did or neither one of us. The words hung in the air between us: "Because you can't."

She dropped her spoon in her bowl and stood up, scraping her chair across the floor with the backs of her knees. "I got up to go. Negotiations were over, as far as I was concerned. But he grabbed me by the wrist." She reached and grabbed me, demonstrating.

I stared at her, dumbfounded, caught up in her grip and in her story both, no longer sure what part I played.

"I just stared at his hand and I recalled the way Lori Leigh had handled him in the back yard that day, while I watched from up in the tree. I said, 'I guess you don't want your suitcase back.'

"He let go." (She dropped my spoon hand.) "That was a start."

I sat and listened.

"I told him, 'I'll be right back.' In my room, unlike in his, I knew where to find things. I tore a sheet of paper out of my science notebook and brought it back with a pen. 'Start writing,' I told him. 'I want everything you promise to do on paper, with your signature, including the headphones and anything else you ever break of mine, paid in full. I'll have my attorney look it over before I agree to anything.'

"'Who? Mom?' he says. 'You can't tell Mom about this, Jeannie. You can't tell anyone.'

"But I had never said Mom. 'You can also stop accusing me of being a rat. Put that in there.'

"'Who, then?'

"'I don't have an attorney,' I said. 'It's a figure of speech.'"

She sat down and resumed her supper, ignoring the soup spattered on the table all around her bowl.

She ended up crossing the creek and talking to Karyn Pendergraft about the suitcase. Karyn said it was too heavy. There was no way Jeannie could carry it.

"Will you help me, then?"

"I guess I have to. I can't have it here when my parents get home. What is he, crippled?"

"Grounded."

"You can tell him for me I said life's a fucking bitch. Asshole. Everybody knows the cops were here last night. My folks are coming back early because of it, and my ass is in a bad enough sling without him leaving his suitcase here, like what? He was sleeping over? Jesus! Like he thought he was moving in with me? What? My folks are fucking gonna freak the fuck out on me!"

"We can push it down this side of the creek, if you'll help me drag it up the other side."

So that was what they did. "What's he got in this thing?" Karyn kept asking.

Jeannie didn't know. They got the suitcase as far as the back door of the Pendergrafts' house and down on the ground. It was an old suitcase from before the days when they started putting wheels on the bottoms and pull-out handles, but the outside had a hard plastic coating, so it slid across the yard easy enough. Once they got it to the gate, all they had to do was let go, and it went sailing down the grassy bank.

"Oh, shit!" Karyn said just before it went *splushhhh!* into what little water was left standing in the creek bottom. They ran after it and hauled it up onto the opposite bank.

"You think it's all right?"

"I don't know what he's got in it besides his clothes," Jeannie said, "and I'm sure they need to get washed, anyway."

Karyn looked at her funny. "His clothes? Really? What the fuck for?"

Jeannie rolled her eyes and shook her head. How was she supposed to know?

"You think it's all right, though? The suitcase?" Karyn couldn't seem to make up her mind how she wanted to feel. "Not like I give a fuck. Really?"

Jeannie said they could let it air dry once they got it up to her yard. So Karyn helped drag it uphill by the handle, while Jeannie got behind it and pushed.

"Is your mom at home?"

Jeannie grunted.

At the gate Karyn said, "That's as far as I go. I'm in enough trouble. Tell him to give me a call. He owes me."

Jeannie got the suitcase through the gate by herself and pushed it to a patch of sun between the mimosa tree and the house. Then she opened it up to see how much water had got inside and right away she saw why it was worth so much to Billy to get it back. His dirty clothes were all stuffed in one side behind a divider that snapped in place. In the other side, he had two heavy blankets folded up nice and tight with a space left in between where he packed his pipes and angle irons, several pairs of drumsticks half beat to splinters, bells, wood blocks, everything. And sure enough, a plastic baggie with what she knew had to be weed, because there were two blunts hollowed out and also an assortment of pills of various sizes, shapes and colors in a second bag tucked inside the first one.

She knew it would nullify her agreement with him, in Billy's mind, if he didn't get back what he was looking for. She also knew that, realistically-speaking, he could sign his name in front of a congregation of notary publics, it didn't mean he'd stick by what he said. She took the baggie out and closed up the suitcase — it hadn't got all that wet inside, after all — and left it beside the back porch while she took off on her bike with the baggie full of drugs stuffed in the waist of her jeans.

She didn't have a plan. All she knew was she'd been tricked, played, like in a movie, conned into smuggling drugs across the creek for her dumb-ass brother. She stopped at the corner of Fair Meadow and Mulberry to fish the baggie out of her jeans and toss it in the gutter. It rolled across the grate of the storm drain and got hung up between two of the bars, so she walked her bike backwards and lined up the front tire to roll over it and push it down in, but before she could do that, a gasp of wind sucked it and a whole slew of dried leaves straight down.

*Sssschloop!* Gone.

She rode back to the house and told Billy where he could find his suitcase, then she took off again. She needed to tell somebody what kind of an idiot she had for a brother and what she'd done about it and to get a second opinion. She didn't want to admit it, but his remark about how she didn't have any friends had hurt. She needed to prove him wrong, so she decided to pay Jarrod Frye a visit.

When she got there, no one was home.

She didn't see Jarrod all the rest of that summer and she forgot about Billy and the drugs until one day in October, when Jarrod was supposed to come over and tell her what he'd found out about Eugene's last name (at the time it was still "Doe") and what it meant.

Jarrod's step-dad drove him. The Lambs had bought the house on Fair Meadow more than a year ago and now that they had finally moved in, Mr. McEarland said, "I'm curious to see what they've done with it." He had a look in his eye when he said it, evasive and haunted, and Jeannie knew there was more to his coming by than mere curiosity. The Lambs had built their addition over the spot where the ladder had broken his wife's neck. Jeannie and Jarrod followed him at a distance, watching as he crossed the lawn to the porch and knocked at the door. Eugene answered.

"That's him," Jeannie said. She and Jarrod hung back. Eugene appeared only for a moment before Mrs. Lamb replaced him at the door, smiling and inviting Mr. McEarland in. She waved to Jarrod and Jeannie, too. "You two, come on in!" she urged them, but Jarrod wagged his head and told Jeannie, "Let's get out of here!" They had business to discuss.

They walked up Fair Meadow past Jeannie's school to a place called Hidden Park which occupied a city block between the highway on one side and the train tracks and grain elevators on the other. Along the way, Jarrod said, "He's working things out in his own way." His stepdad, he meant. It took Jeannie a minute to figure that out. "His therapist told him to let go of what happened, not of my mom, and to stop blaming himself. And for me to stop blaming him, too."

"I thought it was an accident." Jeannie said.

They sat in the swings at the playground end of the park and didn't swing. Jeannie asked if he had to go to the therapist, too.

He shrugged, said he'd gone a couple of times. Then he picked up a pebble and threw it, not at anything. "Dieter still goes."

She didn't know how to ask what she wanted to know. She started to say, "Is it working?" but thought better of it, thinking it might sound like an insult to Dieter, and she didn't mean it that way. "Why don't you still go?" she asked instead.

"Same reason."

"As what?"

"Working things out in my own way."

Jeannie said, "I get it."

"No, you don't."

"I'm not stupid."

"But you still got your mom," he told her.

She couldn't argue with that.

"No offense or anything."

Even though it was October, it was still warm enough for short sleeves. Jeannie started kicking herself back and forth on the swing, watching her big toenail poke its head in and out of the hole in her plaid sneaker. She had painted her toes a color called "Pearl Jam" after the band. It had an opalescence about it like the shell of a snare drum in

70

the window of Manolo's Music downtown that Billy wouldn't shut up about. Her nail color was chipping and she didn't care. Her legs, when she kicked them out straight to make herself go higher, were almost as brown as Jarrod's arms. When he swung forward, the wind opened his shirt up between the buttons, and she saw that his tan was not just on his arms. She swung so high that the chain went slack and then jerked and twisted her sideways. She did it again so she could look at him without his knowing she was doing it on purpose.

He stopped swinging, and so did she. He came over and started turning her around and around so her chains twisted up on each other. "I wish you'd move back," she told him as he wound her up. "We could build another tree house, and your dad wouldn't even know anything about it." She said this without realizing at the time that, in her fantasy, his dad and Dieter did not move back — only Jarrod did. And she moved with him into their tree house world and they both left their stupid brothers far behind. They left the entire City of Keening behind. "Far, far behind," she said with a wistful look in her eye.

"We could build a tree house anywhere in the world," Jarrod said, caught up in her daydream. Then he let go of her chains. She went spinning and spinning and shrieking with laughter, until he caught her and started twisting her in the other direction.

"I found out what D.O.E. stands for," he said later, as they walked back to her house. "Department of Engineering. That's the people who are in charge of all the drain pipes and the waterworks and the sewage treatment plant and everything, basically, except the Police and the Fire Department and, like, the Mayor. They run everything else."

"Oh, shit!" she said. "Shit, shit, shit!" Then she told him about the drugs she'd found in Billy's suitcase and that she'd dropped them down the storm drain.

"That's okay," Jarrod said. "They find stuff like that all the time down there. They must get a lot of money that way."

"Drug money?"

"I didn't even think of that. I just meant, people drop a lot of money, and it ends up down there. I bet those guys are secretly the richest people in town!"

Jeannie wrinkled her nose.

"Does he know?" Jarrod asked her. "Your brother?"

"That's the funny thing. He never even mentioned it."

Surprisingly, Billy had kept his end of the bargain with her. Not that he'd been nice to her, but he hadn't been mean, either. The interesting thing, to her, was that he'd started going to Lori Leigh's church, thinking that if he played his cards right, he could get back with her. Karyn Pendergraft went there, too, to the First Assembly of God. Karyn and Leigh Ann were best friends, supposedly, and Karyn was coaching Billy on the side about how to win her back. So who knew what was going on, really? She tried to explain all that to Jarrod—what she called, in the telling of it to me, the "comic-book politics" of the situation—but she and Jarrod didn't read the same comic books, evidently. She had the feeling that what he heard was something totally different from what she said.

"I'm not ever going to get weird like that about a girl," he told her. "Just so you know. Going to church and everything? I mean, if you believe in God, it's one thing."

"I don't," she said quickly. Then she regretted it, because she wasn't sure.

"I didn't mean like you," he amended. He jutted his chin at the curb in front of her house, where his step-dad had parked their car. "He took off and left me." The fact seemed not to surprise him.

They worked out a plan to take her bike halfway to his house, then she would turn around and come back, and he would continue from there to his house on foot. He steered and pedaled; she sat sideways across the bar in front of him. In her mind, halfway meant the cable swing, but when he glided past it, she didn't say anything, afraid that if she suggested he stop there, he would think she was manipulating him, after they'd already spent all that time on the swing set at Hidden Park. Anything like that, she decided, would have to be his idea. He swooped in a wide arc around the corner onto Washington Street and kept pedaling. At his school, he said, "We came a little more than halfway."

"That's okay. You did all the work."

They stood facing each other across the frame of her bike. Before he passed it to her, she said, "I might believe in God, but I would never make you go to church."

He looked confused at first, then he nodded. "People who live in tree houses are exempt from going to church."

"Right."

He put out his hand, and they shook on it. As Jeannie told me this part, she mooned at the palm of her own hand as if Jarrod had written her a goddamn love letter. It made me want to channel Billy for real so I could slap the stupid out of her.

When she got back to Fair Meadow, she saw Eugene Lamb standing in the front yard of Jarrod's old house, smiling. He waved at her as she sailed by. "Not like he expected me to wave back, though," she said. "More as if to say, 'Like it or not, Jeannie Ivory, I live here now.' "

The next day was a Sunday. Mr. Lamb and Eugene spent the afternoon measuring their back yard, driving wooden stakes into the ground and stretching string from one stake to another. Jeannie watched from the creek, through their chain link fence. Todd Lamb waved. "We're building a tree house," he called. "Want to help?"

Furious, she stalked away, covering the ground between their back yard and hers in no time. She slammed the back door, making the kitchen floor dance.

"What's the matter with you?" Billy said. He was still in his dress pants from church.

"I'd like to know how you can build a tree house in your back yard," she demanded, "when you don't even have a tree!"

# CAN I GET A WITNESS?

I needed to get clear on one thing. "All of this," I asked—"your brother, Jarrod Frye, everything you've been telling me—it's all got something to do with Eugene Lamb?"

"Everything does," Jeannie said.

I had canceled my cable subscription. Living alone like I did (I'd say I was "between men" but I don't want to make it sound like more fun than I was actually having), running a business more than took up any free time of an evening. Most days after we closed up shop and Jeannie took off, I stayed late out in the shop, making something else to sell. So I didn't quite know what to do with her after supper except listen to her talk as I scrubbed the kitchen table with a wet sponge.

Dark had fallen, the snow had not let up, and neither had she. "Now you. He'll be coming after you next."

I wrinkled my nose. "Eugene? After me? How do you mean?"

She chewed at the sleeve of my sweatshirt the way she always chewed at her gloves. "You'll see. He'll get to you."

She was talking about a boy not yet out of high school. Seriously?

I watched the snow appearing out of nowhere, patting its fat paws against the windowpane over my sink in the kitchen. "Would you like something to drink?" She was close enough to twenty-one. It wasn't like we'd be out driving, getting in trouble of any kind.

"All right. I'll tell you," she said, as if I'd asked a totally different question. "I said he sucks the life out of me. Would you like to know how he does it? This is how. He makes you a member of the Sewer Boy Fan Club. You, Vanessa, whether you choose to be or not. Why you, you want to ask? No other reason than because I like you, because I care about you, because you—more than anybody else I could name at this point—you matter to me. I don't mean to come across as overly dramatic, but you play a significant role in my life just by virtue of the amount of time I spend in your company, in your…environment. I've tried-" she hesitated for one split second, then came out with it-"I've tried to minimize your importance to me, but I can't deny it altogether."

"Okay…" I took down two glasses, wondering where this was going.

"I keep telling you, you should get rid of me. This is why."

"You lost me."

"Being important to me makes you important to him. He's already started in on you, in case you hadn't noticed."

"You mean that thing about wanting to write a newspaper article?"

"Just be prepared. That's all I'm saying."

"Prepared for what?" I couldn't fathom how her caring about me made me a member of somebody else's fan club. Or, assuming it was true, why that was a bad thing. "Can I just tell you? You're not making a whole lot of sense to me right now."

"No. I'm sure I'm not." She looked pleased with herself, superior—arms crossed, smiling at the floor—but at the same time, bitter. She wouldn't look at me.

"Could you try?" I took some ice down from the freezer and dropped it in the two glasses, hunted around and finally found the vodka under the sink behind the dish detergent after she had to move out of my way.

"I've never been able to get anyone else to see what he does. If I could just get a witness, just this one time, that's all I ask. Even Jarrod never quite saw it for what it was."

Now, you might look at this from where you sit and see how she reeled me in, made me want to feel special, smarter, more aware, more understanding, however you choose to think of it. I didn't have the luxury of reading about it, though. I was in it, inside the snow globe with her. It was a subtle business, the way she put her pain on display, then concealed it, let the image of it flicker in and out like one of those holographic images where you look at it one way, it's cuddly as a sad-faced koala bear, but just you tilt it ever so slightly and it turns grisly on you. Her pain seemed to take her to a place just out of my reach, beyond a veil of either real mystery or bogus delusion—I couldn't fathom which from one minute to the next.

When she touched my scar, then kissed it the way a child kisses a boo-boo to make it all better, the pure physical sensation of it tickled everything back to the front of my mind—not just the half-buried pain of my own ancient history but also, owing to an old desperation that led me once, and not but that once, to try to—but to try to what, exactly?—to extinguish the pain of my existence? Or just to lance it, the way she did? I won't say she played on my sympathies, but she drew on them. She made our common experience, in a weird way, sacred. Ordinary yet mystical, as if our two brands of loneliness stood side by side, touching. In a way, she woke my loneliness up, not just by touching it, but by putting her lips to it. By tasting it. The way you touch your tongue to the two posts of a nine-volt battery. It gives you just enough of a zing to let you know it's still got some life in it.

In a way I didn't entirely grasp, she wanted to make us blood sisters. And I felt—but this must be how she got to me, how she hooked me into her scheme of things—she made me feel like the mother superior of blood-letting, compared to her little novice cuts. "I admire you," she said, "If I had your courage..." She pointedly glanced at my left arm again. I felt the scar twang like a string that hadn't been tuned properly—plucked hard, not bowed. The harsh twang of it shot to my gut, and deeper, straight down through me. "If I could just get there," she said (as if she knew exactly how she played me, how it felt to be played by her, the way they say a virtuoso becomes one with her instrument), "I don't think he could follow me. I think I could outrun him." She took the glass I held out to her, filled with whatever kind of juice I had in the fridge—cranberry or cherry-pomegranate or I couldn't begin to tell you—and set it down behind her. Her eyes sparkled with a deeper kind of light, darker than garnets.

My laugh betrayed me. Betrayed how hollow I felt. "Now you're really not making sense." I drank from the glass in my other hand, not tasting what was in it. "Nobody on earth wants to go there."

"I do. I want to go there. I want to cross over to the other side."

"You don't know."

"Show me, then. Teach me."

"Teach you what? How to kill yourself?"

"See? That's just it, though. You're alive. I'm the one that's dying."

"No," I said. "You're not. You might be afraid to live is all."

She slid her eyes off to one side. "I've tried that."

"You have not!" I lost patience. "Your problem is, you close yourself off to the world, to everybody and everything. If you want to live, you have to open yourself up first. To life, not death. Whatever this is, it's not about Eugene, it's about—"

"You, Jean?"

"Oh, puh-leeze!"

She looked at me hard, grinning, as if she had trumped me and any-

76

thing I might say to contradict her, now or in the future.

"You were a kid. You had some fucked-up, third-grade idea that you were responsible for another kid that got himself trapped in a storm sewer. And what? You want to blame your entire life on that? It's ridiculous! You're an adult now. You can think big girl thoughts. Idolizing me for no good reason, not for anything worthwhile I might have ever done, not for helping anyone else out or for trying to build a business and a home and a life for myself, but because I cut myself a little deeper than you did? That's just so much fucking bu—"

"A little deeper?"

"I had my baby ripped out of my goddamn arms!" I screamed at her. Without even knowing it, I slammed my glass on the counter, the juice-colored vodka erupting from it in a minor volcano. I balled my fists at my sides. I leaned in against her, rigid, enraged, my face within an inch of hers, spewing at her like a drill sergeant. "I was fifteen years old and two thousand miles from everybody I knew, with no one in the world except a man I thought I loved and a baby I had no fucking clue how to take care of! And they took him! They just took him! They took my baby! My flesh and my blood! To this day, I have no idea where or why or what I did to deserve it! And you want to tell me you look up to me? What the fuck do you know, Jeannie Ivory? What the fuck do you know about me that makes you think I have it in me to give a fuck about you and your stupid-ass delusions of martyrdom in the first place? You want to try and kill yourself? Really kill yourself? You want to go deep?" I no longer knew what I was saying. I think I said, "Be my fucking guest!"

She grabbed my face between her hands, got her fingers hooked behind the hinges of my jawbone. "That's more like it!" she snarled. And she pulled me in and kissed me, full on, on the mouth. I reared back, but she came with me, climbing on my feet to make herself taller than she was, leaning into me, bearing down and pressing and pulling at me and at the same time backing me up across the floor. "I want that! I want your pain!" she demanded, her breath on me, walking me backwards into the other room. "I want your anger! I want your venom, Vanessa! I need it! I want him to have to fight me for it this time! Fight me for you! Fight both of us! I need you to know everything. I need you to see everything he does. I need you to understand, for once, exactly what's at stake and where he gets it from and why." I didn't know the tears were leaking from my eyes until she started kissing them, sipping them from my cheeks, from both corners of my lips, my chin, my throat. "I want your fear," she added in a sudden, softer tone of voice, more urgent than angry, kissing me, pushing me backwards, "I want your weakness," maneuvering me out of the kitchen, "I want your terror," backing me up, unbuttoning me. "I want your strength, I want your love, I want your violence, Vanessa. I want your loneliness."

She reached in and uncupped my breast, scraping my nipple to full attention with the tape on her bandage. And I won't make any excuses, I won't pretend I hadn't seen it coming or didn't know what was happening or that I hadn't been so lonely for so long that any intimate human contact was enough to set me on the precipice, but I will say that as she lifted my other breast out and pressed her lips to it, sucking it like a hungry animal, I gasped out a confession I didn't know I'd been keeping from myself.

"*Please!*"

As I spoke it, the word broke in two pieces, meaning please don't and please do. And as she toppled me backwards over the arm of the sofa and came climbing over it with me, me laughing nervously as I landed with her weight on me, knocking things off the table, knocking the wind out of me, her lips kissing, her teeth biting, her tongue seeking, her fingers finding, forcing their way at first into my jeans and afterwards, more softly inside them, more insistently inside me, silencing my objections until I had curled and crumpled and pounded against the back of the sofa like the swells of an ocean storm, again and again and once again, until the two of us subsided together in an understanding that felt a little bit like peace.

I tucked a damp strand of hair behind her temple. Still bewildered, knowing I'd have to find some way to incorporate what had just taken place into the way I had always before this laid out my thinking—or not always, but knowing I needed to coordinate it, just as I always intended to lay out what to wear the next morning so I wouldn't have to think about it last minute—I said, "What comes next, I wonder?"

She looked at me with a knowing eye, as if the question made perfect sense to her. "Exactly. It's his move. You ready?"

"For what?" I pushed her shoulders back where I could look at her face. "What the ever-loving Jesus are you talking about?"

She sighed and pulled my sweatshirt on inside-out, so it read: "eM tuobA toN eM dnuorA s`tI" and the angel shape was nothing but a mess of threads. When her head reappeared, she said, "I guess I still haven't told you everything you need to know, have I?"

As I fumbled around, looking for clothes to put back on, she resumed her story.

# BETWEEN LIES AND IMAGINATION

That Fall, Eugene Doe introduced himself not only to his classmates in second grade but to each and every student at Murrow Elementary. Extending his hand at a forty-five degree angle, he made his presence known. "I'm Eugene," he said.

"Like this," Jeannie demonstrated, "halfway between offering and begging."

I took her hand and recognized the angle of the handshake. "That's the way that girl shook hands," I said. "The short one." I didn't remember her name.

"They all want to be him. They're like his fucking groupies."

His behavior might have confused the younger kids, but it did not fail to amuse the older ones. A majority of them, at least. His fellow third-graders found him odd at first, until they saw the way the fifth-graders took to him, and then the fourth grade (Jeannie Ivory not included) followed suit. Eugene became a kind of school mascot. He did nothing to threaten the pecking order. He was small, even for a third-grader, and aggressive in his friendliness.

"Like a puppy with sharp teeth," Jeannie said.

"But he's so ca-yute!" Anita Isabel declared. Soon everyone was saying it.

When he approached Jeannie the first few times, she glared at him or turned her back and found a reason to walk away. His foster mother dropped him off every morning and waited at the curb in her dark blue Thunderbird every afternoon to pick him up, even though their house stood but fifty yards from the Ivorys'. Jeannie, who walked to and from school every day—rain, shine, snow or sleet—refused Mrs. Lamb's offers of a ride with as much politeness as she could muster.

The week before Halloween, Eugene found her in the cafeteria and came up to her from behind. She sat hunched over the illustrations in a book called *Voyage of the Basset*, absorbed in the flowing white mane of a unicorn with the tip of its horn plunged into the waters of a brook-fed pool. Her lips moved silently, reading, "*Miranda discovered that she was indeed part of the magic*," when the sewer boy's hand inserted itself between her face and the page.

"I'm Eugene." As always, he emphasized the first syllable of his name. Everybody said it that way now.

Jeannie stiffened, no longer hunched over her book but sitting rigidly vertical, glaring at his small, straight, cleaned-up fingernails. She growled, "I know who you are, Sewer Boy."

Sadie Barnes, Galinda Swenson and Jana Angleton gaped in silent unison. Eugene withdrew his hand.

"We're neighbors," he said, making his voice sound hurt, yet reasonable.

"Get away from me!"

When he didn't go, she tried to push away from the table, only to find that he stood with his hip pressed against the back of her chair, preventing her departure. He took a deep breath, as if he had anticipated such a response from her and had steeled himself in advance. "I just wanted to say thank you, because if it hadn't been for you telling everybody I was trapped down there, I might've never got rescued."

"You're not welcome!" Jeannie scowled.

The other girls exchanged looks of shock, shame, scandal, outrage. She pushed hard, hoping to move Eugene out of her way but instead shoving the table against her lunch mates and tipping Jana Angleton over backwards.

The school acted swiftly. Jeannie found herself in the Counselor's office, talking to Ms. Bergeron. This is a woman I have encountered a time or two in town. Her first name, I believe, is Meredith, or Judith, something like that, a name that ends in a lisp. I see her sometimes at the grocery store, a shawl draped around her shoulders and a pair of glasses a little too wide for the shape of her face, blocking an entire freezer section while she studies the ingredients in a bag of frozen corn. When she acknowledges a person, her lips spread themselves thin and tuck themselves in at the corners, not in a way you might call unfriendly, but not in a smile, either. Jeannie recalled the way her nylons whispered when she crossed or uncrossed her legs, how she leaned forward with one arm braced across her knee and the other hand beside her on the seat cushion, clutching a notepad. She seemed eager to hear Jeannie's side of the story. She led with, "Do you know a boy in third grade named Eugene?"

"I do." Jeannie had watched Law and Order on TV and she knew the criminal should keep her answers short and to the point. "I know who he is. I don't really *know* him, know him."

"He introduced himself to you at lunch today, didn't he?"

Jeannie frowned and nodded.

"He did? Was he friendly towards you?"

"I was reading my book. I didn't feel like being bothered."

"Well," Ms. Bergeron forged ahead, but not in a direction Jeannie had anticipated. "Eugene thinks very highly of you. He says you were instrumental in saving his life, and that's what — that's something that puzzles me and I don't really understand. I'd like your help with it, if you don't mind."

"I never saved his life. I was just there when it happened. I didn't have anything to do with it."

Ms. Bergeron waited, in case Jeannie had more to say, then she pointed out, "Eugene seems to think you helped save his life, though. Do you ever wonder how that must feel, to think that someone else has saved your life?"

"No."

"How do you think it might feel?"

"Okay, I guess."

"Yeah," Ms. Bergeron pondered. "Yeah, I guess it would feel okay. Would you feel anything else besides just okay?"

"I don't know."

"Would you feel, mmmmm…grateful, maybe?"

"I don't know." Jeannie squirmed. She knew she looked guiltier and guiltier the longer this went on. "I might."

"I think I might, too. If I was trapped underground, and someone helped me to get rescued — even if I only thought they helped me to get rescued — I think I might feel very grateful."

"You think he feels grateful to me!" Jeannie said. It came out as more of an accusation than a question. "You think he thinks he owes me something!"

Ms. Bergeron sat back now, cooling. "That's often how people do feel toward someone who's helped them in a big way."

"Like he owes me his life, though? *His* life?"

Ms. Bergeron nodded rapidly. She wasn't smiling. "Mmm-hmmm. Maybe."

"I don't think so! I don't want his life! I never told anyone around here about him. Ever. I only told one person, and he doesn't even go to school here anymore, and then he told Dieter, and Dieter told everyone at his school, and they told people, and it got out of control. It wasn't even a true story! I made it up!"

Ms. Bergeron looked worried.

"I made it up!"

"You made up a story, Jeannie? About Eugene?"

"He wasn't real, though!" Tears stung her eyes now. She knew she'd gone too far. She knew she could never explain to an adult's satisfaction that Eugene Doe was not a real person but a figment of her imagination—that he was not normal or good, that he had never been a normal little boy who fell into the sewer and got lost but something that had come from there, something born of the sewer—that the way a normal person might feel about being rescued did not apply to him.

"What concerns me, Jeannie—and this does not come from Eugene, you understand that? He thinks the world of you. It comes from other people who overheard you. You called him a name, didn't you?"

Jeannie looked straight ahead, at a blank spot on the wall of Ms. Bergeron's office. "Yes."

"What name did you call him?"

"I called him Sewer Boy, because that's what he is."

"Did you tell him to go back where he came from?"

Jeannie's eyes darted to the Counselor's face, to the grim line she made of her mouth. Behind her glasses, Ms. Bergeron's eyes had turned flat, opaque, unsympathetic.

"I didn't say that."

"Didn't you?"

"No."

Ms. Bergeron tilted her head and again assumed an air of concern. "Didn't you say you'd be glad to show him how to get back down there?" She consulted her notepad. "Down there 'with the rats and the worms where you belong.' Did you say that?"

"No."

"Can you imagine how that must have felt, Jeannie? To hear a threat like that?"

"No, because he didn't hear a threat like that. Not from me, because I didn't say that."

"Your mother is on her way to pick you up, Jeannie. She's going to have to know what happened."

Jeannie didn't say anything else. She tried to figure out why Sadie or Jana would make things up about her. Or Galinda, but she didn't think it was Galinda.

"Jeannie, has anyone ever threatened you like that?"

"Huh?"

"Has anyone—"

"No. No one has, and I didn't, either."

"Have you ever been afraid that somebody might want to put you down there or take you down there and leave you? No one has ever suggested such a thing or given you reason to believe the—"

"No. They haven't." She remembered Jarrod suggesting they take a shortcut through the drainage pipe to get to the cable swing, but that wasn't a threat. He was only pretending.

"Because it's natural to wonder about things like that—especially when we know someone that it's happened to. Do you know how Eugene got down there in the first place?"

"I suppose you think it was me that put him there?"

Mrs. Bergeron looked really worried when she said that—worried and interested. "Why would I think that?"

"How could I? He didn't even exist before that. Did you ever see him? Was he ever enrolled in school before? Anywhere?"

Ms. Bergeron's concern intensified.

"Did he have a mother and father anywhere? No!"

"We don't know the answers to those questions, do we?"

"Well, but it makes it all pretty weird, doesn't it?"

"Does it seem that way to you? Like everybody else finds Eugene weird?"

Jeannie didn't say anything. She knew a trap when she saw one laid.

"He does get a lot of attention, doesn't he?"

"Not from me. Not if I can help it."

"I'll bet a lot of kids wish they got as much attention as Eugene gets."

"That's because he goes out of his way to get it."

"What do you mean?"

"I just want him to leave me alone. I didn't ask him to come up to me. I've told him a hundred times not to bother me, but he won't listen, so I told him to go away. But that's all I said. I didn't say another word to him."

84

Ms. Bergeron sat nodding and looking at Jeannie as if she wanted to see inside her. Her glasses magnified her eyes, but they no longer seemed so opaque. To Jeannie, it was like the woman had a switch she could toggle between I-believe-you-Sweetie and you're-a-lying-little-bitch, only "I believe you" really meant, "Why don't you tell me more, so I can get you expelled or locked up or worse?"

Jeannie decided to be finished feeding her information. "Can I go now?" she said.

"Not until we talk to your mother. She needs to know what's going on with you."

Jeannie rolled her eyes. "She's not going to be happy if she has to take off from work to come down here."

"But I think it's best if you take the rest of the day off from school."

"Great." She wouldn't have minded, really, except it meant that he had won, and everyone would know it. They would think it was because she knocked Jana Angleton over, when it had nothing to do with that. It was all about Eugene. "So I'm getting expelled?"

"I wouldn't call it that. Do you have any homework you need to do? Anything you need to take home?"

She felt tears threatening and didn't want to say anything more. She found it hard enough just to breathe.

Eugene must have known about her visit to Ms. Bergeron's office, because he was standing in the middle of the hall, waiting for her with his feet spread wide apart and his arms folded across his chest, grinning. He was little. She could have easily knocked him down, but she only said, "Get out of my way!"

"Hope you didn't get in too much trouble on my account. I told them girls not to say anything, but they didn't listen, did they?"

"I just bet you did."

"I really did."

"Did you tell them not to make up lies?"

"What lies?"

She glared down at him. She towered over him.

"My mom says it's a fine line between lies and pure imagination."

He didn't even have a mom. "Which one does that make you?" she asked.

"Me? I'm not a liar, Jean. I don't ever lie."

"Nice talking to you. I have to get my books."

He uncrossed his arms and spread his palms open, shrugging. "I didn't mean to get you in trouble."

That's when it occurred to her. "Mrs. Bergeron said I threatened to put you back down in the storm drain. Did you tell her that?"

"That would be silly. How could you do that? Did you ever try to lift one of those manhole covers?"

"How did you get down there?"

Eugene looked around, as if there might be someone listening. He lowered his voice. "If you was to ever go down there, you might be scared, but not me. I know my way around the whole system. I could show you."

"That's what makes you so charming."

Nobody spoke to her when she got her books out from under her desk and left the classroom. On her way back to Ms. Bergeron's office, Eugene stood waiting for her behind the door to the boys' room. He opened it just wide enough to whisper, "I could show you how to survive in the dark." He kissed his hand and held it at a forty-five degree angle, then pursed his lips and blew across his palm.

"I didn't raise you to be ignorant," her mom said in the car. "Why on earth did you call him a name like that?"

Jeannie's face scrunched itself up. She couldn't find her voice to answer, because nobody was ever going to believe her, least of all her mom. Eugene would get away with lying about what she said, first of all, and with blowing her a kiss on top of it. Two hot tears splotched the cover of her geography book. She wiped the spots with her forearm and tried to say, "I didn't threaten him," but all that came out was, "I didn't—"

"Don't lie to me, Jeannie! That's the worst thing you can do!"

When they got home, her mom parked the car and said, "When you're ready to tell me the truth, you can. Until then, you don't come out of your room."

Jeannie flung her books from her lap to the floor of the car and stormed into the house. Kneeling on her bed, she screamed raggedly into her pillow, and screamed again, and again, and could not stop screaming even when her mom came to the door and said, "That's not going to help your cause."

As a matter of fact, it did help, because her mom left her alone and she fell asleep.

The next thing she knew, she was riding the cable swing across Jarrod's back yard, weaving her way through a jungle of telephone poles as Jarrod rode with her, pedaling to make the cable swing go faster, because the ground went soft and the telephone poles kept sinking deeper and deeper into the earth.

"These photograph poles go halfway to China," Jarrod said, except that he was no longer Jarrod and something about the way he said "China" made it sound more like "sewer" or like "Keening Creek," she couldn't tell which, and when she tried to climb back in through the window to her bedroom to wake up, the window sill zoomed too high up to reach, and Eugene pressed his face to the screen like a fly buzzing to find its way outside again.

"What are you doing in my house?" she wanted to know.

He said: "How do you know your own name if you don't remember anything else about me?"

He said: "I remember everything."

He said: "I could show you."

With his finger he traced a map of the drainage system just as it appeared on the door of a white City of Keening pickup truck. In an arch over the map—which became, the closer she looked at it, more and more like a detailed map of her name or, possibly, of her body—the lettering read: "D. O. A."

She woke up disoriented, not able to dispel the notion that she still had to climb back inside her room or else face the consequences when her mother found out she had disobeyed.

At supper, the only one who was nice to her was Billy. "You have to admit, Mom, the kid's a little on the creepy side."

"Totally creepy," Jeannie said so softly that only her mashed potatoes could hear.

Her dad advised Billy to stay out of it. Then he said to no one in particular, "I'm just disappointed. I think she's going to have to apologize. Otherwise, this thing's not going to go away."

Jeannie's fork clattered to her plate. She sighed, already wrung out and afraid she might start to cry again. Her voice, still hoarse from her screaming fit, came out as a croak. "May I be excused?"

"No," said her dad. "You may not." He leaned across the table in her direction. "We have to live here, Jeannie." He planted two fingers on the table in front of his plate. "Two things you don't get to choose in life: your neighbors and your family. The Lambs live right down the street from us!"

"They got to choose their family," Billy put in.

Her dad pointed his finger in Billy's face. "I'm warning you."

"I'm just saying. They're going to adopt him. That's choosing your family."

"Thank you for your insight. Are you done?"

"Anytime. If you went to church once in a while, you'd know these things."

Her dad stared at the wall, blinking his eyes, controlling his temper. "Do you really think you're getting the car if you keep it up?"

Billy raised both hands in the air in mock surrender, then he went back to eating.

"They live right down the street from us," her dad resumed.

"We could move," Jeannie suggested.

# Event Horizon

I can't begin to tell you how long I spent traveling the event horizon, the inner rim of Jeannie Ivory's cocao-coffee-caramel-hazelnut-cluster iris, swirling into the void of her left pupil, calculating the infusion of energy it would surely take to alter my course, to back my rocket ship away from what I knew with all my soul to be an endless spiral into her chaos, not mine; her insanity, not mine; her destiny, not mine. I could no more buy into her twisted wormhole of a belief system than I felt I could afford to cash out of my investment in her. I had to figure out a way to believe in her and yet maintain a grip on my own sanity.

It was an old struggle come back to haunt me.

The ghost of my past ordinarily takes the form of my grandma, who raised me from a baby. She still appears in my dreams from time to time. Or else I'll catch myself thinking like her, talking to myself in her voice. The rest of the world regarded old Maggie Cavendish as a hard-nosed, steely-eyed realist, but I grew up inside the cloud of her Native American superstitions. She was three parts Cherokee or ninety-nine percent Crow, depending on the day of the week, but she looked white, married white and lived white on the outside. She described my mother to me as a soul I passed on the night I was born. An angel just like me, she said, traveling the opposite direction, one coming from and the other heading back to the Great Mystery. My father had gone to the West Coast "on business" and had yet to finish up out there and get home again, but to hear Grandma talk, his return was imminent. Soon as he come back, he would lay claim to Grandpa's land and make something of it, make something of himself and, in the bargain, make something of me. That's the way she laid out my life for me, like a quilt she was piecing together. I had no reason to doubt word one of it, until the day she gave up for good and decided to cut him out of her will. On impulse, it seemed to me, but she must have chewed on it for years. She instructed her attorney to give everything, including custody of Yours Truly, to my half-sister Sheila and Sheila's drunk of a pervert husband, Leon, when she passed on.

Don't get me wrong, I adored Leon. At least, I did until I got to know him better, a. k. a. he tried to get to know me better. That's a whole nother story. I will tell you all about it some other time. Not here. This is Jeannie's story. I'm just filling in the background, so you can better understand my part in it and how I come to get in over my head. Suffice it to say, when I was a teenager, I had to get out of the house, away from my sister and her husband, and nobody else would have me. My only ticket, and nothing short of a miracle to me at the time, was a boy of privilege I met entirely by accident, whose real name cannot be mentioned for reasons of national security.

Patterson Price (oops! I said his name) was a political science major down at Norman, half again my age with a fast car and a faster tongue. He meant to run for Congress one day. Eventually he did, and apparently come real close to making a bid for President of the U. S. of A. I shit you not.

I realize now that he was just a kid himself when, for all intents and purposes, he abducted me across state lines, but you cannot imagine how sophisticated he seemed to a hick like me. We were both drunk from a party over at the Bittles' house on the other side of the canyon, a party I was by no means supposed to attend. I left home that afternoon and went with Leigh Ann Bittle under, let's just call it, suspicious circumstances. I had defied Leon and I was terrified of ever going home again, but I had to. Things would only get worse if Sheila was to come in from work (she had the four-to-midnight shift at the State School in Enid) and find me not at home in bed. Unfortunately, Leigh Ann Bittle got too hammered to drive me home. Fortunately, her brother's friend from college had a set of wheels and offered to drop me off, since he was heading back to the City.

Let me back up.

When I said I left the house under suspicious circumstances, I really had no idea how bad. Patterson could sense something was wrong, because I did not want to get out of his car. So I confessed to him.

"Leon drinks." I figured he might take that as the pot calling the kettle black, so I added, "He's crippled. He takes it out on me."

Leon didn't know anything about the party, of course. He didn't know the Bittles were out of town, he just had a problem with me going off anywhere, at any time, with Leigh Ann Bittle or anybody else. He had a problem being left on his own to take care of himself and Lisa Julene, who was three years old and got on his nerves. He had a problem with just about everything, including the skirt I borrowed from Sheila's closet. "What is that, a dish towel? You get that off right now!"

Every stitch I had on belonged to Sheila. He paid no attention to how his wife dressed, but I didn't need to tell him that. He tried to bar the door. "Take it off," he said, "or I'll take it off for you!"

I spent as much of my time as possible, of an evening, either out of the house or upstairs in my room. Problem being, I had to look out for Lisa Julene. I had to do the cooking, I had to entertain her, give her a bath, get her dressed for bed, read her a bedtime story, while Leon sat in the front room watching TV (when he wasn't in the kitchen watching me) and getting drunk. The only bathroom in the house was downstairs, and I never took a bath if I could help it, unless Sheila was home. It hadn't always been like that. When I was little, I adored him. I didn't know any better.

That evening, I had taken care of everything early. All Leon had left to do was read Lisa Julene a story or let her watch something halfway decent on TV and at 8:30 send her upstairs to bed. She didn't have to be carried.

Leon was not an old man, but ever since his oilfield accident and his multiple back surgeries, he walked with a cane. He tried to bar my way and, as I pushed past him, he reached with the curved end of his cane to try and hook my leg and trip me up. So what did I do? I grabbed it and give it a good yank. If he had just let go, like a normal person would do, there would have been no problem. But he didn't do that, because—well, because he was Leon. I was halfway out the door as I pulled him off balance, and he cracked his skull on the corner of the door frame. I will admit, it give me a certain satisfaction, but I didn't stick around to gloat. I run and jumped in Leigh Ann's car and said, "Get me the fuck out of here!" and that was that.

Or so I thought.

"What time you think it is?" I asked Patterson Price hours and hours later in the dark of the driveway. "You got a watch?" If I could but wait right there with him until Sheila got home, I'd be way better off. I'd been thinking I had to get there ahead of her and change out of her clothes, but I now realized I'd feel a lot better about being in the house with her there than alone with Leon pissed off that I had defied him. Strength in numbers, even though my sister wasn't what you'd call an ally and she'd be furious that I stole her dress and was out so late, even though school was out, and that I got a ride with a boy she didn't know. All the same, I would much rather face her music than Leon's.

I tried to explain the situation to Patterson, who was rich and well-bred and couldn't possibly have known what it meant, living the way the rest of us did.

Standing up out of his car—it sat so low to the ground, and he was so long-legged, he had to unfold himself to get out of it—he tucked his shirt tail in and exhaled into the palm of his hand to check his breath for alcohol. "Let me talk to him."

"I don't think it's such a good idea," I said without much conviction.

He held up his hand as if to say, "I got this." He had strong lines to his face. Angular. Determined. He looked to me like a tower of a man in that moment, very competent and trustworthy and like, if he needed to, he could handle himself. He folded the cuffs of his shirtsleeves back on his forearms. My crush on him developed like a Polaroid, before my very eyes.

I had survived the first half of my eighth grade year only by the help of Leigh Ann's mother, who had taught me English the year before and, after a rough beginning, had taken me on as her personal crusade for Christ, having seen something in me worth wrestling away from Satan's clutches. She devoutly prayed—for the sake of my soul, I suppose—that Leigh Ann and I would get to be friends. To her credit, Leigh Ann tried, but in school she had her pick of friends and didn't have to scrape the bottom of the barrel where my social circle would have run, if I'd had one. By the end of that year, even her mother had given up on me. So I can't really tell you how or why I got invited to Leigh Ann's brother's party, whether her usual friends were busy or gone on vacation or she took pity on me or considered me less of a threat than her cheerleader friends or what. Less likely to gossip if she acted the slut in my company, maybe? I was not a worldly enough girl to figure out her angle, if she had one, nor did I care. I never held my breath hoping for invitations, not because turning blue did not become me but because I wasn't in the loop to know what was on the social calendar in the first place. The party wound down pretty quick, anyway, because it turned out her brother's girlfriend had been "seeing other people" while Mark was away at college. In a town the size of Keening, that meant seeing people he knew. People he had invited to his party. When it came time for me to leave, Patterson must've figured my being in need of a ride made a good enough excuse for him to split, too.

I sat in the driveway and listened to the cicadas whirring in the trees out by the road, wondering what in the hell Leon and a boy like Patterson Price could possibly have to talk about for so long. When he come outside again, Patterson slumped in behind the wheel and said, "I don't think you should go in there."

"Is he mad?"

"Mad?"

"Or just drunk?"

I couldn't make out the expression on his face. After a minute, he said, "I think he's passed out."

"Where's Lisa Julene?"

I had to explain who Lisa Julene was.

"I didn't see her."

"She must be upstairs in bed, then." I didn't know what else to do but go in the house. If Leon had passed out, at least I could get changed out of Sheila's clothes. He wouldn't know what time I'd come in. I could check on Lisa Julene and just wait for Sheila to get home. Problem solved.

"I don't think you want to go in," Patterson said again.

So without quite knowing why, I didn't. Patterson shifted into reverse and backed away real slow to the end of the driveway, where he stopped and got out to inspect something in the headlights.

"What is it?"

"Well, I just—I just have to be careful."

Much, much later, after he figured he could trust me, or I knew too much and was too much involved for it to matter, we were in it together, he explained that he had been looking to see if his tires had left any telltale tracks in the driveway. "Your brother-in-law was dead," he told me.

I freaked out, of course, and told him what had happened, about Leon hitting his head on the door. It wasn't my fault, of course—he agreed with me there—but what it come down to was, what did I want to do? He walked me through the likeliest scenario: I was the last one to see Leon alive. We had argued about me going out. By this time, I had told Patterson about Leon walking in on me when I was in the bathroom taking a bath, claiming he needed to pee and saying, "Oh, come off it, Frecklehead! You ain't got nothing I ain't seen before," as

93

he stood there with his hand on his pecker way longer than he needed to. On two different occasions, he stood outside the bathroom door and tried to take my towel away from me when I came out. He was drunk and disabled, though. I fought him off and retreated up the stairs both of those times.

"Means, motive and opportunity," Patterson said. His daddy had been an Oklahoma City attorney before he went into politics. "Exactly what they look for in a criminal trial."

I didn't let myself dwell on the question of what Lisa Julene might or might not have witnessed or how she spent the hours between me leaving the house and her momma getting in at between a quarter and a half past midnight. I never intended on leaving her alone to wonder what had become of her daddy, how he come to be covered in blood and why he didn't answer her when she shook him and pleaded with him. Easier on my conscience to figure she somehow managed, at three years of age, to get herself upstairs and changed into her pee jays and read herself a bedtime story.

That first night with Patterson, we ended up at a motel in Enid. He was shaken up by what he'd seen and wanted to go out to a liquor store while I waited in the room. When he came back, he rolled a joint and taught me how to hold the smoke in. We proceeded to get drunk enough and high enough that none of it seemed real. Come checkout time, it occurred to Patter (my new nickname for him) that at fourteen I was technically a minor, but by then the damage had been done. I said I would never let anyone send him to prison, and he said the same thing about me. He renewed the room and told them we didn't need maid service, then he went out and got some hair color and a pair of scissors and, just like that, I become a fugitive from justice.

Long story short, it made no sense for me to stick around Oklahoma. He said, "Have you ever been to New England?" and I said, "I never been anywhere," so we loaded up his MGB and we moved to Beverly. Massachusetts, that is. Where his family owned property. We stayed for two days in an empty apartment, while he figured out what to do with me.

At one point on that road trip, high up in the Blue Ridge Mountains of Virginia, we weren't in any hurry so we pulled off the Interstate and found us a place to lie back in the grass and just stare up at the cosmos and talk. I did most of the listening, if you can imagine. I just liked the sound of Patter's voice. If I rested my head against him just right, I could feel the rumble of his baritone in the bone behind my left ear. It felt as if all his knowledge of words and of people and of the universe emanated from within my own head. Like if I chose to, if I just could lay quiet enough, I could be part of him, and everything he said would become part of me.

He talked about the Milky Way Galaxy and how big it was, made up of so many billions of stars, and how if you looked off to the side of it, most of what looked like stars weren't stars at all but entire galaxies, each one of them made up of billions and billions of stars and each one with a black hole at the center.

I said, "What's a black hole?" just to keep him talking, and he explained all about it, about what's called the "event horizon," beyond which nothing can get out, and how even if you shined a light from inside there, the light beam would bend around backwards, owing to the powerful effects of gravity, and not get out. "Just like, if you throw a baseball straight up, it comes to a stop and makes a U-turn and comes back down."

"Why's it called a horizon, though, if it's a hole?"

He made me stand up. We were at a pretty good elevation and could see all around. He stood close behind me and held my shoulders as he turned me in a circle to show me what I knew already, of course, I just hadn't thought about it that way—how the horizon is a circle, only we're inside this one, not outside. "What makes it a horizon is that we can't see what's beyond it, because everything drops out of sight."

"Like us," I said, rolling my head to look at the smooth horizon of his cheek. "We dropped out of sight."

He didn't answer me. I now know why. Because it wasn't us dropping out of sight, just me. He had college to attend and a future to pursue, a good family to support him and friends that cared about him. He shone like a regular star, within the visible spectrum of light, whereas I did not emit any light whatsoever. As far as he was concerned, I was a black hole, and he had no intention of crossing my event horizon.

After a couple of days in Beverly, he drove me out to a town in the mountains at the other end of Massachusetts and set me up in an apartment of my own. He said he would send me money to pay for my living expenses, which he did, twice. What neither one of us knew was, by that time, I was pregnant.

I kissed him goodbye.

He said, "I'll be back as soon as the semester's over. You'll wait for me?"

I just laughed and kissed him again.

"You're sure?"

"What else I got to do?"

That was the last I ever saw of him, except on TV.

Years later, during the process of deciding whether to run for office or not, he knew he had tracks to cover. I was one of them, and so was his baby. My baby boy. I intended on naming him Patrick, after his daddy, who never laid eyes on him. We had that in common, my baby and me. Both of us had disappearing daddies. But I didn't name him that or anything remotely resembling Patterson. I named him Marshall Caleb.

Marshall Caleb was stolen from me before I left the hospital. I have never met any of Patterson's family. Though I can probably never prove it, I more than suspect they were behind my baby's abduction.

Fast forward nineteen, twenty years. I'm on my own two feet, just barely, back on Grandpa's land again, trying to make something of it (and something of myself in the bargain). My reputation wags its tongue behind me, I know. Half the good folks of Keening continue to convince the other half I killed my grandma. They were quick to want me indicted for Leon's murder, too, because he died the night I disappeared. I didn't turn up again until Grandma's attorney went out of his way to get in touch with me to say that Sheila had abandoned any claim to the property, and did I want it?

I did.

So here I lay, face to face with a kid half my age and half again as fucked up as I ever was, surfing the event horizon in her eyes and wondering if I dared to cross over it or was I someday gonna run for public office?

# THE MISSISSIPPI MUD BAKING CONSORTIUM

Jeannie and I fumbled around each other's bodies, looking for clothes to put back on. She pulled my sweatshirt over her head, growling, "I'm such a trusting fucking dope!" Apropos of what, I had not a clue. I sat with her jeans in my lap—a pair just like mine, only smaller–looking at her and trying not to take it personally, but was it something I did? Something I didn't do? I laid my palm against the center of her chest. "You?" I teased, "Trusting?" She had my shirt on inside-out.

She smoothed the edges of the tape on her wrist and tilted her head back to get a look at me from a different angle. "I was. You didn't know me."

I cradled the back of her head in my hand, tugged her in my direction, but she didn't come. She'd grown distant suddenly. All right, I figured. So much for afterplay. I let my hand drop.

She pulled her socks back on, dainty ones with lace cuffs, her tiny feet all tendons and frail bone.

"That's what you wear inside those boots of yours?"

She paid no attention. "Before he took off with the car, Billy advised me to go through the motions and make my apologies. Easy for him to say; he was back in Leigh Ann's good graces. His world was in mint condition. I, on the other hand, had to march over to the Lambs' house with my parents flanking me like a prisoner under armed escort."

Just like that, she'd picked up the thread of her story again. As if the sex between us had been just something to do during intermission. I wondered, was it an age thing? Had I been like that when I was young? Able to switch gears the way she did? Or at least more willing to?

"No, wait!" I pouted. I tossed her jeans on the floor and pushed her to one end of the sofa, then went and grabbed a blanket off the bed. When I come back, I stretched out and covered up with my head in her lap. "Okay," I said. "Continue."

She stroked my head, combing her fingers through my hair as I closed my eyes and watched her story unfold across the backs of my lids. I pictured a calm summer evening, the sun reluctant to set, house shadows stretching across the pavement along Fair Meadow Drive, eating the shadows of three striding figures.

"I'm not apologizing for anything I didn't do," nine, going-on-ten-year-old Jeannie forewarned her parents.

"We're not asking you to," said her mother.

"I never threatened him."

"We believe you."

Gay Lamb answered the door and invited them in. Todd pointed the remote at the television set. He'd been watching a program about an expedition to find and recover Noah's Ark. The shadow of an airplane wavered over an ice field high up in the mountains of wherever Mount Ararat was—Turkey, maybe? The voice of the narrator died; the image froze. Todd went toward the back of the house and called up from the bottom of the staircase, "Eugene? Somebody here to see you."

Eugene appeared on the landing, looking concerned, a little wary even. As he descended the stairs, he said, "Jeannie?" as if he wasn't entirely sure of her name.

Jeannie felt the pressure of her father's fingertips between her shoulder blades but she did not step forward. "I'm sorry I called you a name," she said rapid-fire, set to turn and go.

Eugene looked at Mr. Lamb, confusion showing on his face. "What name?"

Jeannie took a deep breath and said it. "Sewer Boy."

"Oh." Eugene shrugged. "That's okay. Kids call me that."

It was Mr. Lamb's turn to look concerned. "They do?"

"Sure. We always call each other names. It's just for fun."

"That doesn't sound like a very nice thing to do for fun."

"It's, um, it's a—" Eugene looked to Jeannie for help in finding what he meant to say. "It's a status thing. Like if you want someone to hang out with you, you have to call them the right name."

Nobody said anything until Jeannie's mother broke the silence. "Are you sure about that, Eugene? You're not just covering for her?"

Eugene rolled his eyes and stepped off the bottom step. He walked up to Jeannie with exaggerated gallantry, clutched his hands to his chest, and rolled his eyes to heaven. "I forgive you your cruel words,

Jeannie Ivory."

Jeannie eyed him with suspicion. He grinned a fake grin, comic and disarming. "You want to see what my dad's building for me? Come on!" In a loud whisper, he added, "The adults need a little time to work this out among themselves." Then he turned back to Mr. Lamb. "Can we put the lights on in the back yard, Dad, so I can show Jean my birthday present?"

"Sure, go ahead!" Mr. Lamb chuckled. "Careful where you step."

In the floodlit back yard, Eugene warned Jeannie to keep away from the two neat rows of holes that pocked the left third of the lawn at regular intervals, the first pair some thirty feet from the house.

"You have a birthday?" she asked.

"I do sort of. My mom and dad said I should pick one. I picked the day you found me. That's going to be my birthday from now on."

"Except I didn't find you."

"You know what I mean."

"But I didn't."

"It doesn't matter. The day I got found, then. Anyway, see this? My dad's building me a tree house. You can come over and play any time you want."

"A tree house?" Jeannie said. "Where?"

"Right here. See all these holes? They go so deep you can't even see the bottom! I bet they go halfway to China!"

Along the hedge between the Lambs' yard and the next door neighbors' rose a stack of what looked like telephone poles.

"Yeah, but—" Jeannie looked around, bewildered. "But you don't have a tree."

The Lambs hired a team of laborers to mix concrete and pour footings, brown men with stocky builds and short, dark haircuts. Jeannie watched from behind the big cottonwood, where the creek bed gently climbed to the back gate of the Lambs' yard. She didn't understand how they could possibly build a tree house without a tree. Two days later, the brown men returned with a small winch truck and stood the poles upright, inching them across the grass one at a time, until one end slid neatly down into a hole. One man kept checking the sides of the pole with a level while the others poured in more concrete, thick with gravel, and tamped it around the base of the pole with long metal rods.

Eugene spotted Jeannie and went to the back fence, calling down to her. "They're using a lot of aggregate," he shouted, showing off his new word. He pronounced it to rhyme with "aggravate."

Jeannie strolled up the bank to stand at the fence, where she could hear the dark men speaking rapidly in a foreign language. She took it for Spanish, but she wasn't sure. Eugene raised his voice to talk over the noise of the cement mixer and the winch truck, telling her the names of the men, which she didn't remember. Then it sounded like he said, "They're watermelons." She narrowed her eyes at him but let it pass. Later on she found out he must have said "Guatemalans." Each time they filled in around a post, they hammered two-by-fours at forty-five degree angles all around to serve as braces until the concrete set. After the winch truck left, they hosed down the insides of their cement mixer and their wheelbarrow and pipes and other equipment and loaded up the trailer behind their double-cab pickup truck and took off, leaving behind a forest of barkless, branchless tree trunks.

"What's it supposed to be?" Jeannie asked, trying not to be mean. "Because it's not a tree house."

"It's way more than that," Eugene assured her. "Just wait and see. This is only the first stages. Do you want to help when it comes time?"

"Why? You're not helping."

"I will be. Just not with this part. I helped my dad lay it all out."

"Your dad."

Eugene nodded. He hooked his fingers in the chain link that separated them and leaned back on his heels, flexing the fabric of the fence. "I told you. They're gonna adopt me. This tree house is my adoption day present."

"Why? Because you don't have a real birthday, just one you made up?"

"I told you. I get to pick one."

"You ought to make it October Thirty-first."

"Okay." He grinned, not like the fake grin he'd given her when she had to apologize to him. This time it seemed genuine and it made her feel rotten, because he didn't catch on that she meant Halloween.

"How do you remember your name if you don't remember anything else?"

He leaned way back, still gripping the fence, looking at the sky. "I remember lots of things."

"Like what?"

"I know the whole way everything goes underground. I could show you."

"Uh, no thanks."

He grinned at her again, his small teeth fanning out from his gums, evenly space, but each one leaning its own direction, like headstones in an ancient cemetery.

She changed the subject. "How'd you end up here, though?"

"With the Lambs?" He shrugged. "They're good Christians. They welcomed me into their hearts." After a minute, he added, "I like it here."

"It's Jarrod's house." She hadn't planned on saying that, it just came out, and she couldn't take it back.

"It's my house now." He didn't seem the least bit bothered by her tone. "Who's Jarrod?"

"He used to live here."

"Is he your boyfriend?"

She looked at him hard. "I don't have to answer that." She didn't know how to. She thought Eugene would have known who Jarrod was, because Jarrod had been there in the tunnel under Bruce Street the day she first invented the Sewer Boy. Never for a minute had she imagined he would come to live on her street and go to her school and be called Eugene.

"That's okay." He seemed to lose interest in Jarrod.

"Remember? His mom died?"

"Oh." He gave her a blank look. She waited for him to say something, anything, about Jarrod or about Jarrod's mom and how she died, but he didn't. He just looked at her.

"You don't have a real mom, do you?"

"Nope. I do now, though."

"Did they just disappear, your real mom and dad?"

"Nope. There wasn't any."

"There had to be."

"Why?"

"Because."

"Because why?"

So she explained it to him. Standing close up against the fence, she told him what she knew about mothers and fathers and babies. Certain parts of it she said almost in a whisper, even though it wasn't a secret, because he seemed so interested and because he asked questions that she hadn't anticipated.

He tilted his head in the direction of the house. "You mean, they do that?"

She hadn't thought of it that way, about Mr. and Mrs. Lamb specifically. "Probably not," she guessed, "because they don't have any real children. Just you."

"I came a different way."

"Right."

"You think they still might?"

"They don't need to," she assured him.

"Yours did."

Jeannie knew that, but she didn't want to talk about it, so she said, "Not anymore."

Eugene looked at his house, at the two-story addition with the sliding glass doors off the back of Mr. and Mrs. Lamb's bedroom. "I think they still do."

Jeannie changed the subject. "I caught my brother and Leigh Ann Bittle doing it. They had their clothes off and everything."

"Did they have a baby?"

"No. They stopped in time."

"She's his girlfriend."

Jeannie rolled her eyes. "Depends which day of the week it is."

"Did you ever do it with your boyfriend?"

"No!" she said sternly. "I don't have a boyfriend."

"I thought you did. The boy who used to live here."

"Jarrod?"

"Well, did you? Up there?" He jutted his chin at the canopy of the cottonwood tree, down in the creek. "Is that why you built a tree house together?"

"No!"

"Because you were going to have a baby?"

"Don't be stupid! You can't raise a baby in a tree house. Anyway, it wasn't just me and Jarrod. Everybody was part of it."

"Who was?"

"Dieter and Sean Cunningham and Donnie Douglas and a bunch of people. It was a whole consortium."

"What's that?"

"It's a club," she told him, "of people who know how to build a real tree house."

Eugene's eyes got big. "Wait right here!" he said. He ran in the house and came back after a few minutes, pulling Mr. Lamb along by the arm and telling him about the Keening Creek Tree House Consortium. "Tell him, Jean! Tell him about the consortion!"

So she did.

"See, Dad? I told you. The Lord answered our prayers, didn't He?" Eugene rested his fingers on top of Jeannie's through the fence and acted like he didn't notice when she pulled away. He explained to her that he and his "dad" had prayed about a tree house and asked the Lord, if it be His Will, to send them a team of qualified helpers to build it.

Next thing Jeannie knew, she and Eugene had mounted their bikes. They went riding together all over the neighborhood, recruiting kids to help build the new tree house. Donnie Douglas signed up, and Sean Cunningham and Logan Reynolds did, too—everybody from the original consortium (with the notable exceptions of Jarrod and Dieter Frye) and a few other boys. By the time they got back to Eugene's house, his mother had sent out e-vites to the mothers of all the girls at Murrow Elementary and to the parents at their church, too. Jeannie's mother got one. She could not have been more pleased that Jeannie and Eugene had settled their differences and had decided to cooperate.

The Lambs' tree house-building party became the social event of the season on Fair Meadow Lane. Jeannie showed up at the appointed time, but Anna Sylvester and her posse had already arrived. Jeannie doubted a one of them had the mental capacity to swing a hammer, unless it was to drive a nail in somebody else's coffin. For instance, Jeannie's.

The Lambs assembled the whole crew in the back yard and instructed them to stand in a circle and hold hands, while Mr. Lamb thanked the Lord for His Mercy and His Kindness and for the Blood of Jesus and for guiding him and Gay to take Eugene into their hearts and home and on and on and et cetera and so forth. When he had thought of everything he needed to be thankful for and said Amen, Mrs. Lamb spoke up and said for all the girls—fourteen of them, counting Jeannie—to come with her into the house to help chop pecans and bars of bittersweet chocolate and to break two dozen eggs in a bowl and mix that glop (Jeannie's word for it) with melted butter and flour and cocoa powder. She divided the mixture into bowls and handed out paddles and told the girls to take turns.

"Fold the flour in nice and slow," she said, "so you don't toughen up the batter, Jeannie."

The whine of an electric saw, followed by the shouts and cheers of the boys outside distracted Jeannie. She handed her paddle off to Sam Corwin and headed in the direction of the back door to check out what was going on.

"Where are you off to, Jeannie? We're not done." Mrs. Lamb ushered her back to the elevated kitchen. "We need you in here."

They mixed the chopped nuts with the batter, and into the oven it all went in separate batches, nuts versus no nuts. Then they all sat in the living room and looked at the fabric Mrs. Lamb had picked out for curtains. Jeannie sat on a hassock and wrinkled her nose. "For a tree house?" she said. In her opinion, a tree house did not call for curtains.

No one showed any particular interest in her view of the matter. The conversation moved on to the Lord's plan for Mr. and Mrs. Lamb to adopt Eugene.

Jodie Clemente raised her hand as if they were in school. "How do you know when Jesus tells you to do something?"

"That's an excellent question!" Mrs. Lamb pressed her hands flat to her knees and scanned the faces of all the girls, including Jeannie. "It's different for everybody. Some people literally hear His Voice speaking to them, just the same as you and I are talking right now. I wish I could hear Him like that, don't you? I don't very often."

"Even though he's dead?" Jeannie asked.

Mrs. Lamb smiled tolerantly and promised her and the other girls that Jesus was not dead. "He is very much alive in my heart. Would you like to invite Him into yours?"

# Soul Decision

"What you believe in your heart is called faith, Honey. I don't really know how to explain it. It's like seeing the color green and knowing it's green, even if someone else tells you, no, that's blue. You can't prove it's green—not to them—even though you still know it is. That's how faith works. Well, kind of. What you believe in your heart doesn't have to match what anybody else believes, that's for sure. If somebody tells you Jesus rose from the dead, they're expressing their faith, which they have every right to do. They believe it in their heart. It doesn't have to make sense to you in order for them to believe it. And it also doesn't mean you have to believe it, just because they do. It doesn't mean one person is right and the other person's wrong."

Jeannie knew her mother was defending her brother, not just the Lambs, because Billy had recently started attending their church. "When it comes to religion, there isn't one correct answer that satisfies everyone. If you believe one thing and I believe another, we have to agree to disagree. That's called tolerance."

"But Billy says Jesus died for my sins, and if I don't believe it, I'm going to hell."

"Well, that's bull, Jeannie. You know it and I know it. But if you were to tell me that you believed in your heart that Jesus rose from the dead, I would have to accept that, for you, that's the truth. Even though, for me, it's not."

"Wouldn't he be all gross, though, like a zombie?"

"I can't tell you, because I don't believe in zombies, either."

"Oh, right."

So when Jodie Clemente, sitting with the other thirteen girls in the living room part of the Lambs' open-concept house, solemnly announced that Jesus had risen from the dead and that she had accepted him into her heart, Jeannie rose up from the hassock and lumbered toward her. Just as she now rose up in my living room, still in her underwear and my inside-out angel shirt, and lumbered toward me with her arms out in front of her like a sleepwalker. Or as she put it, "Like Frankenstein."

We laughed. I warded her off, but she got through my defenses and gnawed on my forehead, "Nom, nom, nom!" then my ear, then started kissing me, my hair, my nose, my cheeks. I held her. She laid her face against my chest, not laughing any longer.

"I believed in my heart," she said, her voice flattening out against me, "that each and every one of those stupid bitches hated my guts. None of them more than Gay Fucking Lamb."

She didn't know when to quit, was Jeannie's problem. She suggested to the girls that they all go outside and help the boys build the tree house while the brownies baked.

Mrs. Lamb did not cotton to the idea. "If you don't want to stay with the rest of us and be of help, I can't make you, but Mr. Lamb only wants the boys outside during construction, because too many people, while he's using power equipment, means somebody's liable to get hurt."

"It's okay. I'm not liable to get hurt."

"We're liable for you, though. Too many people out there, and you might be responsible for someone else not paying attention. You don't want that on your conscience, do you? Someone else getting hurt on your account?"

"I've done it before, though, and nobody got hurt. That's why I'm here. I helped recruit everybody." She looked around at the other girls, none of whom she had helped to recruit, and amended her statement. "Everybody with experience."

"Well, you have a choice to make, then. You can stay and help serve refreshments with the rest of us, or you can leave."

Jeannie ran to the back door and pushed, but Mrs. Lamb had locked it after the first time she'd tried to flee the Mississippi Mud Baking Consortium. By the time she had worked out which way to turn the latch, the woman was breathing down her neck.

"I'm leaving! You can't keep me here!"

"That's fine, but go the other way. I don't want you in the back yard right now."

"I'm the one that got everybody here in the first place, and now I have to make stupid brownies? I don't think so!"

"You don't have to if you don't want to. And they're not brownies."

"That mud, then."

"Goodbye." Mrs. Lamb pointed. "Use the other door."

Which meant Jeannie had to walk past the other girls, whose slack jaws and fervent eyes followed her across the room. She was determined not let them see her cry. She slammed the door behind her.

When she got home, she refused to answer her mother's questions except to say that nothing, but nothing, in this world was fair and that she hated living on the same street with people who ate mud and believed in zombies.

"That's where you still live? Fair Meadow?" You'd think I ought to know. I'd been there often enough to drop her off after work when she didn't have a ride. I don't always pay attention to street signs.

"I can't afford to move out."

"And the Lambs? They still live there on the same street?"

She wagged her head, no. "They moved out ages ago. My brother lives in their house now. They rent it to him. They bought a McMansion up at Gypsum Heights."

Keening had experienced an "aggressive expansion phase," the Klarion called it, back in the early 2000s, while the rest of the country tried to shake off the effects of 9/11. New construction has since slowed down some, but not like you'd expect. They kept building new additions, bigger and fancier than ever, right through the worst of the recession. Gypsum Heights sounded familiar to me, but I had no reason to keep up with every new real estate development in town.

"It overlooks Upper Canyon Lake."

That was new, too. Oklahoma brags about how it has more shoreline than California because of all the lakes, most of which are man-made. Upper Canyon is small and private. If you don't live there, you don't swim there, you don't fish there, you don't put your boat in the water, and you don't tee off on the nine-hole golf course that overlooks it. You don't even get past the guard at the gatehouse unless you get a special dispensation from the homeowners association.

I said, "They had a show on TV once."

"They still do."

"Yes, but not the same one. The one I'm thinking of was all about home schooling."

"You actually watched that?"

"I was starved for entertainment." In fact, I had in mind to buy an advertising spot on local access, and *School at Home with Gay and Todd* was one of the shows I considered. Turns out, they didn't need me as a sponsor. A fact that, if I'm to be honest, made the prospect of their little home-schooled prodigy bringing me free publicity particularly sweet.

"They pulled him out of public school in fourth grade," Jeannie said with a yawn, "because of me."

"Because of you?" I laughed. "What'd you do? Beat him up?"

"No. Didn't I just tell you? I taught him about sex."

"Oh. Seriously?"

She rolled her eyes.

"Well, I hope you didn't teach him like you just taught me."

She fixed me with her slush-brown eyes. "Don't be fucking gross!"

We needed to talk about sex, me and Jeannie. What I mean is, I did. I needed to process what had transpired between us and, by process, I mean contain. I won't try to tell you that I had never found another woman attractive and I won't try to parse that to mean one thing and not another, because I am averse, on principle, to the notion of ruling things out. I do realize, however, that I do not belong to a clear majority in matters that border on the topic of political freedoms and personal lifestyle choices in the Great State of Oklahoma. I would not have predicted—who could have?—that Sooners would follow suit after Massachusetts, New York and Utah, of all places, and be forced to recognize gay marriages. Even if, by divine or—as it turns out—judicial intervention, it up and did just that, I did not, on the basis of a moment altogether lacking in discretion, foresee marching hand-in-hand with Jeannie Ivory to the beat of "Here Come the Brides."

Did I need to make that clear? I was her employer, after all. And don't even ask about the difference in age between the two of us. That would've required the removal of my socks, which I had just dug out of my jeans and pulled back on my feet. Ordinarily, my rocket stove, which was built into the earthen banquette along the front wall of the living room, radiated enough auxiliary heat to last me through the night. I had propane, too, but generally-speaking, I only used it of a morning to take the chill off before I jumped in the shower. "It's freezing in here," I said. "Aren't you cold?"

She didn't miss a beat. "Yeah. Let's get under the covers."

I looked at her long enough, debating whether it made any sense to speak my mind so prematurely, that she gave me a disbelieving half-smile. "You're not gonna make me sleep out here, are you?"

I pictured us calling good night to each other from separate rooms like the Waltons. "Is that why you undid my shirt? So you wouldn't have to sleep on the couch?"

"Exactly."

"Tell me one thing. Have you always been..." There's only so many ways to put it, but I couldn't decide on one. I touched her face, traced the corner of her mouth with my thumb, wanting to kiss her and wanting to resist kissing her at the same time.

"What? Attracted to you?"

That flustered me, I have to admit. "I was gonna say, attracted to women."

"Never." For a girl so young, she had two tiny sets of creases, a pair of them at each corner of her lips. They set off every word she said in quotation marks. "Ever." She turned, ever so slightly, closed her eyes and kissed my thumb. "What do you think about that?"

I pulled my hand away, crossed my legs on the sofa and gripped my toes in my fingers to warm them. "I have no fucking clue." I had not seduced her. Just the opposite. And yet it felt as if the responsibility for what had happened fell to me, being so much older and her boss, it being my house and her being in such a fragile state of mind to begin with. I had briefly imagined us trading secrets. Crushes we'd had on this one or that one. Margo Timmins for me, from Cowboy Junkies. And she would counter with who? A screamer like Brody Dalle, I wondered, or a smoother kind of criminal? Poe? Somebody I'd have to Google, surely. "You don't expect me to believe that, do you?"

She laced the fingers of her hand with my fingers and toes, her other hand so warm against my knee that, for some reason, I wanted to cry.

"I saw the way you looked at Jarrod," she told me. "I felt you looking at him."

I nodded, sniffling, almost laughing. "He is a striking boy."

"I was jealous. Sorry."

"So you just – that's why you melted down like that?"

"Said I'm sorry!" She rested her temple on the back of her hand, on my knee, looking away from me. "Jesus! I didn't know what to do. I couldn't handle it."

"He offered you a ride home, you dope!"

She moved her hand and turned her head over, switched temples on my knee, narrowing her eyes at me now with her mouth hanging open, as if to let me know who she thought was the dope. "I didn't want to go home."

"Oh." I had to rearrange my thinking. She hadn't changed the subject; she was still answering my question. The one I hadn't asked but meant to: how long had she been thinking about me as — not just as her boss, but — I said again: "Oh."

"I was afraid he'd recognize me."

"You said you hadn't seen each other for a while?"

"That's an entirely different story."

"Tell me that one."

"No. I don't think so."

I felt put out. (I don't pretend to understand myself.) "You gonna start keeping secrets now?" I meant for it to come out more as a tease than an accusation.

"You're not ready for that one yet."

I laughed but I didn't think it was funny.

"First you have to know about Eugene and my brother and what they did to me before you can begin to understand Jarrod's...role."

"I'm already in over my head, huh?"

"Way." She looked so sad when she said it, her head on my knee and her eyes on mine, melting me, it didn't matter who she was, employee, lover, lost soul or soul sister. I had to hold her, had to wrap my arms around her and keep her safe from sorrow. She raised up off my knee and wrapped her arms around me, muffling her voice against my heart. "I need you, Vanessa. I need you to understand. And I'm so fucking afraid you won't."

I squeezed her. "I do," I lied. "I understand."

"No, I need you to understand everything about me. Things I haven't told you yet. And not just with your heart but with your head. I need you to really comprehend what you're in for."

"What I'm in for, Jeannie?" Not only did I have all the earmarks of a commitment-phobe, I also had a severe allergy to other people's drama. I only meant to warn her. "What I'm 'in for' is always going to be my sole decision."

She lifted her eyes to me again, her fingers combing through my hair and balling it up at the base of my skull, gently, gently pulling, pulling herself up, exposing my throat and kissing it, kissing my throat, my chin, my lips as she raked her other hand — the bandaged-wrist hand —

roughly down my belly and into my crotch. "Allow me," she said, as her fingers parted me and penetrated me, sending a pang of fear and longing through my body to the back of my brain. "Allow me to inform your soul's decision."

# The Day After Tomorrow

She rested against me, one arm and one leg thrown over me, naked and warm under the covers, the fingers of her other hand twirling and untwirling my hair, her breathing-talking tickling across the skin of my chest. Half-listening, I imagined myself a continent and her a ragged, inconsistent wind, her stories thrashing my semi-dreaming mind awake as tiny cyclones, touching down and skipping aloft again, left behind their minute tracks of devastation. Her mother wanted to know, she said, what happened the other day (twelve years ago? eleven?) at the Lambs' house.

I yawned. I reached to pet her face, to ask if we couldn't pick up there tomorrow, but she grabbed my hand. "You mean after I went and got everybody to help them build their stupid tree house that's not a tree house, and then they turned around and tried to say I was the one that was going to get somebody killed if I tried to help, because all the girls were supposed to keep away from the power tools and from the boys, too, because we're too stupid to do anything except make stupid mud pies, and I left and came home?"

"No. That's not what I'm asking about, and you know it." (Was that her mother speaking? I think so. I was fading.)

"Yes, it is! I tried to go outside and help, but she locked the door! She locked me in their house like a prisoner!"

"Did you tell Eugene about sex?"

"No! I left!"

She remembered then, but it was too late. Her mother already thought she was lying. "The Lambs are upset. They say you talked to Eugene about sex. Now, why would they tell me something like that, if it wasn't true?"

"Yeah, but that's not what happened at their stupid whatchamacallit. You can't even call it a party, because it wasn't one. Just like you can't call it a tree house if there's no tree. Everything about them is fake. Even their boy is a fake boy!"

"Stop that! I don't want to hear another word about Eugene being a figment of your imagination. Do you know how ridiculous that makes you sound?"

"I don't care!"

"What are people supposed to think, Jeannie? What are they supposed to make of you?"

"I don't care what people think. I know the truth."

"Yes, you do. You're a bright, bright girl, Honey, and I don't—"

"Didn't you say you're supposed to respect what I believe in my heart?"

Her mother stopped talking.

"Well, I believe in my heart that Eugene D.O.E. is not real, because I know I made him up. I know I did. And what you say and what anybody else says is not going to change that."

I interrupted, yawning. "D.O.E.?"

"Department of Engineering. I told you that. Try to keep up, Vanessa!"

"I beg your pardon. Go on. Just pretend I'm not here."

"Shut up."

Her mother retreated a step. Her eyes flitted around Jeannie's room like two small birds looking for a way out. "So Mrs. Lamb is making it up?"

"Making what up?"

"You didn't tell Eugene about reproduction? About sex?"

"No. Yes, I mean." So then she had to tell her mother everything. How Eugene didn't have real parents so he didn't know where he came from, how he tried to say he'd never had parents, which was a lie, because everybody did. She tried to make her mother see that she had only told him for his own good. "Would you rather I lied to him?"

Her mother didn't fall for that. "When you learned about it in school, they told you not to be telling other kids about it, didn't they? Younger kids, who aren't ready for sex ed? Didn't they?"

"Yes, but Eugene is going to be in third grade now, so it's not like—"

"Oh, brother!" Her mom must have been hoping that Mrs. Lamb had made it all up. "Well, you aren't allowed over there anymore."

"Fine with me."

"Yes, but I don't think that'll be the end of it. They're up in arms over it."

"Up in arms?" Jeannie figured they could just hold hands and pray about it like they did everything else. "I didn't do anything wrong."

"Yes, you did."

For the hundredth time, Jeannie did not care. "He's going to learn about it anyway. He's in third grade."

"Well, no. Probably not. They're pulling him out of school."

"Oh, I see," I interjected. "So that's how they came to be home schooling experts?"

Jeannie ignored me. I felt like a ghost in her living room on Fair Meadow, a time-traveler watching the first little rift appear between her and her mother.

"So what?" she said, not to me.

"They filed a lawsuit against the Board of Education. They want you to stay away from him. If you see him, no matter where you are, you find someplace else to go. And if he goes there, you go someplace else."

"Suits me fine," Jeannie said. She did that anyway.

From then on, things only got worse when they should have got better, since Eugene no longer attended her school. For Halloween she went as Elfaba from *Wicked*. Her mom took her to pick out a pair of pointy black shoes and green-and-white striped tights and helped her apply the green make-up. Her outfit was perfect.

Until she got to school.

In front of everybody, Anna Sylvester said, "It's so you, Jean! I mean, it's just your color. Don't you think so, Sam?"

"Oh, definitely!"

"You know why everybody's always so nice to her, don't you?"

Sam looked down her nose at Jeannie's costume. "Not really. Why?"

Anna fanned herself. "Only because her brother is sofa king hot!"

"I know!" Deanna Kilpatrick chimed in. "Did you see him with his shirt off, laying the roof on Eugene's tree house?"

"Laying the roof," Sam repeated (Sam Corwin, who had once been Jeannie's best, if not only remaining, friend), giving the phrase another layer of meaning. Then the two of them started barking like dogs, saying, "Roof! Roof! I wish I was a roof!"

I snorted in the dark when Jeannie told me that part. She punched me in the arm, hard.

"What sucked about it," she said, "was I had to find out from them that my brother was now a big fan of the Lamb family. When I confronted him about it, he said Eugene was like the little brother he never had."

"Ouch."

"Yeah. So I told him I knew how he felt, because I never had a brother, either."

"Fuck brothers," I said, reaching for her. "Come here, Sister."

We wrapped each other up tight. She kept talking, telling me the further catastrophes of her childhood as I fell asleep, not knowing, not caring how they infiltrated my dream of a blackbird sitting on my shoulder, sipping the tears that dribbled like tiny black pearls from my left eye.

"Vanessa," she said, her blue-black hair in the shape of a wing, no, a pair of wings, all a-shimmer. "Imagine if your baby did come back. How old would he be?"

He would be grown, I knew.

"He would be my age," she said. Or maybe she said, "He would be a mage." Either way, she made it sound biblical, grander, more meaningful than his having lived a certain number of years. (In my dream, he was ten, going on fourth grade like her, yet wise beyond his years, my Marshall Caleb.) Something in the way she said it made my age sound more like my epoch or my era. Only in my dream there were no equivalents to her meaning.

"Imagine," she said, "if someone saved him as a baby and delivered him to the wrong address." Then she whispered, as if in awe, "He grew up, Vanessa!" But she didn't call me Vanessa. She called me by my other name, a name I had never told her. "He came back to you, Anastasia."

I felt the tears well and the blackbird come again, its beak a like straw. I heard myself say, in the language of the crow, "I'm afraid. I'm so afraid I might not recognize him."

"I will know him," she assured me. And again, her knowing enlarged itself in my dreaming mind to encompass more than mere acquaintance. I believe it was probably, was most certainly a dream because, in my memory of it, she hovered over me. I see her face lit from underneath, her lips whispering, her beak breathing life into the notion that my baby lived, whereas, in actual fact, the room had gone completely dark, so dark I couldn't see my hand in front of my face.

So dark and so cold.

Because I was not accustomed to another body in my bed, I had failed to notice the steep drop in temperature during the night. I had not yet unplugged from the grid completely. I couldn't afford to go wind or solar yet. All I had was a backup generator in the shed next to the greenhouse. It should have kicked in. I lay half-awake, knowing something wasn't quite right but not able to put my finger on it, thinking my dream had left me disoriented, nothing more.

Was it a dream? It must have been.

The bedroom had gone black. No blinking 12:00 am on my alarm clock to let me know that Oklahoma Gas and Electric had abandoned me to my own devices. I couldn't remember where I'd left my cell. Jeannie's bandaged wrist lay across my collarbone. I didn't want to disturb her. Her breath warmed my neck. The rhythm of it lulled me back to sleep. How much time passed before I really woke up was anybody's guess. I pitched the covers back and felt the cold in the room descend on me.

"Fuck!" I muttered. "I've got to get dressed and get out to the greenhouse."

Jeannie pulled me back in. "Don't go."

"I have to. All my plants will freeze."

"No, they won't. Not in the next five minutes. Please?" She wrapped me up in her arms and legs, radiating more heat than you'd think a bundle of skin and bones ought to generate, and sooner than I knew it I was gone down a long tunnel of slumber.

Sometime later, I felt her crawl back into bed, shivering. It was my turn to warm her.

"Had to pee," she said.

When I did finally climb out of bed and layer up in the dark, I discovered I couldn't get out my front door. The storm door wouldn't budge more than three or four inches. I pushed against it and felt the prickle of snow shards dance across the back of my hand. When I located my little LED flashlight and shined it at the gap, I saw nothing but white.

"We are royally, royally fucked," I called. Jeannie didn't hear what I said, so I followed the cone of my flashlight back to the bedroom and told her. "Get up. You have got to see this."

She stood hugging herself in two robes over the angel sweatshirt from yesterday and two pairs of my socks, gaping at the wall of snow at the front door.

"Wow." After a minute, she said, "What about the back?"

So I showed her. The drift at the back door came up only to my chest but it was still too heavy to push out of the way. Even with my full weight against the door, the best I could do was compress the snow a little. The night air blew wild and cold across the top of the drift. I clicked the flashlight off. No stars shone. No lights anywhere, outside or in.

"How do we get out?"

"Worse comes to worst, we break a window, I guess. Help me find my cell phone first."

I last had it in the pocket of my jeans, I remembered, when I came in from talking to Maureen Ivory. I didn't say anything about that to Jeannie. I didn't want to get into what her mother and I had talked about. I knew it had to be somewhere in the vicinity of the couch. We checked under the cushions and reached our hands deep into the crevices behind the springs.

"Here's a quarter. Now we just need a pay phone."

"Finders keepers," I told her. "I can't remember the last time I saw one." A pay phone, I meant, but just at that moment, like the answer to an unspoken prayer, I heard the pathetic bleat my phone makes when it needs a charge. "Shh!" I hissed at Jeannie in the irrational hope that it would bleat again and let me know where it was. "Did you hear that?"

"Yeah." She sounded disappointed, defeated even.

"It's right here, somewhere."

"Did you look under the sofa?"

"I've looked everywhere."

"Give me the flashlight." She turned herself upside-down, kneeling inverted on the couch with the top of her head resting on the rug. "It's right there. Can you reach it?" She sounded so resigned. I could not for the life of me figure her out.

I laid my cheek flat against the floor and followed the beam of the flashlight. "You're a genius!" I grunted, reaching.

I had already formulated a plan. Since I had no idea how much of a charge I had left, I hit the send button twice, to ring the last number I'd called—Jeannie's mom, in other words—meaning to tell her the predicament we were in and would she please call 9-1-1 for me, because in a storm like this, I might not get through right away, and what if my phone went kerplunk while I was on hold?

The phone rang and rang. "Pick up, Maureen!" I willed her mother.

"It's the middle of the night," I informed Jeannie. "Come on! Is your mom a heavy sleeper?"

"Phone's in the kitchen. She won't wake up."

A grumpy voice interrupted the next ring, a man's voice. "Yuh? Who is it?"

"Shit!" Jeannie said, so soft I could barely hear. "Shit, shit, shit!"

I told him who I was and that I had Jeannie with me, in case he didn't know.

Still upside-down, half on and half off the sofa, she started waving her hands in a frenzy, then she dropped the flashlight and covered her face. Whatever I wasn't supposed to say had already been said. Whoever was on the line, I wasted no time filling him in on the situation before my phone gave out one last pitiful bleat. The voice at the other end, more awake now, said, "I'll let my folks know, Ms. Cavendish. You hang in there." Then the phone sang its swan song and shut itself down.

*My folks?*

"That must have been your brother?"

"Nunh-uh." She swiveled her head on the floor, only partially lit by the flashlight. "You didn't talk to my brother."

I repeated what he'd said, whoever it was.

"Oh." Her voice sounded so flat. "Yeah, that's weird."

We left it at that. Help was on its way, was the main thing.

"I still need to get out to the shed off the greenhouse if I can and get the generator going. Otherwise, I'm set to lose everything. I can't believe how much snow we got in just a few hours time!"

"Yeah. Totally nuts." She twisted herself around on the sofa. "I have a better idea." She retrieved the flashlight and shined it at her heavily stockinged feet sticking straight up in the air. "Why don't we go back to bed and wake up in the morning, and it'll all be a bad dream?"

"You can if you want to. I certainly don't pay you enough to do anything else. But I don't have that luxury." I took the flashlight from her and rummaged around until I found my hat, coat, gloves and boots. Then I checked to see which one of the windows offered me the best chance of not getting buried up to my neck in a snowdrift. The one over the kitchen sink seemed like the best option.

Jeannie sighed. "Guess I'm coming with you, then."

"You don't have to. Seriously. It might be better if one of us stayed put, because if help comes before I get back, they're liable to come here first, to the house. If nobody's here, will they even know to come looking for us? At least if you're here, you can send them to find me."

"I don't like that plan."

"Do you have a better one?"

"Yeah. I just told you. I'm coming with you."

So we found her clothes, plus extra layers, and gloves of mine, the kind that come complete with fingers.

I went first, standing on a chair to get up on the kitchen counter so I could hoist the window open. Then, turning around backwards, I snaked my way through the window feet-first and dangled from the sill, already up to my knees in snow. I took a deep breath, let go, and plunged through the cold.

I landed off-kilter and fell over backwards, making a big, Vanessa-shaped indentation in the snow. When I got myself upright again, which took some doing, I guided Jeannie to the ground in a somewhat more graceful manner. Once we got a few feet past the roof overhang, into back yard, the depth of the snow increased dramatically. As we made our way around to the north side, out of the lee of the house, the drift rose higher and higher. I followed the crest of it with my flashlight.

"Jesus!"

"This is bad," Jeannie said.

We couldn't see where the drift ended and the snow on the roof began.

"At least it's stopped snowing." I shut the flashlight off. A gauzy three-quarter moon had risen above the canyon, showing us a deep, gradual basin of snow where we ought to have seen steep red cliffs banded with gypsum.

"It's like that movie."

"Which one?"

"Day After Tomorrow."

"Well, I can't think that far ahead right now. Let's get going."

"There's this, like, super-storm due to the greenhouse effect and it plunges all of North America into a new ice age."

"Great. Come on. There's a shovel on the front porch if we can get to it."

She laughed. "The front porch is buried, Vanessa. You saw that, right? When you tried to open the front door?"

"Yeah." I knew. It was hopeless. If it *was* the day after tomorrow, maybe the snow would be crusted over enough so we could walk across it. But tonight it was fresh, wet and heavy. The best we could do was wade into it and try to pack it down underfoot as we went. The drifts to either side of the house rose ten, twelve feet in places, maybe higher.

"Looks shallower over there." Jeannie pointed, but the moon went dark behind a cloud. Who knew if the storm had passed us by or was just taking a break?

"How far?"

"I don't know. How far is a football field?"

"We don't want to get that far from the house, though. If it starts snowing again, and we lose our way. . ."

"Then I vote we go back inside."

I couldn't argue with that. I felt like a damn fool, dragging her out there in the first place. The wind gusted over the roof and brought down a stinging swarm of ice needles in our faces as we made our way back to the window and started packing a ledge of snow against the house that we could climb on to get back up to the window. I boosted Jeannie through. When she got turned around, she straddled the sink and pulled me in by the coat sleeves.

It felt colder inside the house than before. I shut the kitchen window and lit the oven with a match.

"At least we have propane."

"Goodie," Jeannie said.

# Spare Time

Snow had got all up in my jeans when I fell into the bank, so as soon as we climbed back in the kitchen window, I pulled them off and draped them over a chair to dry out. Jeannie did likewise. We found pajamas and got into them by flashlight, then we pulled the rocker and my other chair from the living room into my little kitchen and sat facing the stove with the oven door open for heat.

And we waited.

How long it might take Jeannie's folks to relay our problem to 9-1-1, and then how long it might take the County to send someone to get us dug out — if they even could do it, if they had the manpower — was anybody's guess. Everybody else was snowed in, too, or so we figured.

"Here. Hold the light for me. I'll make us some tea."

When I ran the water to fill the pot, I discovered that (duh!) the tap had no pressure. Like everything else, the well pump ran on electricity. That's when it hit me. My pipes were going to freeze. All of them.

I wasn't so worried about the house. I could do something about the house. We gathered up every pot, pan, bottle, pitcher, bowl, glass and bucket I had and collected what was left in the hot water heater. Then we bled the lines dry in the kitchen and bathroom. The lines in the shop and in the greenhouse were at the mercy of the elements.

"I'm gonna lose everything I've got." I felt my eyes begin to burn and my lips to twist around my words. I hate to blubber, so I shut up, but two things I could not stop from running: my nose and my mind. I counted on sales from the greenhouse in the spring to keep me going through the rest of the year. Not only was that gone, the cost of replacing everything and repairing the damage from busted pipes would set me back even further. "I don't know what I'm supposed to do!" I blurted. To make matters worse, Jeannie was on her feet holding me, wrapping me up in a blanket she'd pulled off the bed to keep herself warm. She guided me through the dark, back to the kitchen, where she set me back down in front of the oven door. Then she disappeared with the flashlight and came back with the toilet paper roll so I could blow my nose.

"We're not going to talk about that right now," she informed me, clicking the flashlight off, "because there's nothing we can do about it. Why don't you tell me something completely unrelated? Tell me a story."

I wiped my eyes in the dark. "A story? What kind of story?"

"I don't know. The story of your life. You're a writer, aren't you, in your spare time? You must have lots of stories."

A writer? I never said I was a writer. I snorted. "What spare time?" All I could think was how long it would take me to recover from this storm I didn't see coming.

"Right now. This is spare time. Come on, we've got a campfire and everything. It's story time."

"You're right about one thing. I am a writer. I write my stories down. Telling them out loud, that's a whole nother kind of undertaking."

What else I didn't see coming, there in the dark, was the knife she inserted in my gut. That's what it felt like, the next thing she said to me: "People in town say you killed your brother-in-law and got away with it. See, now, there's a story."

I looked at her. All I could make out was the outline of her cheek and nose and the bone-white halo of her hair in the little light that leaked into the room from around the broiler. I blinked. I blinked again. I had stopped crying.

"They also say you killed your grandmother."

That was my heart she was going for now. I looked at her hard. I couldn't believe what I was hearing. Was this whole thing some kind of set-up? Her coming to me, inviting herself into my house? Into my bed? "Jesus Christ!" I accused her, "What the fuck kind of game are you playing?"

"Oh, we're not playing yet. We're still choosing up sides, and I want you to know which side you're playing for. I don't have a shitload of good qualities, Vanessa, but one thing I do have going for me is I will tell you the truth. I will tell you to your face if I think you're guilty of something. And right now, I'm just letting you know what other people say behind your back, what they've been saying about you for as long as I can remember. Since I was in high school, anyway, and you first came back from wherever you went. Those people who talk behind your back? They're on the other side, in case you're wondering. You're on my side. I'm the team captain and I picked you. So please don't pretend it comes as any kind of surprise to hear it."

"Well, it's bullshit."

She sat looking into the oven, waiting me out.

My grandmother took her own life. She wandered into the canyon when I was eleven years old, just like she'd been hinting to me that she was going to do ever since I was old enough to put two and two together and deny to myself that it equaled four. She cut the veins in both of her arms wide open—the right way, as Jeannie would have it. She bled out in the middle of a thunderstorm, though the coroner said she died of suffocation, face-down in the mud of Keening Creek.

I found the knife she used the following day, before the Sheriff's search party got to it. I buried it. I buried it out of shame and—I don't know what else you'd call it—horror, I suppose, though I just felt numb when I did it. I sometimes review the memory of it like a scene from a movie that I do not watch of my own accord. Like it's somebody else in the role, not me. As if I'm looking over my own shoulder, watching myself use the knife to dig its own shallow grave. I sat watching that movie again for a long time by the light of the oven before I told Jeannie, in dribs and drabs, what I just told you.

"Sheriff Angley found the knife, supposedly with my fingerprints all over it. That's how the story got out that I killed her."

"What about your sister's husband?"

"Leon? Leon was my best buddy," I offered by way of a defense. "At least when I was little. I didn't have a lot of friends, living out here by the canyon. Just Grandma and me. Sheila didn't much care for me, but that wasn't my fault. She was quite a bit older, and our dad, well, he cheated on her mom, so..."

"With your mom?"

"So I was told. I never got to meet her. I never even knew who she was until after she was dead. Sheila told me. She worked at Enid State School on the night shift. Same place our dad worked, same place her mother worked until she found out he cheated on her. Sheila said my mother was a retarded woman who lived there, and that's why our dad took off for the West Coast. My grandma always said he lived in California, but for all I know, he might just as easily have skipped the country. To this day, I've never heard from him. Not one word."

"Shit!" said Jeannie Ivory, my new best friend and confidante, my lesbian lover. If I didn't know any better, I'd say she sounded impressed.

"You wanted a story," I reminded her.

She scooted her chair closer to me and undid one end of the blanket, then leaned in against me so she could wrap it around us both. "Can I tell you something?"

I waited. I wasn't sure, all of a sudden, how I felt about her being so familiar.

"I've never told anybody this before, male or female, so I don't know if it's exactly appropriate or not on a first date or if it's too soon or even what it's supposed to mean, but—" and this last part she said in a rush, the way you gun the motor to get through an intersection before the light turns red—"I'm-pretty-sure-I'm-in-love-with-you."

While me, I was held up in the traffic inside my head, still wondering if I wasn't being played somehow and what did it all mean in the context of what I had just told her? Did she feel sorry for me? Because I was past needing anyone to do that. Way past needing forgiveness or understanding for any crimes I may or may not have committed. Much less forgiveness for the sins of my father.

"It's entirely possible I did kill Leon," I confessed. "Or that I was— how do they put it?—instrumental in his death. I grabbed his cane, right? As I was on my way out the door to go to Leigh Ann Bittle's party. And he stumbled and hit his head on the corner of the door." It didn't seem like much at the time, but the human body is a frail fucking apparatus, vulnerable to all kinds of mishaps, accidents and miscommunications between one organ and another. If his brain got jarred just the wrong way?

I sat staring into the open mouth of the oven. Jeannie shifted against me, rested her head on my shoulder.

"All my life I blamed Patterson Price, thinking he killed Leon to protect me."

"That's the guy you ran away with?"

"In my mind—the way I always pictured it—while I sat out in the driveway in Patter's car, the two of them got to arguing. About Leon not keeping his hands off me, maybe. They were both drunk, of that I'm sure. One thing led to another, and he killed him and then later got scared and said I did it, so I wouldn't tell on him. And so he could hide me a safe enough distance away from him and his family and his friends and his reputation that I wouldn't cause him any problems."

Don't get me wrong. I won't say I had a sudden flash of insight that night, huddled in the dark with Jeannie. I 'd always had my doubts about the validity of my version of events the night Leon died. For one thing, I had never actually told Patter—not until a day or two later, after we were well on our way from Oklahoma to Massachusetts—that Leon had ever tried anything with me. Anything sexual. Only now, under the clarity of darkness, hearing myself tell my story out loud for someone else to hear—only now did I realize I could no longer kid myself about what had actually happened that other night so long ago.

"Patter never had any reason to do Leon any harm," I admitted. "He protected me from the truth for a while until he figured out how to tell me. He said, when he knocked on the front door, it was already partway open, propped open by Leon's cane. Just the way I left it. When no one answered, he stepped inside and found Leon's dead body."

So what the good folks in town said behind my back was, in all likelihood, at least partly true. I never did anything to Leon on purpose, but I probably did kill him. Possibly, let's say. In self-defense. And not beyond the shadow of a doubt.

Jeannie found my hand and squeezed it. "You're a strong-minded, capable woman. You do what needs to be done. And you know what? It's sexy as hell."

I never stood trial for it. But folks don't forgive and they don't forget. I always had a sneaking suspicion that, even though she wasn't from here, that was the reason Gay Lamb never wanted me to sponsor her lame-ass TV show.

"If I did it," I said, "I don't feel any remorse."

"That's what I'm saying. I read once, in a book about war and PTSD, that approximately one in fifty people lack the usual inhibition against killing, meaning they are psychologically immune to post-traumatic stress. The study focused on men, because most of the subjects were combat veterans from Vietnam, Korea and World War II. It also drew on archaeological evidence dating back to the Civil War. They found a large number of muskets abandoned at all these battlefield sites. A lot of them never got fired, just reloaded again and again, one ball on top of another, because according to the book, most people have an inborn reluctance to taking human life. The point the book wanted to make is we're getting so much better at training people to kill now, with video games and simulated training. But that two percent thing stood out to me. It explains why so many people come back with PTSD, but not everyone."

"Okay..."

"Maybe you're one of the one in fifty."

"Right. That's me. I'm a natural-born killer."

"Maybe." If I didn't know any better—and I don't—I'd say she sounded almost hopeful.

"And you think you're in love with me?"

"What if I am? Do you think that's why? Unh-uh. I'll tell you why. Because I would kill for you, Vanessa. I will kill anything that tries to hurt you and I will never let you take the blame."

"I think you're a very disturbed young woman."

She snaked her arms around me. "I think we're just two ordinary peas in a very disturbed pod."

"That's one theory," I allowed.

# Big Words

Dawn crept across the drifted snow at the tops of the windows. I could see more than just her silhouette now. Jeannie looked tired. "I expect we'll have a long wait before any help arrives, if you want to go back to bed," I suggested. To be honest, I wouldn't have minded a break from her.

"What about you?"

"I won't be able to sleep."

"I'm okay. It's warmer in here with the stove."

I felt so helpless. I needed to be up doing something. I decided to cook us some breakfast. "How do you like your eggs?"

"Scrambled, if you have any cream cheese?"

"You can look. I don't think so."

She used the flashlight to poke around in the fridge. "Ricotta might work." She handed me the tub. "Mix some of that in."

So I did, while she laid out four pieces of bread on the oven rack and closed the door to toast them. "I can't eat eggs by themselves."

I yawned. "Religious prohibition?"

"I would prohibit religion if I could. What's that got to do with scrambled eggs?"

"Ha. All religion?"

"Why? Do you have one you want me to spare?"

"Not exactly. I'm allergic to most of them."

"Preach it, Sister."

"I'd call myself agnostic, only I don't feel like I know enough to be sure."

My lame joke sailed harmlessly past her left ear. I forgave her for it.

"I've never known anyone like you before."

"I should hope not." I yawned again. Couldn't stop myself. "How do you mean?"

"You talk like a hick, but then you come out with something like that. You're more learned than you are educated. Your grammar sucks, but you still have this, like, huge vocabulary."

"Learned," I mused. "I like that. I don't know that it's true, but I like it. I never made it past eighth grade, but I've always spent a lot of time in libraries, reading books and looking up the words I don't know. I always feel like I owe it to a writer somehow, to try and understand what he's trying to tell me—he or she—and also like I don't want to be judged for not knowing what a word means. I guess it comes down to my mother and who she was. I don't want to be thought retarded. I still carry that around with me. The first book I ever bought and paid for was a paperback dictionary, because they won't let you check out reference books from the library. But grammar, now, that's something else. There's book grammar and street grammar, in my opinion. My English teacher in seventh grade, Mrs. Bittle, she used to correct my grammar all the time. I just let her do it, because it give her so much pleasure. But this once I leaned over and whispered to my best friend. (Ha Ha! As if I had one!) I said, 'That ain't the way my Grammar taught me!'

"My friend snickered and got caught. I forget her name.

"'I heard what you said!' Mrs. Bittle accused me. She was so high and mighty. She like to yanked my arm half out of the socket and made me go stand in the hallway. I looked at her and I said: 'You'll have to forgive me? I was exposed to too much lead in my system as a infant and I just ain't quite right. And I smiled at her real sweet. I never smiled that sweet to no one. I guess it didn't look quite normal on me is all I could figure, what with my four eyes and my freckles and my big teeth. That was early in the year. She marked me as a liar and a smart ass from the git-go. I wasn't one, though. Not really. I was a story teller is what my grandma said. Grandma was an atheist. That's the way she raised me."

"Let me guess. You rebelled?"

"Not really. I just didn't believe her. I didn't understand what she meant by it, because she also claimed to be half Cherokee and three quarters Crow and fourteen sixteenths Lakota, and she talked about the Great Mystery as if it was a living, breathing, thinking being. Some kind of planetary intelligence like on a Star Trek episode. She worshiped our ancestors. Always said she wanted to go 'walk in beauty' with them after she was gone, because so much of the beauty in this world's been raped and spoiled by machinery and construction and 'land management' and what all. So go figure. And you—you're not so different. You call yourself an atheist, yet you tell me you raised Eugene Lamb out of the sewer by performing some kind of secret, unconscious magic." I didn't mean to come across as critical in any way, just to lay out what I saw as a potential blind spot in her belief system.

"Paranormal and supernatural are two different things," she pointed out.

"How do you account for it, though? For something that don't...I don't know—agree with the laws of physics?"

"How do you account for things that do?"

"What do you mean? Give me a for instance."

"Like sunshine. How do you account for sunshine?"

"As near as I can tell, everybody more or less agrees on sunshine. But when you start talking about raising a boy up from your imagination and making him walk and talk and go to school—well, you surely understand how that comes across."

"As delusional, you mean? As some form of mental illness?"

"Could you get me two plates? Cabinet to the right of the sink. Thank you. And pour me a glass of o. j. and yourself whatever you want." Then I said, to cover my ass, "I'm not qualified to diagnose anyone. Not even myself."

She set the table and stood the flashlight up on end like a candle.

"Save the batteries," I said.

"It's romantic. Did you ever hear of a guy named Al Siebert?"

I shook my head. We dragged our chairs back over to the table, she fished the toast out of the oven and buttered it, and we sat down to breakfast.

"He was a clinical psychologist who got a position at the Menninger Clinic in—" She waggled her hand. "Wherever it is. He was already kind of a big deal, I guess, when he came up with this theory that a psychiatric diagnosis occurs as a result of a therapist reaching a point of extreme discomfort with the behavior or the beliefs or whatever a patient manifests during treatment." She used her fingers to make quotes around "manifests".

"Okay."

"Guess what happened when he presented his theory."

I waited for it.

"They diagnosed him."

"With what?"

"Doesn't matter. They locked him up."

I watched her eat. "Let me get this straight. Are you saying that if I don't believe you created Eugene Lamb out of thin air and if I dare to suggest that your theory of his origins might be, oh, let's just say, out of touch with reality, then it's because I'm uncomfortable, not because you're fucking crazy?"

"Aren't you?"

"Uncomfortable? Not half as uncomfortable as I would be if I thought there was something to it."

"Exactly." She bit into her toast triumphantly.

"Jeannie," I said, "Girlfriend, you're chasing your own tail."

"Maybe. But enough about me. What about you? You make people uncomfortable, too, you know."

"How do you mean?"

"They think you got away with murder."

I stopped chewing. "We're back to that?"

"Twice."

I couldn't swallow. "Peopl—" I tried to say but couldn't finish. I had to cough and I couldn't do that, either. I stood up and turned my back to her, went and stood bending over the sink, where I spat egg and toast out of my mouth and tried to rinse it down the drain with nothing but air in the line. I cleared my throat. "I don't care what people think," I said finally.

"I think you do, you just don't let it stop you. That's why I said I never met anyone like you. Not that you're an atheist who uses big words."

I wiped my mouth and turned on her. "Is that really what you think of me, Jeannie? That I'm a serial killer?"

"Not sure yet. But I'll tell you what I do think."

"Please," I said. "By all means." My throat was dry, my voice was hoarse.

"I think if you did kill anyone, you must have had good reason."

"I never had reason good enough for that." I sat down again, pushed my plate away. "As for what people think, if I could fix that, I might consider it. But I can't. People aren't cars. You can't just pop the hood and tinker with them until you know what the problem is. If I could, believe you me, Jeannie, I'd have you in the shop getting looked at right this minute."

She looked at her plate and speared a bite of scrambled egg with her fork. "Yeah. My mom told you not to bother, though." She slipped the egg in her mouth and dragged it off the fork between her teeth, studying me. "Didn't she?"

"I gather she's been down that road with you a time or two?"

"Could say that."

"I didn't figure I'd have much success getting you there. Not that it mattered, since Jiminy shit the bed. Unless you wanted me to call you an ambulance." I was curious. "How'd you know I talked to your mother?"

"Do you have her on speed dial? No, you just hit the last number you called, and that was our house."

"Okay. You got me."

"I'm no genius, but I can put two and two together. If Billy answered the phone, that means they all got snowed in, too. Why else would he be there in the middle of the night? So that means we're stuck here for a while, you and me. If they have to go around digging everybody in town out, how long do you think it'll take them to get to us?"

"I know."

"Days?"

The thought had occurred to me.

"Think we'll freeze to death or starve first?"

"Neither one."

"How much propane do you have in that tank?"

"Enough."

"So if it comes down to you or me, you have more meat on your bones. I could survive longer on you than you could on me, so I vote we eat you first."

"Nice."

She pushed back from the table and came leaning over me, wrapping me up in her blanket. "Why don't you come on back to bed with me, and I'll get started."

"I'll pass," I said.

She rested her forehead against mine, trying to look me in the eye.

"Why don't you bring the dishes over," I said.

"You didn't finish."

"I'm not hungry."

She pulled back, pushed my hair behind my ear, still trying to get me to lock eyes with her. "You're mad at me?"

"Not mad," I said. I felt betrayed.

She probably did, too. It was stupid of me not to just dial 9-1-1 when

I had the chance. How much battery would that have taken? But was it so awful that I called her mother in the first place? All of that was rolling around in my head, until what spilled out was, "I just don't need to be reminded what people think of me. Is that too much to ask?"

"Oh, Vanessa! You don't get it." She bent at the waist and hugged me tighter, pinning my arms to my sides. "People are shit. I just want you to know it doesn't matter to me one way or the other if you killed some scumbag who tried to molest you. You want to know why? Because I'm not a good person and I don't value life over every other fucking thing there is. I can tell you in a nutshell what you need to know about me and Eugene Lamb, okay? If you're ready."

"Do I have a choice?"

"No. Not yet." She kept her grip on me. "Do you know where the name Eugene comes from?"

"From 'You, Jean?' I think I got that part."

"No. Besides that. It means 'good seed,' as in 'good genes.' He literally is everything that's good that I'm not, everything normal and wholesome and decent. Everything rated PG. He's acceptable. People like him. Never mind that he's a vampire that sucks all that vitamin-enriched goodness out of me, because guess what? There's a part of me that's okay with that, that thinks what's left of me might be rotten, but at least it's mine. Everything else—everything good, quote-unquote—is in danger of becoming his. Including you. Don't you think that's why he came out here yesterday? Don't you think that's exactly why he played up to you? I know he made you feel special. Why would he do that? I'll tell you why. Because you're the only good thing left in my life. That's the reason."

I said not a word. What was I going to say? That it wasn't all about her? That she was not always the first item on everybody else's agenda? I felt all the anger, my sense of betrayal, drain right from me. My arms hung limp at my sides, my fingers dangling at the chair rungs, no longer pinned by her but unable to move out of sheer weakness. I slumped forward against her and began to weep—for myself? for her? I'm not sure. I just felt so tired and sad and sorry for her that I, me, Vanessa Cavendish, would be the last good thing in the life of a girl who'd been so crushed and defeated, whether by mental illness or bad luck or just the plain meanness of people. I cried and I clung to her and I swore to myself at that moment that I would never abandon her—I couldn't—not for the sake of a boy I hardly knew, no matter what he promised to do for my business. Not even if the way she characterized him was unfair, inaccurate, distorted by the lenses of her own broken self-image. I swore to myself that I would stand by her, that I would do everything in my power to help her cling to—to what, though? To me? To her idea of me? What she saw in me was at least as screwed up as anything else in her head. Let's just say, I resolved to stand up for her capacity to imagine yours truly as something, someone, worth clinging to.

I would be her pillar, I decided, her rock. I would anchor her soul to mine and I would not budge.

I wiped my eyes with the palms of my hands, then planted my hands on either side of her face and my lips on hers. I didn't just kiss her, I inhaled her. I drew her oxygen, her nitrogen, her carbon dioxide deep into my lungs and held it there. I let my blood absorb her madness, her bleak, intelligent, lightless soul, and make it mine. So that I might begin to love her, maybe the way she loved me.

"The longer he's in this world," she said with a note of desperation in her voice, almost hysteria, "the more he takes. The longer he's alive, the less alive I am. I can't stop him. I can't. I can't face him alone. I need you, Vanessa."

"Need me to what?" I won't kid you, I knew what she was driving at. She wasn't so clever or so smooth that I didn't see it coming and couldn't help myself. She would kill anything that tried to hurt me, and she wanted to know: would I do the same for her?

I don't remember how or when I got to my feet. We stood looking at each other for a long time, neither one of us blinking first.

But the grumble of a big truck outside broke the spell. I heard people shouting. I pushed open the kitchen window and yelled for all I was worth.

I didn't think anyone heard me, so I scrambled out of my pajamas and grabbed the wrong pair of jeans off the back of a chair. I knew they weren't mine as soon as I tried to pull them up over my thirty-seven-year-old ass, but I wasn't thinking logically and didn't want to take the time to peel them off and start over. So I cinched them around my waist and zipped myself in, bundled up and climbed out the window, though I could hardly bend. The good thing was Jeannie hadn't fallen through fresh snow the way I did, so her jeans were halfway dry. The day was bright by now, the snow blinding. I waded around to the side of the house closest to where I thought they might be, judging by the sound of their voices, until I stood chest-deep in snow and couldn't go any further. I cupped my hands around my mouth and tried to pitch my voice over the dune of snow that surrounded my house.

"Stay right there!" a voice answered back. "Stay where you are! I'll come get you!"

I heard a plow drop and a truck engine rev far away, out by the road. The answering voice came from closer up by the house, sounded like, so I waited.

Not a minute went by before I saw a head bobbing up over the snow bank in a watch cap with a tassel on top, then a pair of dark goggles, shoulders, arms and legs, until there at the crest of the snow bank, with the brightest blue sky behind him and his gloved hands spread like the savior of the world, stood Eugene Lamb.

# STANDING WAVE

Eugene descended the long tail of the drift on a pair of snowshoes, hardly sinking in at all. He held his gloved hands shoulder-width apart and ran them in a west-to-east direction, perpendicular to the canyon. "This is crazy! This whole swath is snowed in! Just right here. Nowhere else. We got—" he made a face, guesstimating—"maybe two inches in town? If that."

"Two inches!"

"Weird, huh?

"Two *inches?*"

His braces glinted in the sun. I couldn't see his eyes for the dark glasses. "Nothing to speak of until about a mile or two from here. Then it starts building up to this."

I wanted to ask what he, of all people, was doing here, but he beat me to the punch. "We got a whole crew out front. Nobody believed me when I said you were snowed in. They laughed, but they came. Lucky I had my snowshoes with me. We got Gary Purcell with his plow and Pastor Wingate and my dad and a whole bunch of guys with snow shovels and we borrowed the snow blower from the church. We should have you dug out of here in no time."

"What about Billy Ivory?" I asked. Where was he?

"Yeah, sure. All the guys from Trinidad."

*Trinidad?* I wondered, but I didn't ask. I had enough on my mind. "What I most need is to get to the shed behind the greenhouse and see what's going on with my generator."

"Well, here." He walked, I waded, over to the shelf of packed snow underneath the kitchen window, where he sat down and pulled off a snowshoe. "Take these and go do what you've got to do."

"How will you get back out?"

"I'll wait for you."

"Out here?"

He patted the bench of snow with his gloved hand, smiling. "Right here."

I watched him pull the second snowshoe off and bang the aluminum frame against the other one to knock the snow off. I didn't know what to do. Delusional or not, Jeannie was terrified of this boy. I could not leave him here with the window open and her inside, no matter what I thought he was or was not capable of. No telling how long it might take me to get to the shed, figure out what was wrong with the generator, and come back. It didn't make one ounce of sense to try and explain it, but I couldn't do it. I couldn't leave him there.

What did I think he'd do to her?

Nothing. That wasn't the point.

Once again, I felt played. Not by him, by Jeannie. Make that, by Jeannie's irrational fear of him. I had to decide between that and trying to save my greenhouse. If there was anything left to save.

"Give me a minute." I stepped up beside him and pulled myself halfway in the window, where I faced the egg and toast I'd coughed up in the sink earlier. I'm sure I looked ridiculous. It hadn't been that difficult before, when I had Jeannie to pull on my arms, but now I couldn't seem to wriggle my ass through the window. My thighs, actually. In her skin-tight jeans. Something in her pocket caught on the windowsill and dug into my leg. All my layers got hung up, and I had nothing to grab onto but the stainless steel sink divider, which kept slipping out of my grip.

"Can I help?" Eugene offered from behind me. I had an image of him planting his hands on my ass and pushing, but he lifted me up at the ankles instead, and that's all it took. I spilled into the sink and down off the kitchen cabinet with all the grace of a wildebeest at a watering hole. I made my way to the bedroom.

I half expected to find Jeannie in a state of hysterics again, but no, she sat cross-legged as a Buddha in the middle of the bed, still in my pee jays and extra socks, smiling, holding my cell phone like a lotus flower. "You brought him here?"

"I had no idea he would—"

She cut me off. "You called him."

"No, I didn't. I—"

"Your battery's not dead, you fucking liar."

"Jeannie, I did not—"

"It's right here." She held up my phone. "The last number you called—that's not my house, it's his. Oh, and look at this! You got a text. Let's see—who's it from? Oh, that's funny, isn't it? It's the same number. Let me read it to you. 'Srsly pleased 2 meet u. Hope we cn set up a time 2 talk about Repurpose Farm soon. Would heart 2 blog about u.' Isn't that sweet?" Her equanimity evaporated in a hurry. She threw the phone at me and barely missed my head. It crashed against the bedroom door and came apart in three pieces—phone, cover, battery.

"You better hope that's not broken."

"Or what? What could you possibly do to me that's worse than what you've done already?"

"I did not call Eugene. I called your mother."

"Don't even try." She pointed her fingers at me like a blade, all four of them, the way she'd described her brother pointing his fingers at her. "Just keep him away from me!" she said through her teeth. "I don't want to see him. I don't want to hear his voice. I don't even want to hear his name."

I stooped to pick up the pieces of my phone. "I don't do this kind of drama." My voice shook. "I don't need it. I'm sorry if things don't always work out for you the way you want them to, but you don't have any right to call me a liar." I stood up. "Eugene is right out—"

"I said, do not speak his name to me!"

I closed my eyes. "The Dark Lord is waiting right outside the kitchen window. He can probably hear you. I have to go. You can do whatever you want. You can get dressed and come with me, you can invite him in for a cup of tea, you can lock the window and hide under the covers. It's all the same to me."

"You *cunt!*"

"Okay. Gotta go."

I climbed back outside. It wasn't easy. It wasn't dignified. I didn't care. "I can't leave you here, Eugene."

The way he looked at me—he didn't say anything, but—even through the dark glasses, I could tell he'd heard enough to get a handle on the situation inside. He said, "I wish I had another pair of these I could offer you." He dropped the snowshoes and stepped into them, stretching the cords across his feet. "Can you tell me where the generator is and what to do?"

I explained how to get to it, but as for what the problem was, I didn't know.

"I'll have my dad take a look. Brother Purcell is plowing out your driveway, so the rest of us can start shoveling."

I didn't know who "Brother Purcell" was but I wasn't in a position to care. "Quickest, easiest way is to go through the shop. If you can get the back door open, just come straight from there to the front of the house. Less shoveling that way."

"Looked to me like the wind came over the roof of the shop and piled everything right at your front door, so I think you're right. There's less to dig out at the back of the shop than there is around the side."

"Good."

He stamped his feet in his snowshoes. "Weird, huh? How it's so concentrated right here compared to everywhere else?"

"Eugene," I said. "Thank you."

He nodded. "I'm sorry to cause you such a—"

"No." I didn't let him finish. "You didn't."

He smiled, put his sunglasses on and took off walking up the lee side of the drift like it was nothing.

"Eugene!" I called after him.

He turned, looking down at me.

"Was that you I called early this morning? Because I thought I was talking to Billy Ivory."

"Billy Ivory?" I wondered if he looked confused behind his shades. I couldn't tell. "No, I don't think so. You talked to me."

"Never mind. Thank you for coming."

He turned and climbed to the top, where he stood as high as the roof, calling out to someone on the other side of the house: "I found them. They're okay."

"Praise the Lord!" came the other voice.

I sat outside for as long as I could take it. The sun was too bright, reflecting off all the unbroken whiteness that covered the back pasture and the canyon beyond, but it failed to warm me. I had to go back in the house sooner or later and try to square things with Jeannie. I pulled my gloves off and pieced my phone back together and pressed the button to turn it on, but it didn't want to come to life. All I could figure, based on her accusation, was this: Eugene had left me a text message sometime the night before, probably in the evening, and neither Jeannie nor I had heard it, probably because my phone was under the couch. Maybe we were in the kitchen at the time.

"Or in the bedroom," I said out loud to no one.

But no, we were probably right on top of the couch, going at it, Jeannie with her ears burrowed in somewhere south of my moaning and wailing and "Shit!" I said. "Shit, shit, shit!"

I turned around and reached for the windowsill to steady myself, when the snow bench gave away under me and I fell against the house, wrenching my shoulder. I picked myself up and brushed myself off. I wasn't hurt—not seriously—but I had to pack a bunch more snow up against the house before I'd be able to pull myself up again. I was thinking how tiresome it was, crawling in and out of a hole like a rabbit, when Jeannie came and closed the window and locked it.

Evidently, I had worn out the welcome in my own house.

I sat down. My shoulder hurt.

What kept nagging at me was I didn't think a text message sent to my phone ought to register as the last number I had called. I was sure the last person I had spoken to was Maureen.

But no. That wasn't right, either. I called Triple A after that, didn't I? Sure I did. Or did I call her back? But either way, how in the hell did I get Eugene Lamb on the line?

"Weird, huh?" I heard him say in my head.

What happened, I found out later, after I had power restored and could turn on my computer, was this: A big front passed through with a narrow band of intense precipitation that stretched in a pretty purple band (surrounded by wider swatches of paler and paler blues in the satellite image) from basically my house to somewhere east of the Bittles and the Abercrombies on the opposite rim of the canyon. Elsewhere in the country, from the Texas Panhandle to the Great Lakes, got anywhere from one to seven inches, but lucky me, I got walloped. Something about the steep bowl-shape of the canyon, maybe, had caused what they call a "standing wave" to form and halt the progress of one cell of the storm from moving on with the rest. Plus that wind pattern set up a big rotation in the upper atmosphere that bore down on my address with a vengeance, delivering the god-awfulest package of snow I ever saw. On level ground, it amounted to maybe two feet, but the way it drifted, that didn't matter. In short, don't let anybody tell you God don't play favorites; he does. And this time, I won the Devil's lottery.

I got up and paced to and fro in an area of tamped-down snow about the size of a small cage, trying to keep warm. I climbed up and pounded on the window to no avail. I sat and waited and rubbed the ache in my cold shoulder and listened to the growl of a big truck pushing snow around out front and the higher-pitched rattle of a snow blower, on and off, interspersed with the laughter of young men muffled by deep snow as they made steady progress to the front door of my house. I rested my eyes for, seemed like, no more than a minute, and as I did, my grandma said, "Get up, Ness! Let me fix your hair." Seemed like she meant to say, "your head."

But when I looked, it wasn't Grandma blocking the sun, it was Eugene Lamb again.

"She won't open the front door," he said.

# Take Everything

Come to find out, Eugene had coordinated the entire Repurpose Farm Snow Emergency Rescue Operation more or less on his own. After I'd hung up (thinking I'd been talking to someone at the Ivory house) Eugene went and dragged his father out of bed and made the calls to Pastor Wingate and half the young men of the First Assembly of God himself. Wingate offered the use of the Church's snow blower and told Eugene to call and ask Gary Purcell, who owned a dump truck with a snow plow attachment, if he might be available to help out. The crew descended on my shop that early morning like a battalion of angels armed with snow shovels and thermoses of coffee and hot chocolate. They had my driveway and parking lot cleared out in no time, then set to work on a trench from the back door of the shop to the front door of my house and two side trenches, one that veered a few feet from the main trench to the woodshed and another, longer one to the shed off the greenhouse, so I could get to the generator, which was running again.

"It needed gas," Eugene said.

He took off his snowshoes and handed them to me. "I should've thought of this before," he said. He had me climb up to the top of the snow drift, then take the snowshoes off and toss them back down to him. Then he climbed past me and tossed them up to me. Doing it that way, like a game of leap frog, we both managed to get to the trench in the front of the house, where I could walk the rest of the way to the shop and the greenhouse without sinking up to my hips.

I lost some inventory, but my pipes—everything above ground—were the kind of plastic that expands to something like six times its original diameter before it lets go, so I had no damage to speak of. Nothing I couldn't take care of. Mr. Purcell (the boys all called him "Brother Purcell") had pushed all the snow to one end of my parking lot. I lost no more than a day's business. In fact, I got so many curiosity seekers over the next few days, I sold more knick-knacks, wind chimes and whirligigs than I ordinarily did all year long. Local folks, most of them, who hadn't darkened my door since the day I opened. They damn near cleaned me out. The only drawback was I had no time to replenish my stock, because, of course, I was now alone in the shop, greeting customers, attending to the cash register—all the things I normally paid Jeannie to do.

I'm getting ahead of myself.

While Pastor Wingate had me, Brother Gary, Brother Todd, Brother Eugene and all the other strapping young brothers holding hands in a circle in my newly plowed parking lot, offering thanks to Jesus, Jeannie still had herself barricaded inside my house. I kept an extra set of keys on a hook by the back door of the shop, but of course, I had given her that one, and the other one was in my—

I dropped Todd Lamb's hand and slapped my pockets. "Wait a minute!" I interrupted the prayer meeting to announce a miracle. "I've got it right here!" Then I put my hand over my mouth and bowed my head. "I'm sorry!"

But Pastor Wingate looked up at me with a question in his eyes.

"My key!" I whispered. "I have it. See, I—we—" Just in time, I stopped myself from explaining how things had got so discombobulated in the dark that I managed to wriggle into the wrong pair of jeans and—"Anyway, I got mixed up," I said and left it at that.

"Well, hallelujah!" Todd Lamb shouted.

Pastor Wingate raised the hands of the two young men to either side of him and concluded, "Thank you, Jesus!" and several of the others said, "Amen!"

I was practically in tears by this time, I had so much to be grateful for and relieved about and upset over all at the same time. "I don't know how to thank you all!" I needed someone to hug, so I grabbed Todd Lamb (he was closest), then Gary Purcell (who was a much better hugger, though I think I took him by surprise), then the Pastor in his long overcoat and, finally, Eugene. "I am so grateful," I told him. "I don't know how in the world I got your number instead of who I thought I was calling, but y'all have been amazing to me, and I will never forget it!"

"The Lord works in mysterious ways," Eugene assured me, "His wonders to perform."

"Well!" I laughed, still crying. "Amen!"

Let me not overstate the case, but unless I was mistaken, a couple hours prior, Jeannie Ivory and I had been fixing to plot this boy's murder.

"Listen, I don't know if this is the time or place—" he looked around at his friends and the Pastor, including them in our conversation—"but we would love to have you come worship with us. I don't want you to think that's why we're here, I just want you to feel welcome one hundred percent. Any time, you hear?"

"I do," I said. "I hear you." He looked blurry through my tears. They all did.

Pastor Wingate said, "I think we can let most of these boys get on with their day, then. Thank you, fellas!"

Gary Purcell climbed back in his truck and took one final swipe at my driveway as most of the others filed out behind him to their SUVs and pickup trucks parked between the snow banks on either side of the road out front. Three of them hung back, and Todd Lamb motioned one of those three over to where we stood, a tall boy with a thin nose and a pointed chin. He looked familiar, but I couldn't place him until Todd said, "You know Billy Ivory?"

I shook the boy's hand. "I don't think we've met, but I know who you are." He looked familiar because he bore a resemblance, in that indecipherable way some families have, to his little sister.

"We'll let the two of you talk about what you think is best to do," Todd said. "Come on, Eugene. He clapped his hand on Eugene's shoulder, and the two of them and Pastor Wingate went and talked to the other two boys.

"Mom said Jeannie must have got snowed in out here with you. I can bring her home if you want me to."

"That'd be good, if we can get her out of the house," I said, "because I don't have a way to drive her. My pickup—" I almost said, "shit the bed," but changed it up mid-sentence to "went kerplunk."

"I've got a couple of guys with me. She knows them. It should be okay. Eugene's taking off."

"That's probably best."

"The two of them are like oil and vinegar."

"You mean water?"

"Yeah. Oil and water. That's what I meant to say."

I called over to his two friends. "You guys want to wait inside?"

Billy introduced me to them. They were Tommy Isabel and Ben Ambercrombie.

"Oh!" I said, pushing open the door to the shop so we could all get in out of the cold. "I know you. I know *of* you, anyway. You're Izzy, and you're the infamous Crumb Number Three, and that makes the three of you *The Triumvirate*, is it?"

They laughed good-naturedly to let me know I hadn't offended them, at least, but Izzy corrected me. "We don't call ourselves that anymore. We're *Trinidad* now."

"I see." I did a tight little shuffle in my coat, boots and way-too-skinny jeans. "Y'all got a little Caribbean vibe going on?"

Izzy grinned. "Nah. Not that kind of Trinidad. It's Spanish for Trinity."

I stopped dancing. "As in the father and the mother and the holy ghost?"

The three of them shared a look and a laugh, at whose expense I wasn't quite sure, but I figured I'd get stuck with the tab one way or the other. "The Father, the Son and the Holy Ghost," Billy corrected me.

"Oh, right. Well, that's one for me and one for you," I said, meaning "the mother" for me and "oil and vinegar" for him, but I don't think he made the connection. "Anyway."

I told Iz and Crumb they could load the wood stove in the shop and light it if they wanted to warm up, while Billy followed me down the long aisle of snow between the shop and the house to see if we couldn't coax Jeannie into coming out, now that the Dark Lord had vacated the premises.

I knocked like a guest at my own door. No answer. It was still locked, so I fished the key out only to find that Jeannie had pushed every stick of furniture she could think of up against the door. I could only open it so far. "What the fuck, Jeannie? He's gone! They're all gone. The only one here with me is your brother. And Izzy and Crumb," I added, "but they're in the shop."

I waited.

No response.

I put my shoulder to the door — my left one, because my right one was still so sore — and pushed with all my strength. It might have budged another inch, inch and a half. Not enough to squeeze through. Billy had more success. He managed to shove everything back far enough for me

144

to turn sideways and worm my way inside, where I could pull the table and chairs away from the upended sofa. Billy gave another push, and the sofa tipped over on its back.

"Jeannie?" I said. "You can come out now. Olly, olly, oxen free!" She wasn't in the bedroom. I immediately checked the bathroom and found it empty. The kitchen window was open once again. I leaned over the sink and looked out.

"Jesus H. Christ!" I said when I saw her. "Billy, come give me a hand! Quick!"

Jeannie lay stretched out in the snowdrift with no shirt on, swinging her arms in two wide arcs from her hips to as far as she could reach over her head. She had sliced herself open from her wrists to her armpits, painting a bright red angel's wings in the snow as she sang in a hoarse and hazy, far-off kind of voice the lyrics to Courtney Love's "go on, take everything" song.

# PART 2
# EVERYTHING
# I NEED

# My Kitchen Window

I know women in town who do not consider a house a home unless it has one, but I never give much thought to the window above my kitchen sink. Maureen Ivory says she would've been lost without hers, like a woman blind, unable to see what her kids were up to in her own back yard. Maybe somewhere in the recesses of my mind, I thought about it that way, too, about watching Marshall Caleb grow up. Maybe—all I can do is speculate about the way my mind operates behind my back—maybe *not* putting a window there would've meant I'd given up, accepted the unacceptable, come to terms with the idea that I would never get to watch him play, never get to worry if he strayed from sight again, never replace the gaping vacancy in my heart with the ordinary worry most mothers get to feel all day long.

What's funny about it—why I bring it up—is I designed and built my own house my own way and, out of reflex as much as any well-thought-out plan, I put a window there in the usual spot, above my kitchen sink.

I come to wish I hadn't.

It faced west. But for a strip of land at the horizon, where a huddle of naked trees surrounded the Bittles' house on the far side of the canyon, all I could see that February was sky in the distance and, up close, the white expanse of the back pasture. The canyon itself lay hidden from view except, where now the snow had slumped and separated from the flatter, still-blanketed ground at the surface, the uppermost sections of canyon wall gaped back at me, all wet red clay.

I had to stand on my toes and lean over the sink to see it, but I could not abide the thought of Jeannie's blood soaking into my ground, or worse, contaminating the back wall of my house. I had to get out there and clean it up before the snow all melted. I had to, that's all there was to it. I dropped a five-gallon bucket out the window and tossed a shovel after it.

First thing I did, I dug out my back door so I didn't have to keep shimmying in and out the damn window, then I carefully chipped out all around the shape of her arms, the wings of her snow angel, like two crimson ginkgo leaves minus the stems. I chiseled the soft snow down below the level where her blood had seeped in and carved out its own still frozen, still bright miniature system of canyons.

Once I had a bucket full of pink snow, I asked myself, *Now what?*

I carried it through the house to the shop and into the greenhouse, but that was no good. I hadn't figured out what to do about all the dead flowers in there yet, either. I lugged the bucket back through the shop and out the front door to the parking lot.

I still couldn't get from there to the barn. That part had not been plowed out. I stood in the middle of the parking lot, surrounded by bunkers of snow, turning this way and that, not knowing what to do. I shifted the bucket from one hand to the other, took it out to the road and brought it back again, carrying it in both hands now, my shoulder sockets aching from the weight of it. Anywhere I threw it, it would leave a stain until the snow thawed. Then it would soak into the ground and haunt me.

I needed to put it someplace I could forget, but no such place existed.

# HEARTACHE TO LACK OF CLARITY

After the storm, and the aftermath of the storm, things began to turn around for me. Folks from town who hadn't darkened my door since I opened for business started showing up, *ooh*-ing over the little solar-powered whirligigs I made from aluminum cans and and *ah*-ing over my resin-filled bottle cap earrings like they were miracles of modern design. By the second day, my shelves started looking bare. Come Saturday, I had to close up shop and get my ass in gear making new stuff or all I'd have left to show was a wad of cash and a shit-eating grin.

I cleared off a picnic table I'd converted to a workbench and was about to sit down with my hot glue gun and a box of odds and ends to see what I could come up with, when I heard a knock at the door.

"Sign says 'Closed,'" I yelled over my shoulder, in case whoever it was couldn't read. I tried to sound more helpful than annoyed, but they kept it up until I come wiping my hands on my apron as if I'd actually been doing anything yet and muttering, "What do you need, eyeglasses? Cause I'm all out of those, too,"before I pasted on a smile and lifted the sign out of my way to see who it was.

There stood Eugene.

I opened up and said, "I hope you come just to shoot the shit, because I am practically cleaned out of merchandise."

He gave me a bracing grin, if you'll forgive the pun. "I know. I heard."

"What can I do for you?"

"I really did just come to talk," he said, unzipping his jacket and stamping his feet on my Welcome mat. "You don't answer your phone."

"I don't have one. Cell phone's out of commission, remember? I haven't had a minute to get away and call to let the phone company know my land line's dead, too. Or a way to get anywhere to call."

He reached in a pocket and produced his phone. "Ask and ye shall receive."

I took one look and said, "I'm not up on smart phones.

He showed me how to swipe this and tap that to open up the dial pad and get Verizon on the line. After I talked to them, I asked if I could try one other number. I had the paperwork Jarrod Frye had left with me next to the cash register.

Darrel picked up. "Oh, sure," he said, after I explained who I was and that he had Jiminy. "We been trying to reach you." Jiminy had a new generator and was ready to come home. When did I want to come get her?

"That's just it. I don't have a way to get there."

"Of course you do!" Eugene interrupted.

Darrel said he'd wait for me if I wanted to come straight there, so I gathered up all the cash out of the register, and Eugene drove me into town.

On the way there we talked about my inventory problem and how great it was that everybody was so supportive all of a sudden, though I couldn't expect that to keep me going, and how, come spring, I was in dire straits if I had no way to meet the demand for corsages and like that.

"Is that what you always dreamed of doing, selling flowers?"

"Yes and no. I got started raising flowers because I took an interest in essences."

"Essences?"

"The healing properties of flower...well, essences are like extracts, sort of, to try and treat all kinds of, y'know, conditions."

I was already sorry I'd brought it up, because his next question, naturally, was, "Like what?"

I hesitated. "Oh, everything from heartache to lack of clarity and you name it."

He nodded.

"But try making a living at anything that sounds remotely airy-fairy," I laughed, "out here in the Great State of Oklahomophobia."

He let that pass on the pretense of checking his rear-view mirror.

I think you know me well enough by now to understand that quitting while I'm ahead is not one of my strengths. "Might as well stick a wick in a pile of bullshit," I added, laughing at my own joke, "and call it aromatherapy." He made me nervous, Eugene, he just seemed so put together, mentally speaking, so in command of himself for a seventeen-year-old kid.

"Aside from helping people with broken hearts to achieve clarity," he said, "what do you really want to be doing?"

"It's not that easy."

He stopped at a traffic light, grinned, looked out his window, then back at me. "I didn't ask if it was easy."

"I like making things to sell," I said. "I do. It's just junk, really, most of it. But that's what I like about it. I like to take something other folks say is no-account, stuff anybody else would throw away, and turn it into something useful or unique, something folks decide they want, after all, and will even spend good money on. I get a kick out of that. I don't mean, like, taking advantage of anybody or anything, just—I like for them to see the value in a thing they've overlooked before, and maybe next time they'll think twice before they throw it out. Maybe one or two will start to see other things differently, too, see the value in things. That's the whole idea behind Repurpose Farm. Always has been. I kind of got away from it a little, because, well, you try one thing and another and you end up having to do what sells."

"Like flowers?"

"Like flowers."

"What is it about flowers that people like so much?" he asked as if he just wondered out loud, not expecting an answer.

"They're pretty. They smell good."

"You think that's all there is to it?"

"No. They send a message. If a man gives flowers to a woman, it says, 'You're pretty. You smell good. I like you.'"

He laughed and licked the braces on his front teeth. "Messengers."

"Flowers are wonderful messengers," I told him. I thought to myself, I should get some. I had an apology I needed to send.

As he pulled into the parking lot at Darrel's Eight Ball, he offered to wait. I told him not to bother. He said, "Why don't you come to church tomorrow morning?"

"I can't. I've got too much to catch up on."

"Funny thing about messages, Ms. Cavendish, is they can't just be delivered. They also have to be received."

I got out, but I didn't shut the door right away. I had to think about what he said. Finally, I leaned back in and said, "I guess I owe you that much, don't I?"

"No." His face was clear, as transparent as water, as imperturbable as a plate-glass window. "You owe it to yourself, maybe."

I held up my finger. "One time?"

"Nobody's counting but you."

"All right. Thank you for the ride."

Jarrod Frye came to the counter to talk to me about Jiminy. He hadn't given up on me selling her to him. "Did you know, when that model truck was built, it didn't even come with an oil filter?" To judge by the tone of his voice, you'd think he'd discovered a new breed of dinosaur.

"She's got one," I assured him.

"Not original, though."

"She's not for sale. She's all I got."

When he sighed, the smell of cinnamon cut through the general odor of grease in the shop. "I don't blame you. But look." He turned the bill around and showed it to me. "She needs a lot more work done."

"What's this, my ransom note?" I dug the bills out of my pocket and counted them out. The biggest I had was a few tens and fives."

He laughed. "We need ones, I guess."

"I know she needs to be gone over. She needs body work, too. But she's not the only thing I've got to worry about right now."

He looked frustrated. "Well." He balled up his fist on the counter and commenced to bouncing the fleshy part along the little finger side as if he didn't want to say what he was about to say, but I had forced his hand. "I can't do it here. I can't tie up a bay. But what if I come out to your place and do what I can? I'll go through her from top to bottom, grind down the rust, prime and paint."

"I can't pay you!" I said. Was he deaf? "I can't!"

"I know. I'm not worried about my time."

I just looked at him.

"It'd have to be on Sundays."

"I go to church on Sundays," I announced. I was pretty sure that was a lie, but it sounded good.

"That works out just fine, because I sleep till noon on Sundays."

"You're serious," I realized.

He put his big hand out for me to shake. I took it. "You got a nice grip," I said. "Can I trust you?"

"I have lost my mind," he said.

"Well, if you find yours, maybe there's hope for me." I didn't want to let go of his hand. "Finding mine," I clarified. "My mind. Can I have my hand back now? This Sunday?"

When he said yes, I let him go. I needed to wash my hair. I don't know why I hadn't thought of that sooner.

# SEVEN TIMES SEVENTY

I had too much to do, but one thing I could no longer avoid now that I had Jiminy back. I filled her tank, guided her onto Bruce Street where it becomes Highway 60 and followed her rust-speckled nose to Enid. It was a fine, clear day, clouded only by the thoughts in my head.

I had to let Jeannie go. In every sense I could think of, I had to let her go. I had to say those words, I had to do it in person and I had to do it before she got out of the hospital and back to town. "Not today, though," I said out loud. I knew I had to at least see what kind of shape she was in first. Delaying the inevitable would not make it any easier, I knew. Be that as it may, I repeated to myself, "Not today."

Back in the day, I could have written a letter to Miss Manners:

> How long after an attempted suicide is it appropriate to dismiss an employee with whom one has become sexually intimate? Before or after the stitches are removed? Should the bedside severance package include a nice floral arrangement? Should one's timing take into consideration an age difference of two decades, more or less, or the fact that one's employee a) has no health insurance, b) carries a negative balance with regard to self-esteem, c) invokes the slow, sweet, sticky burn of sorghum on the tongue and in the heart, d) wears the emotional armor and the startle reflexes of an armadillo even, yes, in the bedroom and e) is bat-shit fucking loco en la cabeza?
>
> Signed, Bi Bi Blackbird

She was awake when I arrived, still in leather restraints but with one hand free of the cuff so she could eat a tuna salad sandwich from her tray. A sweet-faced, overweight woman in baby blue scrubs sat next to the bed, a yellow thermos in a Hello Kitty sleeve on the floor beside her. She asked my name and wrote it down in a composition book clipped open on a clipboard, while Jeannie glared at me, not chewing.

"I couldn't get here any sooner," I said. "I just got Jiminy out of the shop."

Her arms were covered in gauze taped over bandages. She rested her free elbow on the mattress. She had a bag of chips, unopened, and something clear over ice on her tray table.

I tried to ask how she was doing, how many stitches, how long they wanted to keep her, but she never answered me a word, never moved a muscle.

"I know you hold me responsible," I started, "but I don't really understand what you expected me to do, turn help away when it was offered?" When she didn't answer, I added softly, so softly, "Let you bleed out completely? Let you die in my back yard?"

She shifted in the restraints so she could reach and put her sandwich on the table, then she took her napkin and scraped the bite of tuna salad off her tongue. "You didn't need to drive all this way to justify your actions." She pushed the tray table as far to one side as her fingers would reach and turned to Hello Kitty. "I'm done. Strap me down, please, before I throw something at this bitch."

"I'll go," I said.

Hello Kitty looked uncertain, so I turned to leave.

"You're already gone," Jeannie said. "Gone."

I kept walking.

Before I stepped through the door, she called after me, "You're not the center of my fucking universe, Vanessa. Get over it!"

I stopped momentarily, trying to figure out how to process that, trying not to come up with a retort, wishing she hadn't stolen our privacy from us, from me, because the situation did not afford me the opportunity to explore what might have happened, how my cell phone might have decided, without my knowledge, to call Eugene Lamb instead of Maureen Ivory. I didn't see how I could go into all that with Hello Kitty sitting there, taking notes.

I decided it didn't matter. I left the hospital and sat in my pickup truck in the parking lot and bawled and sniffed and wiped my eyes and bawled again, and when it felt like I might be done, I drove myself home and folded a load of laundry — my sheets and pillowcases, several pairs of socks, some underwear, a wife-beater and a pair of jeans several sizes too small to be mine. At two o'clock in the afternoon, I went to bed and bawled myself to sleep.

In the evening, I cooked spaghetti and ate it without sauce, just olive oil and a little garlic, and went back to bed and didn't sleep except in dribs and drabs. Sometime around 3 a. m. I got dressed and passed through a seriously diminished snowdrift to the shop. There I built a fire in the stove and left the door open to the greenhouse, where I sat looking at a box of crap I meant to hot-glue together into some crap assemblage of glittered crap to sell, and I knew what I had to do.

I went to the shed and brought the wheelbarrow back, right through the shop and into the greenhouse. I pulled up everything: annuals, perennials, seedlings, herbs, everything. It took me three trips to the end of the parking lot, where I took and whipped everything over the big embankment of snow, left-handed because my right shoulder still ached, not really caring where it landed or what it would look like when the snow melted.

An orange Home Depot bucket stood in the far corner of the parking lot where I didn't remember setting it down, the bucket in which I had collected Jeannie's blood. I went over to it meaning, once again, to find an inconspicuous place and pour it out, but the snow in it had melted down and frozen over. It wouldn't pour.

I went back in and sat down with a pencil and a sketchbook and started drawing angels over and over and over, each one a little different from the last one, each one with a mission unclear to me and, as near as I could tell, to them, too. Some of them reminded me of people I knew or had seen before. Not that anybody would look at one and say they knew who it was, like, "Oh, that's Everett Shaw who works behind the deli counter at the I. G. A." Nothing like that, because I can't draw for shit, one; and two, some of them didn't even have faces, just an attitude you might recognize as belonging to some individual, and even then, only if you're me. None of them was Jeannie. Or they all were. I couldn't tell. Only when I took and laid them all out side by side did I realize what I'd done. I began then and there to envision something big, something unheard of. As soon as I knew what I had to do, I went and looked at the clock in the shop, which said the wrong time because I had yet to reset it after the storm, I'd been so busy. I said, "Shit! I'm gonna be late for church!" and I went and got cleaned up and tried to figure out something to put on.

On the way there I began to have second thoughts. Not just about going to church, though that was part of it. I didn't especially believe in God, nor did I have the time to spend traipsing to town and back when I needed to produce new inventory for my store. Spring was on its way, and I had not one growing thing left in the greenhouse. I might have regretted pulling everything up, but what was done was done. I could always order some corsages and boutonnieres and what-not, come prom season, and sell them at enough of a margin to keep my regulars happy and my business afloat, but in the meantime, I had work to do. Which meant I couldn't mind the shop.

I needed to find someone to fill in for Jeannie.

No, I caught myself. Not fill in. Replace. It just that moment occurred to me that I didn't have to fire her. She'd made it clear she wanted no part of me. That made it easier.

In theory.

What nagged at me was, I couldn't explain to her what had happened, that I hadn't intentionally broken her trust by calling Eugene's number. Why would I? It didn't make any sense. Call him? In an emergency like that? A teenage boy I had only just met for the first time that very afternoon?

Had we exchanged contact information? Yes. Did we have a relationship such that his would be the one number, out of my entire contact list, that I would call for help in the middle of the night to come dig me out of a freaking blizzard? No. Of course not.

The reason I couldn't explain to Jeannie how I'd reached him, of all people, was: I couldn't explain it to myself. Eugene had texted me, not called me. And yet, when I hit "Send" and "Send" again to dial the last number I had spoken to, his was the number that came up.

No way that made any kind of sense.

Yet, in Jeannie's mind, it did. In her world, Eugene must have caused the weather that snowed us in, plus somehow reprogrammed my phone to call him in my hour of need. Someone with the power to soften the ground to cause a ladder to sink and fall on a boy's mother and break her neck just so the right couple could come along and buy the house and adopt him would have no trouble performing a little cell phone magic. Right?

Did I need to worry about explaining myself to a girl who lived in a world where such things were possible? Where imaginary boys took on flesh and blood and came to live next door? Did I need to make myself understood to her, when if I only looked at it for one minute the other way around, from her perspective, I would see just how insignificant and irrelevant would be any rational explanation I might have to offer from my side of the split between what's sensible and what's make-believe?

It occurred to me, probably not for the first time, who had the real power here—not only in my relationship with her, but also in her relationship with Eugene. He might be the popular one, the one everybody wanted to know, the one with the caring, supportive family (even if they were a little odd, those Lambs), the smart one, the one people liked and needed, but what was all that compared to Jeannie's assertion that she had invented him? She had the best of both worlds. She got to be the lazy, no-talent, unfulfilled high school dropout with low expectations and, at the same time, take credit for everything Eugene ever had or did. Everything he would ever become he owed, in her mind, to Jeannie Ivory, rebel debutante in shredded stockings, combat boots and a ratty tutu, all freaked out with no place to go and everyone to blame. "Ha!" I pounded Jiminy on the steering wheel. "The only thing she lacks is anyone to believe her!"

That's what I was supposed to be. That whole business—coming onto me and everything—was nothing but a desperate power play, up to and including the display she put on outside my window. All that bright blood in the snow was a message to me, as sure as if she had literally spelled it out: "This is your fault, Vanessa. This is the direct result of your lack of faith, your disloyalty. You were my witness! You failed me!"

Only my act of disloyalty hadn't been in calling Eugene. Not really. My disloyalty rested in the fact that I was impressed, when he showed up, by the rescue effort he had put together. On my behalf. For my sake. Not only was I impressed, I was grateful. Worse than that, even, I had accepted his help—his and everybody else's. And that, of course, meant that I hadn't believed word one of Jeannie's bullshit.

I still wanted to know what the hell happened with my cell phone. I needed to get it fixed or get a new one, and while I was at it, I intended to ask if there was any kind of logical explanation. If there was one, I needed to know what it was. As I turned into the church parking lot, I jotted a mental note to pay my buddy Clark at the Verizon store a visit.

The lobby of the Assembly of God church was near as big as the sanctuary. Seemed like I saw every one of the boys and men who had come to dig me out the other day milling around in suits and ties, some of them, others in jeans and Sunday sneakers, grinning and talking to one another. I made a point of speaking to as many as I could and saying thank you, before some kind of signal went off that told them to all turn and start shuffling in through the wide double doors to the sanctuary. It was then that Eugene came up to me and called me "Sister Cavendish" when he introduced me to his folks.

Gay Lamb extended her hand to me, fingers dangling like I might want to duck down and kiss her knuckles. It was meant as a handshake, I'm sure, so I took and waggled it.

"We're so glad to have you!" she enthused. She wore a black-on-gray striped pantsuit with a western-style yoke that broke out in a gray-on-white floral pattern in the front and, when she turned to smile at someone else, white-on-gray in the back. Very classy. She turned back to me. "Why don't you come and sit with us?"

I said all right. I had on my best corduroys, so I didn't exactly feel like a slouch, but I was outmatched to be sure. Her entire head—hair, makeup and all—looked like she'd picked it up from the salon that very morning. Todd looked the same in a suit as he did in a parka, like he might as well have one of those bright red buttons stuck in his lapel that advertises "As Seen On TV!" He stepped aside at the second pew from the front to let me and Gay sidle in to take our seats while he shook hands with four or five people behind us and across the aisle. Before I sat down, I happened to catch sight of Eugene taking his place in a glassed-in sound booth at the back of the sanctuary. He grinned in my direction as he slipped a pair of headphones on and swiveled an arm that looked to be attached to a remote video camera on a tripod atop the booth, panning across the audience—I mean, congregation—from one side to the other. Then he raised his hand and counted off on his fingers in the air: three, two, one.

"Are things about getting back to normal for you?" Gay asked me as her husband settled in beside her.

"I don't know about normal," I started to say, but the choir, which had been singing softly as folks continued to spill in from the vestibule, kicked it up a notch on Eugene's count, and the lights went down like in a theater. I turned and looked at the stage, where a giant screen like you might see at a football stadium, broadcast what Eugene was filming. "Oh!" I said. "Y'all got an orchestra and everything!" I saw that Billy Ivory and his two friends were part of it and that Billy had graduated from luggage to an electronic drum kit with those wedge-shaped rubber cymbals and all. He played pretty good. In fact, they all did.

Very bright and upbeat. Not what I would've expected. I adjusted my coat on the pew and sat down.

Pastor Wingate ascended to the pulpit and said a few words of welcome to the congregation, then turned the show over to a slender black woman who reminded me of a radio disc jockey the way she cued up each song and offered a little inspirational commentary in between. She sang lead while everybody else followed along, the words to the songs conveniently printed on the big screen for those of us who didn't know them. The singing part lasted forty-five minutes or so, counting all the commercials for other events the church was putting on. During one of the songs, an entourage of men in dark suits come and stood guard at each end of the four front pews, passing collection bags to and fro, from one pew to the next.

I leaned in and whispered to Gay, I said, "I left my purse out in the truck. Is there some way I can settle up afterwards?"

She flashed me a delicate smile and flapped her wrist at me to let me know that wouldn't be necessary.

Pastor Wingate spoke for quite a long while, telling a story about a woman in Jesus's time who had five husbands, which, that in itself was a revelation to me. "I wish I lived back in those days," I whispered. "I could sure use the extra help around the house," and Gay agreed that wouldn't that be a blessing? Wingate elaborated on the forgiving nature of Jesus with regard to the sinner woman. It wasn't clear to me how she had done the Big Guy wrong, whether if he was one of the five she was stringing along or what, but anyway, they made up in the end. It was the kind of story the regulars seemed to know by heart, the way one or another of them would punctuate it here and there with an "Amen!" like an exclamation point or a "Hallelujah," which seemed more like a dot dot dot to me.

One thing Wingate said that stuck with me. "Forgiveness is only one side of the equation, Brothers and Sisters. It doesn't end there. Someone asked the Lord, 'Lord, how many times must I forgive my enemy for the same offense?' And did the Lord say, 'Once is enough?'"

A few people murmured, "*Nooooo*," and others chuckled as if they knew better.

"Did he say twice?"

No was again the correct answer.

"Did he say to forgive your enemy seven times?"

That wasn't it, either. He kept upping the ante till he got to seven times seventy, and he clarified what he meant by an enemy. "Your brother, your sister, your mother, daughter, father, son, wife or husband, the neighbor who gossips about you, the state trooper that pulled you over for speeding because he didn't like your bumper sticker telling the world that God is your co-pilot; can I get an amen?" (He could and he did.) "The banker, the repo man, the cable company that will not allow you to see responsible broadcasting unless you also allow the Devil's filth into your family room. Oh, I'm only getting started," he said to a ruffle of laughter from the congregation. "The Democrats." He paused, scanning the pews, consulting his notes, before he added, in a softer tone of voice, as if taking care to offend everybody equally, "And more than a few Republicans and Libertarians I could name, too. It all depends on your point of view, now, doesn't it, who you regard as your enemy? Whoever has slighted you or cheated you or reached in your pocket and taken from you more than your rightful share. Whoever has misrepresented your or misunderstood you. Whoever has run his mouth about you. Whoever has humiliated you or owes you money or has turned his back on you in your time of need. Jesus says to forgive that person how many times? Seven times seventy?

"Now before you go looking for the calculator on your smart phone, Sister, Brother, let me tell you; when it comes to forgiveness, there is no such thing as multi-tasking. No. You cannot forgive and keep count at the same time. It doesn't work that way."

Now, I had to admit, that was pretty clever, and it earned him a few more amens. It also got me to wondering if, in a way, he wasn't talking to me. About forgiving Jeannie Ivory.

"Why so many times for the same offense, over and over and over, Lord? Why? Am I not merely encouraging bad behavior if I do that?"

I was tempted to say amen to that, but I kept quiet. Everybody else did, too.

"Forgiveness is only one side of the equation," he repeated, letting his statement hang in the air for a country minute.

"On the other side of the equal sign is where I stand, is where you stand, is where every sinner stands. Jesus forgives you time and time and time again, but all you have to say is one time: 'Yes, Lord. Yes, I accept you. I receive your forgiveness. Hallelujah!" He slammed the flat of his hand on the pulpit.

The choir reassembled quietly and started singing in the background as he drew his sermon to a close, giving the sinners — plural, so I didn't have to take anything personally — an opportunity to step forward and publicly accept the Lord's forgiveness. I had no interest in that, but what troubled me: I couldn't stop thinking about Jeannie and about how, really and truly, you could fill a blackboard with that forgiveness equation, but last time I checked, paranoid schizophrenia did not qualify as a branch of mathematics.

How do you forgive a delusion?

How do you forgive someone for who they are? For what they believe is real?

I saw Eugene again on the way out. He said, "I hope we can still get together and talk about what you do, about your shop and everything."

I said I'd like that. "The only thing is, I don't know if I have much of a business left to talk about."

"Don't be modest, now."

"I'm not. What I need in order to keep going is just inventory right now. And I only have so much time to come up with it."

He grinned a well-applianced grin. "Actually, I think I can help with that."

I laughed. "It's sweet of you to offer. How are you with a hot glue gun and glitter?"

"Probably not my strong suit." He pushed his suit coat back, got his thumbs inside his waistband and hitched his pants. Such an incongruous move for a teenager, an old-man kind of thing, but it matched the suit and tie. "I know people." He winked at me. "Do you have just a minute?"

As Eugene shouldered his way against the throng of the righteous still exiting the sanctuary, Pastor Wingate saw me and raised his finger to excuse himself from another conversation to come talk to me. "Vanessa Cavendish! I'm so happy to see you again!"

He took my hand in both of his and wouldn't hear another word of how grateful I was, but I told him I had an idea for something I wanted to do as a way of showing my appreciation. "I can't say too much about it yet. It's still taking shape in my mind."

"I can't wait to hear more about it. You'll just have to keep on coming to services so you can keep us posted."

"I can't believe how nice y'all are being to me," I told him. I didn't know if I could take a steady diet of it, but it was pleasant, I will say.

"It's because we like you, don't we, Angela?" he said, turning a little. There with Eugene stood one of the two girls who had come to my shop with him and Spider McCormick a little over a week ago, the day of the storm. She was the taller one of the two, with braces like Eugene.

"Angela has a collection of —" he looked at her — "figurines?"

She raised her eyebrows, but not in a way that contradicted him. They were so fine and so blonde they hardly existed.

"Figurines she makes and sells online. But she could use a retail outlet, a brick and mortar like you have. I wonder if you would mind if I bring her along with me one day this week, and she can show you some of what she does?"

"I love your store!" Angela said, beaming.

I had never thought of myself as a retail outlet before, for other people's products, so I didn't know what to make of the idea. I said as much.

"Can't hurt to take a look," Eugene prodded.

I thought about it, but he had caught me off guard. It didn't seem like I could say no. We set up a time after school when the two of them could come out to the shop and show me her figurines. (I pictured some teenage version of Tender Moments.) What worried me about it, she was just a high school kid. I didn't want to discourage her, but what if I didn't like what I saw? Would I be able to say to her face that it wasn't up to my standards? I didn't even know what standards I had. I just made what I made and put it out on the shelves.

I spent the ride home thinking of ways to take the sting out of saying no.

Slush from the traffic of the past four days spattered the dwindling walls of snow that lined my driveway. I normally parked in the barn, but it was still snowed in. As I pulled into the parking lot in front of the shop, I saw that I had a visitor. "Can't people read?" I asked Jiminy, because I was sure I had turned the sign on the front door around from OPEN to CLOSED before I left. Then I saw a pair of cinnamon-colored insulated coveralls leaning against the back of the car. "Shit, Jiminy! I forgot to tell you. You got company."

First thing Jarrod Frye said to me was, "God damn! Where'd you get all this snow?"

I told him I had it trucked in from Ottawa, Canada, he should have seen it three days ago, and he said I must've got a good deal on it. We stood there and shot the shit for a couple of minutes before he brought up the question of where he was supposed to work on Jiminy, since he couldn't get to the barn.

I told him how bad snowed in I was and how Gary Purcell and the kids from the church come and busted their asses for me. "As you can see, he plowed up to the barn, but the doors swing out, so... It's just, after all they'd done for me, I couldn't ask them to dig that out, too. I didn't think I'd need it right away."

He just nodded. "You don't have electricity in the barn, either, do you? I don't see any power lines."

"I run an extension cord from the house when I need to."

"That'll work, I guess. How long before all this melts, I wonder?" He folded his arms and studied the situation. "You really must have pissed off the weatherman. It all fell right here in this one spot?"

"It goes like this for about fifteen miles, from what I'm told, straight across the canyon in a swath about four miles wide."

We agreed there wasn't much he could do today and if the snow wasn't gone by Saturday, enough so I could get Jiminy into the barn, I'd give him a call so he didn't waste another trip. "I hate that you drove all the way out here for nothing," I said. "Can I fix you some lunch?"

"I ate before I came."

"At least come in for a cup of coffee, then."

He looked at his boots, then off at the wall of snow at the end of the parking lot. "All right, then. If you insist."

I insisted.

While the pot brewed in the shop, I showed him out the back door where the boys had cut me a path to the house. The snow to either side of the walkway was still over my head in places. He let out a whistle.

"Picture another two foot on top of that," I said. "That's how much has melted."

Jarrod turned out not to be much of a talker, but he helped me get a fire going in the wood stove. When I told him I managed to get along pretty well on my own under most circumstances, he said, "Just you and your daughter?"

"I don't have a daughter." When I realized who he meant, I didn't want him to get the wrong idea. I said, "That was a girl who works for me." Then I corrected myself. "Worked. Past tense." I kept a couple of chairs by the stove. We sat down.

I could tell he wanted to say something just by the way he looked at his coffee.

"I'm sorry. You take anything? Sugar? Milk?"

He held up his hand.

"I drink it black, too." Finally, I told him. "You know her. She knows you, anyway."

He blew on his coffee and set it down. "To be honest, I didn't get a good look at her face."

I said her name. He nodded. After another minute went by, I said, "I think she's got a crush on you."

"I doubt it."

"I don't."

"She used to, maybe."

If I wanted to pull teeth I'd go to school and become a dentist. I let it drop. But then I got to thinking. Why did he want to work on Jiminy so bad he'd come all the way our here on his day off and not want to charge me a red cent? I'll tell you why, because he thought Jeannie was my daughter, that's why, and that she lived here.

"What about you?" I said.

He looked at me with his cinnamon toast eyes, completely innocent. "What about me?"

"She talked quite a bit about you, that's all."

That got his attention. His eyes said, go on, even if he didn't.

"She told me about you and the Keening Creek Tree House Consortium."

"The what?"

I laughed. "The Keening Creek Tree House Consortium."

He pressed his lips together and wagged his head.

"That don't ring a bell?"

"Sorry."

"She told me about your mom," I said gently.

Nothing.

"About how she died."

His brow creased a little. I thought I had touched something, at least, but he only said, "Huh." It wasn't a question.

"I'm sorry," I said. I let it drop. We talked instead about Jiminy and what needed to be done.

# FACT FROM FICTION

I refilled Jarrod's coffee cup and kept him longer than he probably intended on staying but I had a lot of questions to ask. A lot of sorting, fact from fiction.

"Jeannie's from the old neighborhood," he said, "where I grew up."

"And then you moved?"

"Over to Cortland for a while, then up on Parker Street."

"Who bought your house on Fair Meadow?"

"I couldn't tell you. I was just a kid when we moved. I think the bank might've taken it, to be honest."

When I asked what he could tell me about Eugene Lamb, he drew a blank.

"Let me ask you this, then. Did Jeannie Ivory ever make up a story about a kid wandering around in the storm sewer? A lost boy?"

"Yeah," he said, but not right away. "Yeah, I remember. That was a long time ago."

"Jeannie says she made it up."

Jarrod Frye's eyebrows did most of his talking for him.

"Before it happened," I added.

His eyes drifted across the room like he was chasing a scent or a memory.

"Any truth to that?"

He winced. "She took a lot of crap for some of the things she said."

"What kind of things?"

He took his time answering. I was about to repeat the question, when he said, "One time she told my little brother he was going to fall."

"What was your brother's name again?"

"Deetz. Dieter. That's not the way she put it, though. She said, 'You fell through that hole.' Like it already happened."

"Okay."

"And then it did happen."

"She told me something about him falling through a hole. Was it in a tree house?"

"That's right."

166

"I thought you said there was no tree house?"

"No, we had a tree house."

"I get it. You just didn't call yourselves a consortium."

He scrunched up his eyebrows like, *What the fuck are you talking about, Vanessa Cavendish?* but he didn't say that; he said, "That sounds about like something she would say."

"You didn't like her, did you, when you were kids?"

"Truthfully? Nobody did."

"Why not?"

He took a deep breath and give me a look. "Deetz always felt like she made him step through that hole. Not like—" He waved his big hands around in the air in a half-hearted impersonation of a magician or a voodoo priestess. "Just like—if she hadn't said it, it wouldn't have happened. Like she put the idea in his head, kind of. Can I ask you something?"

Turnabout was fair play. I said, "Sure."

"How did she tell you my mom died?"

I told him about her holding the ladder for—was it his dad? his step-dad? (he said yes, step-dad)—and how the ground was soft and so on.

"Things like that," he said.

"Meaning?"

"She'd say things like that to people. Things that were supposed to happen to them. That's why nobody wanted her around. She got beat up for it more than once at school. She told one girl her dog got run over."

"Did it?"

"Yep."

"Before or after?"

"Long time later. Maybe two months."

"You think it was a coincidence."

"I do now. Sam let her dog run loose all the time on a busy street, and it liked to chase cars, so..."

"So what she said came true?"

"Anybody could've called that one. I guess she just played the odds, but you don't say things like that to people. Not the way she did."

"You said she took a lot of shit from other kids. Anyone in particular."

"Everybody in particular."

"She get beat up?"

He nodded. "She didn't fight back. I mean, there wasn't much to her."

"Did your brother beat her up?"

He said no.

"You didn't, did you?"

He looked at me like, *Seriously?*

"Sorry. I think—" I didn't know how to put it. "I think you were kind of important to her, Jarrod. Did you ever get the sense you were?"

He looked like he just sat down on an ant den and didn't want to admit it.

I'm not sure why I asked him that, except he seemed to have survived her latching onto him the way she had me. Maybe I wondered if there was some trick he knew that I might learn from him. Or maybe I was just being nosey.

"Well?"

He let out a snort. "She asked me to marry her? Does that count?"

"Oh. Really?"

"Every day. When we were in high school."

"Were you going out with her?"

"No. Hell, no. We lived in different neighborhoods but we rode the same bus. She was more of a nuisance than anything, but I always tried to find a seat where she couldn't sit next to me or in front or behind me or across from me. I wasn't always that lucky."

"That's kind of sad," I said. "For her, I mean. It must have been embarrassing for you."

"Just...awkward."

"What? You don't like aggressive women?" I teased him.

At least I got him to smile. "It depends, I guess."

"On what?"

He shrugged and set his cup on the floor. "Why? You want to arm wrestle or something?"

# A Key to Get to the Key

Late in the afternoon on, I think it was Tuesday of that week, Eugene brought Angela Dunhof out to show me what she made. I led them into the greenhouse, and the three of us sat at my picnic table-workbench. Angela unpacked a boxy-looking makeup case and laid out a row of what looked like tiny mummies wrapped in pastel tissue.

I made her wait. I said, "Before you show me, we need to understand a couple of things. I've never done anything like this before, so I don't exactly know how it works. That's one thing. The other thing that scares me is having to say no to you if I'm not a hundred percent sold on the idea, even if I like what you do. I don't want to hurt anyone's feelings, but I'm picky and I have weird tastes."

"Oh, I don't think you do," Angela said with a smile full of glitter.

"I'm just warning you that—"

Eugene reached out and unwrapped the first one, a slender angel made of sticks varnished in their jackets of bark and wrapped in yellow raffia, with clockwork wings. For a halo, Angela had stacked three brass gear wheels one on top of the other so the inside holes lined up, each one a little smaller than the one on top of it. They made not a head but the step-down space where a head would be. No face, yet it wore the most angelic non-expression ever. In the middle of the chest, the raffia parted around a tiny winged key (the wings looked to have come from an actual bee) encased in a honey-colored resin with a keyhole stamped in purple ink on the outside.

"Okay," I said. "I love it. Show me another one."

The second angel's wings were made of antique-looking lace, very finely made. The body had been carved out of the cork from a wine bottle in the shape of a heart with a zigzag crack down the middle, all the way through. Each half had a tiny brass arrow sticking out of it, with insect wings again for the feathers. The arrows held the two halves of the heart together.

"I made it like that," said Angela, "because...well, I don't know if it's possible to be in love with two different people at the same time, but that's what I think it would feel like. Like how could you possibly choose between them and still have a whole heart?"

I looked at her and didn't say anything. I just nodded.

"The first one's more like, here's the key to my heart; I'm not ready to give it up. So that's why it's sealed up and there's no key to get to the key, because I don't want to get stung."

I couldn't stop the spread of my grin. "Go on. Show me more."

She had fingers the size of tweezers. She had to, to work so small. She unwrapped a stained-glass box in which she had mounted the wings of a moth, cut from the body and attached, instead, to a red-and-white candle, the kind you'd see on an ordinary birthday cake. The candle had been lit and allowed to burn down a little. The wax had beaded up along one side.

"Did you melt the wings right into the wax?"

"First I made two little slits in the candle before I sealed the wings in with wax from another candle. They're from my birthday cake. It's just about the beauty of desire and how dangerous it can be at the same time."

"You're how old?"

She smiled in answer, but not at me. Her eyes shone on Eugene as if they shared a joke or some other secret I was too old to get.

She showed me more. Angels made from the filaments of tiny light bulbs, watch springs and filigree stripped from Christmas ornaments; angels decorated with temporary tattoos rendered permanent with fixative; angels shackled and linked together in a chain-gang necklace; angels with miniature scrolls inserted in their mouths like trumpets or megaphones. She showed me painted ladybug pins made from ha-zelnut shells and walnut-shell turtles with legs carved out of skinny dowels and wrapped in colored thread.

I pointed at one of the angels. "How much?"

She gave me a list of her prices.

"I can sell these for three times that."

"That's what Eugene said you'd say." She shared her smile with him again. "Can we say fifty-fifty? Whatever you can sell them for?"

I shook her hand before she could change her mind. I didn't know if I could sell them or not, to be honest, but I wanted to have them in my shop. I would've made room for them even if my shelves were full. "I need fifteen or twenty more as talented as you."

"Sorry. She's one of a kind," Eugene said. "But it shouldn't be hard to find other people who make things you can sell."

"I had a crazy week," I explained to Angela. "Eugene probably told you." I looked around at my empty greenhouse. "I haven't had time to think about what I'm gonna do with this place."

"What I wouldn't give for a space like this to work in! I know exactly what I'd do with it."

"What would you do?"

"I'd hold classes in here."

"Classes?"

"We don't really have art classes in school any more like you probably did. You could teach people how to do what you do."

I never thought of myself as a teacher. "I don't know if I could ever explain to someone else what I do." Anybody can use a hot glue gun or a soldering iron or whatever, but how to think up ideas? How to know what to put with what? I turned it around on her. "Could you teach people to do what you do?"

"I could try. This summer. After that, well—I've sent out applications for art schools. I'm hoping to get into the Kansas City Art Institute."

"Eugene, where did you find her? I didn't think they grew them like her around here?"

The two of them exchanged another mischievous look. "Under a rock," she said.

Eugene said to me, "They grew you around here."

# UBUNTU BLOX

I built my place by grunt force and the gifts my grandma, the good earth and folks who live hereabouts have given me: a falling down house stripped of its copper and other essential ingredients, red gum clay, bales of straw, hard rain, wilting sunshine, and a vast assortment of cast off appliances, car tires and batteries, mattresses, bottles, cans, plastic, styrofoam, you name it. A body wouldn't know to look at it, but a fair percentage of that trash went straight into the construction of my house and got covered up by a thick layer of mud and straw. I learned along the way about a method of compacting plastic into a lightweight building material called "ubuntu blox" if you want to look it up on the Internet. I still have the contraption I used as a compacter out in the barn: a long metal box with a hinged lid and a long screw attached to a plate that crushes whatever you toss inside it down to an eight- by sixteen-inch mass that you then bind with baling wire or, my personal preference, polypropylene ties. A Texas man by the name of Harvey Lacey invented the process and uses it to help women and children in Haiti to rebuild after their country was demolished by an earthquake.

What trash I had left over after I built my house I pushed off to the end of a patch of ground that soon become the parking lot for my shop. I continued to pick through that pile for odds and ends to turn into something I could sell, but it remained an unsorted and unsightly mess. When I saw the wall of snow Gary Purcell had pushed up against it when he cleared the lot, it looked so clean and white, I half-wished it could stay that way, just in that one place, and not melt. Then, when the Pastor gathered us all in a circle and the boys all leaned their shovels up against it, a vision come to me of a more permanent wall. A week or so later, when for no reason I started drawing angels that reminded me of people I knew, it come to me what kind of wall I wanted it to be: a wall of angels, to commemorate what they all had appeared out of thin air and done for me.

So when Angela Dunhof come and brought me her angels, it just seemed to confirm that idea. Even before the snow had melted enough so that I could get back into the barn, I set to work replenishing my supply of cast-off plastic. I went and talked to the guys at the Transfer Station in town. They remembered me. "I got a new project in mind to build," I told them.

Pete, who operated the front end loader, asked me how much I wanted. I let him know it would take me a few trips and could I come once a week until I had enough?

"Make it on Wednesdays?"

"Whenever you tell me to."

I filled up Jiminy's bed with whatever kind of plastic they had: bags, bottles, broken toys. I didn't have to have recyclables only; that's the beauty of it, and that's what they liked about me, too. I took it all home and rinsed it out—milk jugs and yogurt containers and like that can get pretty foul—and spread it out in the sun to dry. Then I turned around and went back for more.

It rained that Thursday pretty near all day and made a slick lake, ankle deep, of the path between the shop and the house, but by Saturday I was able to shovel out the barn door enough so Jarrod could get in to work on Jiminy if he still wanted to. I knotted two extension cords together where they wouldn't come unplugged when I wound up and flung them across what was left of the snow bank in the direction of the barn, so he'd have a way to plug in his power tools. When I got home from church on Sunday, he was in there snooping around.

(No, for your information, I had not taken him up on his offer to "arm wrestle" me, even though, yes, I am that kind of girl.)

He asked me what I was doing "over there" and pointed with his chin in the direction of my fledgling stack of ubuntu blox and my compacter. So I told him.

"Ooboo what?"

When I explained the concept to him, he wanted to make one. I laid out a pair of polypropylene ties in the channels along the bottom of the compacter box, and we tossed in all the plastic we could fit. "Now, close the lid and latch it," I told him.

He did, and I instructed him to turn the big wheel-end of the screw until it wouldn't turn no more. We opened the lid and tied the two ties nice and tight, and I said, "Nine down, six hundred and sixty five to go."

He tossed his block in the air and caught it. "You're gonna build with this? Will it hold up?"

"My shop ain't falling down yet. I ran out of used tires after three courses on the house."

"Used tires?"

"Yep."

"I can get you all the used tires you'll ever need. There's no shortage of them."

"I'm sure you can, but they're a lot of work to fill with dirt and pound solid with a sledge hammer. I switched to straw bale for the rest of the way up on the house. Tires at least got it up off the ground where it'll stay dry. I don't know how it's fared in all this snow, though."

"I've heard of straw bale," he said. "Jim Overstreet built his house out at Ringwood out of straw bale."

"Well, then I heard about this idea."

I told him about Harvey Lacey and the women and kids in Haiti. "Once they're compressed, these blocks are load-bearing, unlike straw bale. Plus it's no big deal if you get a little moisture inside your walls, because plastic won't rot. Only thing breaks it down is UV light, which, that's bad news for a landfill but great news inside a cob wall."

"Can I make another one?"

"Make as many as you like while I get changed. Then you have to show me how to grind the rust off a bumper."

Later on, when I went back to compacting plastic, he shut his grinder off and said, "I could make you another one of those compactor boxes. Go twice as fast if we both had one.

I pushed the hair out of my eyes with my wrist. "You want to help me build my wall?"

"Why not?"

I went back to spinning the wheel, thinking I might have to add another angel to my design.

When I showed my drawings to Angela, she wanted to help, too. So did Eugene. It was her idea to make plaster casts of the faces of all my angels from the faces of all the guys who'd helped shovel snow.

"You know how to do that?"

"It's easy! We'll throw a casting party!"

First we had to get the wall built. Once all the snow was gone, I rented a Ditch Witch and dug down about three feet by two feet wide where the wall would go and a series of skinny trenches running perpendicular where I laid pipe to drain any runoff from the parking lot into the ravine behind the wall. Then we poured a footing. The entire thing, when all was said and done, would stretch some thirty-two feet long by twelve high with buttresses at both ends and two in the middle. At first, a few people heard what we were up to and stopped by to see. Then more and more took an interest until, little by little, my wall of angels had turned into a community project. Eugene's dad wanted me to come talk about it to the youth group at the church, where I got a whole bunch more volunteers to come help mix cob and throw mud at the wall. That was the first party we threw.

Trinidad set up under one tent, and some of the ladies from the church set up under another one to serve lemonade and iced tea and soda and chips and dips and what-not and — you guessed it — Gay Lamb brought Mississippi mud.

I had tarps laid out and three batches of dirt and straw ready to go. I raised my voice and said, "I hope y'all come prepared to get dirty!"

A cheer went up among the teenagers and little kids.

"Get your shoes and socks off, then, and roll up your pant legs. I need four to five per tarp. Gather round me here." I was already barefoot so I could demonstrate. "First you make a cone of dirt in the middle of your tarp like this, then you step right in the middle of it to make a crater like a volcano. Zack," I said to one of the older boys, "would you pour some of that water from that five-gallon bucket right in the crater here?" As he did, I begun to fold the dirt in with my feet. "I'll tell you when to stop. Now, if someone would toss in a few handfuls of straw." I kept stomping and mixing with my feet, the red mud squishing betwixt my toes. "I'm sure someone, somewhere has come up with a precise formula for how much straw to add per how much clay and water, but it ain't rocket science. You just want enough mud to cover the straw and enough straw to hold the mud together, so later on when we throw it against the wall, it goes splat! about like a fresh cow patty will do."

That drew a few eeeew!s from the younger ones, so I knew they were listening.

I stepped out and demonstrated cleaning my feet off in one bucket, then rinsing them in another. "Y'all think you can handle it?"

They jumped right in, while I got another three crews set up to rub big clumps of clay through some wire screens I'd built to make smaller clumps fine enough for making a nice, smooth mud and to get rid of any rocks and twigs. "Soon as one batch gets mixed and ready to apply, you guys'll get a chance to get your feet dirty," I promised. Those that weren't doing anything yet watched and asked questions and waited their turn, and soon we had a steady rotation going—three teams screening clay, three teams dancing in the mud and three teams plastering the wall.

Once the front was mudded yea so high, we moved around and started in on the back side and on the four buttresses with the younger ones, while a group of men set up scaffolding in the front. We then lifted batches of mud up to the older teenagers in big tubs, and they kept going until we all had big, mud-spattered grins, tired backs and one big, beautiful wall of mud. The day ended as it had begun, with all of us standing in a gigantic ring of prayer and thanksgiving, and as corny as it felt and probably sounded, I cleared my throat and addressed a god I had no idea if I believed in or I didn't. I said, "Lord, if you're looking down on this day and if you can see into my heart, then you know how much I appreciate your people, how glad I am to know them, and how bad I wished I'd known them back when I was building my house, because would you just get a load of how fast and how smooth everything went today? Oh, and by the way, I hope you will help Genevra to forgive Kyle for his bad aim, if that's what it was. Amen!"

"Amen!" they all said, and I have never hugged so many tired and dirty people in one day in my entire life, nor cried so many cleansing, joyful tears. I waved goodbye until my shoulder like to fell out of its socket. Then I weighted down the tarps with shovels and buckets and tubs turned upside-down and left everything just as it was, went and scrubbed myself clean in the shower, the red mud trickling down the drain until I felt clean again and lotioned and loved and about as beat as a dead horse. I took myself to bed and dreamed of Jeannie Ivory and how disappointed she was in me that I had not invited her to be a member of the Tangled Angels Consortium. "Since the fucking thing was my idea!" she told me. I think she actually said "flocking," not "fucking," and I grew very much confused in my mind as to whether she lived in my asylum or I lived in hers. I fell down a steep embankment, only not of dirt but tiled like a subway station, and watched blood trickle from my vagina and run like live snakes down the drain directly into Keening Canyon.

# Cinnamon Buns

What with Angela making a new angel practically every other day and Eugene scouting out local talent willing to sell on consignment and scouring the web for artists and crafters who would wholesale to me, little by little, I had my shelves full again. He built me a website, too, and kept it going, posting photographs and videos, writing my "Mission Statement" and a page about the history of Repurpose Farm and yadda-yadda. He got me subscribers and built me a bona fide email list where we announced each new line of products as well as Angela's classes and documented the progress of my Wall of Gratitude.

We shot instructional videos on all sorts of things for folks who couldn't make the classes, not just on Angela's subjects but also on building with unconventional materials, starring Yours Truly. How that got started was, unbeknownst to me, Eugene had shot footage of the mudding party and of me demonstrating how to mix cob and screen clay and of everybody slinging mud at the wall. He time-lapsed most of it to make it so a full day's work got accomplished in three minutes and thirty-seven seconds flat, including certain parts where he slowed the frame-rate way down to emphasize the camaraderie of folks laughing together and dancing arm-in-arm in the mud, not to mention the righteous form of Zack Angleton's sidearm, the perfect splatter of cob across the surface of the wall, a still shot someone else had taken of Eugene himself washing Billy Ivory's feet and, as the credits rolled by, including the names of everyone who had participated, a circle of bowed heads bathed in the afterglow of sunset to the tune of Trinidad's wordless version of Amazing Grace.

"You should've let me borrow your camera while you and Angela did your mud dance," I teased him, remembering the two of them in their rolled-up jeans with their hands braced on one another's shoulders, touching foreheads as their toes kneaded the mud in time with a song I hadn't heard in decades. I knew it as *Everyday with You, Girl* by the Classics IV, but Billy Ivory corrected me.

"The original title was *Every Day with Jesus Is Sweeter than the Day Before*," he said.

I said, "Oh."

Jiminy made her debut on my blog when Eugene discovered I had taken befores and afters of her as Jarrod ground down her rust and primed and painted her back to her original Windsor Blue. I didn't let him see the durings, because of one in particular with Cinnamon Buns up on his tiptoes and the top half of him, shirtless, burrowed deep in her motor cavity. I didn't want Jarrod showing up on the blog at all. I had my reasons; don't ask me to list them. I had a hard enough time justifying it to myself.

The gist of it was: Suppose a certain someone happened across my website and saw him there; i.e., what would Jeannie think?

I had nothing to hide. I'd done not one thing I ought to be ashamed of. I hired a man to do some work for me was all. Or not hired; he volunteered to begin with. As things turned out, I had begun to do a pretty steady business that spring and could afford to pay him for his time. In spite of what I knew to the contrary, I still managed to secretly convince myself that his real reason for getting involved with Jiminy — at least in the very beginning — was he'd wanted to get close to Jeannie, thinking she lived with me or at least still worked for me. I figured he was disappointed to learn otherwise, regardless of what he said. He was just too much a man of his word to renege. He did not want to take my money, but I made him.

"I don't want to be in your debt, Jarrod. If you don't take this, I won't be able to look you in the eye." I had a hard enough time, as it was, because he so rarely wore a shirt in the hot weather.

"I wouldn't like that," he said.

I took his hand and stuffed it with a roll of bills. "Neither would I."

Then he asked me out on a date. "You can pick me up in your pickup truck," he said. "We'll drive real slow up and down Bruce Street, showing off your hot new wheels. You can take me to Wild Horses for dinner, and I'll pay because I just now came into some money."

"Oh, you're a big spender!"

"Seven o'clock?"

I said, "No. I have to make a run into Enid."

"Even better. I'll take you to a real restaurant. We can see a movie."

"I can't," I said, and then I confirmed it. "I can't."

"Can you another time? Or you can't, period?"

"I don't know," I said, frustrated. I didn't like feeling cornered. "Jarrod Frye, I am twice your age. You do realize?"

"No, you're not. You're in your forties?"

"Not yet. That's not the point."

"Jiminy's old enough to be my great grandmother."

I just looked at him. "What the hell kind of argument is that?"

"She's in good shape," he said, "for now. But she needs someone to look after her."

I rested my hand on his shoulder and patted him a time or two. "Do you think I need looking after, too?"

"That's not what I —"

I reassured him I did not.

I didn't have a real reason to go to Enid. That was just the first excuse that popped into my head. Now I felt like I had to go and I needed to come up with a reason when, in fact, I knew exactly where and why I needed to go.

I stopped at the front desk of the hospital to ask for the room number, figuring Jeannie had surely moved upstairs to the psych unit. They don't keep you that long just for stitches.

*What? Mental stitches?*

Woman at the desk in the lobby took off her glasses to search the computer files, then put them back on to tell me what she'd found. "Ms. Ivory has been discharged."

"Discharged home?" I thought I would've heard something if that were the case.

"Oh, they don't tell us that."

I didn't have a working cell phone, but my landline was back in service. I drove all the way back to the shop and called Maureen.

"Did Jeannie come home?"

"No. Who's calling, please?"

I apologized and told her who wanted to know.

"I don't think she'll be coming back to work anytime soon, Vanessa."

"No, I don't —" I almost said I didn't want her to. "I don't expect her to. Did she come home? They told me she's not at the hospital."

"They moved her." After a couple of seconds, she said, "Out to Fort Supply."

"Oh." Fort Supply used to be an actual fort. If I'm not mistaken, General George Armstrong Custer was stationed there once upon a time. Now it's just a town where a prison and a state psychiatric facility are located, out near the Panhandle, back in the opposite direction from the way I'd come. "That's another three hours."

"Two and a half," Maureen said, "yes."

"I wish I'd known that before I went to Enid."

"Oh, you went there to see her? You should have called me sooner, I would've told you."

"I guess I should have."

"You've been awfully sweet to her." I might have imagined it — most likely I did — but I thought I detected a note of accusation in her tone. It didn't matter. I couldn't dwell on that.

"It must be so hard on you!" I said.

It sounded like she caught her breath. "I always paid more attention to Billy when they were kids. I know I did. I worried more about him. He was the one always testing me, always pushing the limits. Jeannie was so good! I don't know what happened to her! Billy's involved in the church now. He's got his music and his friends, and that Lori Leigh is just a doll. A doll! I credit her a lot. I do. He's done a complete one-eighty. Well, you must know what I mean. You've been going, too, I hear."

"There must be some comfort for you in that, at least. In Billy." I hoped that didn't come out sounding sarcastic or condescending or whatever. I didn't know how to talk to a mother about her children. Not really. It brought up so many conflicting emotions in me. I could be jealous and relieved all in the same instant. Jealous of her specific worries, her specific fears and triumphs and disappointments, where all I had was ignorance and wondering, vague apprehensions and imaginings. One of my greatest fears, I shit you not, was that I would one day cross paths with my own son and not recognize him, not know, ever, how close I'd come and that I'd let him slip through my fingers. The worst of it was thinking it might have already happened. Or that it might yet. Or that maybe he was somebody I saw all the time and didn't know. Nobody needed to tell me how astronomical those odds might be, because the real odds favored me never seeing him at all, ever, for reasons I didn't have to think about if, instead, I held onto the fantasy of him passing in and out of my life, all unbeknownst to me, as my greatest fear.

Did I want what Maureen was going through? The tribulations she had faced over the past two and a half weeks? Never mind the past two decades! Could I not be grateful, in even a small sense, for that?

No. I did not permit myself that gratitude, because I envied her even her heartaches. I would gladly have borne the most wretched state of grief and self-recrimination, just to know my child existed.

And then what? I wondered. What would I do with that knowledge?

I climbed in my pickup truck and started driving, racing the sun to see which one of us could get across the horizon first.

# FOLLOW-UP QUESTIONS

I don't pay a lot of attention to politics. Not my thing. But a young man paid me a visit back in the winter of 2008, sporting a dark over-coat, kid leather gloves and a haircut not more than two days old. He left a Lexus the color of deep water parked in the mud and gravel out in front of my shop. He wanted to know if I had heard of Patterson Price.

"Heard of him?" I said. "I've heard of him."

He seemed keenly interested in my responses to his follow-up ques-tions, of which he had a few.

"What have you heard?"

"What specifically? Oh, I couldn't tell you. If he comes up on the radio, you know, or TV. He has an unusual name. Kinda stands out." I left it at that.

He smiled. Nothing about him seemed to contradict me. "That's an interesting way of putting it. Overall, would you say you have a favor-able impression of him or an unfavorable one?"

"Oh, you're asking the wrong person."

"What makes you say that?"

"I don't like talking about people behind their backs, do you? Good or bad."

I noticed him noticing things I had for sale by the register, little mag-nets and hair clips and note cards and things. I felt like he found every little detail, from the streaks in my glass counter top to the business li-cense on the wall behind me and the state of my hair, every bit as inter-esting as my answers to his questions, as if everything his gaze touched was part of a massive calculation he did in his head. He had the kind of eyes that seem to absorb everything at once and yet stay focused on one item at a time. "As a public figure, would you say that other people think well of Senator Price?"

"People around here?"

"Yes. Yes, the people you know."

"Most of them probably never heard of him, would be my guess."

"Oh? Funny you should say that."

"Why?"

"Do you know the Bittles over on Ringwood Road? Cecil and, ah—"

"Delores."

He raised the kid-gloved index finger of his right hand. "Delores. That's it."

"She taught me seventh grade English."

"Seventh grade," he said, as if that meant something to him. "You must have known her kids, too? Did you know that Mark Bittle went to school with Patterson Price up at O. U.? They were fraternity brothers, if I'm not mistaken."

"I think I might have heard something to that effect. That they knew each other, anyway."

"Mark was a friend of yours?"

"Not really. He was always nice to me, but I was closer in age to his little sister."

"Does Leigh Ann ever mention Mark to you?"

"To me? No. We haven't stayed in touch, really."

"They seem like good folks, the Bittles." He leaned on my counter, smiling in a way that seemed friendly. Or was meant to. "I guess they haven't seen Mark for a number of years, is that right?"

"What are you driving at? You know, when you first walked in, I took you for one of those Bible salesmen or whatever they are. I figured you wanted to talk about the end times." (This was years before I ever started going to church or knew much about it.)

He had an easy-going laugh. "Is that what you thought?"

"Then you start in about Patterson Price like you're taking a survey that's either for him or against him, and next thing I know you want to gossip about my neighbors? Who are you?"

"I'm sorry." He reached out. "My name is Andrew Blake. I have been, like you say, canvassing the area." His glove felt smooth in my hand.

"What is it, then? What's your interest in the Bittles?"

He seemed to go to a different place, like his internal gps detected a wrong turn and had to recalculate his route. When he come back, he said, "There are some people who believe that Senator Price may have ...ambitions beyond his current level of employment."

"Okay."

"Others think we should be more concerned about his past."

I said nothing.

"About certain events that transpired during the summer of 1990."

I smiled. I'd been down this road with people before, back in Massachusetts when I lived there. I had no intention of giving a perfect stranger anything he didn't need to know. "What exactly do you think transpired?"

"That seems to be the question."

"Well, Mr. Blake, I don't have the answer. If you want to know something about Patterson Price, maybe you should go ask him."

"Oh, I have," he said. "I have. I can't help thinking your story might prove more interesting than the one he tells."

"I doubt it."

"Let me put it another way. A lot of people would find your story very interesting, especially if Senator Price were ever to gain national attention."

"What's he thinking about, running for President?"

"I couldn't say what he's thinking or not thinking at this point, just that other people are taking notice of him and asking questions. We would just like to be out ahead on any of the more difficult ones, if and when they come up."

"You want to know what I'll say if somebody else like you comes sniffing around?"

"I just want to know the truth."

"The truth, huh? I guess you'll just have to take a number."

"I'm sorry. I didn't come here to upset you."

"You haven't." I was ready for him to go.

"I won't ask you any more questions, then, all right? Just let me tell you what I know, and you can tell me if I'm right or wrong."

I laughed. "True-or-false question is still a question."

"True," he admitted.

"False."

He looked confused.

"That's my answer to every single one of your questions: False. I've had enough of it. I've been through it all a hundred times, and I'm sick of it. So you just tell whoever sent you — "

He cut me off. "You gave birth to a baby boy in 1991. Marshall Caleb Anatoly."

My throat seized up on me. When I tried to swallow, my tongue made a loud click against the roof of my mouth.

"On the same day, May 7, 1991, Mark Bittle disappeared. He has never turned up." Mr. Blake stood up straight and folded his gloved fingers together, resting them on my counter top. He studied me more intently than ever, but when he spoke again, he changed his tone, made his voice go soft and supple. "Two days later, your baby went missing, also never to be found."

Last time I saw Mark Bittle was the night I met Patterson, the night I took off across country with him because, evidently, we both thought I killed my brother-in-law. That was the last I saw of a lot of people — practically everyone I knew — until I came back to Keening in 1998. I didn't know what to make of this new information. "You telling me there's some connection?" I asked.

"What do you think?"

"I never had any reason to think anything at all until you just this minute brought it up. If you know something I don't, I wish you'd stop playing games and tell me."

"I'm happy to tell you what I know. Maybe you can help me connect the dots."

So we talked. I found out that shortly after he started his senior year of college, Mark Bittle dropped out and went to work for Patterson's father, Edmund Price. The Price family had made it big in the oil business going back three generations. At one time they owned their own refinery. In the eighties, they sold everything. Old Man Price ran for a seat in the State Senate and won. He hired Mark Bittle as a driver, technically, but Mark also took on other duties, delivering messages, sorting mail and so on, more along the lines of an aide or an intern than a chauffeur. That was in late October of 1990. He worked for the Senator up until May of '91 when, according to Mr. Blake, he and my baby went missing within days of one another.

"Nobody around here even knew I was pregnant," I said. "Not my sister, not Mark Bittle, not even Patterson himself. Nobody."

"Patterson didn't know?"

"Nope."

"You registered at the hospital under an alias."

I nodded. I didn't see how it made any difference.

"How did you come by the name Anastasia Anatoly?"

"Just a name I used. I was afraid I'd be blamed for Leon's death. My brother-in-law. That's why we — that's why I ran away in the first place."

"With Patterson."

I couldn't tell if he already knew or if he only suspected and was fishing for confirmation. Either way, I waited a little too long before I asked, "What makes you say that?"

He dismissed the question. "If you tell me what happened between the two of you, there's a chance it will lead us to what happened to your baby." He held up his kid-leather glove to stop me from saying anything. "I can't promise you the news will be good. You understand that."

"Yes." One part of my mind said, yes, I understood. The other part will never be satisfied with just the truth and not my baby. I didn't let that part answer. "It'd be better to know," I said, "whatever it is."

"I would think so."

"Can I ask you something first?"

He didn't say no.

"I'd like to know who you work for?"

He fished a little silver case out of his suit coat and handed me a business card. "Andrew Blake, Attorney at Law," it said. It had a telephone number and the name of a firm out of Oklahoma City.

"But who hired you?"

"That I'm not at liberty to say."

"Why do you care about helping me find my baby?"

"That's a very good question, and again, I can't promise anything. But the answer to your question is that my client cares what happened."

"Why?"

"What my client actually cares about is whether Patterson Price is a fit public servant. That's something that, potentially, a lot of people may end up caring about."

"Define 'fit public servant' for me."

"In a democracy?" He tucked one corner of his mouth into his cheek, giving himself a dimple on that side. "I guess you could say it's up to the people to decide who's fit and who isn't."

"That's not an answer."

"Maybe not, but it's the best I can provide. The best any of us have, isn't it?"

"So," I said, still putting two and two together, "what your client really cares about is whether Patterson Price can get elected. Whether I've got anything to say that might get in the way of that." I held his business card up between my two fingers, like a cigarette. "Which means this is bullshit, what it says here, and so are you. You want to know where I got my alias? Probably the same place you got yours. You either work for Patterson Price—or the Republicans, at least—and want to nip something in the bud, or you work for the Democrats and want to make sure it all comes out."

"No, on both counts."

"I'm sorry. I'm just not interested." That was a hard thing to say, believe you me, but I didn't want to get sucked into whatever game he was playing only to find out he didn't know any more than I did. "I don't have anything else to tell you." My instincts said, if he really knew anything, now would be the time to tell me. I handed him back his card.

He didn't take it. "Fair enough. Thank you for your time." At the door, he turned and looked at me. "If you think of anything you do want to talk about, you know how to reach me."

"Hold on," I said. I took and dialed the number on his card. A few seconds after the second ring, the horn started blaring on his Lexus. I hung up. "That's what I thought." There was no office in Oklahoma City, and he was no practicing attorney. More like a journalist or a private investigator.

Ten years I'd been back home, after eight years in Massachusetts. I was thirty-two years old and I kept to myself. People like to talk. I've known that since I was young, and it has always been my practice to give them as little to go on as possible. Where had I been? New England. What did I do there? Worked on a farm. What kind of farm? Small. What brings you back to Keening? The farm. Did you kill your sister's husband? Not that I know of.

You might think I'm joking, but I'm not. One thing people like to say about small-town living is everybody knows everybody's business. Not true, unless you let them wear you down. Plus I lived on the outskirts of the outskirts of a small city. Let me say this again: In those days, nobody around here ever knew I had a baby. Not one person. Before Jeannie Ivory come along and pushed my buttons, I was determined to live out my days as a devout mystery.

That hasn't exactly worked out, so let me back up now and tell you the story of my life.

# PART 3
# MY NAME IS MUD

# Inheritance

Walter Martin did right by my grandma. When she no longer could attend to the details of her appearance, he made certain her blouse was buttoned straight and her ruffled collar laid flat, that her lipstick matched her nails and didn't bleed into the fringe of smoker's wrinkles that radiated from her lips. He did wonders with her hair and makeup. Everybody said so. Walter had such fastidious fingers.

He called no attention to himself when friends and visitors entered the parlor but saw to their needs quietly and without fuss, then busied himself in another room. I won't say he loved her, but he cared for her as well as any man could a woman in her condition. She looked contented (everybody said so), her face as relaxed as I 'd ever seen it. Her gnarled fingers no longer fidgeted. He'd seen to it, too, that the stitches at her wrists stayed tucked inside her cuffs.

I stood a long time by her casket, appreciating Walter's handiwork. Grandma looked as if she'd washed up there in the little chapel, pre-composed on a raft of bronze and satin, flanked by sprays of lavender and lilies, as if her head and shoulders had come to rest on that pillowy beach by none but natural means.

Whatever you might have heard to the contrary, I did not take her life, nor were the two of us witches but ordinary law-abiding citizens.

I can't help what I inherited. Red hair runs in my family. Mine is the color of bricks, whereas Sheila got my daddy's coal-black eyes and the intensity of his mind. That is my impression, anyway. I never met him.

Sheila said that was nobody's fault but mine. Not even my mother's.

"Your momma couldn't help herself," she told me with the gentle reassurance of an older half-sister. "She was a retard."

That was the real reason Grandma took a bread knife to her wrists. Because my momma was a retard at Enid State School, and my daddy took advantage.

# SUSPICIOUS CIRCUMSTANCES

Of an evening, oftentimes, I laid a small hand soft and freckled in an old hand hard as knot wood and accompanied my grandma down along a path our feet had driven through the back pasture. There a belt of winter wheat had sprung up volunteer, and the smell of muscadine cloyed the air from vines my daddy'd planted ages on ages ago, before I was born. Unattended like me, they grew wayward from their trellises, trailing to the ground to grapple with the roots of weeds and bushes, fence posts and antique tractor parts. Grandma insisted he would come back one day from California (Alaska, she said one time but later denied it) to make something of the place. And to make something of me in the bargain.

My sister Sheila lived in Enid with her momma, whose name was Starla Cavendish before she went back to using her maiden name, Gray. That became my sister's name, too, until she married Leon Keefe. Her momma made her come and visit us once in a blue moon, because, though we lived like paupers, Grandma secretly was well off. Land rich, anyways.

Most of what acreage we had she leased out to Andy Goslin and his herd of beef cattle, a section and three quarters across the road plus, over here on our side, the little strip of pasture that run behind the house. The rest of Grandpa's property, as she always referenced it, was canyon land too steep to farm and not worth terracing. Nothing but a few stunted cedars grew there, twisting in the wind like yellow-green candle flames about to stutter out.

She walked out the back door at the end of almost every day, made her way down to the edge of the canyon and just stood there. I always knew what was on her mind to do that she hadn't done yet. Don't ask me how. I just knew. I didn't question her about it. I didn't have to.

"This old canyon gonna take me one these days," she muttered time and again under her breath as if she meant me not to hear, though she knew I did. More of a prayer than a warning, I think.

Keening Canyon is not a big deal. Just an extension of the back pasture is all it really is. Textbook example of soil erosion gone demented.

When I was little, it seemed like all there was of the world outside of me and my grandma's house was, in one direction, wheat sawing in the wind of a pale morning across the road, with the Keening Co-Op elevators on the far horizon like the full-bellied sails of a fairy ship or the conjoined towers of an alabaster castle, while in the west, lying in wait just beyond the back pasture: the gaping mouth of a dragon fixing to swallow the world whole — earth, sky, everything — and belch it back at me all aflame to consume me.

We're talking the northwest portion of Oklahoma, before the panhandle. The earth here is red. Almost as red as a red velvet cake. Around the lip of the canyon run a rim of selenite like that at the Glass Mountains to the northeast. Which, I always thought the Glass Mountains were named for the broken beer bottles scattered all over everywhere like glitter on a seashell. Careful where you step. But for a skim coat of dead grass on top, that rim of gypsum might be the frosting on a cake. Down the middle (like someone served himself up a nice big slice of dessert and ate it) is what's known as Keening Canyon, all crumbly and dried up most of the year. Except after it rains cats and dogs, the creek bottom will fill up just as if that same someone used a little too much red food coloring and it all run out the bottom.

Am I painting too sweet a picture for you? I don't mean to. It is the quintessential red state, though, Oklahoma is.

I remember the very first time I encountered anyone from Massachusetts. Patterson waited in the car while I went in a little corner store for something to snack on. (I didn't have to worry so much about being spotted way up there, so far from the scene of the crime.) Girl behind the register says to me — she was a college student from the look of her, she says — "Are you all set?"

I was not but fourteen, going on fifteen. I wondered to myself, Now, what in the ever-loving world does she mean, am I all set? I had no idea what she was getting at. I finally opened my mouth and said, "What, like concrete?""

She looked at me like I had three heads and of course was real ignorant about it. It took me I don't know how many years after that to figure out she must've thought I was getting smart with her, when it sure seemed the other way around to me.

That's how different people can be over something as simple as "Are you all set?" versus "Have a nice day!" or "Will that be all for you?"

Never mind the Right to Life versus Free Choice or whatever that is. I don't mean to imply that she was an abortion rights activist or anything like that. I didn't know her from Adam. All I'm saying is you got to do more than travel around the country to see both sides of it, no matter if you start out in a red state or a blue one.

Where was I?

Oh. The Bittles. They lived on the other side of the canyon from us. They still do. Old Lady Bittle and her husband do, anyway. No one has seen hide nor hair of Mark for twenty-some odd years, and Leigh Ann has long since up and married and moved to town and got divorced and remarried and what all. She was about my age. Mark was the only one that was ever sweet to me. Their dad had a welding truck. He worked the oil field and odd jobs on the side, spot-welding horse trailers and like that. A welder made decent money, plus Old Lady Bittle taught seventh-grade English. So they never hurt for anything.

I had nothing against her in the beginning, but Old Lady Bittle didn't care much for me. Reason being, I was just as likely to get the correct answer as to blurt out whatever come into my head, and neither God nor the Devil could predict what that might be. I guess it rubbed her the wrong way. She once accused me of having Tourette's Syndrome.

"Tourettes don't make a wrong," I said. I thought that was real clever. Nobody else did.

I got detention for it. I was all the time getting into some kind of trouble or other. There was nothing I could do about it, because you couldn't predict what was going to set her off. Except if someone wrote an essay on befriending a crow and keeping it as a pet and teaching it to quote John 3:16 backwards like Tommy Isabel said you could. She was bound and determined to go into a tirade then.

She hated crows so bad!

They were an unclean animal according to her and the Bittle Bible. They hopped around like the Devil in carnations and they had no problem whatsoever with eating carrion. Which at the time I thought was spelled carry on. Like luggage. I didn't care what she said, I hadn't ever seen one eat a suitcase in my entire life.

"Can anyone tell Miss Cavendish what carrion is? Carrion is road kill."

"Human beings don't have no problem eating road kill, neither," I pointed out.

She give me another detention for that one.

"Is that your answer to everything?" I slammed my *Explorations in English Grammar* shut there and then for all eternity.

Honestly? I didn't know what was wrong with me except I had the Devil in me is all. Better him than Jesus, I figured. Jesus wouldn't know what to do with the likes of me.

"You will burn in Hell!" Leigh Ann told me when I said that. We were the same age, but she was light years ahead of me in school, having a teacher for a mother instead of a retarded woman. They were church-going Baptists, those Bittles, whereas my grandma brought me up atheistically. I didn't know any better. I just figured Baptists went to Heaven and Atheists went the Other Direction. Which worked out to my advantage.

"I ain't much good with a harp," I told her, "so pass me a pitchfork if you think that's more my speed."

Leigh Ann was a cheerleader and she thought I was a hot shit. That's as close to popular as I ever got.

Long story short, my grandma died wandering around the canyon in a hailstorm.

Under suspicious circumstances.

# How In Love I Was

Friday, August 12, 1983. Grandma invited Sheila and Leon to come for supper. Leon's workmen's comp had run out, and Sheila had yet to get back to work after the baby. Grandma and me had not laid eyes on Lisa Julene but once, through the window at the Bass Hospital nursery, when we got a ride to Enid in the back of the Goslins' Buick. Grandma refused to drive.

Last we'd seen of my sister and Leon before that was in June, when they come to borrow money. We all knew that was the reason behind the visit, but we had to pretend otherwise. Sheila come waddling up the front steps pressing on her back with one hand and pulling herself up by the railing with the other. Stork legs and a beach ball belly. Grandma and me met her on the porch.

"You want to sit down out here, Sheilie?" Never in all my life had I heard Grandma call her that before: Sheilie, like she was a little girl. "It's cooler out here than in the house," she said, sweet as a licorice stick.

Something was up.

"In a minute I do, Grandma. I been sitting. It feels good to stretch." They hugged and kissed in the vicinity of one another's cheeks.

"Vanessa, go get us some iced tea out of the ice box."

I went and got some and cut up a lemon in wedges and stuck them on the edges of two glasses like I'd seen it done somewhere before. I brought them out on the porch.

"You put sugar in mine?" Sheila had already got over being tired of sitting and had taken up residence in my porch rocker, next to Grandma in hers.

I knew I was going to get it wrong one way or the other. If I said yes, she wouldn't want any; if I said no, she would. So I made it easy on myself and said, "I don't think there is any."

To which Grandma replied, "Yes there is, too! You go get her some!"

So I did. I put a tablespoon of sugar in my mouth and spit it in Sheila's glass and brought it back out. By that time, Leon had shut the engine off in the driveway. He had to listen to a song finish on the radio first — that's just how he was — and now made his way across the yard to be sociable. Leon walked with a cane but he was about the handsomest man there ever was. I called him Elvis Presley and he called me Frecklehead and that's how we got along.

I was the only one to say, "Hey, Leon! You want some iced tea I made?"

"Get over here, Frecklehead!"

I run and give him a hug, quick, before he changed his mind.

He squeezed me back, one-handed. "You're getting big!"

"You like sugar in it?"

"Yeah. Not too sweet." He set down on the next to the top step and leaned on his elbow on the top one, stretching his leg out straight such that it didn't look so wasted away.

I made him one and me one and I tasted his and decided I liked it that way too: not too sweet. When I give it to him I made sure I handed it so when he took a drink from it his lips were bound to touch where mine had touched.

"Go on!" I said. "See if it's how you like it."

I privately swooned to see him take a drink, because it was like we kissed, even if I was the only one to know it. Just the way his Adam's apple bobbed up and down as he swallowed was enough to make me weak.

He wore a white tee shirt. Which, I believe that was the only color they come in back in the day. He had the narrowest hips and the biggest biceps you ever seen. Which again, biceps were the only muscle group anybody knew existed, either. Nowadays we have a whole host of others to be concerned with: deltoids, abs, lats, and my hands-down favorite, the gluteus maximus, which I took to be the name of a Roman Emperor the first time I heard of it. And no. I am not being funny. He carried his cigarette pack rolled up inside the sleeve of his tee shirt like they all did back then. He unrolled it and tapped one out against his good knee, then grabbed it with his lips and pulled it the rest of the way out. He had to dig in his front jeans pocket looking for a book of matches, all the while his cigarette dangling. Every little thing he did like to give me a heartache. That's how in love I was with my sister's husband.

"You want me to hold that for you?" I offered, so he didn't have to set his iced tea down to light up. When he handed me back his glass for a second, I quick took a sip while nobody was looking and touched my lips where his had just touched to make it complete: him kissing me and me kissing him back.

The only gimpy thing about him was his leg. He worked construction in the oilfield before his accident. A Wetback had been the cause of it. They run that son of a bitch off. Called Immigration and sent him high-tailing back to Mexico where he belonged. At least, that's what Sheila told Grandma and me happened to him. Only that didn't do Leon one bit of good, did it? He still couldn't work. Not like he used to.

He was a working fool, they used to say. They said he one time picked a whole engine block up off the ground and set it under the hood of a car they were working on that belonged to a certain welder I don't need to mention by name and started bolting it down while everybody else stood and gawked at him. That's how he was. And now just look at him, everybody said.

It didn't change him one bit, though. Not in my eyes.

Bad timing was all, what with Lisa Julene on the way. Him and Sheila were up Schitz Creek.

What happened was a load of pipe had not been secured the right way to the back of a flatbed truck. By that Wetback, like I said. Before the truck left the yard, the straps let go. Leon was in the exact wrong place at the exact wrong time. Lucky he wasn't killed.

"Won't be so lucky for Filipe, I ever get a hold of him," is what Leon said in the hospital. But of course that was just talk, for all I or anyone else knew at the time.

"Filipe won't be coming back this way anytime soon, now, will he?" Sheila reminded him.

"Not likely," he said and left it at that.

A lot went unspoken between the two of them. Their doctor bills were out of this world. That was how they come to be sitting on Grandma and me's front porch, talking about this, that and the other thing and Sheila looking miserable and fanning herself in the heat. Out of the blue she said, "You got everything you need for supper, Grandma?"

"Pretty sure I do. Why? Is there something you need?"

"Just if there was anything you could use at the grocery store, Leon would be happy to go pick it up. Wouldn't you, Baby?"

Leon took a drag on his cigarette. When he got around to answering, he spoke in smoke signals. "Happy to." You could tell how thrilled. I loved the way his cigarette smoke hung under the porch roof until the wind caught it and pulled it away. You could hear a cicada whirring away off down by the road and my Grandma's rocking chair creaking over the floorboards.

"We could use some bacon, if you're planning on being here for breakfast."

"We hadn't intended on staying over, Grandma Cavendish," Leon said.

"Leon, we could too! Why? You got an important business meeting to go to in the morning?"

"Yeah!" I chimed in and nudged his good leg with my bare foot. "You got an important business meeting, Leon?"

That didn't sit too well. Nothing I said ever did. Sheila give me a look like, *You shut your trap, Piss Ant!* while Leon, you could see his mouth get real tight and the muscle in his jaw start to jumping. He flipped his cigarette out in the grass and exploded a big double stream of smoke through his nose.

Grandma said, as if it didn't matter to her one iota whether if they stayed over or they didn't, "Nobody's twisting your arm, Leon."

"I have sat in that car enough for one day!" Sheila said.

It was about a thirty-minute ride from where they lived in Enid. Thirty-five at the most.

Leon took his cane. "What else besides bacon?"

"You like orange juice?"

"I do," I said.

"Vanessa, go on my dresser and get my purse."

"We can pay," Sheila said.

Which was a big fat lie, because Leon said, "No, Sheila. We can't." He give her a look like, *Go on ahead and contradict me, why don't you?* and it was her that had to shut her trap then.

"You want to ride along, Frecklehead?"

Of course I did. I looked at Grandma.

"Go get my purse like I asked you to."

On my way back by I dropped it off in her lap and said, "Come on, Elvis! I'll race you!" I shot past him across the grass.

"You win!" he grunted, using his cane to pry himself off the steps and get his feet under him. I would have won, too, but Grandma called me back to go find her an ink pen in the house. By the time I come back with one, Leon had gone and got in the car already and was gunning the motor like as if to take off with or without me.

"Here. Take this." Grandma tore a signed check out of her checkbook and handed it to me to pay for the groceries. When I went to take it from her she held on tight and said, "Don't let him go fast!"

As if I had any control over that. I said, "I won't!"

Then she let go.

"I won anyway!" I declared, climbing in beside him in his maroon Mercury.

He didn't answer me back.

Something had happened between the time Grandma called me back and him going and getting in the car. As to what that might be, I was in the dark as usual. But something. Words had been exchanged, and somebody had got their feelings hurt. Your guess is as good as mine what it was about. All I knew was Leon had got his tit in a wringer.

No sooner did I open my mouth to say, "What's wrong?" than he laid the pedal to the metal and *barooom!* we went flying ass-backwards down the driveway at about a mile a minute, spewing dust and throwing gravel out in front so bad I like to had a fit. Once we slalomed out into the road, he hit the brakes and spun that old Mercury halfway back around sidewards. I got flung like a rag doll one way and then the other as off we took in forward gear. I couldn't tell who was screaming louder, me or his motor. I hung onto my armrest with both hands and squeezed my eyes tight shut. Under my breath I said, "Don't go too fast, Leon," so if she asked me later I could say I told him so and I wouldn't hopefully get in trouble for it, even if it was at my own funeral and his, too. That's how fast he drove all the way to the Keening City Limits.

He didn't say word one, even after we pulled into the parking lot at the I.G.A. He just set in the car and stewed on whatever it was that went on back there between him and Sheila or between him and somebody. I didn't know who or what and I didn't want to.

I got bacon and paid with the check she give me, all wrinkled from me gripping it so tight. When I come out again, he still wasn't exactly in a conversating mood, so I turned the radio up loud, and off he drove at a more civilized rate of speed.

He did not go far.

Down at the corner of Main and Cherokee stood what, anywhere else in the world, would be known as a beer joint, but in Keening, by city ordinance (I shit you not) it had to be called a Cigar Store. Leon pulled into the gravel parking lot off the alleyway.

"I'll be back in a minute or two. You want a pop?"

I said sure, and he went in the back door, stepping over a litter of kittens that had their nest in an old Miller High Life box.

A minute later he come back out with a Dr. Pepper and said, "I'll leave you the car keys if you want me to. You like to listen to music?" So that's what I did while he was in there drinking beer, it getting later and later until I finally went and put my face against the back screen door to try and see inside.

It was too dark in there and too bright outside. I sat down and petted the kittens for a little while. They begun to be looking for me to give them some milk or something I didn't have to offer, until I finally thought of some of that bacon.

Try as I might I couldn't tear into it without a knife, so I went inside and told Leon we better be getting home or else they'd wonder what happened.

Him and the old boy at the bar looked at one another and at me and then Leon paid him some money that supposedly he didn't have and come on out with me back to the car. I started around to get in and he stopped me and asked me had I ever driven a stick before.

I give him the hairy eyeball. "I never drove anything, Leon!"

"That is about to change. Get in over here!"

So I climbed in on his side. He made room for me to sit between his legs where he could work the clutch with his good foot. His gimpy one flopped over on the gas pedal, but it wasn't totally lacking in strength and coordination. That was the way he normally drove. I didn't think anything of that.

He showed me where all the gears were and made me go through each one a few times and say which one it was—low, second, neutral, high and reverse—before we took off out of the parking lot, him doing most of the steering and me just wiggling the gearshift from one slot to another like he told me to. Once we passed the city limit sign, he let me put it all the way down in third gear and take over on the steering wheel.

"All right, you got it from here. I'll just close my eyes and take me a little snooze and you wake me up when we get there."

I laughed and said, "No you ain't, either!"

I thought nothing of it at the time. I was so intent on keeping us from going in the ditch that it didn't fully register. But Leon had somehow or other got his hand up under my sun dress and had it there the whole rest of the way. It never dawned on me until a few years later to wonder what that was all about.

Not all the way up under. I don't  mean that. Nothing totally indecent. But I never quite forgot about it. Not really. I wasn't traumatized by it. It didn't go into my deep, dark, suppressed memory banks and it didn't change how I felt about him one way or the other.

Later on maybe it did. But not right then.

Yet I am bound to contradict myself, because it slid across my mind again two months later, that afternoon of August 12, when Grandma said they were coming again and bringing the baby.

I said, "Do they have to?" I had the feeling that Grandma might know something, like she might be onto me about Leon, so I felt like I had to act like I didn't want to see either one of them, when really I did. Don't get me wrong, I didn't especially want to see Sheila but I did want to see the baby. And I did think about Leon and about him letting me drive their Mercury again and how even if he did have his hand on my leg, so what? That didn't mean I didn't have to not like it.

"When I'm gone, Vanessa, you are gonna need someone to look after you."

"I can look after myself just fine," I assured her. In my mind, I already did as much looking after myself as anyone.

"Can you pay the taxes on this house? And put groceries on the table and clothes on your back? You can't even wake yourself up of a morning and get yourself off to school on time!"

"I wouldn't have to if you didn't make me," I said back.

"I guess that answers that."

I don't remember an argument she didn't win, but I had no intention of going to live in Enid with Sheila and Leon after she died, nor to California where my daddy ended up. Or so she said he did. According to her, he had married into a vineyard the second time around, somewhere north of San Francisco, and he now had kids of his own out there. Of his own. That's how she put it. Like what in the hell did that make me? Not to mention Sheila.

I don't know if there was ever a word of truth to it. He might have been dead or in prison for all I knew. He never contacted me except one postcard one time, before I was old enough to even read it. To this day, I have never put myself out to find him. Not out of anger or disgust, but just—why would I?

All that afternoon, she'd been antsy, my grandma, stepping up behind me and patting me on the head to calm herself. I suspected something was up. Like the barometric pressure in her brain or something. What did I know? But something had sure got into her.

"There, there!" She pounded me on top of the head like I was a nail she had to drive home. "There, there, there!"

Her eyes were far sighted. She rested them on a level with the door lintel. I could tell she was thinking of going down after supper to look at the canyon.

"You said Sheila and Leon's coming?" I ventured. I needed to make sure.

She didn't contradict me. But other than to say she wanted to bake a loaf of bread, she hadn't made any preparation for supper nor asked me to do anything, either. So I didn't. There was an outside chance that Sheila planned something special to bring, but even if she said she would, you couldn't count on it happening. So I was puzzled. Grandma didn't leave things to chance like that.

I give her a look. Deadpan. I figured supper had "slipped her mind" in the hopes that Sheila and Leon would head home early, before sunset, or else get something in town at the cafe. To be honest, it was a longer drive to Enid back then than I let on, because it wasn't all paved highway like it is now. It didn't seem likely we'd get away with not feeding them. Much less going down to the canyon. That had always been something just between her and me, anyway, Grandma's obsession with the canyon.

Ever since Leon's injury, or since Sheila getting pregnant, or the two things combined, maybe, my sister had developed a hobby. Some take up needlepoint or jogging or Tupperware. Sheila took up worrying. Grandma's bones were frail! What if she was to take a spill? That kind of a deal. She became a worry wart about every little thing. Way before her time, if you asked me.

Yet that morning early, Grandma had stripped her bed. With my help she leaned her mattress up against the wall and opened her windows, just as if company would be spending the night, and she intended on taking the sofa for herself. Three of them now and only one of her, that's how she saw it.

"Might just as well strip yours, too!" she said and sent me upstairs for my sheets and pillowcase. We had a spare bedroom across the landing from my room, but Leon had trouble climbing stairs, plus they had the baby now. Grandma didn't sleep well on the second story, so it was just me up there. And I thank my Lucky Charms, too. I was most of a teenager by this time and I liked my privacy. We threw our linens together with a few articles from the hamper and agitated them in the wringer washer. We were the last people on the planet to have one, but Grandma wouldn't give hers up for love nor money. She said electric machines would eat your clothes.

"Whites and colors together?" I marveled.

"Won't matter." She was not acting her usual self. I tugged on a corner of a sheet as she cranked the wringer. "Just this once," she amended.

She sent me to stand on the chair in the yard and pin the laundry. When that was done, she tied her sweater around her waist and rolled her sleeves up to mix bread. She had a way of making a waltz out of kneading the dough. Her brown shoes repeated the same steps to and fro over the kitchen linoleum, and a certain loose board in the floor kept time with a low groan on the off-step. She paused to shoo a thought or a ticklish hair from her brow with a swipe of the clean inside of her wrist, then dusted the tabletop and sifted flour through her fingers like plaster through old ceiling lath. Once she'd kneaded it enough, she tucked the undersides of the dough up under itself to make a smooth white belly on top, oiled it and laid it like a newborn in the big zinc bowl, covered it with a lid of towels and fit the bowl over the mouth of a stoneware crock full of warm water.

We sat together in the front room. Her hands rested oiled and clean in her lap like a woodcarving, and she spoke to me for the umpteenth time concerning the stipulations in her will.

"In my will, I left this house and most everything in it to your sister. She needs the help. Just till they get on their feet. And five acres," she added, "from the back pasture, there where it's fenced off, that the surveyors come already and marked and mapped and is all drawn up."

I remembered.

"I discussed this with Sheila. Also with the bank manager. He recommended that attorney up at Fairview, so that's the one I used." She looked at me. One hand patted the other, and she went on: "Sheila don't know I'm telling you this."

I didn't have to ask why not. She would get to it. Again.

"Land is no good to her. She don't know how to work it. Leon won't make any kind of farmer, not with his leg the way it is. I thought his accident might teach him a lesson, but it won't. Some things ain't meant to be. Not for some people. I don't know what I expected. Him to learn some patience, maybe? To be more humble? Not humble enough for farming, though, that's for damn sure. This is the best thing I know to do, Vanessa. Maybe it seems unfair to everybody. What else could I do?"

I listened for as long as I could sit still. She'd been over it all before, point by point. Then, lo and behold, she took a sudden turn from her usual spiel and started talking about my daddy, and in a whole new vein. "He'll never amount to nothing, either. I cut him out," she said with a swipe of her hand the way you might sweep the peelings off a cutting board. If I don't, there won't be nothing left for either of you girls."

What that meant, what had happened to lead her to that conclusion, I will never know. She never gave me reason to think she needed to justify her actions to me. But then, she had always before maintained that my daddy would come save us from having to work things out our own way, that her decisions were only temporary fixes, a way to get by until his fateful return.

Now, regardless of what he did or didn't do, I am not hateful or resentful towards my daddy. I don't want to give that impression. I just never knew him but through Grandma's stories. Make that, hers and Sheila's, which up until that day could not have been painted in more contrasting colors. Grandma maintained that Starla Gray had so badmouthed him to her that Sheila didn't know any better. She didn't remember him right.

I said to Grandma once, "I don't remember him at all, do I?"

"Sure you do. He loved you."

We had a black-and-white photograph of him on top of the upright piano. The piano is long gone. I figured the photo was, too, but it turned up again. I don't know where it was taken, but in it you see him posing with a group of other young men just like him, hippies with long hair and no shirts. He stands second from the left in the front row, wearing a belt that hangs way too long for his skinny waist, a foot or more of it looped back on itself like the flourish under a signature.

I seldom brooded on him. It was hard to tell sometimes if I vaguely remembered him or I just knew my Grandma's stories so well it seemed I ought to know him but didn't. Her sudden mention of him caught me off guard. I found my eye attracted to that picture, which was my favorite one of him and must have been hers, too, because in the two other ones that got packed away with all the extra photographs in three shoe boxes, Starla Gray appeared.

We had not one picture of him and my momma together. I knew that for a fact. Not one picture of her whatsoever. I don't know if none ever got taken or what? I'd been told on the one hand (and not just by my grandma but, years later, by her attorney) that my mother was "capital B Beautiful." To this day, I don't know what to make of that. Maybe she was. Maybe that's why my daddy thought he couldn't help himself. Who was I to argue with how I come to be? Then again, maybe people told me such things because I didn't know any better and couldn't prove otherwise.

Grandma flung the backs of her fingers at an apparition of him I couldn't see. "Shoo! Be on your way!" she told him. "Run off to Alaska! That's what you're bound and determined to do, ain't it? Don't you take it to heart, Vanessa. It's not on account of you, though you're the one to suffer for it." She fiddled with her collar. "I told him you would."

"On account of who, then?"

She narrowed her eyes. "That Starla Gray. She drove him off. You wouldn't know it the way she acts now, but she had a wild streak in her. Jealous? I guess she was jealous! And so cunning. Your daddy didn't have sense enough to see it and steer clear of her and not give her reason to get that way. She laid trap after trap for him, until finally he got caught with your momma, and that was all she wrote."

"What was she like?" I wanted to know. I didn't believe half of what Sheila said.

"Your momma? She had the sweetest disposition."

"Yeah, but what did she look like?"

"You have her chin."

That didn't help. My chin was pointy. "What else? What color eyes?"

"I believe they were blue."

"You're just saying that."

"No, I believe they were."

"What about her hair?"

"Blonde!" she said with certainty.

"What kind of blonde?" (Sheila said "dishwater blonde," which was not a color.)

"Well, let's see. Like the color of maple."

"Maple?" I said. "Maple's red!"

"No, it's blonde."

"It is not. It turns red."

"No, you're thinking of cherry. Don't you know what maple looks like? We don't have any." After a minute, she said, "Not the leaves. Like maple furniture."

"Oh." That didn't help, either. "I wish I had a picture of her."

"Listen to me. You need to hear this. Andy Goslin up the road holds the leases to most of this land. He plants one whole section and a half to wheat, plus another three quarters that he uses for winter pasture, to the south and west of this five acres. You know where I mean? Where the trail leads down to water his herd? He ought to drill him a well but he won't listen to an old Indian woman like me. Now, those leases are five-year leases, guaranteed income. I made them renewable for another five years, until you come of age. Once I'm gone, that rent goes to Sheila. It's hers to do as she sees fit, so long as you're clothed and fed and taken care of until you turn 21 or else get married. Or if you're going on and getting your college education, it continues until you graduate or turn 25. Depending on whichever way you go in life, that's how long the lease money lasts. You understand all that?"

I made known that I did.

"It's all spelled out. You understand why it's got to be that way?"

"To make sure her and Leon keep a roof over my head," I recited.

She give out a sigh and closed her eyes like it exhausted her to have to go over it all one more time. Then she said, "You might turn out pretty when you're grown. Your Momma was. It only caused a lot of trouble in her case. Too soon to tell yet about you, one way or the other. Sheila will try to keep you away from that kind of trouble right up to the last minute. At least, I hope she will. It won't be for my reasons but for the reasons I give her. That's the purpose of having a will."

I sat quiet while she chased her thoughts and I chased mine, then she raised her head in the air like a wizard or a Bible prophet, half-blind, eyes scouring the ceiling. "A Baptist," she said—and by "Baptist" she meant the Bittles across the canyon—then she chuckled somewhere way off by herself, kind of evil. "A Baptist will tell you the soul goes on after the body. They confuse it with the will."

# SKEWER

"Is your room picked up?"

I had a library book open in my lap. "Don't worry, it will be."

Grandma fixed her eye on me.

I got up. "I just this minute got the sheets in off the line!"

"Get up there and make your bed!" She slapped my rump like you do a horse to get it moving.

I stomped halfway up the stairs and turned around, out of her range, with my hand on my hip, a finger marking my place in my book. "Nobody's allowed in my room, anyway. Not without my permission!"

She pointed a finger like a bent twig. "This will be your sister's house sooner than you think. She might have different ideas."

"Just let her try!" I tromped up to my room.

Yet the minute they brought Lisa Julene across the threshold, I knew I was going to have to change my tune and play second fiddle. She was about the cutest, most pitiful-looking thing I ever saw, with her face rumpled up in the crook of her daddy's arm.

"This here's your Aunt Frecklehead," Leon informed her, hoisting her up to get a look at me. She clobbered the side of her face with her little knuckles and studied me like I was a problem she didn't have the faintest idea how to solve. The feeling was mutual.

Sheila stalked into the kitchen and took a deep sniff. "*Mm – mm – mmm!* Something sure smells good!"

"It's bread," I volunteered.

"Homemade bread? Oh, it smells so good! Doesn't it, Leon?" Her eyes did a quick scan of the counter tops and the stove, her brow pinching itself into a deep V, no doubt wondering what else was for supper. Then it quick smoothed itself out. "Oops! I clean forgot! It's past Lisa Julene's feeding time. I won't hold us up too much, will I, Grandma?"

"Bread's got to cool a minute. You can go in my room."

"Bring me her diaper bag, will you, Nessa?" When I did, she pulled me into Grandma's room and shut the door.

"Wasn't she expecting us?"

I didn't know how to answer. I just shrugged.

She slumped down on the bed with the baby and pulled her tata out of her dress and got started. I hadn't ever seen breast feeding before. Lisa Julene made a cranky face, arched her little back and begun to fuss. "Oh, look, You!" Sheila said, kind of cross, in baby-talk. "What do you think you're pulling, a hunger strike, you?" She took a minute trying to get her nipple plugged back into the baby's mouth, but Lisa Julene wasn't having it. Finally, Sheila give up. "I guess she ain't hungry." She scavenged in the diaper bag for something else. "You didn't answer me, Vanessa."

"I don't know," I said.

Her breast was still hanging out. I couldn't take my eyes off of how big it was. I didn't have any idea what I was supposed to do or say. "Grandma's dead set on dying," I blurted. "And pretty quick, too. Like, any day."

"What in the world are you talking about?"

"Don't let on I told you."

"What did she say? I won't let on. Tell me what she said!"

I inched my way toward the door, but she reached for me, flapping her hand. "Get back here! Tell me what she said, why don't you?"

"She must've just forgot she invited you is all."

Lisa Julene begun to squall in earnest. Sheila jumped off the bed, trying to quiet her in one hand and keep me from leaving with the other. She pulled me back to the bed. "See what you can do with her!"

She transferred Lisa Julene over to me.

I didn't have a choice. Either take her or drop her on her head. So I sat on the edge of the bed and begun to sway from side to side, the way you do, and to and fro, and tried to get her to hush some.

"She ain't hungry," Sheila said, "but sometimes just a pacifier will quiet her. You want to see what it's like?" It didn't take but my two top buttons and she had my shirt laid halfway open. "It's okay. Go on ahead!" She pressed Lisa Julene's little squirming face up against my flat chest. I let her, too, as much to cover up as anything. I didn't have anything to show yet, but just the same!

It did muffle the baby's crying, at least, as I stroked the soft back of her head and bounced her up and down a little until, lo and behold, she took to me, muckled onto me with her little mouth and went to town.

"That feels completely weird," I said as Sheila's lip curled up one side of her face. She turned away to button up. "Ain't she gonna figure out something's wrong here in a minute?"

Sheila shushed me and come stroking the baby's head and crooning at her. "Lisa Julene, this here's your Aunt Nessa. She likes you."

"Not if she ever decides she's hungry, she won't."

"Ain't it something, though?"

"It halfway between hurts and tickles." Not that I minded. I just didn't want Sheila to go thinking the wrong thing. Mind you, I didn't know what the right thing to think would be. I just didn't want her thinking the wrong thing, and the wrong thing had to do with me pretending to be Lisa Julene's momma, which I wasn't. She was. And Leon was her daddy. And I was old enough to know, all pretense aside, that him having his hand up under my dress fell under the category of him thinking the wrong thing about who was what and who was not what. And here I set with Sheila, acting like nothing ever happened.

"Bread ought to be cool by now," I said.

"Vanessa?" She laid her fingers on my wrist like she was taking my pulse. "Has Grandma mentioned to you what's going to happen when she does pass on?"

I nodded my head real slow. I thought, *Here it comes.*

"That she wants us to move out here with you and look after you?"

"She told me." I didn't think it would happen, though. I didn't think she had any interest in living out in the middle of nowhere, as she called it. And no way in hell was I moving to Enid with them. I was determined to run away before I let that happen.

"Did she tell you something else?"

I looked at her fingers on my freckled wrist and felt my own pulse jumping. "Like what?" I lied.

"That we'll be proud to — to, if and when, I mean, if it's meant to be — Leon and me'll be proud to have you with us. Lisa Julene will, too."

I don't know if I blushed or blanched or turned blue, but I stood to hand her back her baby and said, "I better go set the table."

Sheila wiped her eyes as I went to leave. She had choked herself up. She stopped me yet again and mouthed the words, "Button your shirt!"

I set out the butter knives and the little plates — we didn't need much else — while Grandma poured four glasses of wine and called Sheila to come on.

Out she come with the baby yowling and fussing again.

"What'd you go and wake her up for, Stupid?" Leon said.

210

He received an evil look from Sheila. One from me, too. "That ain't nice!" I told him.

"Why? I didn't call you stupid."

"Good thing you didn't!" I said, and I reminded him, "She's still my sister."

"Come sit down," Grandma interrupted. "Come on, Leon. Vanessa, scoot around! I'll take her a minute, Sheila, you sit down."

"She's awful crotchety, Grandma. She takes after her Daddy."

"Let me have her a minute. Did you burp her? You couldn't have!"

Sheila took one look at me, and the corner of her lip curled up into her cheek again. I glared at her, like *Don't you say a word about it!* But she all of a sudden noticed what else was on the table and said, "Grandma, what's this in these glasses?"

"Muscadine wine. Taste it."

"Leon and me don't drink, Grandma. We gave it up ever since Lisa Julene arrived."

"I don't much either. I brought it up from the cellar special for you."

"Special for me?"

"I thought you might make an exception." Grandma took a dish towel over her shoulder and proceeded to give Lisa Julene a few good blows to the back, until the baby let out a belch and spit up a dribble of milk, looked like—which was weird; she hadn't taken any. Grandma landed a few more blows for good measure before she took and laid her on the sofa in the living room and propped her all around with pillows and cushions where she wouldn't roll off, then she come on back in the kitchen. "I'll sit here, where I can see her." She held the warm loaf of bread against her chest and sawed off several slices before she sat down with the rest of us.

"Your Daddy made this wine," she said. "This is the last of it."

The way the windows were situated, the late sun slanted under the leaves of the old maple outside and laid its light on the bias across the table. Even with the swamp cooler going in the other room, the butter melted in its dish and slid off the butter knife when I tried to spread it.

Sheila sat fanning herself and said grace so fast she must have been afraid me or Grandma might interrupt her if she took too long. She tossed in a word for "the hands that have prepared this bread for the nourishment of our bodies" and something about the Lord keeping us steadfast in his ways, amen, and when she raised her head again, the sun burnt pure white behind her head like she was by God anointed. The curtains hung still in the open window, the maple leaves hung still in the hot air, and the sweat prickled on Sheila's forehead, smooth and bone-white, not frowning one least bit, and on Leon's forehead under his thick black Elvis Presley do, and on mine in all my freckleheadedness. Grandma's face and hands gleamed with oil and sweat, too, as she lifted the bread to her mouth and bit into it, cupping her hand to catch the butter that spilt from it, and likewise the butter spilt onto each one of our palms and run down my chin, it was so warm and so good. We all laughed together and lifted our glasses in a kind of toast where no one had to say word one, including me, who had never tasted a drop of wine before in my life, and even Sheila, who believed it now to be a sin, and Leon, who give me a wink on the sly.

"That's good bread, Grandma," Sheila said. Me and Leon spoke up at the same time, agreeing, and soon everybody was talking all at once, Sheila describing how quick the baby had taken to me, and me and Grandma both saying what a beautiful baby she was.

"Every Cavendish baby's a beauty," Grandma said. "Every one I ever seen."

"I've seen pictures," Leon said, and everybody laughed again and sighed over the warm buttered bread and drank the wine, dividing the last drops from the second bottle amongst us. A little of it spilt onto the tablecloth, and a stain spidered through the lace, a stain that never did come out. We laughed with a fierceness like the sun burning a hole through the windows, through our souls, and everybody's teeth laughing made me think we exposed the bones of our faces to one another, not in a ghastly way but as the beautiful skeletons of who we were if we could but shed the skin of ourselves, of how we pretended so hard to be the family we weren't and forgot to be the fucked up, beautiful one we were. And no, of course I didn't think all that in my head, not at the age of eleven, not in so many words, but that's as close as I can get to the way it felt in my heart after a glass and a half of my long-gone daddy's muscadine wine.

When our supper of nothing but bread was finished, Grandma fished a scarf out of the pocket of her sweater and drew it over her head. "I'm going out for a little walk," she said. Her fingers tied a stiff knot under her chin. "You coming, Vanessa?"

"Where to?" said Leon.

"Just down to the canyon."

"That's kind of far, Grandma, for Leon to walk and me to carry the baby."

"Well, I'm going down to see the sun set like I always do. You all can watch from the yard if you want to."

"I'm going," I said.

"You are not going down there!" Sheila glared at me, that V shape stamped between her eyes again. "The two of you alone?"

"We do all the time."

Grandma give her a look, mild but firm. "Ain't a power on Earth can stop me, Sheila."

"Vanessa ain't big enough to—what if you should fall?" Sheila's eyes begun to glisten with emotion, with worry or, in hindsight, plain guilt and foreknowledge. "The three of us together ain't enough to carry you back up to bed!" I have often wondered how much Sheila knew, or suspected, deep in the secret corners of her mind, like I did, of what Grandma intended that night, because when Leon pushed back his chair and reached for his cane, Sheila warned him, "Stay out of it, Leon!"

"Well, I can make her stay put, if that's—"

"Don't be an idiot!" Then, to Grandma, "If you go, we're all going!"

Insects chittered and thrummed in the tall grass. High overhead, the clouds gathered at the edge of the sky, but down where we were, the wind held still, the heat like a vapor rising. Sweat slid down my neck, down my flanks. We crossed the back pasture Indian file, down where the stunted cedars twisted out of the ground every so far apart and the yellow grass rasped against our legs. I felt a sudden chill from the heat, and the sun, like a hot skewer drawing us into its fire, threw our shadows across the uneven ground.

Grandma went first, scarf and sweater, long skirt swinging over the tufts of dead grass. Then come me. Sheila next, shielding Lisa Julene's face with her hand, and Leon brought up the rear, prying himself along on his cane, his bad foot scuffing along after him. He made as good a time as any of us down the first shallow runnels, where drought had baked the earth to a crust. I caught up beside Grandma, and we never stopped. Right on down into the canyon we went, just as I knew we would, just as our many trips before had always prefigured.

Sheila lost her nerve. "You're not going down *in* there! Vanessa, stop her!"

I was strong for my size and useful to her over that first steep, stony ground where Andy Goslin's cattle had churned and crumbled the lip of the canyon to make a path that washed out every time it rained.

"Remember this place," Grandma instructed me. She jutted her chin in a small arc, for me to look around and mark where we were. "This is the best way back."

"I know it."

"It'll be dark, though."

I answered not a word.

# Descent

Clouds piled above us as we stepped down into the canyon, me and Grandma. Sheila stood hollering down at us from as close to the edge as she dared to hold the baby. Loud enough so we could hear, she told Leon to run back in the house and call the police, but that didn't stop us. Leon argued with her. He said the police don't respond outside the city limits, he'd have to call the County Sheriff.

"Then call the goddamn Sheriff!" she screamed.

I found out later it didn't matter one bit what number he tried. He never even got a dial tone. Unbeknownst to any of us, Grandma had called the telephone company that afternoon (probably while I was upstairs making my bed) and had the line disconnected.

She kept right on down into the canyon, swaying with every step like a cypress tree in a high wind, her hand on my shoulder for support. I felt the grit loosen underfoot, hard red clods and splinters of selenite burning through the soles of my shoes like a bed of coals. Where any sizable chunk of wall had slipped and tumbled to the canyon floor, it left slivers of crystallized gypsum strewn in its path until, after hundreds of thousands of little avalanches, the whole canyon glittered in the late sun.

Eventually, we come to a long spur that let us down at a more gradual slope all the way to the end, where it dropped off. She wanted to sit there and rest a minute.

"Ow!" I stood back up. "It's hot!"

We watched the sun sink behind the horizon. The sky in that direction turned so red it looked like the earth had caught fire. I stood behind her, resting my hand on her shoulder. Maybe this was as far as she meant to go. Maybe she just wanted to sit and watch the storm gather. She didn't say. The wind picked up again and drove a handful of low, dark shreds of cloud across the canyon, herding them toward the opposite rim. There they fattened, and more clouds come, swollen with anger, and the lightning beat them black and blue and made them rain off in the distance.

"You got a colorful imagination!" she said.

"Why? What do you mean?" I hadn't said a word that I was aware of.

She didn't answer me. The wind dipped down into the canyon and snatched at our dresses, snapping and popping them and whipping my braids in all directions. It beat against the walls of the canyon, picking up dust in crazy swirls like snakes writhing down into the gullies to either side of us. The far clouds reared up in columns like heads peering down at us, watching over us as the moon rose up on our side, faint as glass, and the last rim of the sky burned a deep violet-red for one long minute before it went pink, then purple, then blue-black, and the moon rode behind a cloud.

She never moved until finally I asked her, I said, "Is this the place you're always talking about? Where you and Grandpa always come?"

She sighed and cradled one hand in the other like she was ready to wait out the next geological age. "A little further. Then you can head on back."

"Further where? What you looking for?"

She refused to answer me for the longest time, just sitting there, letting me and my questions aggravate her. Then at last she said, "It's an Indian thing."

Which was a lie. Nothing she said or did ever struck me as outlandish—I guess because so much of what she said and did, by most standards, qualified as outlandish—but I could always tell when she lied, when she made up a lame excuse to shut me up. No one behaved the way she did just because they had a little Cherokee in them or Choctaw or whatever. I let it go. I stood and waited, beset by strange and contradictory winds, my hair and my clothes pulled in opposite directions.

I had enough finally. I said, "We're only a quarter Crow."

"Half," she corrected me. "Your father's a quarter; you're an eighth. That ain't the point." She unfolded herself and leaned on my shoulder again to stand up and turn around backwards so she could negotiate the steep face of the spur, clawing into the sand, her feet sliding out from under her.

I like to choked, watching her. I was sure she was fixing to veer sideways, stumble, and break something. I'd be left to explain to Sheila how come I to let such a thing happen to her, I knew I would. I turned and scrambled down the way Grandma did, scraping my knees and the palms of my hands. I meant to get to the bottom ahead of her so I could hopefully break her fall, if she did slide, and scold her for the stupid old woman she was. But she managed fine. When she caught up to me at the bottom, she pounded the top of my head and pulled my face against her before I could open my mouth to say anything, her old fingers hot and brittle as sticks pulled from a fire and laid against my cheek.

After a minute, she let me go, and on we went.

Packed red clay run in braided channels at the wide creek bottom, where like on Mars the wind had long ago erased any last trickle of water. We reached a certain gnarled cedar overhanging a cleft between an irregular block of sandstone and a secondary spur off the one we'd climbed down.

She said, "Here."

I give her my shoulder to lean on one last time. She was breathing heavy now as she squatted on the canyon floor and stuck her legs out.

"This—" she said and she slapped the hard ground like she meant it— "this is the place!"

In my memory, I see her fierce white smile gleaming at me out of the shadows. I cling to that memory, though I know it's false. The smile and the memory of it both. The moon hung like a lamp between two clouds. In the shadows of the cranny where she sat, I could hardly make out the shape of her. Yet I remember the fierce persuasiveness of her smile, as if she willed me to believe her, as if I had no choice but to believe her: this place was special–to her and Grandpa, anyway–and she meant to die here. She did not want me nor Sheila nor anyone else to interfere.

I crawled in on my hands and knees and planted a kiss on her forehead where I always kissed her at bedtime, then I backed out of the shadows again.

A faint few stars had crept into the sky in the east. In the west, thunderheads and lightning.

"You'll have the moon with you but for a few minutes. You get on back. You got time before the storm gets here. Go on."

I did not cry. I wanted to, but I thought it would not dignify the situation to do so. I climbed back out the way we'd come, my feet slipping out from under me several times as I made my way back up the side of the main spur. Beneath the lip of the canyon, where the path turned at a steep rise back up to the back pasture, I stopped and looked behind me, surveying the canyon. Everything not in shadow the moon had lit to a dullish pink. And I saw — or I sure thought I saw, moving across the flat bottom, out, away from the cedar cleft where I had left her — where she had led me to believe she meant to die — the dark shape of my grandma swaying to and fro, looking for a place she never intended me to know.

# Mud

It took five men with flashlights to find her in the wee hours of the morning and dig her out of the creek bank. They had to carry her up to the road by hand on a stretcher and put her in the ambulance. The gurney would not make the trip. We had golf ball size hail that night and one report of a funnel — sighted, not confirmed. That held things up. If anyone had asked me, I would've told them Grandma planned it exactly that way. She'd waited there with me at the end of the main spur, made sure the storm was coming our direction, before we proceeded to the bottom. Something in her bones must've advised her.

She'd lived on the rim of Keening Canyon her whole life — all of her adult life, anyway. It meant something to her to die there. I wasn't sure what or why, but I respected her wishes. That's what I told myself, that's what I told everybody else, and that's what I believed.

Near dawn, Sheriff Angley come and got Leon to step outside and identify positively that it was Margaret Cavendish in the back of the ambulance in the driveway. The emergency lights were not flashing. Angley made Sheila and me stay put, even though we were next of kin, not Leon. Leon come back in the house and said, "It's her all right. You don't want to see her the way she is right now."

Sheila begun to cry. I begun to tear up, too, but I stopped myself.

The ambulance took off toward town, lights going, no siren. Sheriff Angley come up on the porch again and just stood there holding his hat. His shoes, his uniform pants and even the sleeves of his jacket were spackled in mud. He wouldn't come inside. Everything on the porch was soaked, so we couldn't ask him to sit down out there even. He just stood and waited.

After a while he come and poked his head in the door and said, "If there's anything I can do for you folks…"

Of course, there wasn't anything.

He made his voice gentle, considerate. He said, "At some point, maybe in the morning, I'll need to ask y'all some questions. When you first noticed she was missing and all like that. If you could try and remember anything she might have said that led you to—"

"We didn't find her missing," Sheila snapped. Her eyes were blood-shot from crying, wild-looking. "We knew where she went. Vanessa can show you."

That's when he changed his attitude and stopped pussyfooting around. He went and got his flashlight again and a roll of that yellow tape and wanted me to show him right then and there. So I did. I don't mean to suggest that he was ignorant about it or anything. He just all of a sudden shifted gears. He took me by the hand, and we went slipping and sliding back down the same way me and Grandma had gone just a few hours prior. I took him straight to the cedar overhanging the cleft and started in on my hands and knees in the mud to show him where I left her sitting, but he held me back and said, "No, I don't want you going in there."

So I didn't.

He said, "Why didn't you tell me this before?"

I asked him what he meant, and he said in an angry tone of voice, "If I had known where you last saw her, we might have been able to track her from here and get to her sooner. She might still be with us."

That was the last thing I needed to hear right then. I had held it to-gether pretty damn good up to that point. But his accusation pushed me over the edge. You know how you sometimes know you're gonna cry—there's no way of stopping it—but yet you can't draw air enough to get it started? I couldn't shut my mouth, I couldn't say anything, and I couldn't breathe. He knelt down in the mud and grabbed me and held me, and I squeaked a few times, until at last it all come blubbering out of me, tears and snot and all, and I didn't think I would ever be able to stop once I got started. It probably wasn't the most professional thing on his part—hugging a suspect like that—but that's what he did. He kept apologizing for what he said.

I never told anybody about it, but if you were to ask me, that's prob-ably how come I to not end up in prison for murdering my Grandma. Because I showed remorse for not telling him sooner. And to this day, whenever I see someone on Death Row, I always have to stop and won-der: Did you just not break down and cry at the right time or in front of the right person? Is that the difference between Cold Blood and Not Guilty? Because I don't show a lot of emotion, either, as a rule. Not ordinarily until I get mad.

Don't get me wrong. I'm no bleeding heart. If somebody did it, by all means, flip the fucking switch! All I mean, from my own experience, is just how close did I come?

At the same time, I didn't tell him everything he probably wanted to know. Not for lack of trying, I just couldn't get the words to come out about how I turned around and saw my grandma wandering off from one place to another. How at one point it looked to me like she had crossed over to the other side of the creek. If I had told him that, then he or one of the others might have found the bread knife, not me.

He tied off the area with his yellow Do Not Cross tape, and we climbed back out.

At eleven years of age, I didn't particularly want to know how she went about taking her own life. I wanted it just to be, like, Grandpa come and collected her, like in some kind of Native American spirit ceremony. That was the way it appeared to me in my imagination — Grandpa in the form of a star cluster shaped like a wolf or a buffalo and her beginning to fade and twinkle simultaneously until they were two the same. Somehow that idea seemed worth preserving. There was a truth to it that I could not then, nor can I now, explain to my own satisfaction, never mind anyone else's. The knife she left behind for me or anybody to come along and pick up and say, "Look at what I found!" on the other hand — that was a dirty, commonplace lie.

Now, I can play dumb as dirt, that don't mean you have to fall for it. Take Old Lady Bittle. I never could get her to understand why I had to go get that bread knife and bury it. I wasn't trying to hide it to protect myself in any legal sense of the word. I think I could've found a better hiding spot, if that was the case. I hardly expected her to tell the Sheriff and for him to go and dig it up. I just didn't want people thinking the way I knew they would be thinking, once they found out about it. I knew people would talk.

I come across it that same afternoon. As soon as I could get off by myself. While Sheila and Leon and the baby were catching up on a lost night's sleep, I run off into the canyon, and there it lay flashing in the sun, not far from where I'd seen her from above, in the dark, as she headed down the creek bottom. I brought it back to where it seemed to me like it ought to belong, underneath that cedar tree where her and Grandpa long ago made love and conceived my daddy. Where my daddy must've took my momma, too, the way I pictured it, and conceived me. And where, if I was ever to get my way, I would one day go with the future boy I loved and conceive a baby of my own. Down in the canyon. On the ground. Buck naked like people been doing since Adam and Eve.

In a private place, a native place of intimate secrets. That's where I buried Grandma's bread knife.

There was no blood left on it when I found it. That part of the gossip really is a lie. What did people expect, after it had rained half the damn night? All that was left to forensically examine was mud.

That was my name around town for years to come: Mud. And that's all I'm guilty of, aside from tampering with evidence and crawling under a Police Do Not Cross line to give it a proper burial.

# The Problem

Sheila and Leon didn't have but a little roach-infested, two-room apartment in Enid and they couldn't hardly afford that. Which is why Grandma stipulated in her will that they were to move in with me after she died and get the income off the land leased out to Andy Goslin until I come of age. After that, it reverted to me, but I didn't care. As far as I was concerned, we could split everything down the middle and go our separate ways.

It must have complicated matters some for Sheila when I took off with Patterson Price. Especially considering she no longer had Leon, either. Not that he ever contributed much, but he did at least look after Lisa Julene some of the time and almost always waited till I got home from school to start his drinking.

By the time I made my way back to Keening in 1998, Sheila had married a Texan and moved, I think to Houston or someplace. Grandma's house stood battered by the elements and other vandals, stripped of its paint and emptied of its contents, all but for a few boxes left in the attic that nobody saw any value in. Someone had come along and stripped all the copper out of the walls and under the floors, so it had no running water, no heat, no electricity. The foundation had caved in along one side, and the window panes had made for some fine target practice. Not but three windows left intact, and of those three, not one would budge in its frame, the house had settled so. The front door had gone AWOL as well as two bedroom doors, most of the trim, the mantelpiece and every stick of furniture. Even the porch railings and the fancy brackets that once supported the eaves — anything remotely of interest to an antique or restoration dealer — gone.

Before I had it bulldozed, I salvaged what I could of the lumber and one box from the attic that had a picture of my father in it, the one that used to sit on the back of the upright piano, and my old school papers, including this one, riddled with red check marks and squiggles and comments in the margins:

Mrs. Bittle                              *September 17, 1988*
*English*                               *Vanessa Cavendish*
*7th Grade*                                    *4th Period*

### The Wind

*The Town, The County, The Creke and everthing around here is name after the wind. You look east to see the sun rise an the wind git dirt in your eye. If you turn south it slap you acrossed the face. No telling wich way you turn you can not exape it. It swoop around a corner an git you. If you turn a way it will chang on you. If you turn another way it change back. The wind is all ways in my hair it is all ways at my close it is constint. The wind what carv out Keening Canyen. What drive the cadle out of the pastcher and it pick up the hauk in a spirel. Down in the creke in the winner time it freses over ice clapses in the dry creake and the water run out under The wind sings down in Keening Creke. I seen a slab of jipsome slide down the wall of Keening Canyen crack and rumbble and spilt apart it give a way for no a parent reson. It was the wind. Ever year are barn leen backword more an more them doors do not close nomore. It is not sqare. It want to lay down flat it is so wore out by the constint wind. At nite my windda radles if I want to come out doors an play. Some days I stand at the egg of the canyen and sprade my arms out wide wide wide and leen forword it is the wind holden me up. My Grandma tole me I am to skinny the wind mite pick me up and carry me a way.*

### The End

Mrs. Bittle made me stay after school. "I want to talk to you about your writing," she said. "You have a wonderful imagination!"

Sheila had always told me the same thing. It was her polite way of calling me a liar.

"It's the truth." I said.

"I didn't know you had this in you."

"My grandma used to tell me the truth is the hardest thing in the world for some folks to imagine."

"Is it?"

"No."

224

"We all need someone we can tell the truth to, Vanessa. When I correct your spelling or your grammar, I need you to understand. I'm not correcting what you say, only how you say it."

I didn't understand the difference, really. She said, for one thing, I needed to pay more attention to the correct spellings of the words I used.

"Oh."

"And how to use them to say what you want them to say."

"I just say it," I said. "I just say what it is."

"Exactly."

She explained to me that saying something and writing the same thing down were two entirely different forms of communication, with different rules. "If you tell me something in person, if I don't understand you, I can ask you questions about it. But if you write it down, you have to get it right the first time. That's why there are more rules, and the rules are stricter."

"And if I follow the rules, I can tell about whatever it is?"

"I will never correct you for telling me the truth, Vanessa. You can count on that."

I'm sure she never imagined, at the time we made that deal, how her words would come back to haunt her. I didn't need but a dose of encouragement here and there, and I took to paying attention to the way a sentence come apart and fit back together on the blackboard, though I have long since forgot the names of all the parts, and when I write a story down, I try to follow the way an actual person might tell it and not a person following a diagram in a book. I kept turning in my papers to her the following year, even though she was no longer my teacher. Not assignments but stories I wrote just for her. One of the rules we agreed to was that fiction could be my way of telling the truth, even though the details could be things I made up. Up until I gave her this one particular story, she encouraged me to keep writing and to keep sharing what I wrote with her, but after this one, she called our deal off. I had gone too far for her liking.

I 've taken the liberty of revising this one, cleaning up some of the grammar for you, and tons of spelling errors, which in this instance Mrs. Bittle did not bother to correct. I never gave the story a title. I think I meant to call it "The Problem with Cynthia."

What was left of them and their crew rolled down the hill with Jolly in his pickup truck and Jess and Brandon in back and Roy up front. Jolly was older than them, not really part of their crew, though he worked with them most of the time as an independent contractor the company hired. He was a welder. Adulio used to be with the crew but no more. Roy had run him off for causing what happened to Leo. "That's his car," Roy said. "He's still here, that shit-for-brains. That's his car. Pull up behind it." Jolly cut the motor and the lights and let the pickup tires drift up against the curb. Then they all piled out. Jolly and Roy walked slow and steady up the sidewalk like nothing was the matter. The other two ran the other way around the corner of the block to the alley that cut behind the houses on that side. Roy and Jolly stepped up on the little concrete porch with no roof and opened the screen door that had no screen in it. Roy knocked three times hard, real hard.

A face appeared in the window then disappeared again. They heard talking behind the door. "Prisa! Prisa!" the woman said inside.

"Open the door, Adulio! We want to talk to you."

Jolly laughed. "He ain't coming to the damn door, that's for sure." He pushed Roy to the side and raised his boot up high. He planted a kick right above the door knob. The door splintered around where the lock was located. Roy rammed it with his shoulder. It come open easier than he expected it to. He stumbled into the living room and seen Adulio's woman, wife, whatever she was called on the sofa with her feet pulled up under her and her kids huddled up against her, one boy and one girl. The boy started crying. Cynthia put a hand to his mouth. Cynthia looked like a white woman but she was a Mexican like Adulio. She could pass for Italian if she never opened her mouth.

"Not here," she told Roy in Spanglish. "Adulio no aqui."

Roy put his hands up in the air, showing her the palms of his hands. He talked real slow to her and stayed real calm. "Nobody's going to bother you, Cynthia. Not me, not Jolly, not nobody. No way. We just want to talk to Adulio."

Jolly walked past him into the kitchen. "He's gone out the back."

Roy told Cynthia to just stay put because nobody wanted to bother her. They were just after Adulio was all. He looked in the front bedroom, in the closet, in the bathroom that connected the two bedrooms and in the kids' bedroom in the back, just to make sure Adulio wasn't hiding anywhere inside the house. Then he come back and told Cynthia to just stay put again. "Aqui," he said. "You stay aqui, all right? All right." Then he chased after Jolly into the back yard. At least, he thought that's where Jolly went. He saw a flash in the alley and heard a gun go blam! and he run ducked over in that direction, saying, "God damn!" A woman screamed. Not Cynthia. It come from across the way. Two shadows raced down the alley, one in front of the other. He recognized them both, and neither one was Adulio. It was his two men, Brandon and Jess. Brandon had the weapon. He didn't know where Jolly had got to. He took off after the other two down the alley, but they were too far ahead. In some of the houses, he saw lights go on. In other houses, the lights went out.

A car started in the street. He run back to the house and through it, yelling, "Cynthia! Cynthia, goddamn it, I told you to stay put!" Cynthia was gone. She had taken her two kids with her. From the front porch, he saw the taillights of Adulio's car disappear around the corner.

Jolly come thrashing through the bushes between Adulio's house and the house next door. "Who brought the fucking artillery?" he wanted to know.

"Where did you get to?" Roy asked him.

"I thought I heard something. I was making sure he didn't climb out a window."

"Who the hell is Brandon firing at?"

"Fuck if I know. I didn't see hide nor hair of him."

Time was wasting. "She took the car. Let's get after her." Jolly followed him. They got in the truck and come up on Brandon and Jess several blocks away, leaning on their knees and breathing real hard. Brandon still had his Sig in his hand. Roy told him to put it away.

"Safety's on."

"Put it away. Nobody told you to bring the fucking thing."

"Nobody told me not to." Brandon grinned. "I think I got him."

"You better hope you didn't."

"No, I think I did. Tell him, Jess. He went down, motherfucker! Didn't he?"

"He did," Jess said.

"Where?"

"In the alley."

*Brandon laughed. He was out of breath yet and fell down on the ground, pretending to be Adulio. He still had the gun in his hand.*

*"In the alley?"*

*"Yeah, but he got up again. A car stopped and picked him up and took off this way."*

*"Jesus Christ! Get in the back."*

*"It was his car, I think. Was that her?"*

*"Get in the back."*

*"I thought you guys had her in the house."*

*Jolly leaned across Roy and hollered. "Get in! Or I'll leave your asses right here!"*

*They climbed into the bed of Jolly's pickup.*

*"Stupid fucks," Jolly said. "What do you want to do, go after him?"*

*"Shit. I don't know. What if she takes him to the hospital?"*

*Jolly didn't answer right away. He slipped the pickup into gear and tore off in that direction, the way they said the car went.*

*It all started because of her. Because Leo got it in his head that he had to be with her. Now he was out on workman's comp. Before the accident, so-called, Cynthia had tormented him something awful, but when he tried anything with her, she said she was married. She was Adulio's woman. Then one night after work at the Denim Blues Lounge, Leo got fed up with her. He saw her standing off by herself near the back door while Adulio wasn't paying attention and he took her outside and pushed her against the side of the building and kissed her. When that wasn't enough for him, he took her behind the building and pushed her down in the grass and did what he did. Nobody heard anything. It was Karaoke Night. He made her swear she wouldn't say word one to Adulio. "If you do, I'll make sure he gets picked up and shipped back to Mehico. Comprendie?"*

*But she didn't listen, did she? That was the problem with Cynthia.*

### The End

I understand a little better, these days, how a woman can come to make certain compromises in life, but I only meant to let Mrs. Bittle know, on the sly, what I had pieced together from the late-night knock-down drag-outs I overheard between Sheila and Leon–namely, that her husband, Cecil, and Jolly the welder in my story were not entirely different people. Cecil was maybe not a rapist and maybe not a murderer, but almost as bad as both. I figured I was doing his wife a favor letting her know. That was part of it, anyway — the part I told myself in order to justify my story to myself. The real reason I wrote it and gave it to her, I now think, was I needed somebody else to know I was living under the same roof as the one I so carefully disguised as "Leo."

I needed a witness, somebody besides me to know the reason Leon walked with a cane. To my thirteen-going-on-fourteen-year-old mind, the best way to describe my situation was to make up a story.

Mrs. Bittle handed it back to me the next day after school with not a single mark on it, though I can assure you it had plenty of mistakes. Without looking at me, she said, "I don't believe I want to read any more like this."

And that was that. She never said to stop telling her the truth. But I got the message.

# PATTERSON PRICE

Patterson left me on my own in Massachusetts. Not right away, but eventually he had to. I was fourteen and dangerous. We'd crossed state lines. He hadn't thought things through. He had school yet to finish.

We stayed in Beverly for only a couple of weeks. In August we took a ride through the back-country hills and ended up on a highway that went snaking alongside a broad, shallow river, then a steep drop on my side of the road where a different river leaped and squirreled its way between gigantic white boulders as the road twisted higher and higher into the mountains. Patter pulled off on a wide gravel area and we traipsed down to the river so he could pee. Then we took off our shoes and picked our way across half-submerged rocks to a flat-topped boulder in the middle of the stream where we could sit and talk.

He said, "I could live in a place like this."

So of course I said, "Me, too."

I knew he was leaving, I knew our time was short, but I had every expectation that he'd come back between semesters and on spring break. Then he would graduate from O. U. He said Massachusetts had the best law schools in the country. Harvard wasn't out of the question. His considerations swam in the air above me like dragonflies, darting, iridescent, out of my reach yet all mine to behold. I studied the rise of his cheek as I lay back across the hard slant of the boulder, listening to his dream of building a house on a bridge, right where we sat, with the little river running underneath the glass floor of our living room.

I had not a doubt in the world that he loved me, that he would come back to me when he could. We hopped from rock to rock across the frigid water to reclaim our shoes, then climbed back up the bank to the car. The mountains grew steeper and greener until we crested one that looked down across a broad green valley with a town nestled in the forest. I gasped. I was born and raised a flatlander, and even though we had traveled through the Smoky Mountains of Tennessee and along the Blue Ridge Mountains in Virginia, we had done a good deal of that driving late at night. I had never felt as high up as this, never seen the Earth stretched out at my feet before. I realized for the first time in my life—what I mean to say, I understood with my own two eyes—that I lived on a planet, that it was round like they said. It changed something in me that would never change back, that moment did, that view.

Patterson pointed at the mountains in the distance. "That's New York over there." Then he swung his arm in another direction and said, "That's Vermont."

Little did I know the town down below me would become my home, that I would live cradled between these mountains, hemmed in, with no way to get back up where I could see the world again as it truly was. Patter found me another apartment, little bitty, in a blue house with five other apartments in it, furnished.

He had another surprise for me, a card. "It's your birthday," he said, though it wasn't.

Let me back up.

He had asked me once, on the long ride out (I think it was in a motel room in Tennessee), if I could pick a name, any name in the world, what name would I choose to go by?

I didn't hesitate. I said, "Anastasia." Not that there was anything significant about that name. If he'd asked me the same question on a different day, I might've said Marylin or Cleopatra or Christ knows what.

The card he handed me was a driver's license. It said my name was Anastasia Veronica Anatoly and my birthday was August 3, 1972. He said, "You were born in Georgia. Not the state, the country."

I never even knew there was a country named Georgia.

"In Eastern Europe. It's part of the Soviet Union. Your parents defected in 1974. They raised you in the South, in the other Georgia. That explains your accent."

"My accent?" I knew I had one, but I didn't think it was that bad. I couldn't take my eyes off my new name. I was a princess!

"Trust me, nobody will believe you just stepped off the boat."

My story had gaping holes in it, as you might imagine. I knew as much about the Great State of Georgia, the U. S. one where he said I was brought up, as I did about the country where I was supposedly born, but the town of North Adams, Massachusetts, was foreign enough to both of those places that, with a little practice and him to coach me, I figured I could fudge it. We spent the next two weeks pretending, telling each other stories about my loving parents, Tamaz and Anamaria, and how all in the world they ever wanted was for me to be happy and free and to become a United States citizen and a big success.

"I'll send you money," he promised, "but if anybody asks, you can say it comes from your father. We should get you a job."

"I don't know how to do anything except go to school, and I ain't very good at that, either."

"College, maybe. You're too old to go to high school."

I snorted.

"No, seriously. You graduated from Northside High School in Columbus."

"Oh, yeah. I remember now. I was a cheerleader."

He liked that idea, I could tell. We fucked our brains out for those two weeks, knowing it was all we had left. I cried a few brave tears, missing him already but knowing as deep down as I knew my multiplication tables that it was only temporary, that he loved me, that our separation would be as hard on him as on me but that, in the long run, it would be worth it. Once he had his law degree, I would be eighteen for real, and he could tell his parents to shove it if they didn't like it. I would be his lawfully wedded.

"You *are* eighteen. For real. Nothing is more real than what's documented. You have to believe in it yourself, Ana. You have to believe in it one hundred percent, or none of this is going to work."

I kissed him to make him shut up, because it hurt too much to hear him call me that and to know he wouldn't be there to remind me and that I could so easily forget and fuck it up, fuck it all up and ruin it for him and disappoint him. I was scared of that more than anything, more than dying, more than being alone in a strange place, more than being found and convicted of murder and dragged off to prison for the rest of my life, more than all my nightmares put together.

And then he was gone.

Until you try, you have no idea how easy it is to be someone you're not. And no idea how impossible it is to not be yourself. The lies rolled off my tongue as fluid as the truth, until I discovered nobody was listening. My neighbors' concerns did not concern me, and vice versa. Three were students at the college in town, one was a couple with two kids. The wife, Lillian, screamed at them all day long. I took to not being in my apartment as much as possible and wishing I did have a job to go to. I intended on going to college myself, since I legally could, but I knew I'd have to get smarter, or at least sound smarter. I spent most of my days at the public library, looking up words. Big words. The nicest thing about being Anastasia Veronica Anatoly was Anastasia never had a mentally retarded mother.

One of the students must have graduated that year. She moved out shortly after I moved in. Her apartment stood empty for a while before an old guy took it. From day one he did not put up with Lillian's bullshit. I overheard him telling her he just got out of the House of Correction and he didn't mind going back if she didn't shut her goddamn mouth. His name was Franklin.

Franklin was not one bit shy about looking at me. "Yuh not eighteen," he said in what I would come to find out was a Boston accent, very different from the way other North Adams people talked.

I sat on the front stoop, which is what they call a porch up there, looking across at the side of Mount Greylock of an evening, where it rose up behind the rooftops with its summit among the clouds like a judge's head in a powdered wig. Franklin perched next to me, leaning against the post that held up the little porch roof. He studied me. He shook out a cigarette and offered me one. I said no thanks, I didn't smoke.

"Bother you if I do?"

"Nope."

He shifted around and poked my knee with his bare big toe. "Yuh not eighteen," he said again.

I didn't answer him.

He poked me with his toe again, higher up on my leg. I was in cutoffs. "How old are you?"

I slapped his foot. "Nunya."

"Oh, well, I beg your pahdon!" He laughed a raspy Marlboro Man laugh and said yet again, "Yuh not eighteen, I know that."

"Whatever."

"Where you from, kid? Or is that none of my business, too?"

I said, "Georgia."

"Oh, yah? What paht?"

I was glad he asked that, because I knew the answer. "Columbus."

His smoke drifted high and disappeared against the gray of the clouds. "What brings you up here?"

Nobody had come right out and asked before. I figured he already didn't believe me, so I might as well practice my powers of persuasion on a skeptic as a regular person. "I'm here to establish residency. I'm going to college next year."

"Uh huh."

"Uh huh," I said right back at him. "It's cheaper that way. I don't want my folks throwing away good money for nothing."

He laughed again. "I'm not the college type."

The funny thing about a lie is it has just as much power to make a person feel superior as the truth, if you let it. "What type are you?" I said, "The prison type?"

He ran his fingers along his cheek as if checking to see if he needed a shave. Which he did. I could tell he was calculating some kind of response I didn't want to hear, so I got up and went inside and locked the door to my apartment.

I knew how to do most things. Grandma taught me how to cook, and I basically took care of everything after she died, what with Sheila working the four-to-midnight shift in Enid and sleeping most days until noon, while Leon did nothing twenty-four seven. He did watch Lisa Julene while I was at school, but I did all the cooking and cleaning when I got home. I bathed Lisa J. and played with her and put her to bed and all like that. The one thing I didn't know how to do was grocery shop at a Big Y instead of the I.G.A. back home. That, and entertain myself.

So I took a notebook and pen and went up and down the aisles at the grocery, listing everything they had that I knew what it was and how to cook with it and I made myself a diagram. Patterson had left some money in a bank account in my fake name, and he paid my rent and utilities, I guess by mail. I knew he was rich, but I didn't know how rich until I went to the bank to draw out some cash and asked how much was in there. I gaped at the teller when she handed me the slip with my balance on it. Twelve hundred was more than I could ever imagine spending on myself. I figured Patter must have meant it to stretch until he came back in December, but there was a lot I didn't know, a lot I didn't anticipate.

Franklin soon got work at a bar on Union Street, which left no one to keep Lillian in check. She had some kind of Franklin radar that told her when he stepped out, so she could jack up the volume on her shrieking and dropping the f-bomb on her husband and kids (the boy was four years old and his little sister still in diapers) while I knelt over my toilet bowl, hurling. Something in the New England climate made me sick, I figured, until I mentioned it to Franklin.

He brought home a motorcycle one day and wanted to show it off to me. "Hop on! I'll take you for a ride."

"I don't feel so good."

"What's the matter?"

"I just feel sick. Don't matter what I eat."

He diagnosed me on the spot. Leaning back astride his bike with his arms crossed on his chest, he made a face like I was trying to put one over on him. "Yuh pregnant."

"No, I'm not pregnant. I'm sick."

"Yeah, all right."

"I wish I could," I said. "I'd get you to take me up on top of the mountain, so I could look down again. I only been up there once."

He asked a battery of questions that confirmed my condition—in his mind, anyway. "How about I take you to a doctor instead?"

The next day, I heard his bike pull up and shut off and him come knocking at my door. When I answered, he handed me a white paper sack with a home pregnancy test in it. I handed it back to him. "Very funny. I'm not pregnant."

"Listen, Red." He always called me Red, not Ana. Lillian and Tom were the only ones who called me Anastasia. "I'm not being funny. I know it's none of my business, but you need to know, don't you? Just fucking take the fucking test. You don't have to tell me what the results are."

I told him.

He was the only person I told. The only person in the world. Except, obviously, my doctor, later on.

I had a notebook I wrote letters in, one after another, to Patter. I never mailed them, because I didn't have an address. I planned on just giving him the notebook when he came at Christmastime. I didn't call him, either. I had a phone but no number for him. (We had to keep everything secret for a few years until he finished law school.) I didn't even write it down that I was pregnant. What if I wasn't? Or what if I was but something happened and I, you know—got over it? Franklin Swansea was no doctor.

He said I needed to make an appointment with one.

Of course, they wanted to see my insurance card, and I didn't have one. "I got money," I told them. I had no earthly idea how expensive it was just to get looked at and weighed and have blood drawn and to pee in a cup.

Long story short, I was totally preggers.

I couldn't wait to tell Patter. I wrote all about it in big block letters in my notebook before reality set in. He still had years of schooling left in front of him. I had no way to get in touch with him, to warn him. When he showed up in December, I'd be, what? Four months along? I'd be looking like I swallowed a watermelon seed. It was already hard to remember him exactly as he was, the exact shape of his jaw line, the right shade of blue in his eye. What I most remembered were his hands, the way he could squeeze my middle so tight he could touch his thumbs and middle fingers around me, that's how long they were. That's how skinny I was. How skinny I was supposed to be.

I ripped those pages out of my notebook.

"What am I gonna do?" I asked Franklin.

"Yuh not getting an abortion," he said, "that's for damn sure." With his accent (he grew up on the Noth Shaw) "abortion" came out ab-washion.

So I wasn't getting one. Franklin was Catholic, and that was that. I had no one else on Earth I could ask, even if I wanted to. He took me to sign up for all kinds of things, because just that one appointment had close to wiped out my bank account. That was the first of many problems I encountered. All I had for identification was my fake driver's license. No Social Security, no birth certificate, nothing.

Franklin drove me up the hill to the Emergency Room at the hospital. "You need anything, you come here," he said. "They can't refuse you treatment." Then he wanted to know who I was, really. "Don't lie to me, Red. I hate being lied to."

I told him everything except Patterson's name. I told him about Leon, how I hadn't meant to kill him, how I had been blamed already for my grandmother's death, and how I couldn't go back to Oklahoma, not for any reason. He had done time. I figured he would understand.

"You're a hot tomato, aren't you?"

"I guess so." Whatever that meant.

"So that makes you what? Twelve? Thirteen?"

I couldn't even pretend to be insulted. "Fifteen next month," I mumbled. It was already October.

"I got news for you, kid. You're not gonna want to hear it."

"What?"

"This so-called boyfriend of yours? He's not coming back for you, I guarantee you that."

"You don't know."

"I don't know much, but I know that."

You might not think so—I certainly didn't at the time—but that remark ranks among the kindest things anyone has ever said to me. I knew it was true, though I resolutely did not admit it to myself. Patterson Price was no longer real to me. I couldn't touch him or talk to him, couldn't even conjure him at night, alone in my bed, or remember what it felt like to kiss him. I could call to mind the coils of his pubic hair and the way his penis nested in his balls when he slept, but only because I had never seen one before his. It came as a shock to me to lift the sheet off him early one morning in a motel room—not the first one, but one of the many—after he'd fucked me with it how many times by then? to find it so much smaller than I thought, like a bald little mouse curled up and hibernating.

I didn't want that to be my single most durable memory of him. For that reason as much as any other, I clung to the belief that, come December, I could count down the days until I saw his face again and heard his voice. I would do so much better at remembering him the second time around. I would study him like there was going to be a test.

Only there wasn't. Franklin was right about that, too.

One thing he wasn't right about.

"Yuh sister's got to be looking for you. This guy, whatever his name is, he's already been picked up by the police. I mean, just logically speaking. He's the last person anyone saw you with, right?"

He waited for me to acknowledge the obvious, but I didn't.

"Then he goes missing for how long? And so do you?"

"All summer." The words deflated me.

"So let's say he shows up again. He's had time to make up a story for Mumsy and Daddy, but what do you think he tells the cops?"

"I don't know."

"He can't tell them anything about you, that's for damn sure. He's got to say he dropped you off at your house and that was the last he saw of you. Nothing else he can say. Now, let me ask you something. You think the cops are gonna buy that story?"

How could I possibly answer that? I didn't have to.

"Not for a goddamn minute. They're still watching him. He could be locked up. At the very least, the cops are watching every move he makes. If they found so much as a single fingerprint of his in your house, he's their number one suspect, not you. They've got to have him figured for two murders, not just one."

"Two?"

"Sweetheart, if no one has come knocking on your door in all this time, it's because they're too busy combing the forest for your grave."

"What forest?" I laughed. There was no forest within a hundred miles of Keening. It wasn't a happy laugh, it was just that I hadn't ever looked at it the way he did. Why would I? I was still alive.

"I beg to differ. Anastasia Goddamn Whatthefuck is still alive. Whoever you used to be, that girl is dead."

"Okay." I needed a good reason not to believe his theory. "I've been honest with you. Will you be honest with me?"

"Sure," he said. Shoowah.

"What were you in prison for?"

"First of all, I picked up a county bid. The House of Correction is not prison. State time is prison."

"Jail is jail."

He just looked at me and nodded. "Weed."

"You're a drug dealer?"

He laughed. "I'm on parole, so no. I have to go piss in a cup every so often down in Pittsfield, whenever my number comes up. I step outta line, I go back inside, no questions asked. That's not happening."

"You told Lillian you wouldn't mind. I heard you."

"I was bluffing."

I laughed.

"Worked, didn't it?"

"Sure did! Oh, my gowad!" I said and made myself laugh. I sounded just like him. "You must be rubbing off on me."

I cried and cried at Christmastime, but I was secretly — and by that I mean, it was a secret I kept even from myself — secretly relieved that Patterson didn't come. I had a job by that time that I could walk to, at Burger King, so I could afford to buy my own groceries. I never saw the landlord or even thought much about paying rent. In retrospect, Patterson must have paid my entire lease up front, which included utilities. A large sum of money did appear one more time in my bank account, but never again after that.

I cooked for Franklin a time or two. He never made any kind of move or anything. He gave me the creeps in the very beginning, but it turned out he wasn't actually like that. When he got back from visiting his family in Charlestown, I asked if he had a girlfriend there. He said no, and I said—not right away, but later on in the conversation, "Do you think I'm gross?" I was showing pretty good by then.

He answered real slow. "No. I don't think you're gross. I think you're barely fifteen, and that's as far as this conversation's going."

"Anastasia Anatoly is nineteen."

"But you're not."

"Nobody else knows that."

"Too bad. I do."

My eyes filled up. I looked away so he wouldn't see, but my voice betrayed me. "What if I never told you?"

"You didn't have to."

Which was true but beside the point, as far as I was concerned. I was over Patterson but I wasn't over being pregnant by a long shot, so call it what you want. Maybe it was part of my biological nesting instinct to be on the lookout for a suitable baby daddy, but as I saw it, I had fallen in true love with the kindest, toughest man I knew, and why not? At least I could call up his face in my mind's eye.

I can to this day. He had three little lines underneath his right eye and a crease at the opposite corner of his mouth, plus a dimple in that cheek that crinkled when he smiled and sometimes when he just talked. He had freckles on his forearms, not as dark as mine and nowhere else that I knew of, and hair that varied in color according to the light. Sometimes it had a reddish tinge but more often it was the color of sand or (since sand can mean almost anything) the color of trees in winter, far off against the mountains of Massachusetts—not when it snows but the rest of the time, like the color of cardboard, like the back cover of my notebook where I no longer told my secrets to Patterson Price but, without his knowledge, to Franklin Swansea, drug-dealing motorcycle man whose voice grumbled like a Harley in the morning and smoothed out some on the long, straightaway of an afternoon.

MY NAME IS MUD

My due date was still a ways off when my water broke in the middle of the night. I banged on Franklin's door. He stood there in his boxers with a baseball bat in his hand, and I stood there in a fresh pair of panties and pajama bottoms and a long jersey, holding my belly.

He leaned the bat against the wall. "I'll call an ambulance."

He went to find his phone. I braced myself in his doorway, spasming so hard I couldn't speak. When I could, I said, "I don't know if I can wait that long."

"You're gonna have to. Come in and sit down." He came back in a pair of jeans and a sweat shirt, talking on the phone, giving his address. He pointed at his sofa.

"I can't!"

He moved me by the shoulders. "Lay down, then." He repeated the address to the dispatcher.

"I can't do that, either." I sat down.

He sat beside me and put his boots on. I must have looked at him funny. "I'll follow the ambulance," he said.

Another wave hit me. I half-stood, half-laid down, my mouth making an o because I couldn't breathe or think or know what to do. He brought me a long-sleeved shirt to put on and a pair of his socks and led me downstairs to wait on the stoop.

The next time it hit me, I grabbed him and buried my face against him. When it passed, I said, "You have to take me."

"On my bike? You out of your fucking mind?"

"If we leave right this minute, we've got time before the next one comes."

"No way."

I leaned against him, sweating in the cool night air. "Then you have to carry me."

"Not happening."

"I just want this over with."

He smoked a cigarette.

I was going to have a boy. I knew that, and I knew he didn't have Downs Syndrome or anything else obviously wrong with him. I didn't have any complications to speak of, no sugar diabetes or anything. But I was as scared as I could be that something would come up last minute. I knew I could hemorrhage and die. I knew the cord could wrap around the baby's neck and strangle him, or he could get turned

240

around and try to come out backwards and they'd have to cut me open. Right that minute, I was most afraid I would deliver there on the front stoop in the middle of the night, and as competent as Franklin was in every other area of life, as near as I could judge, I didn't think he was cut out for midwifery.

He smoked his cigarette all the way down and tossed it in the yard before I had another spasm. After it came and went, I said, "See? You could've got me there by now."

I doubled over two more times before the ambulance pulled up. I won't take you through the entire ordeal. You've either been there or you haven't. It was light outside before I pushed one final time, and out slipped Marshall Caleb Anatoly. I picked that name figuring I could later have it changed to Marshall Caleb Cavendish, which sounded more like it. They cleaned him up and rested him on top of me, skin to skin, both of us worn out, and everything so perfect, really, outside of everything that wasn't, that I just cried and cried and held him and fell asleep before they came and took him and told me I couldn't do that. I might roll over on him and suffocate him.

Franklin came and saw me before he had to go to work in the afternoon. He brought me flowers in a vase with a little teddy bear tied to it with a ribbon.

"Did you see him?" I asked. I had never been so proud of anything in my life. I kept asking all the nurses and the aides and doctors and everyone who came in to check on me for any reason, "Did you see my baby?"

"Looks just like his ma," Franklin said. "If you shaved your head, you'd look just like him, too."

I laughed because I was just so happy. Worried, too, don't get me wrong. But the reality of my situation hadn't set in yet. Not fully. I mean, I had thought and thought about it. I had no job now and no money coming in. The landlord had sent me a letter saying my lease was up come the end of July, which was two months away, but Franklin said to just stay put. They couldn't kick me out, he said, not with a baby. He said social services would be on my side. He had already taken me around to so many places, getting me set up in advance with Food Stamps and WIC and everything, so at least I knew what to do, and I felt like I could almost manage. At least until I got on my feet again.

I say "again" like I ever knew what it was to be on my own. I remembered my grandma telling me how and why I had to live under Sheila's dominion, because I couldn't take care of myself, and part of me wanted to say I guess I showed her.

The other ninety percent looked at Franklin and said, "How am I gonna do this for real?"

"You'll manage."

"I couldn't manage anything if it wasn't for you."

I saw in his eyes that he agreed with me, and the truth of what I'd just said bore down on me so hard it broke me, and I sobbed. He held me, and I clung to his shirt and breathed his stale cigarette smell, knowing it wasn't good for me or the baby, and his closeness only drove home the fact that, though he was by far the closest, most familiar friend I had, he remained, for all intents and purposes, a stranger. He wouldn't be around forever for me to lean on. I saw that, too, in his eyes.

"You don't give yourself enough credit," he said, rubbing my shoulders and squeezing me.

But I was alone, and I knew it. Worse than that, my baby was alone with me. "I have to get back to Keening, that's what I have to do."

"Is it?"

"I know it is. Even if I do end up in jail. At least Marshall Caleb will have an aunt there to look out for him and a cousin to play with." I didn't know if it was the right decision, but it was a decision. I felt like I needed to make one. Yet no sooner did I make it than I second-guessed myself. "What would you do?"

He held my head against his heart, his big fingers pressing the side of my face. "You're asking the wrong guy," he said. His voice sounded like tires on a gravel driveway, pulling away. "I can't leave the Commonwealth."

"I wish you could."

I wanted him to say, why didn't I wait the four months until his parole was up? But he didn't. Or why didn't I just stay put? But he didn't say that, either.

"I'm gonna miss you when I go."

He didn't even say, "I'll miss you too."

"You gonna come see me, at least, when you get off parole?"

"In Oklahoma?" He made it sound like the moon. "You'll have to send me directions."

"Don't think I won't," I lied.

I let him go. It was about time to feed Marshall, and I hadn't had much practice yet. I went down the hall to see him, but he wasn't in his crib, so I went back to my room, figuring they must be bringing him to me.

He never came.

I went back to the nursery, and he still wasn't there. I tapped on the glass to get the nurse's attention. "It's past time for my baby's feeding," I said. "I don't see him."

The nurse or assistant or whatever she was, holding someone else's baby on her shoulder, shaking it up and down, said, "Let me see who's got her."

"Him." I told her his name and pointed to his crib.

I went back to my room to wait, but he never came.

He never came.

Different ones kept telling me to be patient, they'd find him. My milk let down and stained my johnny. Someone came and cleaned me up and brought me a new one, but it didn't matter. They still hadn't found my baby. I went right in the nursery with them pulling at me and telling me I couldn't, but I shook them off and slapped one of them pretty hard across the shoulder and kept going from crib to crib, thinking he had to be in there, they just got him mixed up, put him in the wrong crib. "Did you give him to somebody else to feed?" I pushed my way back out to the hallway. "Who's got my baby?" I went from room to room. "You got my baby? You got my baby?" I honestly don't remember what all I did and said. I do remember trying to fight off two security guards who grabbed me and carried me by the arms as I tried to twist and kick my way free to go find my baby, until we all ended up on the floor, and they got the better of me.

I woke up god knows how many hours later strapped to a bed in a different room in a different part of the hospital, groggy as all hell. I don't remember them shooting me up with anything, but they must have.

The police came, a man and a woman. They wanted to know who had been in to see me, and I told them it had nothing to do with Franklin, but of course they stayed pretty focused on him and on who the father was.

"It's not the father, either." I didn't say his name. "He doesn't even know. Why aren't you down there talking to the nurses? They're the ones who know where my baby is."

Instead of that, they wanted to know all about my parents and where they lived. I had enough presence of mind to say "Georgia. Not the country, the state. They moved from there to here." I tried to think of the name of the city in Georgia where they lived. "I'm not even sure," I said.

It got very confused after that, because they kept insisting I said my parents had moved here, meaning Massachusetts, but they didn't believe that, either, nor Georgia, because earlier I must have said something about Oklahoma. It had been such a long time since I practiced any part of my story that finally I just said. "No. They're dead."

"Now your parents are dead," one of them said, the guy cop. It wasn't a question. He was looking at his partner when he said it.

She said, "Do you have any siblings?"

"No."

"Aunts? Uncles? Cousins?"

I wasn't sure. We'd never talked about that.

"Any other family who might know about you and your baby?"

"No," I said. "Nobody. That's just it. I never told a soul. Not one soul except, you know, people who knew me, like my neighbors. People I couldn't hide it from."

"Why don't you tell us who the father is?"

"I can't. It's not important. It wasn't him. The only people who know I even have a baby are right here in this hospital. They're the ones who are supposed to be in charge of him." I needed to get up and go do something, not lay there and talk. "They can't keep me here like this, can they?"

Turned out they could.

Some days, none of it feels like it was ever real. Like I never actually had a baby. And yet it never gives me any peace. A doctor—not my doctor—came and informed me of what I already knew, explained to me what I already understood. He had a black mustache that moved like a cartoon mouth, only approximating the shapes of the words I heard him speak. Marshall Caleb was not in the hospital. Someone had apparently taken him.

"Why have you got me tied up like this?"

He said I had assaulted people. He said I was understandably upset, but they could not let me continue to hurt people or violate hospital rules.

I sat propped up on my elbows, the restraints pulling at me. "I just want to know where my baby is. You bring me my baby, you won't have to worry about me yelling and screaming and upsetting everybody else that thinks their babies are safe in your hospital."

He didn't want to hear that.

The more helpless I felt, the more frantic I got and the more I wanted to get out of bed and go find my baby. But the more I tried to get up, the more they wanted to keep me there, and the more helpless I felt.

"You lost my baby!" I screamed at him the next time he came. "And I'm the criminal?" I cut him off before he could answer. "This hospital lost my baby! And they have to be protected from me?" I tried to explain the backwardness of the situation, but Dr. Mustache was fixated on something else.

Apparently, I wasn't who I said I was.

I failed to see how that mattered, really.

He seemed to think it did.

"What's it gonna take for me to get out of this goddamn bed so I can get out of this goddamn hospital and find out what happened to my baby?"

"Why don't you start by telling me your real name?"

No way I was doing that. I repeated my question, until finally he told me something I'd hear a lot over the next few days.

"You'll have to contract for safety."

I said, "What?"

He let me know on behalf of the entire staff of the hospital how they wouldn't feel very safe if he let me out of restraints and that I would have to convince him that I wouldn't try to hurt anybody else.

"I never tried to hurt anybody in my life," I said. "Not ever."

"You'll need to convince me that you can remain in control of your behavior."

"You mean not get upset that y'all can't find my baby?"

He changed the subject. "I have some news for you, if you're ready to hear it."

"What news?"

"The police may have a lead. They might know something."

"What? Tell me!"

It turned out a nursing assistant, one who hadn't been working there very long and who had been on duty the last time anyone saw Marshall Caleb, a woman by the name of Ellen Haddick, did not show up for her shift the next day. She also did not finish out her shift the day Marshall disappeared. She left without saying anything to anybody and without punching her time card. The police went to her apartment, but she did not answer her door. They got a search warrant, but when they got inside, it was empty. It looked like no one had been living there for weeks, maybe months. The same woman cop told me this. When I asked how they could tell, she said the place was dusty.

"Does that name mean anything to you? Ellen Haddick."

I said, "No."

"Is she related to you?"

"No. I don't think so."

Maybe she was related to Anastasia, though — the girl I was supposed to be? I've had a lot of time to think about it over the years. I've tried everywhichway to make sense of it. Somebody wanted a baby, and they decided to take mine. Maybe Ellen Haddick wanted Marshall Caleb for herself or maybe she stole him for money. There are more mysteries in life than solid facts, has been my conclusion, and my baby's disappearance falls into that category. I did have a theory now, thanks to Mr. Andrew Blake, but I couldn't prove it. If it was true, it provided me no comfort and no hope. Quite the opposite.

Patterson Price did end up going to Harvard Law School. There was a reason he picked Massachusetts to take me to, because his family had connections there, in Boston. Powerful ones, names you might recognize. He did very well for himself up at Harvard, all unbeknownst to me.

I still didn't know if he ever found out he had a son. By me, I mean. He did have three boys that looked like different versions of how he must have looked at their ages. They had smiles that must have cost a fortune apiece. I would've liked to believe he never did know about Marshall Caleb, that somebody else found out about me and him and had us followed and figured out the rest. Or just came and found me and reasoned the easiest thing to do was get rid of the evidence.

My baby, in other words.

If nothing like that happened, why send Mr. Blake to talk to me about it? Where did he get his information? I tiptoed around and around these questions in my head and found no comfortable place to sit with them.

You know by now that I exaggerated when I told Jeannie they ripped Marshall Caleb out of my arms, but not by as much as you'd think. That was how it felt. That's how it still feels. Like one minute he was in my arms and the next he was gone. And I have never had a good enough imagination to make myself believe in a fairy tale ending where the Price family took Marshall Caleb in as one of their own, or one where they found a good home for him, a nice family. Or any family at all.

Evidently, I did not give Mr. Andrew Blake the answers he hoped to hear, because Patterson Price never mounted a campaign for President of these United States, and though there was speculation about him in the news, no one took him as a running mate, either. Which may or may not have had anything to do with me and the story I never told.

# PART 4

# SHE TALKS TO ANGELS

# BUDDHISM 101

I almost didn't recognize her, she'd cut her hair so short. Or had it cut. Chin length, dyed the color of dark chocolate. Unsweetened. Her makeup had a more refined edge to it than her usual battered-junkie look. And she'd put on weight.

"I like it," I told her. We sat in a day room on a locked ward with posters of sunsets and inspirational sayings on the walls.

Jeannie scrambled her brow. "You like what?"

"Your hair."

She jutted her chin in acknowledgment, a kind of reverse nod. Even her mannerisms had undergone a makeover. She changed the subject. "You came a long way."

"I drove out last night and stayed over."

"They let you do that?"

"At a motel."

"Oh." She let a beat pass. "Why?"

"I went to the hospital in Enid. You weren't there, so I called your mom. She told me you'd been transferred. By the time I got here, it was past visiting hours.

"That's not what I meant."

"Right," I said. Then, "I need to apologize."

She gave me a lop-sided grin. "Hasn't God granted you the serenity to accept the things you cannot change?"

"I guess not."

"You can't change the past, Vanessa."

"No. I can't."

"I've had some time to think."

I waited.

"About you and me." She reached across the table and scratched the backs of my fingernails with the tips of hers. The gesture surprised me with its tenderness. "They want to wash your sins away," she said. "And you want to let them try, don't you?"

"They who?"

She made an exasperated sound with her lips. My question evidently did not merit more of a reply. "Thing is, Vanessa, I don't just come out in the wash. I still see you for who you are. You know I always will."

"Who am I, in your eyes?"

"A sinner."

I rolled my eyes.

"A sinner in the hands of an angry god." She winked. "Like me."

"What kind of drugs have they got you on?"

She wagged a finger in my face. "Oh, no, no, no. I'm not taking anything, and neither should you. That's what forgiveness is, you know. It's a drug. You take it, it makes you think everything's okay. But everything is not okay, because you can't change the past. You do know that?"

"Yeah, I think I got that."

"Forgiveness won't unkill your grandmother."

"No," I said evenly, "it won't."

"It won't unkill your sister's husband."

"That is also true."

"It won't unkill your baby."

I did not have a reply to that. Not right away. Finally I said, "You like to twist the knife, don't you?"

She sat back, looking pleased with herself. The gesture of her hand said *Look at me!* Her mouth said, "I am the new high priestess of bloodletting. I wear the crown now."

"Congratulations."

According to Pastor Wingate, the word "sin" was originally an archery term meaning you missed your mark. It made me think of the stories I used to turn in to Mrs. Bittle, of all the misspelled words and grammar mistakes and half-assed logic. She liked to point out my writing sins to me with her red felt-tipped pen to make them stand out even worse. I wondered if there wasn't something about the color red that scratched an itch for her, satisfied the urge to draw blood. "We are born in sin," Wingate preached. "Born in blood, marked by blood. Medical science tells us that every cell of our bodies is fed by blood. The Bible tells us God demands a blood sacrifice for our sins."

That sermon played in the back of my mind as I sat there, looking at Jeannie Ivory. "I didn't come here to have my blood let," I informed her.

"Did you come to ask my forgiveness?"

"I came to apologize."

"Somebody once told me apologies don't mean shit. You were right about that. An apology is about yesterday. I only care about right now. Did you come to tell me you love me?"

I wondered whether she might be making some kind of joke.

"Because you still haven't done that."

"No. No, I haven't."

"You didn't come to apologize to me, Vanessa. You came because you want me to apologize to you, so you can forgive me. So you can wash my sins away. Maybe then you can love me."

"I wouldn't know where to begin."

"No. You wouldn't."

"I'm open to suggestions."

"No, you're not."

"Okay. This was a mistake." I looked around at the day room with its heavy, wipe-able plastic-covered foam chairs and fake oak tables bolted to the floor. "I hope they can do you some good here."

"Like what? Change the past?"

"No, look. You're wrong about that. I was wrong. Forgiveness is not about the past. The way I see it, it's about the here and now. You have to let a wound close, so it can heal, instead of always probing it and picking at it. It's about understanding the other person's point of view and why they must have done something to you in the first place. I don't want to forgive you, I want to understand you. If I can."

"Oh, you want to understand me! You want to understand my point of view! Why? So you can correct it? So you can explain to me how your point of view is superior to mine? The problem with that is, I already understand your point of view, Vanessa. It's just like everybody else's point of view: Jeannie Ivory is some special kind of crazy. But you know what's funny about that? They still haven't given me a diagnosis. The truth is a little simpler than mental illness. The problem is, I know what nobody else is willing to admit."

"What's that? That other people are a figment of your imagination?"

"No. That's just Buddhism 101. One thing you did for me. To give credit where credit is due, you helped me figure out it's more than me and my imagination. Eugene is a figment of the collective imagination. Everybody's. Yours, mine, the whole town's. Thanks to you, I got away from the insanity. I put some distance between me and everybody else.

It allows me to see the situation a little more objectively than the average bear."

"And that's thanks to me?"

"Yes, thanks to you."

"Glad I could help."

"Before I met you, all I could do was feed him. A little bit at a time, then a little more and a little more, until he gradually took everything from me. Before you, I was afraid to care about anything or anyone, because I knew if I did, he'd find a way to take it from me. He did, anyway, didn't he? He took you. Didn't I tell you he would? But never mind that. You showed me the way. You said I needed to go deeper. And that's exactly what I did."

"Go deeper? I said that? And you thought I meant with a knife?"

"It doesn't matter what you meant. You think understanding your point of view means I have to adopt it as my own, but I don't. You think going deeper with a knife is one thing and 'going deeper' in the abstract, is something else. And guess what? I can forgive you for thinking that way, because that's how they think, and you're one of them now. That's how they operate, separating fact from imagination, the body from the mind, the literal from the metaphorical."

"You lost me."

"Christians. Everybody."

"Uh, okay." I had my purse strap over my shoulder, one foot pointed at the door.

"The whole religion — most human religion, in fact — is based on human sacrifice. Sit down, please? Hear me out."

God knows why I didn't just leave. I had driven all that way, put an extra three hundred miles on Jiminy's odometer, and for what? So I could listen to the screws in Jeannie's head work themselves completely loose? But I didn't go. I sat down.

"I've watched them do it, Vanessa. We're all swimming around in the dark, all of us. And they know that. They lure you in with sweetness and light, the way an angler fish lures its prey. They make you want to belong to them. They want your soul. That's how they pay for their sins. Not with blood. That's old school. Christians pay in souls, in the souls they collect for Jesus. We don't use real money anymore, we use plastic, and they don't use real blood. But there's always that one stubborn one. That one soul they know they can never have. That one gets marked for sacrifice."

"And that would be you?"

"Not anymore. I gave at the office. I'm paid in full, in real blood. I went deep."

"Come on, Jeannie! Do you even hear yourself?"

"All I can do is warn you. You have to kill yourself to be part of them. A little bit every day. They'll tell you so if you listen closely enough. But don't you worry. I'm here for you. I'll be watching. When you need me to, I'll remind you who you really are."

"You don't even know who you are."

"I am you, Jean."

"What?"

"I am you. I am the second person. I am the second coming. I am the finger you point in the mirror. When you come for me, I'm already coming for you. When your brain tells your right hand to move, my left hand obeys. I am the negative image of who you are, who you believe yourself to be. Where you see angels, I see the demons standing in their shadows. Where you see evil, I see good. You think you're free, but I see how you chain yourself to them. You think I'm locked up here, but I go where I want to go. I'm an angel riding on your shoulder. I go where you go, see what you see, hear what you hear. I know what you think."

"Okay," I said. "I really have to go."

"I will make a cameo appearance, Vanessa, when you least expect it but when you most need to remember."

"Uh huh."

"I am the Menninger Clinic, remember? I am the meningitis that makes you so uncomfortable you want to diagnose me, don't you? I am the disease you don't see in yourself, that makes you want to deny me, deny that I mean anything, deny that I happened, deny that I am as much a figment of your imagination as you are of mine. But I did happen, and I am your imagination. It's nothing but you yourself that you need to deny, you need to sacrifice. I'm just the excuse you need to do it. So go ahead. Do it to me. Slice me open. Reach inside me and take my beating heart. I'll still be with you. I will rise up like Jesus from the dead. I will recreate you in my image, and all the blood and all the whitewash in the world won't make you clean again. All the bloodletting on all the altars in all the churches and temples and synagogues in the world won't drain me from your veins, because I am you, I am your

Jean Sequence, and you are part and parcel of me."

"I really wish you would take the medication, Jeannie."

"Yeah, I bet you do."

I stood to go. "I'm just saying."

She stood with me and raked her sleeves up to her armpits, stretching her arms out wide to expose the fresh pink scars that squiggled up the insides.

"This is you, Baby. This is what it means to be you."

Her laughter chased me out of the day room and down the hall to the exit, where I had to wait for an attendant to come let me out.

"Watch for me, Vanessa!" she cried after me. "Watch for my appearance!"

# EARTHLY DESIRE

Even after he'd run out of work to do on Jiminy, Jarrod continued to turn up at my place on Sunday afternoons. True to his word, he got a hold of some sheet iron and a long screw and the steering wheel off an old Allis Chalmers somebody had junked, and he welded me up a second ubuntu blox compacter. We made a good team. I no longer kidded myself that his intentions had anything to do with Jeannie Ivory.

After a particularly hot day's work, we took my pretty new Jiminy out for a spin and ended up at the "new" bridge south of the canyon, where it broadens and flattens out into more farmland. At that point, the creek becomes just a creek again, its bed lined with cottonwoods and blackjack, green and dark and pretty. I let him drive, and that's where he decided to pull over and stretch his legs. We walked down to the creek and rested there in the shade. He took off his shoes and rolled up his jeans to go wading, so I did, too.

I remembered a funny story and started telling it. "Do you know Delores Bittle?" I said. "She and her husband live across the canyon from me. She used to teach seventh grade English in town. Anyway, she give me a ride home from her place once. I was in a little bit of trouble with the law, you might say, and I ended up running off across the canyon. I didn't have a plan or anything. It just so happened I come out the other side on her property. She knew who I was, of course. At the time, it seemed like I was all anyone had to talk about on account of my grandma's suicide, and well, anyway, long story short, Sheila and Leon had gone to Enid to see the attorney about her will. I had no intention of going with them, so I run off into the canyon. Once I was down there, I dug up the knife Grandma had supposedly used to—well, not supposedly; she actually did use it to kill herself, I guess, I just didn't want to believe it. I'd found it and hid it from the Sheriff and then later on I got scared, thinking now it had my fingerprints all over it, so I dug it up and wiped it down and buried it again and took off and, like I said, I ended up in Delores Bittle's back yard."

"You're a hot mess," Jarrod said. He stood closer than he strictly needed to. We had a whole wide creek to wade around in.

But the mud between my toes felt so soft and squishy in that particular spot that I didn't much feel like backing up, so I just agreed with him and went on with my funny story. "I was. I was all dressed up to go into the city, and now here I was covered in mud and all scraped up from climbing back out the other side, which is even steeper than on my side."

He dipped down and cupped his hands in the water to splash his face and stood up again.

"But Mrs. Bittle, she took me in and give me a tall glass of iced tea and tended to my scrapes and bumps and bruises and even had me take a bath in her bathtub while she got me a dress of Leigh Ann's, her daughter's, to put on. I'm convinced she did that just so she could search my clothes for deadly weapons. Hoo!" I caught my breath as he put his cold hands on my waist. "And then she took me home. We talked about—I was going into seventh grade that September, so I was already scheduled to be in her class, and she had known my grandma, but she'd never met Sheila and Leon, who were to be my new guardians. Jarrod," I said, "what are you doing?"

"Listening."

"Well, you are an active listener, I'll give you that."

We stood swaying in the breezy shade, up to our knees in cool water. I felt collected in a way I wouldn't have expected. I won't lie. I had surely thought of how his touch might feel—his deliberate touch, I mean, without the pretense of accidental contact as we worked side by side on my wall—but I could not, in my imagination, have made it feel so normal, so welcome and so right. I would not have predicted that I'd be able to keep track of what I was saying, never mind continue. But I slipped my arms around him, rested my head on his chest, and simply kept on talking, even though, at times, depending on what he did, my breath abandoned me. "Come to find out, Sheila had canceled their appointment in Enid and called the Sheriff to report me missing, so I was in some pretty deep shit. I remember it all in vivid detail, that day, because that was also the day I got my first period, and I was in no way prepared for that. But anyway, that's not what I meant to tell you."

"What did you mean to tell me?"

"About Mrs. Bittle, after she dropped me off."

"Oh."

"She told me later on that she took the road down this way to get back home. She thought it might be quicker. This was only a few days after a big storm had come through. Some said it was a tornado. I wouldn't swear to that, but it did flood down this way pretty bad and it took out the old wooden bridge we had back then, which, Mrs. Bittle didn't know about that when she set out this way. This was just a dirt road in those days. When she hit a patch of mud, she went into a skid and come to a stop with the sun in her eyes. That's when she swore she saw my grandma standing in the middle of the road, barring her way."

"Huh?"

"Right. My dead grandma. It turned out to be nothing but a sign in the middle of the road. Just a plywood and cinder block affair with the words "Bridge Out" painted on it, not an old Indian woman in a long skirt holding a bread knife in her hand. How she mistook one for the other is anybody's guess."

"You think she really saw your grandma?"

"I don't know. I don't have to think one way or another. It's just what she told me. Years later, her daughter Leigh Ann informed me that she thought it wasn't a ghost but an angel God had sent in the guise of my grandmother to warn Delores of the simple truth that God had set a wide gulf between them and me and it was a mistake for her mother to try and help me or to have anything to do with me."

"Wow. What was that all about?"

"Sheila's older brother, Mark, disappeared about a year after I did and has never been heard from again. Kind of like me, only I showed back up, and he didn't. So somehow I'm to blame."

"Do you believe in ghosts?"

I shrugged against him, enjoying the contrast of his warm body and the cool water, the breeze, his stale but honest sweat. "Weird things happen all the time." I thought of Jeannie Ivory and the conviction she clung to that she had literally conjured Eugene Lamb out of the sewer. "It only gets to be a problem when you attach a belief system to something you don't have a rational explanation for. People get so attached to their beliefs, sometimes they can't see straight."

"You don't care much for attachments, do you?"

I pulled away, only enough so I could look him in the eye—those warm cinnamon-colored eyes of his. "Not to ideas, maybe. I don't have a problem forming attachments to people." And then, but to myself and not to him, I said, "Do I?"

258

And like a helium balloon, he attached his laughter to my self doubt and made it not go away but rise beyond where I could reach it. I knew it would sink eventually and come to ground again someplace inside me, someplace I probably couldn't see, but in that moment I was free of it, free to attach myself to Jarrod Frye in ways I have no earthly desire to write about.

# ZENTANGLED

Weeks passed.

Eugene and Angela took me shopping in Enid to get supplies for the mask-making party. We first hit Hobby Lobby, but Angela knew where to get gloves and Vaseline and like that for cheaper money. I let her take the lead.

"I think we got everything on the list," I said after the last stop. "Where do you want to eat?"

They looked at each other, grinning, and both said, "Sonic!" at the same time.

"Y'all are a cheap date. I thought we might could sit down and eat. We can get Sonic at home."

"But it's so nice out!" Angela pleaded.

So we ordered Sonic and took it to Champlin Park. We sat side by side on the new swings and ate our burgers and fries.

"Do you ever hear from that girl that used to work for you?" Angela asked me. "I forget her name."

I had a mouthful, so I didn't answer right away. I chewed extra slow to buy myself some time. "Jeannie Ivory?" I reached down and took a sip of my Diet Coke and set it back on the ground before I said anything else. "She's not coming back to work for me."

"That's too bad. For her, I mean."

"Probably for the best. She used to tell me at least once a week how she wasn't good for business and I ought to fire her."

"It's none of my business, but did you?"

"Fire her?" I wagged my head. "She saved me the trouble." I took another bite.

Eugene said to Angela, "She's at Fort Supply for a little while."

"Oh."

"I went to see her," I confessed. "She looks better, but—I mean, she's not all gothed out like she used to be." I went to take a french fry and put it back. "It's an improvement."

"How long does she have to be there?"

"Hard to tell. She was refusing medication, so it could be a while."

"Well, I hope she gets better."

Eugene said, "We should pray for her."

Angela's sneakers rested over by one of the legs of the swing set, a pair of white canvas high tops that she had zentangled in purple fabric marker. She scratched at the dirt divot under her swing set with a bare toe. "Yep." By the level of enthusiasm in her voice, if I didn't know any better, I'd have said I just witnessed their first argument, because a couple days later, while Angela and I set up the tables out in the greenhouse for pouring plaster and what-all, she confided in me.

"I feel just awful about that girl," she said. "Jeannie."

"You don't have to. You didn't take her job, you know, if that's what's bothering you. All she did was sit behind the counter and read a book."

She mulled that over. We spread blankets and put pillows on the two tables and covered them in tarps and set out plastic drop cloths to use as bibs and buckets and gloves and two bags of plaster. Then we sat down together in the main shop and tore strips of fabric from old shirts and other garments I'd picked up at Goodwill.

"Eugene prays for her."

My instinct was to not say a word, so I didn't. I concentrated on pulling the threads left behind by a button.

"He prays that she'll find Jesus."

I looked at her out of the corner of my eye. She looked miserable. "I'm not much of a pray-er," I said.

Real slow, as if each word had to be pried off her tongue, she said, "I don't want her to find Jesus. I don't want her to be saved."

"I don't think you have much to worry about."

"Don't you think it's wrong, though? I know it is."

"What? Praying for her?"

"No. The fact that I don't. The fact that I fake it." After a minute, she said, "You won't tell anybody what I said, will you?"

"Not a soul."

"You never married?"

I laughed. Where in the hell did that come from? "No, I never did."

"Do you have a boyfriend, though?"

"I've had a few," I said carefully. "Over the years." My problem was, half of them, I couldn't name names. My first one was now a politician. Then come a couple of sweet, fucked-up boys at the farm where I stayed in Massachusetts, wards of the State, like me. Long dry spells and, more recently than I liked to admit, a string of married men or men otherwise unavailable to me outside the bedroom. Now Jarrod. Not only was he too young for me, it still felt sometimes like I'd stolen him from Jeannie. Even though I knew full well there had never been anything between them (except in her head), it felt—I don't know—shabby on my part to be sleeping with him. Did Angela Dunhof need to know any part of that? Of course not. But it made knowing how to answer her question tricky. "It's complicated," I added.

She nodded.

I wanted to steer her away from asking me any more questions, so I said, "Is it complicated between you and Eugene?"

Her nodding deepened. "Can I show you something?"

She set aside her bag of strips and went to the greenhouse, newly renamed "the classroom" or "the studio" depending on the day of the week. She came back with her purse and produced a corkscrew and handed it to me. "It's completely functional." The opening in the top of it, the part you turn to drive the pointy screw into the cork, she had filled in with red and purple resin divided down the middle by a flat wire bent in the shape of a profile, like something Pablo Picasso might have drawn. The arms of the corkscrew had a lot of glass beads attached to them.

I looked at the other side and noticed the wire line down the middle in fact created two tiny profiles, not just one—kind of like the way that optical illusion of a wine goblet makes two faces—only she had dispensed with the goblet, so the two faces pressed up against each other, the nose of one becoming the eye socket of the other. Each one had an eye made from a teeny-weeny clock spring embedded in the translucent resin. One face was blueish-purple, the other one orangey-red.

"Are they kissing?" I asked.

She took it from me and plunged the corkscrew part down through the ring that fit over the lip of a wine bottle, so the gears caused the two arms to spring up, becoming a pair of wings strung with glass beads, clear round ones interspersed with red teardrops. She withdrew the two-faced head and plunged it again, then again and again, until it dawned on me.

"Oh. Okay. They're screwing. Duh."

"She turns her tears into wine."

I looked more closely at the two faces. "You and Eugene?" I ventured.

"No." She put it back in her purse. "Not me."

I didn't know what to say.

"He wants me to pray for her to get better, so she can get out and come back to him."

"What? Angela, no. I don't think so. She can't stand the sight of him."

"Oh, I'm sure."

"Can I see that again?"

She opened her purse and handed it to me. I studied the faces, the two profiles. I worked it slowly up and down, making the wings flap — not like an angel's wings so much as the arms of a person doing jumping jacks. Ruby teardrops poured out from under the arms.

I cleared my throat. "What do you call it?"

"It's not for sale. It's too personal."

"I know. I understand. I just wondered if it had a name."

"Cameo Angel."

My heart skipped a beat. "What?"

"Yeah. It's like a movie that plays in my head. Not that I want it to." She twirled a finger in the region of her temple. "My doubts are the subtitles."

"She believes—" I didn't know if I should be saying this or not, but it wasn't like I was Jeannie's psychiatrist and I had to keep every word she ever told me strictly confidential, so I went for it. "She believes Eugene is not . . . real. She thinks she invented him. She also believes that he has taken everything good in life away from her. And that's the reason she's the way she is."

"Crazy, you mean?"

"I guess. Maybe he took her sanity away from her, too, I don't know."

"You care about her, don't you?"

I didn't have an answer for that. "All I'm saying is, you didn't take her job. You certainly didn't take her boyfriend."

"You don't think so?"

I saw tears ready to spill. I said, "No." And I thought to myself: *No more than I have.* "No," I said again.

"Then why is he so obsessed with her? I don't get it!"

"Is he?"

She looked away. The tears had overflowed her eyes. One tracked down the near side of her nose to the corner of her lips. She sipped at it and drew a ragged breath, clenching her eyes and her fists. "I don't want to pray for her!"

"Then don't."

"But I feel so guilty! Is it a sin that I don't want to?"

"I'm no expert on the subject, but it might be more of a sin if you did. I mean, feeling the way you do. Wouldn't it make you a hypocrite to pray for her? Anyway, it's not like she's going to come back all healthy and full of sunshine just because you do."

A small bark of laughter escaped her. "Maybe that would be a good thing. Maybe everybody would stop caring so much."

"You really think he cares about her more than he does you?"

"He might." She sniffed, sucked down a tear from the other cheek. "He might care more about me if I wasn't so—"

I waited.

"—if I was more like her."

"I'm having trouble picturing you with albino hair and zombie makeup."

"I don't think I could pull it off."

"You could start with a Day of the Dead tattoo," I suggested, "somewhere tasteful."

"How about just a skull with wings?"

"Definitely."

Her smile hovered and faded.

"Bad girls are over-rated, Angela."

"Except, that's easy for you to say. You're not a guy."

"Just tell him the truth. You don't want to pray for her."

"I'm afraid to."

"Afraid of what he'll think?"

"Yeah."

"Afraid he might think you're a bad girl?"

She looked suspicious.

# Missed Opportunity

The guys were easy. We got them all together of a Sunday afternoon and had them lie down two at a time on the big tables. I fitted them with shower caps and makeshift plastic bibs and greased them from the neck up with petroleum jelly, while Angela laid strips of fabric soaked in plaster over the contours of their faces. They breathed through plastic straws, one in each nostril.

"I catch anyone blocking anybody else's air, you're outa here," I threatened. "You don't come back, and your face does not go on my wall. I don't give second chances when it comes to something like that. We all clear?"

Crumb Number Three raised his hand. I asked him what it was.

"Keep an eye on Pastor Wingate. He's the one you have to worry about."

Wingate sighed, "Oh, ye of little faith! Sister Cavendish, I believe Brother Ben should go first."

We soon had an assembly line going. I prepped the boys' faces, Eugene mixed the plaster, Angela made the molds, and as soon as one had set up, I wrote the name on it in black marker, rocked it loose from the face it sat on, and set it aside to cure. By the end of the day, we had nine molds: Pastor Wingate, Todd Lamb, Gary Purcell, Billy, Izzy, Crumb, Zack Angleton and the Pearson brothers, Josh and Justin. We did Eugene last. While we waited for the plaster to set up, Crumb asked me, "You sure you don't want me to just—" He made as if to pinch off the straws stuck in Eugene's nostrils.

I gave him a look, and he backed off with his hands in the air, saying, "Fine, fine. It's a missed opportunity, though. I'm just saying."

Angela went to strip the tables, but I said just to leave them. "When are you coming back? I want to get one of you, too."

She grinned. "Why me?" As if she didn't know.

"Come here." I squirted some lotion and took her by the hands, massaging them. "Of all the people I have to be grateful for lately, who do you think tops my list?"

She smiled more broadly, showing her smooth white teeth. "All right. Then I get to make one of you, too."

"You got your braces off!" I said, astonished that I hadn't noticed before. "You look so beautiful!" I finished rubbing the lotion in.

"How about a week from today? Can I ride out with you after church?"

"Sure you can. Eugene got something else going on?"

She shrugged, then pulled me into the shop and closed the door to the greenhouse. "We broke up."

"Oh. Really?"

"It just makes sense. He's going to Evangel in the fall, and I'm going to Kansas City."

I gasped, more out of delight than any great surprise. "You got in?"

"I got in!"

I grabbed her and hugged her and told her I was so proud of her and not one bit surprised and I was going to hate her for going away, so just be prepared.

"No, you're not. You don't have a hateful bone in your body."

Then I got serious for a minute. I said, "And it's going to be okay? You and Eugene? That's not an easy decision."

"Easier than you might think. I actually need to ask you for a ride today, too."

"Oh?"

"He wanted me to ride out to Fort Supply with him. I said no."

"No, he didn't! What on Earth for?"

She just looked at me like, *duh!*

"You've got to be kidding!"

"It's been in the back of my mind for a while that we needed to start thinking about what we would do when we go our separate ways. It's not like KC and Springfield are at opposite ends of the Earth, but—"

"I don't think that's a good idea."

"No, it's okay. Really. We talked it over very rationally, and—"

"Is he still going? By himself?"

"Where? To Springfield?"

"No, to see her. To Fort Supply."

"He's a free agent."

"That is such a bad idea." I found myself pacing toward the door, unsure where I wanted to go, then turning and pacing toward the phone on the back wall, unsure who I wanted to call. I turned in the direction

266

of the greenhouse, where Eugene lay with his face covered in plaster. I needed to talk him out of going to visit Jeannie, but why? What would I say? I turned back to Angela. "That is such a bad idea."

She shrugged as if to let me know I was preaching to the choir, or maybe to remind me it wasn't her call.

I had to talk to him. "Do you think his mask is set up yet?"

"One way to find out."

We went back into the greenhouse. I wrote his name into the fresh plaster on his face. The marker left a slight indentation, and the plaster gummed up the tip. "Not quite," I said. "We'll give it a few more minutes."

The others were sitting and standing around the other table, visiting. I looked at Crumb Number Three and wished he would have cut off Eugene's air in earnest. I said, "I appreciate y'all coming out for this." I explained how I intended to use the molds to make their faces appear on my wall. As soon as they realized their part of it was done, they said goodbye and gradually took their conversation outdoors. That left Angela, who was going to ride back into town with me, and Eugene, who still had his face covered in plaster and couldn't speak.

"Eugene," I said, sitting next to him on the bench part of the picnic table. "I understand you intend on taking a ride out to Fort Supply this evening to visit Jeannie Ivory and I want to impress upon you just how unwise I believe that course of action to be." I wished I could erase and rewind and start over, but I couldn't, and it didn't matter. The words to express the stupidity of him going to visit her had not yet been invented. "Now, I think we can both agree that Jeannie is a very disturbed young woman, and while I admire your sense of compassion in wanting to wish her well, you need to understand that you are very probably the last person on Earth she wants to see right now because, in her mind—now, how do I put this? She sees you as her complete opposite. You have everything in life that she does not. I don't know how to tell you this except to tell it the way she told me, so don't shoot the messenger, but she is under the impression that you have taken everything away from her, and I mean everything: her friends, her family, her reputation, her self-esteem. Whatever you and I might make of that is beside the point. What I'm describing is very real to her. She was so upset with me for calling you that day of the snow storm, because she was convinced I'd called you on purpose. That's why she tried to kill herself. I believe your intentions are good, Eugene, I do. But I'm very concerned that if you go out there today, you will only set her back. She might even try and kill herself again. And she might succeed."

I sat quiet a minute, hoping my words had sunk in and he might reconsider.

The door opened behind me. I turned and saw Angela coming into the greenhouse. "Is he cooked?" she asked.

I touched the plaster mask. It was firm. I got my fingers under it and started working it loose. His face gleamed like the skin of a newborn from the heat of the plaster and the residue of petroleum jelly. He opened his eyes and fixed them on me. "I hear the conviction and the sincerity in your voice, Sister Cavendish," he said. (I hated when anybody called me that, and he knew it.) "I know you speak from the heart, out of love for the lost. I'm not going to visit Jean because I selfishly want to or because I think, from the limited perspective we have as mortals, that it's a quote-unquote good idea. I'm going because the Lord has spoken to me. He has called me to go and minister to her in His Name. I believe He has a purpose for her life that is beyond my understanding. I am an instrument in His Hands, that's all. My will is subject to His."

"Oh, boy!" I said. I handed him a towel to wipe the shine off his face.

"Vanessa will give me a ride home," Angela told him.

"Do your parents know what you're up to?" That was me.

He assured me they did.

"Well, be careful they don't find a room for you while you're out there . . . ministering to the sick."

Angela followed him out to his car. They talked for a minute and hugged goodbye in a way that, from where I stood, looked like goodbye for good.

"You okay?" I asked when she came back in.

"No." She threw her arms around my neck. "Yes. I don't know. I will be. He's such a —"

"'Idiot' comes to mind."

"No..."

"You like 'sanctimonious prick' better?"

She sniffed against my neck. "I do, but that's not it, either. More like, you can't argue with him, because he's got the Lord on his side, and I end up feeling like perfect...shit for disagreeing with him."

It required an effort for her to say that word. I squeezed her. She let me go.

I drove her home.

Angela's sweetness refreshed me.

I meant what I said about her not having taken Jeannie's job. I still could've used another body to fill in behind the register. I had so much going on suddenly and, at the same time, more customers than I could tend to by myself. Yet between making her angels and teaching her classes and helping me plan my Wall of Gratitude, I didn't want to ask Angela to run the register, too. She was too valuable for that. With tourist season coming on, I needed to think about hiring someone else. It was a good thing Jeannie wasn't around, because I occasionally caught myself thinking I might be tempted to take her back — on a trial basis, of course — if she ever got well enough to get out of the hospital.

But who did I think I was I kidding? No better way to bring my business to a screeching halt than to hire Jeannie Ivory back, and I knew it. It was more than just that, though. I pictured Jarrod coming around of an evening and on weekends. And just how might that fly, with Jeannie there?

I can tell you. Off the handle, that's how.

So when it came to not particularly hoping and praying for a speedy recovery, all things considered, I found myself every bit as conflicted as Angela.

Maybe more.

I'm trying to put a prettier face on the whole business than I like to admit. I didn't relish the thought of Jeannie moving back to town because, quite frankly, she knew too much about me. And I didn't want Eugene — or anybody else, for that matter — going to visit her because, among other things, she might tell him things that could potentially embarrass me, that might jeopardize my newfound standing in the community and, along with it, my recent uptick in net worth. Bad enough I'd soon be losing both Eugene and Angela to college, without him finding out I'd slept with Jeannie and telling everyone I was not only a serial killer but a lesbian who preyed on defenseless, psychotic women half my age.

I hated the very word, lesbian.

Yes, I know how incorrect it is of me to say that, not to mention hypocritical. But why should I feel obliged to embrace a label not of my choosing? I hated the way it colored my conversation with Angela on the way to her house, when I said, "I'm going to miss you when you go off to art school," because I was thinking three moves ahead to when Eugene told her my "secret" and she replayed that remark in her head and made it sound like it meant more than it did, or something different. It's one thing to step outside the closet and live your life as you see fit and quite another to give your neighbors the impression they're entitled to inspect your nightstand and your underwear drawer.

"You could come visit me in Kansas City," she responded with an innocence that only reinforced my apprehension. "Anyway, we still have most of the summer."

We talked about her coming back over Christmas and Spring Break and the following summer, just to ease my separation anxiety, but I knew a girl like Angela would be presented with plenty of opportunities along the way. We left it that my door would always be open. Still, it felt like she was breaking up with me, too.

At the curb in front of her house, she said, "See you at church?" She meant the Sunday evening service, which was less than an hour away.

"I'm beat. I don't think I'll make it." I wanted to be alone with my introverted, antisocial, asexual self.

She made a face. "It's just—I suddenly don't have anyone to sit with."

"I'll try," I said, "but I can't promise." I had a phone call I needed to make. "How about I come get you on Thursday and we'll do plaster facials?"

She laughed and climbed out. Before she could close the door, I said, "Congratulations, Honey! I'm real happy for you. About art school."

I flew home. I still didn't have a working cell phone. When I got to the shop, I punched in the number of the State Hospital. "I would like to speak with Jeannie Ivory," I said. "She's a patient there."

Ms. Ivory was at dinner, the voice at the other end informed me, a soft baritone, the kind you can't be sure if it belongs to a woman or a man. I ought to try back in forty-five minutes.

"Forty-five minutes might be too late." I tried to keep my voice level. "She's got a visitor coming. Somebody she does not want to see, believe me when I tell you."

"She doesn't have to see anybody she doesn't want to see. She has the right to refuse to a visit."

"Yeah, but you don't understand. I don't know if she'll be able to do that. Be strong enough, I mean. He has a — this — some kind of hold over her. In her mind he does. Oh, hell! Do you even know what I'm talking about? If she even finds out he's there, she'll freak out. He's the reason she's there in the first place!" I probably sounded like a nut job myself. "She thinks she invented him and he's some kind of demon she brought to life and she has to cut herself to feed him. He's why she does it. I'm scared she'll do it again."

"I see. Who am I speaking with?"

"A friend of hers," I said. Then I clarified: "Her boss."

She asked my name (I think it was a woman) and I told her. "Can you do something? Will you just tell him he can't see her?"

"I will relay your concerns to the staff on her unit."

"The name of the one on his way out there is Eugene Lamb."

She had me spell it.

"Yes, Lamb. Like a sheep." I didn't say in a wolf's clothing, or whatever that saying is, but it did come to mind. I sometimes think the line between sane and crazy is mostly just a matter of knowing when to keep your mouth shut and remove all doubt.

—

# TANGIBLE ANGELS

I lost myself, over the next few days, in my Wall of Attitude. I took no particular joy in the work, but mixing a finer batch of cob and molding it to the insides of the plaster casts one by one did comfort me some. It allowed my mind to rest in a way, to stop churning so with worry about what Jeannie might have done to herself this time, whether I'd pissed Eugene off completely by calling and warning her of his visit, how I meant to stay afloat without help from him and Angela, who in the space of two and a half months had become damn near my partners in business, responsible in more ways than one for better than half of my recent jump in income.

What would happen to me if they no longer operated as a team? Not if, but when they both took off in September, going their separate ways? Eugene had set me up with Facebook, Pinterest, Instagram, a blog and an online shop, none of which I had the foggiest how to keep up with on my own.

"I'll just have to get him to show me," I whined to the plaster inside-out face of Todd Lamb before I smooshed it full of mud.

I wished I had the clarity of purpose Eugene and all those other Children of God exhibited. They never seemed to doubt themselves. Angela, for example. Did she think twice about breaking up with Eugene? Not that I blamed her, but she made it seem so easy, so clean, whereas I had no clue how to proceed, not in love nor in business nor in life. I was no good at letting anything go. Anything or anybody. Why had I called Jeannie to warn her? I'll tell you why. Because I sucked at minding my own business. I sucked at letting go — not just of Jeannie but of her stories — of the ridiculous, paranoid, delusional, egotistical world she'd created like a micro-cosmos inside my head where the laws that govern ordinary reality got themselves temporarily suspended enough so that she, Jeannie Ivory and nobody else but Jeannie Ivory, had the power to call forth a spirit from underground and make him real. Are you kidding me? I slapped another handful of mud in Todd Lamb's face and called it good.

On days when she had classes, Angela came and went. Sometimes one or the other of her parents dropped her off and picked her up, sometimes she borrowed her mom's car, sometimes I went and got her. I was often up and out of the house by first light so I could work on my wall before people started coming and interrupting. One morning in particular, I had just got Billy Ivory's face mounted and had to hold it in place to keep it from slipping and falling to the ground while I mudded all around it, when the phone in the shop started ringing.

"I can't talk to you right now," I snapped at whoever it was and kept on working. Every time I took my hand off Billy's face, it started to slide. It was nothing but lime plaster — mud with fine straw and a little manure mixed in. If it fell, it would shatter.

The phone kept ringing.

"I see what your problem is," I told Billy's face. I had embedded sticks in the wall that were meant to support the weight of his face, but I hadn't angled them upward enough. "I need to start over, don't I?" I lifted his face down and set it on the deck of the scaffold, then scraped all the fresh mud off the wall so it didn't harden in place. A couple of the sticks broke off in the process. I pulled the rest of them out and tried to reinsert them at a steeper angle, but the mud of the wall was too stiff, too dry. I needed to break some of it loose and start fresh. Then it occurred to me I could use a drill to make new holes for the sticks. "If I make them a little too big and then fill them in with fresh mud, that ought to anchor them." I looked at Billy face. "What do you think?"

He didn't answer. He had his eyes closed. All my angels did, for now, until I painted them open later on.

The shop phone rang again. I ignored it. Wet mud would not adhere to dry, I knew. I'd have to soak the wall and the back of Billy's head and roughen up both surfaces, then glue them together with fresh mud. I climbed down and went inside to find my drill. Before I did, the phone started in again. I looked at the clock. It was after nine o'clock, so I answered. "Repurpose Fa — "

"Vanessa, did you forget me?"

It was Angela.

"What day is it? Oh, shit!" I held the top of my head. "You're teaching a class today?"

"Yeah, in twenty minutes."

I told her I'd be right there.

She was at the curb with her tackle box and a shoulder bag full of handouts and binders when I pulled up.

"I am so, so sorry!" I said.

"I know, I know. Just go, please?" After a minute, she said, "You were working on your wall." It wasn't a question.

"Don't be mad at me."

"I'm not. You have mud in your hair."

"Okay, but you're gonna be if you're not yet."

"Why?"

"Because my stuff is all over the place."

"On the tables?"

I winced and nodded. "Everywhere."

"Oh, Vanessa!"

"I know. I'm sorry!"

I pushed Jiminy as hard as I dared.

"You haven't been coming to church."

"Yeah, I've been a little preoccupied."

"Obsessed is more like it."

I knew the guilt trip had more to do with me forgetting her class than missing services, but that didn't get me off the hook. "I said I'm sorry."

"You haven't been for three weeks."

"You keeping track?"

"I care about you."

"No, you don't," I said to lighten the mood. "Three weeks is nothing compared to four years."

"What?"

"Never mind." We were almost there, and she was going to see what a mess I'd left. "Bad joke."

"College, you mean?"

"Told you it was a bad one."

"You can't be mad at me for that!"

"I'm not."

"You are, too."

"Am not!" I stuck my tongue out at her.

"Okay. You can be mad at me, but you can't punish me by sabotaging my classes, because that hurts us both."

"You think that's what I'm doing?"

"And by not coming to church. That's worse. Are you avoiding me?"

"Not you." I pulled up my long driveway only to see that two cars had showed up already. Ana Kopchik and her daughter Stephanie, and Carlie Hardcastle, all here for Angela's class. Another car pulled in behind us.

"We're not finished talking about this," Angela warned me.

I had to apologize to her students and enlist them to help clear my stuff off the tables, when what I really wanted was to find my drill, a fat bit and an extension cord. That was going to have to wait, though. I couldn't abandon my shop while class was going on. Customers could see through the window in the door to the greenhouse, and often thought nothing of interrupting a class to ask Angela for help, even if they'd seen me right outside. I had got myself in deep enough water with her. The last thing I needed was for her to think, on top of everything else, that I neglected the store.

"Jeannie wouldn't give two shits," I muttered, nostalgic in my twisted way for counter help that kept intruders at bay, or at least in their place once they got past the Closed sign she always felt it was my job to remember to flip over.

Her voice in my head, a whisper as rusty-sweet as a dirty razor, continued the conversation Angela had started but couldn't finish. "Are you avoiding her?"

"No. Not really." I stood at the door, looking out at my wall, wishing I could just get that one head mounted on it. I flipped the sign over to Open.

"Who, then?" I turned and looked at her, where she used to perch on the barstool behind the register with a book closed on her thumb and the toes of her thrift-store Doc Martens propped against the back of the counter. "Eugene?"

"No," I said. "I don't know. Maybe."

"But why? He's been so good for you!" She went back to reading her book. "Didn't I tell you he would be?"

"I know you did."

"Then why?"

"Because he didn't need to come bother you."

"Awww," she purred, sarcastic. (This was all in my head, mind you. I knew she wasn't there. I wasn't hallucinating or anything, just having a polite conversation all by myself.) "That's sweet of you! Always thinking of me. Since when is it your problem who comes to visit me in the loony bin?"

"It's not. I don't know."

"Since I know you too well? Since I know too much about you?"

"Maybe."

"Loose lips sink ships."

"Shut up!" I pushed open the door, stepped outside and slammed it behind me. I didn't need to listen to that. I didn't know why I was afraid to face Eugene, exactly, except that he seemed to have confirmed for me that both Angela and Jeannie were right about him—in one regard, at least. He did seem fixated on her, and not in a healthy way. I don't mean that I suddenly started believing he had the power to psychically drain her world of light and sweetness, to render her psychotically shriveled soul allergic to optimism, fragile, defenseless, friendless, suicidal. But maybe she did have good reason to recoil from him, to protect herself the only way she knew how.

I wondered what had happened when he arrived at Western State Psychiatric Facility? That was the thing I didn't want to know. But yet I needed to know. My best estimate was that she had refused his visit, and that was that. But I couldn't be sure. She'd gone over some kind of edge when she did what she did to herself. That in itself made her unpredictable. What if she told him about the two of us? What did she have to lose?

I wasn't afraid of mere judgment, was I? I told myself I wasn't. But I cringed to think of it, of her saying what had passed between us. Saying it to him, I mean. To anybody, but especially him. What bothered me about it was feeling like she'd turned me into some kind of battle ground between the two of them, a country divided. Like I was supposed to choose between them when I had no idea what the choices involved. Eugene had swept in on me with his ideas, his practical charm and sociability, with business savvy beyond his years, his influence, his people. He had saved the day for me, saved my business. By rights, the storm last winter should've wiped me out. Instead, I prospered. Yet I had to admit that Jeannie still commanded at least some part of my heart. I guess my heart. I didn't know what else to call that dark little territory in the pit of my chest. In spite of all the evidence to the contrary, I wanted to believe in her.

I wanted to believe in her, you might say, because I wanted to believe in myself. In certain parts of myself that ordinarily didn't get much play. The furtive parts, the light-shirking parts, the parts that distrusted the moral high ground, that preferred to burrow in. The nocturnal parts.

I was a house divided. What had I done to deserve my good fortune? I had no answer to that question other than to say that, truthfully, I had benefited from Jeannie's misfortune.

Not as a direct consequence, though, so let me rephrase that. I benefited from the same forces that did her in. And that force had a name.

Was that my fault? Did I subconsciously look to undermine my sudden success — through neglect or by sabotaging poor, good Angela — because I felt guilty? Because I secretly (knew) thought I didn't deserve it?

But I'll tell you how it felt. It felt like Jeannie had infected me. As if I'd caught her virus, her disease. Like I'd gone through a latency period where everything seemed great, but the whole time the virus kept replicating in the dark, in my blood, and now, suddenly, I started to show signs and symptoms: little eruptions of self-doubt, of indifference to normal things. It manifested as a kind of feverishness over my stupid wall.

I stood in the middle of the parking lot now, looking at it. It was taking shape. I was making progress. In a way, building that wall constituted the one thing I myself could do about my good fortune, whether I deserved it or not. I could at least accept it, couldn't I? Couldn't I at least say thank you?

I mixed a fresh batch of mud and wrapped it in plastic before a car with Virginia plates pulled in and a couple with two kids got out.

"You must be Vanessa!" the woman said. "I'd know you anywhere. Look at this, Justin, Rachel! This is your Wall of Gratitude, isn't it?"

I looked at my hands, caked with mud, and rubbed them on my jeans.

Her name was Nadine. She and her husband, Thomas, subscribed to my blog, which was not my blog, it was Eugene's. But it had my name and my picture plastered all over it, just like "my" Facebook and "my" Pinterest did. Thomas wanted to inspect my wall and ask all kinds of questions about wind shear and lateral stability and what all, because he was an engineer and wanted to show off. He took particular interest in the buttresses that supported the wall from behind and separated my stashes of various raw materials: plastic from glass from metal from styrofoam and assorted god-knows-what. Meanwhile, Nadine and the kids wandered into the shop, so I steered him in that direction, too, in case they had any questions I could answer.

"I want this, Tom." Nadine showed him a hanging lantern made of wine bottle bottoms I had cut and pieced together several summers ago using stained glass caning. A circle of circles with a round base in the center to hold a candle, the whole thing glued to a sherry goblet turned upside-down with three holes drilled in the base where a chain was attached to it.

Justin picked out an angel from Angela's shelf, one made of two belt buckles soldered to either side of a door hinge. Rachel was keen on a pair of earrings. They brought all their loot up to the register and left it, and as I swiped Tom's credit card, Angela's class let out on break.

I looked past his shoulder and called to Nadine. "These are my real angels," I said. "Stephanie, Rachel here is making off with your earrings. The blue wire with the spirals. You want to show her, Rachel?"

Rachel was at that age where her two front teeth were too big and one of her eyeteeth was still too small. It gave her the most adorable grin. Stephanie Kopchik, meanwhile, had just moved past the most awkward stages of adolescence and could suffer a relapse at any moment. She glided down on one knee like a water bird coming in for a landing just in time to see Rachel turn her head one way, then the other, modeling.

"You made them?" Rachel asked in tones of awe.

Stephanie nodded and looked at her mother. It was her first sale.

I passed Tom the slip to sign and his receipt. He wanted to take Rachel's picture with her new BFF, so I suggested he get one of Justin with Angela, too. Then I remembered to ask if they would be sure to Like us on Facebook, and I told Tom if he would send me the pictures he just took so I could get them up on my blog, I'd email them a coupon for 25% off anything in the shop next time they came through.

He said that might be a while, they were on vacation, but how would it be if I took a shot of the four of them in front of my wall? So we did that. Then Stephanie took one of the four of them with me, then I had Angela join us, and next I took the camera back and got the whole class in there, and we finally sent the family of Virginians off with stories to share and memories to keep.

"Y'all just made their day," I said to Angela's peeps before they all filed back in for the remainder of their class. "Mine, too."

Ana Kopchik hugged me and whispered in my ear that Stephanie was so proud of herself, and thank you!

"She should be! Did you see that little Rachel light up?"

"I know!"

Later on, as I helped Angela pick up and put away after her class, I said, "I'm changing the name of my shop. I just decided."

"Oh?" I could practically feel her trying to act normal, like she wasn't still pissed off. "What to?"

"What do you think of the name Tangible Angels?"

"I like it."

"That's what we make, whether if they look like literal angels or not. Like even Stephanie's earrings. Just little things people can take with them and store their memories in them, because those memories are the thing. They're the angels. We just make them — wait for it…tangible."

She smiled. "I'm sorry I was so mad at you."

"You had every right to be."

"I know."

"I have every right to be mad at you, too."

"If you say so."

"I won't take it out on you again."

"That's good."

"I promise. I still need to make a mask of you."

"And I get to make one of you."

"You just want to see me with straws sticking out of my nose, don't you?"

"That, too," she said.

# UPGRADE

I was overdue for an upgrade. I figured I might as well join the 21ˢᵗ Century at get a smart phone. I could afford the data plan, at least for now. A lot of what Eugene did for me—taking pictures and videos, tweeting, Facebooking, even blogging—he did from his cell phone. If I wanted to pick up my own slack, I'd need to learn how he did it. I closed the shop early and drove into town.

I didn't mean to get into it—it was all water under the bridge—but I had to explain to Kyle at Data Solutions what had happened to my old phone, how I got snowed in last winter and lost power and used the last of my charge to call for help. "I just hit 'Send,' meaning to call the last number on my call list. You know what I mean? I never knew it would call the last text message."

"It won't," Kyle said.

Kyle is prematurely bald and more interested in devices than in people, so I talked to the top of his head while he disassembled my phone. "Well, but it did."

"Nope."

I had no intention of arguing with him, so I changed the subject. "If I change phones—"

"You can keep all of your contacts and your history," he said, not letting me finish.

"My history? I'd just as soon you got rid of my history."

He looked up at me, squinting through his lenses.

"That was a joke," I said. "Never mind."

He went back to my phone, inserting a different battery and putting it back together. I thought about telling him it might improve his customer relations if he let me paint a smiley face on his bald spot, but I doubted my suggestion would be given the consideration it deserved. He turned to his keyboard and typed one-handed, then swiveled his monitor so I could see. "Here's the last outgoing call. 4:43 a.m., February 22nd." He pointed to a number I had since learned by heart: Eugene's cell. Then he shifted his finger up one row. "Same as the previous call at 11:17 p.m., February 21st."

"That doesn't make any sense. I only made one call. What's the number before that?"

He rattled off an 800 number, which would've been Triple A.

"And before that?"

He read a number I hadn't called in a while, but I knew it had to be Maureen's. Maureen Ivory, Jeannie's mom.

"See, that's the number I thought I was calling. She found out I called Eugene, and that's when she threw my phone at me and missed and it smashed against the wall. Not her. Her daughter."

"That voids the warranty," Kyle said.

I looked at the top of his head. "You've been very helpful. Could I get you to print that out for me?"

I bought a new phone, which required that I upgrade my data plan and practically sign up for college to learn how to use it, but the whole time Smiley Kyle spent tutoring me, all I kept thinking was: I did not call Eugene Lamb twice that night. I didn't even know his number. I knew I didn't, because the first time I ever called him on purpose, I had to do it from my landline in the shop, reading his number off a sticky note he'd given me.

Which, I now realized, I had folded and shoved in the hip pocket of my jeans that afternoon, before the storm hit.

"She called him!" I blurted. "That lying little —"

"Huh?" Kyle squinted and pushed his glasses up on his nose with the knuckle of his forefinger.

"She's the only one who could have. Never mind. I have to go. Can we wrap this up?"

I always wondered how my phone got so far under the sofa. She must have called him and then threw it under there, where she later "found" it for me, on its last leg.

I wrote Kyle a check and left with my new phone, my old phone and a printout of my calls for the previous twelve months.

Why, though? Why did she call Eugene?

I turned around at the door and went back inside. "One more question. Can you call up my text messages, too?"

He pointed at the plastic Verizon Wireless bag in my hand. "They'll be on your phone, unless you deleted them."

"My old phone?"

"No, your new one. Your old one is deactivated. You can do whatever you want with it."

"Thank you."

I searched and searched. Not right then but as soon as I got behind the wheel of my truck. Either Jeannie had deleted it, or I never received a text message from Eugene.

Had she made the whole thing up? For some reason, she had called him earlier in the night. I looked at the times again. Five hours and twenty-six minutes between the two calls. She called him after we finally went to bed, before we knew we were snowed in.

But she knew—she *knew*—that when I hit Send twice, my phone would call the last number dialed. His. Eugene's. She knew that, because she was the one who dialed it, but still she accused me of calling him on purpose. Then she made up the story of him texting me and pretended to read it to me, all to try and cover for the fact that it was her fault I called his number instead of her mother's. Then she threw the phone and smashed it against the wall so I couldn't check and see that she'd lied to me.

She knew.

The thing I couldn't figure out was why?

Did there even have to be a why, though? Really? Practically everything she told me that night had been a lie. If not a lie, then some form of delusion, which, in practical terms, amounted to the same thing: I could not trust a word she said.

Even so. It made not one speck of sense. Eugene terrified her. She hadn't been faking it when he showed up with Spider, when she left the shop without her jacket, sitting out in the cold till her lips turned blue. She wasn't faking it when she cut herself the first time, and she certainly wasn't faking anything the second time. Something had happened between her and Eugene, something worse than anything she had told me. Worse than not getting to help build a tree house, worse than getting in trouble at school or taking shit from other girls over a Halloween costume, worse even than somebody else's mother getting her neck broken.

Something she said that she never got back to kept tickling at the back of my mind like a spider crawling across my brain stem. She said I had to know something else about Eugene before I could begin to understand how Jarrod figured into her story. Whatever it was, she didn't get to tell me because she tried to kill herself rather than face Eugene.

But after so many lies, what made me imagine the one thing she didn't say might be the truth?

I stopped wracking my brain and decided to try out my new phone. It took me a minute to remember what to swipe and what to tap, but I finally managed to call Jarrod at work. "I need to talk to you. Can I see you when you get off?"

"Sure. You want to meet somewhere?"

"Not really. I just want to talk. I'm in town."

"All right."

"I don't know where you live."

"My house?" He sounded surprised.

"If you don't mind." Was there some reason he didn't want me to see where he lived? I hadn't given it much thought before—I mean, I hadn't obsessed about it—but he knew a lot more about me than I knew about him. Jeannie had talked so much about him that night, it felt like I'd known him for a long time, like I knew him better than I did. But I hadn't, I didn't. In fact, I knew what she had told me about him, and I knew what he had told me, but the two versions of Jarrod Frye didn't necessarily add up. I assumed his version to be the more reliable one, but what did I know, really? I tend not to ask a lot of questions of other people, probably because I don't want a lot of questions asked of me, if you can imagine. The few things I did ask Jarrod had more to do with Jeannie and her stories than with my curiosity about him, per se. Which I now realized might be a problem, something I might have overlooked. "Why don't you want me to know where you live?" I teased him. Sort of. "You lead some kind of double life? You got a wife and kids in town you don't want me to know about? Is that why you don't want me to come over?" By this point in my routine, I noticed he was no longer chuckling. I wondered if there might be an edge to my voice or something too close to home in what I said. "Am I just a little sumpn-sumpn you got going on the side, Mr. Man?"

"Vanessa," he said, all serious. "I still live at home."

"Oh. You do?"

"Yeah."

"And that's why you haven't invited me—oh," I said again, realizing. We had been a little secretive, Jarrod and me. I thought he was just following my lead.

Let me explain. Jarrod was so much younger than me, and I had so much on my plate, we didn't go out a lot. We mostly hung out at my place. I didn't want to worry about how people in town might react, seeing us together. Also, the business with Jeannie made me shy of attracting that kind of attention. I don't mean because I'd slept with her — even though, sure, that was part of the equation — but because it seemed to me, and Jarrod had confirmed, that she had never got over her childhood crush on him. Keening's a small town. People talk. I didn't want to add fuel to her delusion that everything good in her life had to be taken away from her. Even if the thing in question had never existed outside of the reality in her head. Preposterous as it might sound, carrying on with Jarrod made me feel like a tool, as if Eugene — the Eugene of her twisted imagination, at least — had used me to deprive her of Jarrod.

"So you don't have a girlfriend besides me?"

"No."

"And you're not secretly still in love with Jeannie Ivory? You don't have pictures of her all over your bedroom like a shrine or something?"

"Jesus. I gotta get back to work. You want my address?"

He gave it to me.

I didn't have a whole lot else to do in town, so I ended up on Cortland Street earlier than I needed to. I pulled up facing the wrong way, with his house on my left. Rather than turn around, I parked at the curb across the street and waited. The house was pale yellow with dark green trim. The porch had two front doors, like it might be a duplex. One door faced the street; the other one came off the side of an ell that jutted out a little ways beyond the porch. Jeannie said Jarrod and Dieter and their dad had moved to Cortland from Fair Meadow, though I distinctly remembered Jarrod saying they'd moved more than once.

I got out and crossed the street, walked up the driveway to the garage — the old-fashioned square kind with a pyramid-shaped roof and a big bi-fold door rather than the overhead kind. It stood about two feet from an ancient fence, which matched what Jeannie had said about her and Jarrod sitting with their backs against the outside wall of the garage and their feet up against the chain link, her grilling him about spreading the rumor of a boy trapped in the sewer. Two bicycles occupied that space now. Grown-up bikes. One his, I figured, and the other one Dieter's.

"Can I help you?" a woman said behind me. I like to jumped out of my skin.

I have this nervous laughter that comes over me at the oddest times, like when I'm interrupted trespassing on private property. I can't control it. I read once where anthropologists theorize that laughter must have originated as a kind of all-clear signal among our primate forebears. With a lion on the prowl, they had to all keep perfectly still and not draw attention to themselves. But if the lion went after an antelope instead of one of them and tackled it and started chowing down, then whichever one of our ancestors was on guard duty at the top of the tree that morning would let out a bark of what we might today call laughter, as much as to say, "We're good, we're good. She got somebody else this time." And they'd all share a good round of laughter before going back to picking each other's nits and bickering over immigration reform and who had the biggest banana." Which explains why, to this day, we get such a kick out of the misfortunes of others. And don't say we don't.

I also tend to talk too much. I said, "Oh! Hahaha! No! No, I was just entertaining myself while I wait for Jarrod. Jarrod Frye," I clarified. "He lives here."

She gave me a blank stare. I took her to be the neighbor lady. Hair the color of last year's leaves, a soft, unkindly face and the crossed arms of a cop interrogating a known suspect. "And who might you be?" she wanted to know.

"A friend of his. Vanessa Cavendish. I live out on Canyon Road. Jarrod's been taking care of some body work for me, and I just—I had a question I wanted to ask him."

"About what?"

I laughed again. She wasn't messing around, this lady. "I just need to talk to him."

"How do you know him?"

"I just told you." Up to this point, I had tried to keep it light, figuring, in a way, it was kind of sweet of her to keep an eye out for the neighbors. But she had taken matters a little too far for my liking. It really was none of her business, but I had nothing to hide, so I told her again, in no uncertain terms. "I had him out to my place a few months back to give me a jump. He took a liking to Jiminy." I nodded in the direction of my pickup truck across the street. "Ever since then, he's been taking care of her for me. Now, I'm not bothering anybody, I'm just waiting for him to get home from work so I can talk to him about something that is frankly just between him and me, if you don't mind."

She uncrossed her arms slowly and rested her hands on her hips, sizing me up. "I think I do mind," she said. "He's my son. Now, can I help you?"

"Oh? You're his mother?" I said, knowing full well she couldn't be. Jarrod's mother had died when he was a boy of, what? I forgot how old Jeannie said he was when that happened. The ladder, the soft ground. "I'm sorry. I didn't realize. He never mentioned his dad had remarried. No reason he should, of course," I back-pedaled. "We just never talked about it—about that part of his life, I mean."

She looked at me harder. "Are you referring to Jarrod's biological father? I don't believe Jarrod would know or care if he did remarry. Harlan was the only father he ever knew. Or needed."

"No, no," I said, waving my hands in the air to dispel any confusion. "I meant his step-dad. I meant Harlan. After Jarrod's mom—" I hesitated, because I didn't want to say his real mom and make matters even worse. "After Amy Frye passed away."

Her hands slid off her hips and hung at her sides. She looked at me with her mouth open as if she wanted to say something and decided not to.

"Or so I've been led to. . ." I never finished. The words unraveled on my tongue. My certainty unraveled. The threads of a hundred thousand facts, so-called, that Jeannie Ivory had woven together in my mind, tying them one to another with such authority, in such eye-witness detail, caught and tangled up on one another and left me speechless. I moved my lips, but no sound came. I found my tongue unable to shape a thought. I looked at Amy Frye—if that's who she was, if that's what she called herself—and I saw a walking miracle, a woman with a severed spinal cord made whole again, a history of some nine or ten years once lost and now restored to her. Or not to her but restored to me, you might say, though I was entirely ignorant of most of it, of all that had transpired in that time, or transpired differently from what I might have imagined–had I bothered to imagine the life of someone I never knew, that is.

When Jarrod said, "I still live at home," I jumped to the conclusion that he meant with his step-dad—with Harlan. But I seemed to recall asking him about his dad when I first met him. He said his dad had been dead for six or seven years. So did he mean he lived with his mom? He must have.

I begun to laugh. In earnest this time. "You never died? You never —?" I couldn't say what I wanted to say, for laughing so hard. I could only wave my hands in the air in a weak attempt to illustrate a ladder sinking into soft ground, a big man (in my mind, Harlan was not fat, but solid) clinging to the topmost rungs as they twisted with him like a tree in a high wind, knocking her backwards, crushing her, catching her across the jaw. I could only pantomime, and not very well — I found it too comical, all of a sudden — the snap of her neck, her paralysis, her death on the operating table. I roared. I howled. I had to support myself. I reached for her as she backed away from me, horrified. I doubled over with my hands on my knees, tears rolling down my cheeks. I like to wet myself, I laughed so hard.

By the time I pulled myself together, she had vanished. She'd had her fill of me, I suppose. At the end of the driveway — her driveway, Jarrod's driveway, somebody's driveway — I turned around, still laughing in little spurts, and called out to her, wherever she was, "Tell Jarrod I —" but I busted out laughing again and had to try over. "Tell him never mind." I wiped my eyes. The front door slammed.

I couldn't remember what I'd wanted to talk to him about, anyway.

# ORDINARY ANGELS

I had Angela over. We closed the shop and mixed a batch of plaster. "You first," I said. "I'm chicken."

She tied back her hair, stuffed it up inside a shower cap and stretched out across the picnic table on a pallet of blankets and tarp. I draped her in a plastic drop cloth and tucked it in around her collar. Just as I finished coating her face in petroleum jelly, she decided to ask me if it was true that Jeannie Ivory and I were lovers.

I wiped my hands on a towel. "Where did you hear that?"

"It's what some people say."

We had the plaster mixed and several old shirts and dresses cut into strips. I took a fistful and tossed them on top of the plaster in a bucket.

"Eugene said Jeannie told him so when he went to see her."

"I see. So it comes from the horse's mouth?"

"I don't like gossip. I make it a policy to go the person and ask."

"Mm-hmm." I took a plastic straw in one hand and a pair of scissors in the other and snipped the straw in two. "You want to do this or you want me to?" I greased up one end of each of the two pieces of straw. She took and inserted them in her nostrils, breathing experimentally.

"You good?"

"I'm good."

"Good." I pushed the strips of cloth into the plaster and stirred them around. "Anything else you want to ask me before we get started?"

"You can say it's none of my business."

"I know I can." I pulled a strip out of the plaster and slid it between the fingers of my left hand so the excess plaster glopped back into the bucket. "You sure you don't have any more questions?"

She did have one more. She asked, "Do you think it's a sin?"

I maneuvered the first strip carefully, carefully under the two straws and stretched it across her mouth the long way, pressing it down at the corners and along the seam of her lips the way I'd seen her do a dozen times to get the plaster to conform to the shapes of a face. I tilted my head to examine my work before I took another strip. "I'm a little fuzzy on the concept of what is and is not sin, so I'm going to leave that question alone and go back to the first one. Eugene said Jeannie said she and I were lovers, and you'd like me to confirm or deny."

Her eyes followed my movements. I was tempted to lay the next strip across them. I laid it across her forehead instead, letting the ends drip plaster down over the shower cap. Next I went across the bridge of her nose, then her cheeks, giving myself time to think. At last I said, "It is none of your business. I think you know that. But since you asked, if I don't answer, I might as well just say yes. But the real question isn't if we're lovers, is it? That's a complicated one to answer, anyway. What I think you really want to know is: have we had sex? And there's a part of me that wants to punish you for asking, especially because of your follow-up question. So let me just point out that I would never ask you about Eugene that way. You understand that, don't you?"

She closed her eyes, which I took to mean yes.

"I remember Pastor Wingate talking about sin, how it comes from a word that means missing your target. By that definition, you asking me if Jeannie and I were lovers, when you really mean, did we have sex, qualifies as a sin. Or maybe me assuming you meant something other than what you said is a sin. So let me save us both from going to hell by answering the question you actually did ask me, which was whether Jeannie and I are lovers."

I thought about it while I laid a plaster strip across the side of her face and patted it smooth. "I can only answer for myself," I sad. "Do I love Jeannie Ivory?" I laid a strip along the other side and one under her chin. At last I said, "I guess I do. I must."

Angela opened her eyes. A tear leaked out the corner of one of them, ran a short distance and filled up a depression in the petroleum jelly and stayed there. I continued laying strips across the planes and hollows of her face until all that was left of her face were her eyes. They looked up at me, slick with tears, the color of two regrets.

"I find it hard to believe a word she says," I confessed, "but that doesn't stop me caring about her. I find it hard to believe much of what anybody tells me, including myself. You need to close your eyes now."

The eyes are the most complicated features of the human face. Two soft domes, set inside a hollow of bone with ridges of different heights set on every side, two rows of lashes and a fold of skin that relaxes across the top of the domes as they close. It took me a while to get the strips to conform to all those shapes without buckling. When I finally had her covered, I took the rest of the strips and started layering them up on top of each other, building up a solid mask. Then I scooped up what was left of the plaster in the bucket and spread it over the top. I sat and talked to her while it set up. Just thinking out loud, really. "You know how they say seeing is believing? That's true to a point, because Jeannie told me the most outlandish stories I ever heard. I knew they couldn't be true. Yet in a way I believed every word, I pictured it all so clearly in my head. Once I've seen something, I can't unsee it. She told me about a woman dying of a broken neck. I have since seen that woman with my own two eyes. I talked to her just the other day. So now I have two sets of memories in my head, one true and the other not, yet the one is just as vivid as the other. So I have a choice to make. Do I believe the pictures Jeannie Ivory put in my head? Or the ones my own good senses put there for me? Do I call her a liar because the pictures in her head don't square with the pictures in mine?

"She believes she invented Eugene? *Invented* him! Out of thin air! And he's been siphoning energy from her ever since, taking everything good from her, so eventually all that's left of her will be the empty shell of a human being. Now, what's crazy is, she told me what would happen. She predicted Eugene would take me from her. I was one of the last good things left to her, and Eugene would rob her of that. Of me. 'It'll be good for you,' she told me. She predicted the success I'm having, which you are so much a part of. In a sick way, it all makes perfect sense. At least, to me it does. I wonder if it does to you?

"We create our own realities, right? We each put our little part of the puzzle together in our own way, depending on the pieces we're dealt. If your picture comes out a little different from mine, so long as we make our edges line up somehow, what difference does it make? When our pieces don't line up, we have a problem. Then I'm gonna tell you you're doing it all wrong and you might need therapy. I might come over and look at it from your point of view and try to show you where you got off on the wrong foot. But if you're like most people, you'll be thinking I'm the one that's screwed up, and you'll try and fix my way of seeing things. I'll enlist somebody else and convince them to see it my way, you'll get your friends to see it your way, and the next thing you know, we've got two different religions and we go to war. But do I have to be right and you wrong? Or do you have to convert me to your way of thinking? It's just a puzzle, and we don't have half the pieces.

Why not leave space between us for what we don't know? If things line up, fine. If they don't, we know we're still missing some pieces is all.

"I don't have the answers to most of my own questions, much less yours. Am I Jeannie's lover? You got me. She tried to kill herself in my back yard because I called a wrong number and got Eugene to come dig us out of a snow storm. I can't begin to fathom that logic. I think she needs at least one other person in the world to look at her part of the puzzle and say, 'I never thought to put it together that way,' instead of, 'You're a fucking lunatic!' and I wish I could do that for her, I do. But does it have to be at the expense of my own sanity? That's the kicker."

Angela raised her hand off the table and groped in the air until I took it in mine. She squeezed, and I squeezed back. And in a way, there was more truth, more common sense, in that hand clasp than in all of my words put together.

Once the plaster had set up, I eased the straws out of her nose and got my fingers under the edges of the mask at her jaw line. I gently worked it free. She helped. We soon had it off and set to one side, while I wiped the Vaseline from around her eyes, then gave her the towel and let her do the rest. Her face had turned pink from the heat of the plaster.

"I think we got an eyelash," I said, inspecting the inside of the mask.

She cleared her throat. "I'm sorry, Vanessa. I shouldn't have asked you that the way I did. I wasn't judging you. I just wanted to know if you thought it was a sin or not because I'm not sure. When I go away to school, there are going to be girls who are into other girls and boys who are into other boys. It's not like I've never encountered a gay person before. But Eugene says art schools are havens for homosexuality. I need to be strong in my faith if I'm intent on going. But I'm pretty sure he only said that because he wants me to go to Evangel with him."

"You asking my opinion?"

"If you have one."

"Then I think it has more to do with biology than faith. Four years spent in one place or another isn't going to affect your sexual orientation, unless you're wired that way to begin with."

"I don't think so, either."

"Is that why you broke up?"

"It might be what he thinks."

"What do you think?"

She seemed to consider it, but then a grin crept up one side of her face, and she said, "It's your turn." She pulled off the shower cap and handed it to me. I put it on. She snipped a straw in two and handed me the pieces. Then she showed me a baggie full of different-sized holes she'd punched out of card stock. "I want to try something."

After she'd slathered my face with petroleum jelly, she started taking and placing the dots of paper across my nose and cheeks and chin and forehead, everywhere I had a freckle. "I hope they're thick enough the plaster will pick up an impression of them. What do you think?"

I wished she hadn't brought up the way I felt about Jeannie. I wanted to say how lonely it felt, now that I understood how much she'd lied to me. And I thought how lonely Jeannie must feel, having no one left to hear her stories. Eugene did take me from her. I'd known that since he appeared over the crest of snow that morning. What I hadn't taken into account was that he had also taken Jeannie away from me.

I'd made a choice—a no-brainer on the surface of it, but a choice nonetheless—between two operating systems. I picked the one that seemed better supported, the one that came bundled with its only little network of compatibility. I no longer had to feel so isolated, so self-reliant. I had a community I could call on.

Which trubled me, since I no more believed the stories my new community told than I did Jeannie's. The biggest difference between Jesus dying on the cross to rescue me from my sins and Jeannie conjuring a lost boy who comes to life and robs her of her soul is in the number of people who believed in one and not the other. People need to ground themselves in one kind of fiction or another. But why? Why is that? What do we need that simple, unadorned reality does not provide?

Meaning? Direction? Insight? A set of rules? What?

When Angela finished applying her paper freckles to my real ones, she mixed a new batch of plaster and began to cover me in a new version of myself, one strip at a time, an inside-out version from which I could later fashion a public face, an angel-self to express my eternal gratitude for calling a wrong number.

Moving my face as little as possible, like a ventriloquist, I asked, "Do you believe in angels?"

She squeegeed a strip of fabric between her fingers, applied it to my face. "I've never met one. Not the kind in the Bible. In the Bible, every time an angel shows up, it's not like we think of them. They're not beautiful and they don't watch over us and protect us from harm. When an angel appears to someone, it usually means that person is in for a rude awakening. You have to stop talking now." The next strip went across my mouth. "I mean, imagine what it must have been like for Mary. I don't know how old she was, probably my age or younger. Girls married young then, and she was a virgin. Yet an angel appears to her and turns her world upside-down. I doubt people believed her when she said an angel came and told her she was going to have a baby and that baby was the Son of God. Do you think Joseph believed her? He stood by her. But do you really think he believed her? I don't make that kind of angel," she concluded. "I make ordinary, everyday angels."

My mind flashed on an image that tormented me: Jeannie, bare-chested, arms scraping a bloody pair of wings out of the snowbank. Me, scrambling out the kitchen window, screaming at her brother to call 911. Her voice going drowsier and drowsier. "Take everything! Take everything!" I caught her arm as it dragged across the snow, an open flap of skin, blood gushing. I took her left arm, close to her heart, and stopped it from moving. There was no strength in it. I jammed the heel of my palm into her armpit, applying pressure to try and stop the bleeding. She'd lost so much blood already, who knew if it did any good. Billy came through the window and knelt in the snow on the other side of her, picked up the shirt she'd pulled off and twisted it around her upper arm, as close to the shoulder as he could get, to make a tourniquet. He slid the belt out of his jeans and cinched it around the left arm. Her eyes began to fade away. I screamed at her, "You stay here!" and slapped her face, like something you see in a movie. "You stay!" Her eyelids fluttered but didn't open.

Seemed like hours before the paramedics arrived, calling from inside the house, climbing through the window, strapping her to a stretcher and passing her back through. Last I saw of her was the soles of her Doc Martens, twitching. All that was left of me was a stunned feeling.

I ended up at the hospital. Izzy drove. I somehow know that but I don't remember it. Someone had picked up Jeannie's mom and brought her. We clung to one another, me covered in her daughter's blood. At some point, Billy brought me home and waited while I bathed and changed, and we went back. The details are a blur to me. I saw Jeannie in bandages, sedated, her face flush with donated blood. I cried. I cried for the mystery of who she was, and the misery of it, for how lonely it must be to be her, for the paths her mind traveled where mine balked, turned back and walked the other way.

Here, now, stretched out on the picnic table in my greenhouse-turned-classroom/studio with my eyes and mouth sealed shut, I felt Angela's fingers patting my face through layers of cloth and plaster. In that darkness, I caught a glimpse of myself as I had never quite seen myself before: from a distance, magnified, the way I imagined Jeannie saw me. Through her telescopic vision, I saw all that Eugene had done for me, how he brought me clear evidence of a reality that was not available to her—at least, not acceptable—a reality in which the good people of Keening no longer whispered behind my back but accepted me, upheld my virtue. Truth to tell, I think they had not forgiven me so much as they collectively agreed to forget I wasn't one of them. Unlike Jeannie, I chose not to remind them. I let them focus their silent ire, their blame and, if need be, their pity on her. On Jeannie Ivory.

She had re-enacted for them, in a way, the story of my grandmother. Only this time, I had witnesses to the fact that not only did I not try to murder anybody, I actually helped *save* a life. That became the new story of who Vanessa Cavendish was. The old version got overwritten.

Somebody—it might have been Franklin Swansea, or somebody in a book I read—once pointed out to me that most people don't think, they just rearrange their prejudices. Some folks saw me as Jeannie's victim, while others saw me as her hero, but either way, the new storyline was no less a fiction than my old one. The part of me I'm least proud of wished I'd let her bleed out and not come back to haunt me. The better part of me wished I'd paid closer attention to what she tried to tell me that night before she did what she did.

In my experience, nothing's harder to pin down than actual fact. No matter which way I turned the picture-puzzle in my mind, I couldn't find an angle, a point of view that demonstrated a truer or more complete way of looking at Jeannie Ivory than any other. If I was to paint her portrait, it would end up looking like a fake Picasso, with her nose going one direction, her eyes another and the rest of her from a third angle. In a way, I think that's how folks still see me. Jeannie was right that, in the popular imagination of Keening, Oklahoma, I was responsible for both Leon and my grandmother's deaths, and nothing save my acceptance of their religion could ever redeem me in their eyes. It was only a matter of time before they stepped over to my side of the table and started rearranging my puzzle pieces to better fit their own.

But I had got a taste of social redemption, and it was sweet. I had yet to go through all the motions of their religion, but I knew that public acceptance was available to me in a way it never had been before.

When the time came, I felt Angela's fingers probing the edges of my mask, little by little releasing the rigid plaster from my pliable skin.

# BROKEN HALLELUJAH

Late July. I stood back from my Wall of Gratitude and called it done. Done in the structural sense, at least. I still had a few surface refinements to make before I painted it. Eight snow shovels flanked the blade of a snow plow, four to a side, to form the base of the wall. The handles angled upward and inward. The angels' snow boots hovered in mid-air, their elongated bodies maybe half again as big as life-size. They floated this way and that, converging in an overall way toward the middle. Their overlapping wings took up most of the wall's expanse. I had positioned them in such a way that the faces of the men and boys who had come to dig me out that day in February, had they been notes on a musical staff, would spell out the melody of Leonard Cohen's "Hallelujah" song. Not the whole thing, just that one word sung twice the way he does. My little joke. I didn't expect anyone else to make the connection and I never said a word about it to anyone, not even Angela. But of all the music I knew, that song best summed up for me the profound mystery and downright ignorance I felt as regards my relationship to other people and myself, to rotten luck and divine providence: a holy and a broken hallelujah.

At the top in the middle I put the shape of the sun with its rays burning through the clouds and showering down on everyone, myself included, and Angela, who had come to my rescue every bit as much as Eugene, probably more. Originally, I meant to put the two of them side by side in the middle of my composition, but that no longer seemed like such a good idea. I mixed a final coat of lime plaster and applied it and, when that was dry, I painted the whole thing white and feathered in a few irregular streaks of veining to make it look like a marble frieze. I wished I had the skill to paint the whole thing in a more lifelike manner, but I am no Michaelangelo, and even if I was up to such a task, it would have taken way too long, so I called it done. I sewed together twelve white flat sheets and made a drape to cover the entire wall. I anchored my drape at the corners and at several points along the front and back to keep the wind from picking it up. The second Sunday of August I set as the date for my unveiling, and we made arrangements for a potluck dinner after church, everyone invited. I borrowed tables and chairs to set up in my parking lot. Come that Saturday, we had everything in place, all my plaster casts cleaned up and set out to serve as centerpieces, the forecast sunny and warm, pop-up tents set up for shade. I had in mind what I wanted to say and I wrote it down in case I got nervous and forgot, but I didn't think I would.

I had worked for months on this project. It had come to mean so much more to me than just a Texas-size Thank You. It signified my acceptance of, as well as my acceptance by, a community I felt had always excluded me. The unveiling of my wall was to be, for me, a chance to celebrate with the good people of First Assembly. They had become, in a way, a kind of extended family. Something I had never had before.

I went to bed with a smile on my face.

In the morning I showered and dressed for church in a new outfit I allowed myself for the occasion: a flouncy white broomstick skirt with cowboy boots and a gauzy white blouse with full sleeves that some might have considered immodest but for the sage-green western-style vest I wore over it to disguise my lack of feminine amplitude. I spent half an hour with the curling iron and put on lipstick, eye shadow, the works. I folded my notes in a neat square and slipped them into the pocket of my vest, just in case I felt the urge to look them over during the sermon, and set off for the barn.

Jiminy started like a charm. I cruised by the shop and could not resist one last peek at the parking lot, all set up for the afternoon's festivities. My eye zoomed down the long aisle that stretched between all the tents and tables to a wall of darkness at the far end.

I did a double-take. My foot slammed on the brakes. Jiminy skidded to a stop. "Holy fuck!" I mouthed. I opened the cab door and slid to the ground, already striding in the direction of my wall. "Are you fucking shitting me?"

My sewn-together flat-sheet drape had been pulled down and trampled. The wings of every singlle one of my angels had been spray-painted black. Their eyes and fingers dribbled blood.

Discarded cans of spray paint littered the rumpled drape. I kicked one and sent it flying. I screamed. I balled my fists. I paced to and fro, fuming and flailing at the empty air until, at last, I crumbled to my knees with my head in my hands and bawled.

# MORAL SUPPORT

I showed up late to Sunday service, furious and defeated. Standing at the wide double doors at the back of the sanctuary, scanning the backs of the heads of the congregation, I wondered who? Who among them? Which one—or which ones—had done this to me, to my wall? Nobody outside the members of this church had any reason to know that today was to be my day. It had to be one of them. I saw Eugene in his light-and-sound booth and did not return his smile. I walked slowly up the aisle to the right of the center section of pews and found Gay and Todd Lamb in their usual pew, second from the front. I did not sit with them but leaned and whispered in Todd's ear. My voice shook with anger, more than I yet knew how to spend or who to spend it on. "We have to call it off. Can you tell the Pastor for me?"

There were always a few announcements made at some point during the service, but I didn't know if that moment had passed.

Todd looked confused.

"It's ruined," I said. "In the middle of the night, somebody—" But no. This was a mistake. I couldn't tell him in front of everybody. I was afraid I might break down and start crying again—or worse, start screaming. Whoever had wrecked my wall, I had no intention of giving them that satisfaction.

Todd must have sensed how bad off I was. He stood and motioned to Gay, who also got up. The three of us walked out to the vestibule.

"You've got to tell Pastor Wingate to call it off," I said again. My whole body trembled with anger, with fear, with humiliation! "Somebody come and spray-painted all over my wall. Black and—and blood and—and I can't have everybody come and see it like that!"

"They what?" Gay Lamb shook me by the shoulder, as if I were an unruly child lying to her face. "What did they do?"

"Red and black." I pantomimed spray-painting, in case she needed a visual aid. "Blood on everybody's hands and—and faces and—and black all over the wings and—" Neither one of them had seen the finished wall, so I started to explain, in fits and starts, what I meant, what I had done, what had been done to me.

"What a horrible thing!" Gay said. "What a horrible, horrible thing!"

"The worst of it is thinking it might be someone—" I pointed at the sanctuary doors— "someone sitting in there right now, gloating!"

"Oh, you don't really think so! Do you?"

"Who else even knew about it, outside of this church?"

"Why everybody, Silly! It's been in the newspaper and on the radio and all over."

I gaped at her. I closed my eyes, trying not to picture TV cameras broadcasting my humiliation to the world.

Todd rested a hand on my shoulder. At least he didn't shake me. "Let's not jump to conclusions, Sister Cavendish."

I had been called that a few times. Sister. I didn't like the sound of it today.

Gay said, "What about that girl who used to work for you? The one who—" She didn't have to finish. I doubt she intended to.

I didn't have anything to wipe my nose. I used the heel of my palm. "She's still in the hospital as far as I know."

"Isn't she the likeliest one?"

"It doesn't matter now." I turned to Todd. "We need to call it off."

Gay laid a hand on his arm to remind him: "All the ladies have brought dishes."

"Seriously?" I said.

"Well, no. I just mean, maybe we could have the potluck here. In the Fellowship Hall."

"The tables and chairs are all out at my place," I pointed out.

"We might have time to go get them," Todd said. "Would it be all right with you if we shifted the location?"

I didn't know what to say. It seemed the priority for them was everybody sitting down to eat. But if that was all it took to get the spotlight off of me... I sniffed and nodded.

"I'll get a few fellows to help."

So it was decided. The announcement was changed. Todd Lamb and Gary Purcell headed out to my place with a few young men to collect the folding tables and chairs so nobody's Sunday dinner plans had to undergo a major revision. They would see what had been done, and they would tell everyone, but that couldn't be helped.

I did not stay for potluck. I could not abide to sit through Sunday dinner wondering how many of the people I broke bread with secretly enjoyed my humiliation, much less had caused it. Over Gay Lamb's and Pastor Wingate's objections, their attempts at comfort, I went home and confronted my angels.

I stood in my empty parking lot in my done-up hair and Sunday finest with my hands on my hips and I demanded answers.

"Why do you mock me?" I said.

I said, "I have never done a goddamn thing to a goddamn one of you. Not one of you. I don't understand it. You come here to help me when I'm in trouble, yet when I try to say thank you, this is what I get? Black wings and bloody eyes? What's it supposed to mean? Is it some kind of message, because if so, I'm not picking up what you're laying down, so why do you fucking bother? I'm not one of you? I get it! I don't believe in your religion! I don't believe you get clean by washing in the blood! I think you're all a bunch of sick fucking psychopaths, if you want the truth! Do you want the truth?" I asked them again, "Well, do you?"

They didn't answer.

I searched one face after another: Izzy, Crumb, Billy, the Pastor, Gary Purcell, Todd, Josh and Justin Pearson, Zack Angleton and the group in the middle that included Angela, Jarrod, Eugene and me. Only then did I realize that one of us was not like the others. I had no blood on my hands. Instead, my hair was spray-painted red. Like I wore a wild halo in the same bright bloody color as the others wore on their hands and faces. I did have tears running down my face like the rest of them, but my hands were clean. I wondered why?"

Then I noticed something else. Something about the black.

I had not given myself wings. That was the whole point. I meant to show myself surrounded by angels, not count myself as one of them. But by painting all their wings black and leaving the space around me and behind me white, my vandal had given me a pair.

I knew by now who did it. I didn't need to call and find out she'd been released.

When I went to gather up the spray cans, I found a note weighted down by one of the red ones. She hadn't signed it. It just said, "I thought your sculpture could use a little color."

I shook the can. It still had a little in it. The black ones and two other red ones were all empty. I now had a more organized recycling system behind my wall. I gathered up the empties and tossed them in the metals section and carried the one can of red inside, along with the note. I set them on the counter by the register.

I sat and thought about what to do.

She was right.

In a way that I knew but didn't want to admit to myself, she was right.

I heard a car in the parking lot and wished I'd taken the time to drape the sheets over my giant eyesore of a wall again. I spied Eugene's car through the front window and saw that he had Angela with him. They stood looking at the damage for a while before they let themselves in. Eugene carried a styrofoam container. "We brought you something to eat."

Angela said, "It's just awful."

I pointed to the counter. "She left a note."

Angela went to retrieve the note. "She?"

I told them who I thought it was. Who I knew it was.

Touching it only at the plastic nozzle, Angela tipped the can at an angle to study it. "She's not the brightest bulb. You called the police?"

I shook my head. "You think I ought to?"

"Malicious destruction of property," Eugene said.

"I suppose."

"I just feel sick about it, Vanessa." That was Angela. She read the note out loud. "You can't let her get away with it."

"She's right, though, you know."

"She's *right?*"

"I don't mean what she did, but what she said is right. I got lazy. I got scared is more like it, and that made me lazy."

They didn't understand what I meant, so I explained. "I let myself get in a hurry. Summer's about to run out. I wanted to have the wall done in the nice weather, so I could have everybody over to see it and to celebrate with me. So I painted the whole thing white, thinking I could always add some color later if it called for it. I needed to be done with it before the two of you take off for school and leave me back in charge of my own business. When am I gonna have time to paint all those faces and hands and all the other details the way they deserve to be painted? I don't even know where to begin! I could read up on how to paint a faux marble wall. That was easy. But I'm no artist. Now I'm gonna be alone here to run the shop, with no time to spend out there, and just look at it! I can't leave it like that!"

"You're not thinking of taking her back, are you?"

"No."

"Vanessa, you can't!"

"No," I said again.

"Not after this!"

"All I said is she has a point."

"You need to call the police and take out a restraining order on her. She's a sick puppy, Vanessa. I'm sorry, I feel bad for her, I do. But you can't trust someone like that." Angela said this to me, of course, but I couldn't help thinking she spoke for Eugene's benefit as well.

"It was sweet of you two to come," I said. I wondered, partly because of how outspoken Angela was about her feelings toward Jeannie, if maybe Eugene had come to his senses and the two of them had patched up their differences. "I'll talk to the Sheriff about it. Keep in mind, I don't know for a fact it was her."

"She left evidence. There are fingerprints in the paint on the can."

"I know."

"If you won't do it to protect yourself —" She didn't finish.

"What?"

"Never mind."

I looked around the shop. She had a point, too. What if Jeannie decided to break in and take out her grievances on my inventory, a lot of which was not mine but Angela's and her students' work, which I had not paid them for? I sold it on consignment.

"I'll call," I said.

"I'd feel better if you did."

"I will."

Eugene, I noticed, had very little to say. It seemed he was there primarily for moral support.

# El Greco

A deputy sheriff came and investigated. He took photographs and put on rubber gloves and bagged up all the paint cans. He wanted to know all about the wall and whose faces were on it and why I had made it, so I told him the whole story, including Jeannie's part in it, about getting snowed in and how upset she was when Eugene showed up to help and what she did to herself as a result.

He seemed to know the story of her attempted suicide. "You think she's the one that did this? Jeannie Ivory?"

"I think so, yes. Assuming she got out of the State Hospital, that is."

"Easy enough to find out. Anyone else who might be upset with you about your wall, or hold a grudge against you?"

"Not that I'm aware of."

He handed me his card and said to call him if anything came up or if I thought of anything else. He seemed about ready to go, so I asked him about a restraining order. "What's done is done," I said. "I'd like to go ahead and repair the damage, if that's all right. But I don't want it to keep happening."

"Do you intend to file an insurance claim?"

I hadn't even thought of that. "I don't know if it'd be covered."

"Then go ahead and do what you need to do. As for a restraining order, if we find out Ms. Ivory is the perpetrator, it would be wise. What was the nature of your relationship with her?"

"She was my employee."

"Is that all?"

"Yes," I said. "That's all."

"What about her relationship with Eugene Lamb?"

"You'd have to ask her," I said. "I would not expect to get a straight answer."

He looked at me funny. "Why do you say that?"

"Aside from the fact that she's nucking futs?" I said. "You talk to her, you'll find out."

As it turned out, Jeannie had been released from Fort Supply less than a week before the spray-paint incident. She wasn't living at home—at least, not according to her mother. Where else she might have gone was anybody's guess. You can count the number of homeless shelters in Keening on, let's see, no hands at all. Long and short of it? If the Sheriff couldn't locate her, he couldn't serve her with a restraining order.

I kept my wall covered during business hours and went out of an evening to try and do what I could to make it less hideous. The white paint I had did a piss poor job of covering the red, never mind the black. The thought of making it all white again no longer appealed to me, anyway, so I went online to find out how to mix a good flesh color. Not as easy as they make it look, unless you're painting manikins. Not everyone is the same color, a person's hands are not necessarily the exact same shade as their face, and even a face is not just one color but a whole range of different ones, unless you want it to look like total pancake. One video said to use a toothbrush to flick speckles of different shades of tan and orange and yellow and blue and even violet, the lighter, warmer colors for the highlights and darker, cooler ones in the shadows. As for the wings, after several coats of paint, I had a grayish white that I thought I could work with. Problem being, my own "wings" still showed up whiter than everybody else's, when I wasn't even supposed to have any.

Cooler weather was not far off. The days were already getting shorter. I set up a pair of flood lamps on yellow stands so I could work late, but they only threw my shadow stark against the wall and made it harder to work, not easier. Plus I found out the hard way that artificial light changes the way colors work together in broad day.

Come the end of August, I said goodbye to Angela and Eugene and decided to close my shop on Tuesdays to give myself one full day a week just to work on the wall. By the end of September, I had it looking better, all the red and black more or less covered up and the angels looking more like the people they supposedly represented and less like ghosts and ghouls. The wings came out a sort of dove color, except my own, which I painted blue to look like sky. The blade of the plow I made a deeper shade of bluish-gray with piles of snow at the bottom that I added by building up a layer of new mud that then had to dry and be painted.

I posted pictures of it on my blog—I had to manage that on my own now, too—and a girl who saw it (I assumed she was a little girl because of her username) asked me if it was inspired by El Greco, which,

304

I didn't know what that was, so I Googled it.

I commented back: "No, Miranda Panda. I never heard of El Greco before, but I'm inspired by him now. Thank you!" I added a smiley face.

That night, my vandal struck again.

# A NEW FACE

No spray paint this time. Instead, she left an ax—my ax from the woodshed—leaning against the wall next to a big hole she'd chopped out of the center of the wall, out of the blade of Gary Purcell's snow plow and the lower half of my body, leaving rebar and blocks of recycled plastic exposed.

Where the attack with spray paint had left a message I could decipher (my so-called angels had blood on their hands), this one struck me as a simpler, more brutal gesture. Way more personal. She had mutilated me, my body, my sex in particular. I got that. But to go after a snow plow? The rationale behind that eluded me.

Then again, how much sense did it need to make? She hated me now. She hated what I stood for, what I was trying to express, because it did not accord with her version of reality, which I rejected.

I rejected her.

Which, in its way, was also brutal.

I took the ax and put it away. I didn't call the Sheriff's Office again. I brought my new smart phone out and took pictures of the damage and posted them to my blog. I wrote:

> *I know who did this.*
>
> *I don't know why you did it. Not entirely. I can never predict what's on your mind. Rage? The feeling that you've been cheated out of your life some way? Well, I wish I knew how to get your life back for you but I don't. It's a safe bet that blaming me and trying to get even with me won't help. Blaming an imaginary enemy won't help, either. Blaming, period, won't help.*
>
> *What's yours, really and truly yours, can't be taken from you, never has been, never will be. You just need to claim it is all. You need to own it.*

Over the next several days, between my blog and my Tangible Angels Facebook page, that post elicited hundreds of comments: questions, rants about online bullying, notes of sympathy, outrage and other forms of support for me and condemnation for "whoever did this."

I spent my evenings reading, responding, ignoring and deleting. Most of it was "positive" in one form or another, but underneath it all ran a current of something that, if I looked at it not from my point of view but from Jeannie's, probably came across as, let's just say, unhelpful. Assuming she read any of it.

What I mean is this: All that positivity flowing in my direction only promised to alienate her that much more. What good would that do? My bad, I realized now, to take our feud public. But would keeping quiet about it have produced a better result? I figured, in all likelihood, she never saw my post. Come to think of it, she probably didn't have access to a computer unless she went to a library. How did she even know I had a website?

Turns out she did know.

I get a lot of spam comments. Every blogger does, I guess. Eugene had installed a plug-in to catch most of it and delete it automatically, but every now and again, something gets past the filters, usually from someone who wants to sell me on a better way to run my business or improve my website's search engine standings. Once in a blue moon, I get something from a pervert who's figured out how to fly under the radar. One of those caught my eye. It contained a link to a page called …com/sister/iamyoujean.

I knew better. Eugene had taught me better than to click a link that came in unsolicited like that, but this one caught me off guard. I don't know if it took me to a phishing site or not. When I got there, it just looked like porn. A video started playing as soon as it loaded: of a skinny girl groaning in her bed and evidently masturbating inside her pajamas.

I was more annoyed than offended and went to click the back button when I heard the girl moan, *"Jarrod! Please, Jarrod!"*

The camera zoomed in on her mouth, open now in a strained, shaky kind of silence. I couldn't make out enough of her pixelated features to recognize her one hundred percent, plus she had her forearm thrown over her eyes. But plain to see, from her wrist halfway to her elbow, was a series of hash-marks, a dozen or more parallel lines, slightly raised and angry red in color.

It still could have been anybody, but I knew it wasn't. I also knew the video had not been made recently. The lines on her arm were too neat, the cuts too superficial. It was Jeannie, all right, but a younger Jeannie with a rounder, fuller face. I felt sick, sad and sorry all at the same time. Why did I need to see that? It felt like I'd walked in on something I was never meant to witness. Yet I had been taken there deliberately, to that specific page, that video, that bedroom, led there by a knowing hand.

And I knew whose.

"I don't want to play this game anymore," I said out loud to the computer.

"*Jarrod!*" she cried, louder, going at herself with a more insistent and determined attitude. "*Jarrooooooooood!*"

I clicked away. The back arrow returned me to my blog, but I didn't want to see any more of that, either. I shut down my computer and went to the shop. I could not stop thinking of Angela's corkscrew, of her "Cameo Angel" flapping its ruby-beaded wings, and I couldn't stop thinking of Jeannie half-naked in the snow, her strange, broken heart pumping itself dry, and of how the snow melted under her as it drank her hot blood.

I wanted to scream.

I wanted to vomit.

I wanted to purge myself of her, of the toxic waste she had dumped into my system. As attacks go, her video scored a more direct hit than anything she might have done to my wall.

My wall.

I needed to work on my wall, needed to repair it. I seized on that as the one thing I could do that might make sense, if only because it meant physical activity. I had so much nervous energy to expend, I needed to use my hands. I needed to be doing, not thinking. I went to the greenhouse for my tools: a shovel and a hoe, the garden hose, a tarp. What else did I need? I had a little straw left in the barn, a few bales. The wheelbarrow and the screens were in the greenhouse shed. I started in that direction when I saw it.

A new plaster mold. A new face.

When they came for the folding tables for the potluck in the Fellowship Hall, the guys from the church had carefully stacked all the plaster centerpiece molds on one of my picnic tables. I moved them to a shelf in the greenhouse, and that's where they stayed. This was a new one, perfectly clean, with no stains from the red clay I'd used to make the cob for the angel's faces. It threw me for a loop. Had I forgotten someone?

The mold was an inside-out face, of course. They all were. But this one had a weird protrusion on the inside, as if whoever it was had got a mouthful of plaster, so I couldn't make out whose face it belonged to. I tossed my tools in the wheelbarrow and carted them out to the parking lot and counted my angels. I had the right number. I knew I'd included everyone. The one in the greenhouse had to be an extra. Had Angela goofed one up and done it over without saying anything? Surely I would have known, though. We worked side by side on all but hers and mine. I decided she must have done a practice one, maybe of herself. Maybe one of her students?

It didn't matter.

I screened some clay and mixed up a new batch of rough cob to fill in the hole in Gary Purcell's plow and to give myself a new pair of legs. The work took my mind off the video for a while. Or it put me in a different zone where, if I couldn't help thinking about Jeannie (given the damage she'd done both to my wall and to my peace of mind), at least I felt constructive again. Like I was in control of something. Less of a victim.

But I wasn't the victim, I decided. Not really. I was more of a bystander who got caught up in Jeannie's crossfire. Her drama was around me, I reminded myself. It was never about me, regardless of how hard she tried to make it mine. That realization allowed me to consider what I'd seen in the video, and my reaction to it, in a more neutral, unbiased light. What upset me most about it was the clear impression I had, watching it, that I was not supposed to be watching it. I mean, yes, whoever sent it to me (Jeannie, beyond the shadow of a doubt) had meant for me to watch it. But she had never purposely made it for me to watch. Not originally. The making of it had clearly preceded me. It had been made before I knew her, before she came to work for me. In the video her hair was neither bone-white nor black and blue as when I first met her, nor was it the dark brown she'd dyed it more recently, but a soft mouse brown, and longer than I had ever seen it.

I would not have put it past her, considering what Jarrod had told me about the way she'd stalked him in high school, to have made such a video of herself for him. She'd hardly be the first teenager to demonstrate her desire for a boy she liked in such a graphic way. But to post a link to it in the comments on my blog? That was a stretch, even for Jeannie.

"Why? Why? Why? Why? Why?" I wondered out loud, using a trowel to feather the edges of fresh mud into old. Did she still trust me at least enough not to approve the comment, which would make it public? Because no way was I going to do that.

Maybe she just didn't care.

Had she found out about me and Jarrod? Was I supposed to feel guilty about that? I could've told her I didn't need any help in that department. I could also have told her that I hadn't seen Jarrod once since the day I met his mother, alive and well, back in August. Between the business with the wall and running the shop by myself, I didn't have much time for a social life. Plus, the whole thing just got too weird for me after that. We talked on the phone a time or two. He reminded me that his offer to take Jiminy off my hands still stood.

"I dunno," I said. "She's worth a lot more now. She's mint."

"She won't be if you keep beating her up."

"I don't beat her up."

"You treat her like she's your everyday vehicle. I see you in town with her all the time."

"She is my everyday vehicle. She's all I got."

"Jiminy's a boy's name, anyway," he said, not giving up.

"No, it's not. It's a cricket's name. Do you know how to tell the sex of a cricket?"

He didn't answer. It was general knowledge, by this time, that Jeannie had become something more than my employee. Jarrod didn't ask if he could see me, and I didn't offer. I never mentioned having met his mom, either. If she ever said anything to him about me, he never brought it up.

After a couple of hours, the first stage of my repair job on the wall was complete. The hole was filled in, at least. I still needed to lay in a course of lime plaster to bring it back to where it had been before the ax job, then try to match the paint. On top of being furious, I was now sad, confused and sick over the video. I still couldn't fathom why she'd sent it, but I think it sealed the deal for me on sleeping with Jarrod ever again. I had no desire to have Jeannie's voice in my head, wailing his name at a crucial moment. And that's exactly what would happen. I knew it would.

Maybe she knew that, too. Maybe that was her intent.

I hosed off my tools and put them away. I had mixed more cob than I needed. I wrapped the extra up in a tarp to keep it from drying out and set it in the wheelbarrow with the screened clay. Don't ask me why, except, I'd gone to the trouble to mix it. Why throw it out?

# PART 5
# CANYON GIRL

# FAMILY REUNION

That night, she paid my wall another visit.

She took the extra cob I'd set aside in the greenhouse and used it to build up over my repair job and to add another angel, her upside-down self, naked, emaciated, eyes closed, mouth open in a scream, just the way it appeared near the end of the video she sent me, at the point of her most excruciating pleasure. She made her face from the new mold I'd come across in the greenhouse, the one I didn't recognize. She left it lying on the ground, mud-stained. The open mouth answered the question of the glob of plaster protruding from the inside of the mold. What did she do, I wondered, pour plaster straight into her mouth? How did she not suffocate? I looked again and saw a nipple at the end of the protrusion, like she might have used a balloon. Pretty good trick, I must say, to make a mask of herself, working blind at least part of the time.

Her upside-down legs intertwined with mine, one over, one under. The one that went under mine bent at the knee, with the calf of that leg crossed over my belly to form an upside-down figure 4, like the Hanged Man in a Tarot deck. She had also reconstructed the lower half of my body, naked like hers, as if I was part of her orgasm, our legs woven together like a Celtic knot.

"Goddammit, Jeannie!" I said when I saw that.

The cob she'd applied was still fresh. I could've scraped it off with a hoe, could've taken it back down to where I'd left it yesterday.

Coulda-woulda-shoulda.

It was Wednesday. I needed to open the shop. I went to the greenhouse to get my sewn-together drape and cover up what she'd done. I couldn't find it.

Something ten feet wide by forty feet long doesn't get up and walk away. Jeannie had broken into the shop, that much I knew. She probably still had a key. For one creepy second, it felt like she knew what I was thinking, like she had anticipated my next move, knowing I'd want to cover up the wall, and hid the drape so I couldn't. I decided to go get Jiminy and parallel park her in front of the wall to hide the naked angel, in all its orgasmic, anorexic glory, from prying eyes.

I found my bed sheets in the barn, draped over a couple of bales' worth of straw she had taken apart and strewn over the floor. More straw filled in between the sheets to make a mattress under her and a blanket over her. The heel of her jump boot stuck out at one end and a few strands of mouse-brown hair, tangled with straw, at the other. I could not decipher the rest of her body from the extra folds of stuffed drapery.

I walked up to her. "Jeannie?"

She stirred. A thin hand appeared, the fingers waving, then collapsing on the straw.

"Jeannie, what the fuck?"

She wrestled her head free of her coverings and looked at me, eyes groggy, hair full of straw, mouth slack. "I need a job," she said, yawning, "and a place to stay."

"You have got to be shitting me."

"I don't have a lot of options." She let her head fall back, the skin slack as an old hammock between her jaw and cheekbone. Even the palm of her hand, caked with mud and resting next to her head, looked wasted. I think she fell back asleep.

"When did you eat last?"

"Hunh?"

I wanted to shake her. "When was the last time you had something to eat?"

"I'm fasting."

She didn't say anything else. I climbed aboard Jiminy, slammed the door and started her up.

Wouldn't you know it? I had customers. An SUV with Texas plates and a family of four stood right smack in the middle of the parking lot, gawking at Jeannie's nude luciferous angel. The woman looked oddly familiar, even from the back: short dark hair, long coat and heels, cute purse—something in the way she held it by the strap in the crook of her arm, something old school. I don't know. They all turned to look at me as I come rumbling across the gravel. No sense parking in front of the wall now, they blocked my way. So I pulled up beside their car and climbed down out of Jiminy.

"Good morning!" I called out to them with all the cheer I could muster.

"Vanessa?" the woman said, coming at me with two vertical creases in her forehead, converging between her brows in a capital V. My first impression was she looked pissed off, then I saw she was fixing to cry. "*Vanessa!*"

"Oh, my god!" I said. "Oh, my god!" And because I couldn't think what else to say, I said it again. "Oh, my god!"

She like to knocked me over backwards when she got to me and threw her arms around my neck, her purse flailing my backside. I grabbed onto her for dear life and held on. "Sheila? Sheila, what on earth are you doing here?"

She squeezed me so tight I thought she might break me in two. I had all I could do to stand my ground and squeeze her back.

"It's so good to see you!" she kept saying, "Lord have mercy, it's good to see you!" until it occurred to me she must've still thought I was dead.

She got to bawling, and then I started bawling, too. Don't ask me why. As sisters go, we'd never been that close. I had long ago formed the habit of thinking she blamed me for the death of her husband — her first husband, obviously, Leon — but if she did, she evidently had got over it.

Her new man and the two kids stood grinning at us. I say kids, but they weren't little, not even teenagers, both of them were full grown. The girl stood slender as a broom handle with tri-color hair: dark brown streaked with blonde and, just in front so it framed her narrow face, the softest, prettiest, cotton-candy blue, or more like teal.

"Oh, my god!" I said yet again. I seemed to have lost the whole rest of my vocabulary. "Lisa Julene? Is this Lisa Julene?"

I disentangled from Sheila and went over to her. She held her arms out straight, her fingers stretched as wide apart as they'd go, just the way she used to do when she was two and wanted to be picked up. Only the angle of her arms was different, pointing almost at the ground but ready to grab me. I stepped inside her hug like it was yesterday. "Do you remember me?" I asked her, touching her, holding her.

"Kind of," she sniffed and rubbed my back the way you do a stranger.

"You were just a baby! I can't believe it! You're taller than I am!" I turned to Sheila, not letting go of Lisa Julene. "She's taller than I am!"

I could hardly see anymore, the tears come so fast, so brutal. I couldn't speak for several minutes. The years collapsed on me. The

316

weight of them, all rolled into one, come crashing over me like a tsunami. I wasn't sure I could stand up.

"This is Ryan," Sheila was telling me, "and this is Paul." I couldn't have told you which name belonged to who until later on.

"Hoo, boy!" I said, fanning my chest with my sweatshirt at about the same speed my heart was pounding. "You want to come inside? Come on through here." Quicker to cut through the shop than go around by the barn. I hadn't let go of Lisa Julene but pulled her along with me. I could sense them all slowing down, looking around at all the angel paraphernalia. Angel books, angel fortune-telling cards, angel incense, angel this and angel that.

When Sheila followed me and Lisa Julene out the back of the shop, she stopped dead in her tracks.

"Grandma's house is gone!" She looked stunned as only my sister Sheila can look stunned, that deep V stabbing between her eyes again.

I thought, *Uh oh! She's not gonna be happy about this.* "Wasn't much left of it," I said. "I salvaged what I could."

"Huh! Well, that's a relief!" Sheila is sixteen years older than me, making her what? I had no head for math at that particular moment, but Jesus! Fifty-something? Age had softened her corners some. "I was dreading seeing it again, just ask Paul."

I didn't have to. Paul confirmed. "You can say that again!"

Lisa Julene patted the wall of my house by the front door like she was petting a horse. "I just adore adobe!"

"It's similar to adobe," I said. I brought them all in and gave them the tour and a quick run-down on my eclectic building methods and materials.

"We watched the video about ubuntu blox on your blog," Ryan said. Ryan was the son, I deduced, and Paul the father. Taller than his sister, with a stud in his lower lip and his long dark hair tied back in a pony tail, in a way, Ryan reminded me of his grandfather, from the one and only picture I had left of him, the one my grandma always kept on the upright piano in the parlor of the old house and someone — must have been Sheila, come to think of it — had left in my box of school papers in the attic. "And the one about your wall," Ryan added.

"Oh," I said, wincing. "About that wall." And then it occurred to me. I had completely forgotten about my overnight guest in the barn. "Shit!" I said. "Y'all make yourselves comfortable. I'll be back in a minute."

I ran out to the barn.

Jeannie smelled of body odor when I knelt beside her and touched where it looked like her shoulder might reside amid all the layers of straw and bed sheet. She hadn't bathed in god knows how long. "You awake?"

Her voice come muffled. "Not really."

"I got company," I said. "Somebody I haven't seen in ages. I'm trying to decide whether or not to call the Sheriff on you. He's been trying to serve you a restraining order for going on...shit! three weeks? Has it been that long? I kinda hate to let a golden opportunity pass him by. Like you camping out in my barn."

She stirred. A hand emerged and pulled the sheet from her face.

"So if you could give me some idea of your inten—"

"Two days," she said.

"Two days? No, it's been more than—"

She waggled her hand in front of her face. "You asked me how long since I've eaten."

I stood up, brushed the straw from my knees, wondering what I was going to do with her. "Last time I let you in my house didn't turn out so well."

She yawned. "Not for me. Turned out great for you."

I left the barn still undecided. I went to the shop and flipped the sign over from Open to Closed and locked the door. Then I went out to the road to fetch the new feather flag I'd bought to replace the old sand-wich board, when I changed the name of my shop, and tossed it in the back of my truck on my way back to the barn.

Jeannie sat on the one bale of straw that remained intact, hugging her knees and shivering in a tee-shirt and filthy jeans. Part of me screamed bloody murder at the rest of me for it, but I said, "Come on in the house, then. Let's get you something to eat."

She climbed off the straw bale and followed me. Her jeans puckered at the waist where she'd tied some of the belt loops together with yarn to keep them from slumping off her nonexistent ass, and her arms stuck out of her sleeves like two saplings stripped of their bark. "Been more than two days," I wagered. "Listen. My sister and my niece are here. I haven't seen them for—" I mentally subtracted 14 from 37— "twen-ty-three years. And her new husband and a nephew—I think he's my nephew — that I just met for the first time. So we got some catching up to do. Just so you know."

"Your family. That figures."

I turned on her. "What's that supposed to mean?"

"Nothing." She smiled. Lines appeared in her face where I didn't remember there being any before, pencil-thin ones at the corners of her mouth and her eyes. "I'm happy for you." Maybe I hadn't ever seen her smile before. "Truly."

"First we're gonna get you in the shower. No offense, but you smell."

"Tell me about it!"

"Then I'll get you something to eat. You like oatmeal?"

"Beggars can't be choosers."

"Some things none of us get to choose," I said. I'm not sure why. Those were just the words that come tumbling out of my mouth. Some days I really need to buy a filter.

"Like family?"

"That's not what I said."

"Oh."

I pushed into the house and announced, "Everybody, this is Jeannie. She's gonna jump in the shower real quick, and we'll make introductions later, okay? You go on ahead," I said to Jeannie. She knew where the bathroom was. "I'll bring you something to put on."

I found her jeans — the pair I had put on by mistake that morning some nine months ago — still on the shelf in my closet where I didn't know where else to put them. I took a flannel shirt down off a hanger and got socks and a tee shirt from my drawers and brought them to her. I set everything on the toilet lid. "Everything but underwear," I said. "I can't help you there. You'll just have to go commando."

She narrowed her eyes at me and said, "Thank you."

"Do I need to take the razors out of my cabinet?" I asked.

"No."

"Seriously?"

"Have I ever lied to you?"

"Let me count the ways."

"Never."

"You're not gonna cut up?"

"Been there, done that."

"Good God, girl, you stink!"

I stepped back out to the living room. My company looked at me expectantly. "Sorry about that. Jeannie used to work for me," I said by way of an explanation. "She's been—" I didn't know how else to put it—"missing in action for a while, and I just discovered—I mean, just this minute, just before you got here, I found out she's evidently been living out in the barn. For how long, I don't know. Anyway, where were we? Can I get you all something? Are you hungry?"

"No, we stopped and had breakfast," Sheila said. She'd changed. Her hair was shorter, the color of it softer—she dyed it that way, I'm sure—but besides that, she was just more put together, if you get my drift. I don't mean that in a bad way. When I knew her, she always seemed so frazzled and anxious and quick to put me down. I could tell there was something on her mind that made her uneasy, but even at that, she felt more settled into herself, less on edge than I remembered. That might have had something to do with Paul, I figured, as opposed to Leon. I'd just met the man, we'd hardly exchanged a word, but Paul sat with his arm behind her on the back of the sofa, his legs crossed at the knee. No Elvis Presley, but lean and tall and gentle in a rugged kind of way. Sheila had always attracted men with a certain sense of presence. Only this one wasn't a brooder, I could tell. He had kind, gray eyes and a weathered air about him. You never know about people, but he did not strike me as the hard-drinking type, at least. Much less a creep and a rapist. At the very least, he had two good legs.

Lisa Julene had her cell phone out and was showing her brother something. Ryan glanced up at me with a curious expression, shy and a little apprehensive, as I scooted my rocker over to sit and get acquainted with him and Paul and reacquainted with my sister and my niece.

"So tell me everything," I said, "because I am just too overwhelmed to know where to begin. Where do y'all live? Can I get you some coffee, at least?"

"No, sit," Sheila said. "We have a lot to tell you."

"Oh?" I immediately figured she must have got information about our daddy out in California or Alaska or wherever. That kind of news would have affected her more deeply than me probably—she at least had known him as a girl—but I could see where she'd want to share it with me. Especially if he'd died, or something else awful had happened. "What is it?"

"Well, it all goes back a ways." She watched me as she spoke, gauging my reaction. "Back to the time when you disappeared. Now, I'm not asking what happened," she was quick to add, "where you went or who with or what you did. You can tell me if you want to, all in your own good time, but if you don't, I understand."

"It's a long story."

"When you're ready," she repeated, her eyes wide open and direct, letting me know that this might not be the best time, in any event.

I said, "Thank you."

"I can't begin to tell you how worried I was. I thought for sure you'd been kidnapped or—well, murdered. God knows what. Everybody did. But be that as it may."

Lisa Julene had closed her phone, I noticed. She and Ryan paid close attention. It occurred to me for the first time that maybe they weren't brother and sister. He could be a friend, a boyfriend, even a husband. Not that brother and sister always have to look alike, mind you. He could just as easily have been her half-brother or her step-brother, but what I'm trying to say is, I did not detect a strong likeness between him and Paul, either.

"I can't get over you," I said to Lisa Julene. How big she was. "You were what? Three?"

She smiled, shrugged. "So I'm told."

"I'm sorry." I took a deep breath. "Go ahead, Sheila. No, I mean. I was not kidnapped. Not really. I went voluntarily. I was scared."

"Of Leon. I know."

I wasn't prepared to go there just yet. And from the way she said it, she wasn't asking me if it was Leon I was scared of, she was telling me. Like she didn't really want to talk about that, either. So we didn't.

Paul closed his fingers around her shoulder and squeezed. I liked the way he looked at her. He wasn't anything at all like Leon.

"Anyway. A man paid me a visit some time ago," she resumed. "It's been close to four years now. A man from Oklahoma City. He came asking all kinds of questions about you. About you and a Senator from here. A Senator Patterson. Did you know him?"

"Patterson Price. He wasn't a Senator when I knew him, but yes. Somebody came asking me about him, too, right about the same time. Was this guy's name Andrew Blake?"

She and Paul exchanged a look. "Yes, that's him. He wouldn't tell me if he knew whether you were alive or dead. You say he came to see you? Here?"

I nodded.

"Well, how long have you been back?"

"Since 1998," I said.

That knocked the wind out of her, I could see. She leaned her elbow on Paul's knee and rubbed her forehead with her fingertips. "All this time," she said. "Vanessa, why did you never let me know?"

"Let you know?" What did she want me to let her know? "I figured I was the last person in the world you wanted to hear from."

Her head snapped up. "You *what*? Of course, I wanted to hear from you!" She scooted to the edge of the sofa, fixing to stand up. "If I'd had an inkling you were still alive!"

Right about that time, Jeannie emerged from the bathroom, toweling off her head. She looked at me and said, "Family reunion?"

# DNA

I made oatmeal for Jeannie and put on a pot of coffee. "There's honey, maple syrup, brown sugar," I opened the cabinet to let her see, "all right here. Milk and butter in the fridge. Make it however you want."

Ryan came over to the stove. The only separation between living room and kitchen in my house is the way I arrange my furniture. He said, "I don't drink coffee. Do you have tea?"so I smiled at him and turned the burner on under the teapot, too.

"So you must belong to Paul?"

"Oh. No," he said. "Mom—" he hesitated, then, "adopted me before they, kind of, met."

"Oh. Well," I said. "We'll give this a minute to boil. You wanna help me carry? I don't know how everybody takes their coffee, so…"

"I got it," he said. When he and Jeannie both went for the fridge, he said, "After you."

I caught him staring at the scar up her left arm as she reached for the milk. He scratched the side of his face and waited while she poured and set the carton beside her bowl. She waggled her brows at him and turned her wrists up so he could see them both. "Matching set," she said.

He took the milk. "Whoa!" he said to no one in particular and poured a little milk into two mugs, a lot into a third, then stirred in sugar in roughly the same proportions. "That one's Jules," he said of the light sweet one and took the other two over to Sheila and Paul on the sofa.

I brought mine and Lisa Julene's. "Jules?" I said. "Is that what I should call you?"

"Mm-hmm. Thanks!" she said. "I spell it J.O.U.L.E.S. Like the unit of energy."

"Oh. *Joules*." I smacked my head like I coulda had a V8. "Of course."

I figured Jeannie would sit at the kitchen table and eat, but she brought her oatmeal and sat with Ryan and Lisa on the long earthen bench along the front wall of my living room.

I said, "Jeannie, this is my sister, Sheila, and my niece, Lisa Jule—Joules."

Lisa Julene—it was going to take me a minute to get adjusted to calling her anything else—leaned past Ryan and gave Jeannie a little half-wave, half-salute.

"Ryan you met." Ryan held out his fist to her, and Jeannie, bowl in one hand, spoon in the other, gave him an elbow bump. "And that's Paul."

"Hi, Jeannie."

I took a deep breath and turned to my sister. "Remember after Grandma died, how at first everybody said I killed her?"

"Still do," Jeannie put in, stirring her oatmeal.

"Thank you, Jeannie. Yes, some of them still do."

"Small town assholes. You know. Lack of imagination."

"Jeannie, please?"

"Just saying." She spooned a bite of oatmeal into her mouth and winked at me.

I waited, wondering what to do with her. I looked at Sheila. "Do you remember what it was like?"

"I hated it here," she said. "Everything about it. I'm shocked you ever came back. I'm just so glad I never had to put Joules in public school here."

I let that sink in. "When I come back, it all started up again. They were convinced I murdered Leon, too. You were gone. Mr. Goslin was dead. The pasture was overgrown. The house had been shot up. Everybody used this place like it was the town dump. I'm sorry, Sheila, but I assumed you thought the same thing about me. I didn't blame you, but I honestly didn't think you wanted anything to do with me after that."

"I don't understand. About Grandma, yes. But how could anybody think you killed Leon? He drank himself to death."

"All that blood?" I suggested. "When he hit his head?"

"What blood?"

Jeannie wiped her mouth with her sleeve, eyes on me.

"There wasn't any blood," Sheila said. "It wasn't pretty, but there wasn't any blood."

I didn't say anything. I felt like I all of a sudden stepped into an episode of *The Twilight Zone*.

"But he was dead? He died that night. Didn't he?"

"I came home and found him. Thank God Joules was upstairs asleep! I didn't know where you'd gone, but no way I thought you'd killed him. I called around later, after the ambulance came. Mark Bittle said you'd been over to their place and that you got a ride with someone. He never said who. I just—I had no idea where to look for you."

"That was Patterson," I said. "That was Patterson Price. He's the one who gave me a ride."

"The Senator?"

"Well, like I said, he wasn't a Senator then. He was just a guy, a friend of Mark's."

"Mark acted like he didn't even know who you left with."

"He might not've. It was a party. Their folks were out of town, and Mark and Leigh Ann had a lot of kids over. Some older guys that Mark went to school with, both from here and from college. Leigh Ann got shit-faced and couldn't take me home, and Mark wasn't in such good shape, either, so Patter said he would. He was sweet, really. He never hurt me or anything. But I was scared to go in the house, because—I told him what had happened, how pissed off Leon was and, Sheila, I don't know if you were aware of it or not, but Leon could be a—" I decided to just come out with it. "Leon was a pervert, Sheila."

I had to back up and tell her everything. How I borrowed one of her dresses, and Leon thought it was too short and didn't want me going out like that, how he tried to trip me with his cane and I grabbed it and give it a jerk and he hit his head and how that was why I always thought maybe I did kill him, even though it wasn't murder with malice and aforethought, as they say. I told her how Patterson went in the house and found him dead. "He led me to believe I killed him," I said. "I guess I never questioned it. I always assumed you believed it, too." In the middle of my trying to tell her all this, Sheila got up and come over to me, leaning over me in my rocker and hugging me, crying and saying, "Honey, I wouldn't have cared if you did kill the son of a bitch! I would've helped you do it!"

"Well!" I said with a hitch, because I was crying, too, by this time, "I didn't know that."

When we'd both quieted down some, Jeannie said, "I guess I picked the wrong sister."

"Jeannie," I said, "how would you like to go open up the shop for me?"

"Happy to." She sidled off the banquette with her bowl. "How do you take your tea, Garçon?"

Ryan looked at her.

"You know—milk? sugar?"

"Yeah, sure. Two teaspoons."

"Gotcha covered."

As Sheila talked about Leon's condition when she came home and found him, I watched Jeannie out of the corner of my eye, fixing Ryan's tea. When she'd finished stirring, she took a sip, then came back by and served him. "Go on, taste it," she said.

He sipped. "It's good."

"Vanessa, could I borrow another layer? It gets a little chilly out in the shop."

"Help yourself," I said.

On her way back from my closet, wearing my I Ching sweatshirt that says "Consult with Innocence" across the front, she bent next to my ear and whispered, "I just made out with your nephew." Then she was out the door. I didn't need to ask if she had a key to the shop.

I breathed a little easier with her out of the house.

Lisa—Joules, I mean, asked, "Is she a homeless person?"

"To be honest, I don't know. Before, when she worked for me, she lived with her mother in town and rode her bike back and forth, but now I don't know. She might have burned some bridges. She has a certain way about her, you might've noticed."

"She's hard core," Ryan said. He pointed at one wrist, then the other, grimacing.

I closed my eyes and opened them again, quick, before that scene could start looping across the backs of my lids again. "Where were we?" I asked Sheila.

"Well, I don't want to beat around the bush. Is that okay?"

"Of course." Did she want to contest my right to Grandma's land? All I did was pay taxes on it. "Say what you have to say."

"The man from Oklahoma City, the one who came asking all kinds of questions, he said he thought you had had a baby in Massachusetts."

That wasn't where I was expecting the conversation to go. "I did."

"He wanted to know if I knew anything about it. It seemed to me like he was trying to dig up dirt on Senator Patterson."

"Price," I said. "Patterson's his first name. He was. Trying to dig up dirt."

"That's right. I keep getting the name turned around. He seemed to think that Senator Price might have been the..." It seemed to cost her an effort to say it. "...the father of your baby?"

"What else did he say?"

"Well, he said that Mark Bittle went to work for Senator Price's father, who I believe was also a Senator."

"A State Senator," I said, "Yes."

"And that Mark Bittle disappeared just like you did."

"Later," I said, "That's what Mr. Blake told me, too."

"He said your baby disappeared, too."

I nodded.

She looked at both of her kids, then back at me. She took her husband's hand in hers before she plunged into what she had to tell me: "We have reason to believe that Ryan might be your son."

"You what?"

"We've thought so for a long time. We just never imagined you would come back here to Keening. We didn't even think you were still alive."

"Well, I—" I didn't know what to say. The pressure in my throat was too much. I couldn't form a word. I didn't know if it was true. I didn't know if it wasn't true. I had no room in my chest to take a breath and ask, "What makes you think so?" I tried to look at Ryan, to see if I might know him, but my eyes swam so, I couldn't make him out, and my legs were too weak to get out of my chair and go to him.

I felt Sheila next to me, holding me on one side, and then Lisa Julene on the other side. I could tell she was pulling him over—Ryan, or I mean, possibly, Marshall Caleb—pulling him by the hand. Sheila said, "We've had dna testing done, Vanessa. It matches up."

This hurt. I can't begin to tell you how much it hurt. Like someone had stabbed me from behind with a spear, and the point of it pushed my heart straight up into my throat so hard it felt like it might explode. I gasped with the pain. And then the pain burst, and it all come raining down on me. I was afraid of it, afraid of the joy and, at the same time, of the cruelty of it being not the truth. Afraid of it being the truth, too. Afraid of it being the truth and then being taken away from me. And I reached through that pain to find him and blindly pull myself to him, and him to me, this boy, this man, this baby of mine.

Part of me knew that it could not be true, that no way could my baby have ended up halfway across the continent from where he was born, from where I lost him—with my sister? The logical part of my brain would not shut up, would not suspend its judgment on this ridiculous, convoluted set of circumstances, would not stop trying to calculate the odds against it, and I could not make it shut up. *I would have known!* I told myself. *The minute I laid eyes on him, I should have known him.* How was it possible—what kind of missing instinct did I not have that I did not recognize him immediately? I groped and found his face and forced myself to look at him through my tears, through the distortion of my own emotions, wondering if and when it would begin to make sense, and I could not see him, could not see him at all, could not even see that he had a face, never mind that it was or was not the face of my baby. But he touched his forehead to mine, and the all uncertainty flooded out of me. I pushed up with all my might, his arms encircling me, hauling me up, and I stood and held him and bawled for all I was worth, hitching and bucking in his arms.

"I can't take it!" I choked on my words. "I can't take it!" Then I lashed out at Sheila, because it was too hard to come to grips with the fact that she had raised my son out of my sight, behind my back, without my knowledge. "Are you sure about this, Sheila? Are you sure!"

"I am now," she said, laughing-crying. "Yes."

"You're my baby?" I asked him.

He was bawling, too, now. I think he said, all congested, "If you're my mom, I am."

"They stole you!" I told him. I wanted him to know that. "They stole you! I never gave you up! I went from room to room of that hospital, looking for you. They came and took me and strapped me down and shot me up with tranquilizers! I was out of my mind! They said she took you and just vanished!"

After we all calmed down some, Sheila explained.

"For a while, after Leon died and you disappeared, I stayed on at the State School. I didn't know what else to do. I left Joules with my mom in Enid, because I didn't want her staying out here, not with just anybody. Not after everything else. Well, one night, while I was at Pine Cottage, somebody came and banged on the front door! so loud it scared us all. Nobody ever knocked, you know, because we never locked the doors back then. Us supervisors came and went all the time, between one cottage and another. There was no need to lock the doors. I grabbed Danny Carlisle and he and I went to see what in the world was going on, and there was—well, there was Ryan, in a car seat with a note pinned to the front of him addressed to me. It said, 'Sheila Keefe, Take care of this baby. He is not retarded.' And it was signed, 'M. B.' Nothing else. No other explanation or anything."

"Mark Bittle?" I asked.

"Had to be him. That was right about the time he went missing. He dropped out of college, I guess, the year before and went to work for that Senator, and then they said he just never showed up again after that. He's never been found."

I had a thousand questions, but I couldn't take it all in. Not in one sitting. "He looks like Daddy," I said. "I thought that when I first saw him. But I thought because he was yours, you know? And then he said he was adopted."

"He does," Sheila said. "And he takes after you."

"I'm standing right here," he reminded us.

"I named you Marshall Caleb. Your last name on your birth certificate says Anatoly, but that's just—it's a long story. I always figured I'd change it to Marshall Caleb Cavendish eventually."

"Marshall Caleb!" Joules said, giving him the once-over, like she was trying it out on him to see if it fit.

"I gotta get used to having two moms," he said. "I guess I could get used to having two names."

"You're twenty-three years old. And I don't know one thing about you since the first day of your life. Do you even know your birthday?"

He looked at Sheila. "Not really. I mean, I have one, but—"

"May Seventh, 1991."

He mouthed the date and grinned. "I could get used to having two birthdays, too."

# WANDERING KING

Ryan lived in Austin, Texas. 510 miles away. He had friends there, an apartment he shared with one of them, and a degree in computer science. He worked for the family business. "Paul's a picker," he said. "They run a flea market, him and Mom. I help out more at the information gathering end of things, doing research on whatever they bring in to sell, so they know what it is, kinda what its story is, how to price it. I see what else is out there like it on eBay and Craigslist and wherever. Is it weird if I call her Mom? I mean, I know you're my mom, but she's been my mom my whole life."

I sat with my face cradled in the palm of my hand, looking at him, watching him talk. "I don't know. You just walked into my house and turned my life inside-out. I don't think I can name one thing that's gonna be normal for a while. So I'm okay with weird."

He had the most perfect angle to his jaw, the clean way it swung out from under his ear, like the sweep of a dove's wing or a — or, in a way, the lines of a sports car. Don't ask me to explain that. He had a few freckles, not many, not like mine, and faint. They didn't dominate his face the way mine do. His hair was dark, not quite black, and not quite all of it contained by the clasp at the back of his neck, where the pony tail went soft and curly. I could not, for the life of me, make him resemble his baby self except, maybe remotely, in the flare of his nostrils when he grinned. I had no pictures to compare him with, there hadn't been time for that. He had good teeth. That was one thing I worried about when I saw Patterson's three other boys in a magazine with their big, expensive smiles. I used to worry that my baby wouldn't get that kind of dental care. Not unless he had been secretly taken in by some other branch of the Price family. That was one of the fantasies I entertained in order to stave off knowing what had "really happened" to him. But none of it was real. Nothing I imagined turned out to be true. Not the best case scenario and certainly not the worst. Turned out he just had good honest serviceable teeth, a little jagged along the side like upside-down mountain peaks when he grinned. Strong hands, shapely ears, a clean jaw and dark eyes like my daddy's that looked so far away at times, but when they made the return trip, they came back soft and full of laughter. Quiet eyes, I thought. A quiet soul.

His full name, the name he went by, was Ryan Noah Gray. Sheila told me it meant "Wandering King."

"How're we gonna work this out?" I asked her. "Y'all are gonna take him back to Austin with you, aren't you?" I didn't mean it to sound like such an accusation, but I could feel the prickle of tears threatening to fall again. We sat alone, talking, just the two of us, because Ryan, Joules and Paul wanted to see more of the shop before, according to plan, we'd all head into town together for a bite to eat.

"Ryan's the one who has to figure that out," she said sensibly enough, warning me: "He does have a life there. In Austin."

"I know, I know! It's not — I'm sorry. I'm a little emotional right now. I don't mean this in a bad way, but I feel like I've been run over by an eighteen wheeler."

"I bet."

"Next time you do this to somebody, you might want to call ahead." I attempted a smile to let her know I meant it as a joke, but the smile came out crooked, and my breathing went funny again.

"We did, Honey!" She held me. I hardly recognized her, she was so much less guarded and more loving than the Sheila I'd known as a kid. "Several times. We never got through and we could never leave a message. It always said your mailbox was full."

"Oh. Yeah, that's probably about right. I don't check it like I ought to. I've been so focused on that stupid wall." I let my head rest on her shoulder. "For a while there, I didn't have a phone at all."

"We finally left a message on your website, in the comments. It's still pending approval."

"You did? I haven't paid much attention to that, either. Not since —" But I brushed that away. I didn't want to think about Jeannie and her video right that minute.

"That's how Ryan found you. He came across your website, looking something up for Paul. I forget what. A hood ornament or something. He saw Keening, Oklahoma, next to your picture and your name and recognized it, because of course I'd talked about you. I never kept anything from him. He got mad at first. He thought I'd lied to him about believing you were dead, because there you were, plain as day and very much alive. We read every word of your blog together. He's read it more than once, I'm positive. I still can't believe it's you, that you came back here to Keening, of all places, and that you did all this and that I'm sitting here talking with you in your own house that you built all by yourself! And that wall out there! I know it's not finished yet, and you've had to fix it how many times? But it's just beautiful! I hope you catch whoever it is that's been defacing it like that!"

"My vandal?" I laughed. "You just met her."

She looked at me with that V stamped in her forehead. "That girl?"

"Yep. She's got some issues." I sighed. "I better get out there and check on her."

"You let her run your store?"

I shrugged. "I didn't know what else to do with her. We needed to talk, and she was gonna keep interrupting."

But Jeannie wasn't in the store. Joules was standing at the card rack by the door, while Paul investigated the whirligig aisle. I didn't see Ryan, either. I looked in the greenhouse, but no one was in there. "Where'd she go?"

Joules looked up. "Outside." She waved a card she was holding in the direction of the parking lot. "With Ryan."

The two of them stood together looking at the wall, specifically at the freshly mudded fallen angel Jeannie had added overnight. Her upside-down nude self-portrait.

Ryan turned when he heard me come outside. "This is so great!" he enthused.

"You like it." I didn't mean it as a question. I could tell he did.

"There was just a big blank space here. I wondered what you were going to put there."

"It was a snow plow, before Jeannie took an ax to it."

"Oh." He looked at Jeannie, then back at me. "It was?"

Jeannie, looking past him, arched an eyebrow. She spoke to him but for my benefit. "You couldn't really tell that's what it was, could you?"

He played the diplomat, holding his first finger and thumb about three inches apart and saying, "I only saw it this big."

"You think it adds something, though?" I asked him, willing to consider his opinion. "This upside-down angel?"

"Well, yeah. It's, like, epic now!"

"It does change the story."

"Completes it," Jeannie put in.

"This wall had a purpose," I told my son. "I wanted to express my gratitude to a group of people who came to my support when I needed them. They've been there for me ever since. I wanted to do this for them. It came from the heart. Now I can't even show it to them. Can't even let them see it."

Standing on the other side of him, Jeannie lobbed her question. "What does that tell you about them?"

I exploded. "They're good people, Jeannie! Just good, decent people who happen to believe things I don't necessarily believe! They still show up for me when I need them!"

She nudged Ryan and pointed. "That one there? That's my brother. We sprang from the same womb. That one's Eugene Sewer Boy Lamb. And that's Jarrod Frye. Jarrod's a hottie. Vanessa certainly seems to think so."

"Do we have to do this now?" I cut in. "Do we?"

"I thought so, too, when I was fifteen. Pathetic story. But here's the funny part. I mean America's Funniest Home Video funny, right? When my brother moved out of our house, I got his room. Little did I know, my brother and his little buddy Sewer Boy had installed a nifty little spy cam in the ceiling. Don't ask me why. Maybe they recorded Billy fucking his girlfriend. None of my concern, right? Except they used it to record me, too, after he moved out and I moved in. Twenty-four, seven. My two very own guardian angels watching over me by night, my soul to keep. They got some excellent footage of me, Ryan Baby, if you ever want to check it out."

"Stop it, Jeannie!" I said. "Just stop!"

"So I guess you can understand why she doesn't want to show these good, decent people her Wall of Gratitude, now that I'm part of it."

"Jeannie, stop!" I wanted to strangle her. "How do you expect me to believe anything you say? For all I know, *you* made the video."

"I'm sure they've all seen it." She waved her hand at my wall of angels, then pointed at Jarrod specifically. "All except him. And no, Vanessa, I did not make a video of me finger fucking myself and calling your boyfriend's name." She turned back to Ryan. "He was the only one I cared about in the world. Sewer Boy knew that. He told me he'd show Jarrod the video unless I did what he wanted, whenever he wanted." She raked back her sleeve. "This is what he wanted."

Ryan looked at her arm, not saying anything.

"Not the big one. The little ones. See?" She pointed at the fine, parallel scars in her forearm, fading now, disrupted by the big, jagged one running across them. "He wanted me a little at a time. As long as I kept up my payments, it was all good. But I couldn't leave home. I had to do it on camera, so he could watch, then go in the bathroom and let my blood run down the drain. Maybe there was a camera in there, too, I'm not really sure. He always said he'd know if I didn't let it run down the drain. This one—" she traced the long ragged scar with her finger, looking at me—"this was Vanessa's idea. Give him everything all at once. Go deep and be done with it."

"I never said that! Don't you dare put that on me!"

"Then what does she do? She goes and gets Billy! Gets my brother to stop me from bleeding out and getting free."

"You were dying! You were bleeding everywhere! All over the snow! What was I supposed to do? Leave you there? Do nothing? How was I supposed to know Billy was part of it? Part of some—some—"

"You were too late. You didn't know that, did you? I went out—" Her eyes scanned an event horizon I could not see, somewhere beyond my wall of angels, beyond my woods, beyond the canyon, beyond the sky. "—out there. Do you know what I saw?"

I didn't.

"I saw the white light, all right. Bright as the fucking sun. Blindingly bright. But I had no way to get to it. I saw people. People standing in the light, looking down at me, some of them reaching down, but between me and where they were, where the light came from, there were dark iron bars. They reached down through the bars but they could only reach so far. And I couldn't reach them. My arms weren't long enough. I was way down below, down in the cold, in the dark. At first, I was only cold from the knees down, but the cold kept seeping up and pulling me further and further down. My dad was there. I saw his face. He looked so worried. Jarrod's mom was there, too. My grandparents. But the cold kept pulling at me. It was all around me, up to my neck. The light, and all the people who were in the light, who were part of the light, kept getting farther and farther away, out of reach. Then I felt this tug from deep inside me, this pull that I couldn't resist. It ran through me like a big soul flush. Tugged me backwards, back down that long tunnel, too fast to even think about it. I landed back in my body. I wasn't conscious, really, but I knew what was going on. They were sewing me back into my body, stitch by stitch. I wasn't happy about it, but there was nothing I could do. Vanessa 'saved' me."

She looked not at me but through me, her chin pulled up, resolute.

"Would you rather have died?" I asked seriously, softly.

"I did die."

"Would you rather have stayed, I mean — dead?"

Her eyes flickered into focus, looking at me, then looking away. "You know where I was, don't you?"

I didn't.

"Down there. Down in the sewer. Up to my neck in earthworm soup."

I shook my head, not getting it.

"Down in the storm drain, Vanessa. Because I was supposed to be his replacement. He's been grooming me for it my whole life. That was my future. That's what I've had to look forward to."

I felt a cold wind run through me, a downdraft from my throat to the pit of my soul. I realized for the first time that every word she spoke was utterly true, nothing a lie, nothing invented. The world she occupied worked according to a plan and a schedule altogether unlike this one. She followed a set of rules as absolute as gravity and as foreign as Jupiter or Venus. I could no more convert her to my way of thinking, my sense of what makes sense, than I could ask water to run uphill.

"I was supposed to be his replacement," she said. "But I'm not. I came back. Just like Ryan here."

"Why?" I asked, putting every ounce of my own logic on hold. "Why do you suppose?"

"Why'd I come back?"

I nodded. I needed to understand, even if I couldn't.

"To take back what's mine." Her eyes shifted like ice melting, like dirty ice in the bottom of a bucket, and settled on me. "Starting with you."

I laughed a small, hopeless laugh. There was a limit to my understanding, and she headed right for the border. "I'm not yours, Jeannie. I never have been." Yet as I spoke, cold little fingers of dread, of a fear that she might be right, traced up and down my spine. "I'm not Eugene's or Jarrod's or anybody's. I'm not a piece of territory you get to claim."

She snorted. "I don't mean you, you narcissistic fuck! I'm taking back what's mine *from* you. What's mine that you've taken from me."

"What? What have I taken that's yours?"

"The truth. Right there." She pointed at her depiction of herself on my wall. "Where was I in your story? You conveniently edited me out of it. You're so ashamed of me, aren't you? So ashamed of the part I played in your little ego drama! So you just delete me? No fucking way. I belong there. I put myself back, because none of this happens without me. Without me in it, your 'Wall of Gratitude' is just a pile of bullshit, and you know it. You're so 'grateful' Eugene came and took me off your hands, aren't you? You were so willing to let him erase me from your story. But I don't give a shit anymore. I'm still part of it. I have nothing left to give him. Nothing left he can take from me, because not even my blood is my own. That was fucking brilliant, Vanessa, even if you don't want to take credit for it."

"You called him," I said. "Not me. You called him that night. You made it so his number would be the one that came up when I hit Send."

"Why would I do that?"

"I don't know, Jeannie! Why did you?"

"Because I'm such a genius, I knew you wouldn't do the logical thing and call 911? I knew the lights would go out? I knew the battery in your phone would die? I timed it all so perfectly, didn't I? I knew you'd think it was Billy and not a wrong number, certainly not Eugene. I knew you wouldn't recognize his voice or even, again, do the logical thing and say, 'Who the fuck is this?' didn't I? Because that's just how much of a diabolical fucking genius I am."

"I never thought you planned it all out that way. I never said that."

"No, I didn't. But I did call him. I called him after we made love. I got up to pee and I called him and told him to fuck off. I told him to do his worst. I no longer gave a shit who he showed his fucking video to. Not anymore. You know why?" She advanced on me, her voice rising, her finger in my chest. "Because I had you! I. Had. You. I had you!" She grabbed me by the front of my jacket, wadding it up in her fist. "Not like property, you stupid shit!" She sneered at me. "Like territory? Fuck you. I had you because you believed in me. I had a witness!" Her voice broke on the word, her tears burst like rain, and the rest came ragged. "I thought I did. I thought I could put my faith in you!"

She let me go, dragged her sleeve across her cheeks to wipe them dry. "I didn't know how bad the storm was. I didn't think it mattered. But the power went out, and you got scared. You were so worried about your goddamn flowers! You had to call for help. I didn't want you to. We weren't gonna die, for Christsake! But I couldn't stop you. I even helped, remember? I got you your phone. I knew where it was, because I threw it under the couch after I called him. But I didn't tell you to call him! You just did it. You just fucking did it. It happened too fast for me to stop you. I couldn't even say anything. That's when I knew he had you." Her tears kept coming. "Yeah, and I did lie to you about one thing. I did lie to you about the text. I wanted you to think it wasn't my fault you called him instead of my mom. And I broke your phone on purpose, so you wouldn't find out."

"I did find out."

"I know."

"Thank you," I said. I meant, for telling the truth. I didn't mean it to sound sarcastic.

"If I hadn't done that, you know — if I hadn't called him — you'd be shit out of luck. You owe me that much, at least."

"What do you mean?"

"I had to give you up, Vanessa. Like everything else. I had to give you up to him, let him rescue you, let him be your savior. Not from me, not from a freaking snow storm. He got you in with his parents and the rest of the children of fucking God. He hooked you up with Angela Twinklestar and made you famous. And now we know why, don't we? So you could get your life back. You even get your family back."

Ryan's eyes swiveled from her to me and back again. I wanted to say to him how sorry I was that he had to endure all this, that I knew it didn't make any sense, that I would explain it all to him when I could. But the truth of it was, I had no idea how to begin, and Jeannie wouldn't let me.

"But it wasn't about you, Vanessa. It was never about you. He just wanted to get you away from me. He wanted you to never let me back in, because I told him — when he came to see me with his ultimatum, at the state hospital — I told him what I meant to do."

"What? What are you going to do?"

"Here's what I'm saying to you, Vanessa. I belong on your wall. I'm part of the story. If you want to express your gratitude, you don't get to pick and choose. Either you're grateful or you're not."

"What do you want? You want me to tell your story?"

"That's what you do, isn't it? Tell stories? Repurpose people?"

I needed to think. I stared at the wall, wondering. No way could I know if she was telling the truth about Eugene and her brother and the video. No way could I tell it was a lie. Lie or delusion, did it matter? It was all the truth to her. That much I knew.

"I'd tell your story if I knew how," I said. "I don't know where to begin, and I certainly don't know how to make it believable."

"Fuck believable. Tell the truth."

"That's just it. I don't know what the truth is. Your truth? My truth? I don't even think there is a comprehensible truth to all this."

"Then let me tell it. Just stop fucking whitewashing it."

Ryan stood there, taking it all in. How much of it he understood, how he managed to make sense of it, I couldn't tell, but he had a suggestion. "Why don't you work on it together? Take turns. Add on to it if you need to. Go all the way around if that's what it takes to get it all told." He drew a circle around us with his finger, enclosing the parking lot.

I could almost picture it.

"See? He gets it."

I looked at Ryan, then I looked at her. They were looking at each other.

"Jeannie, I need to tell you —"

"I already know," she said.

I looked at Ryan.

"I told her. She wasn't surprised."

"Why would I be surprised?" Jeannie said. "Of course you got your son back. I knew the minute I laid eyes on him. He's you all over again."

Joules, Sheila and Paul came filing out of the shop, unaware of the drama that had unfolded in the parking lot. "Why don't we all go get a bite to eat?" Sheila said. "Jeannie, you come with us. We won't all fit in our car. Ryan can ride with you, Vanessa. Wherever you think."

Jeannie wiped her eyes and cheeks again. "Wild Horses is the best place in town," she suggested, "on Bruce Street."

"We'll follow you."

Jeannie took my hand. "This all right with you?"

I had too much to think about. "All right?" I said. "Sure." I was a little stunned.

She stepped up on her toes, with her hand on my shoulder. I thought she meant to whisper something in my ear, but instead she touched her lips to the corner of my eye and sipped a tear I didn't know I'd shed.

# Wild Horses

Ryan climbed aboard Jiminy with me, watching Jeannie get in the back of the SUV with Joules. "She's kind of intense," he remarked.

"Kind of." I changed the subject. "When did you all get here?"

"Last night." He searched the door post, patted the seat beside him. "Whoa! No seat belts? No way!" Then, "We stayed at Nana Gray's in Enid."

"Is that what you call her? I meant to ask Sheila about her mother." I had the key in the switch, but I could tell he had something he wanted to say. I waited.

"I want to meet my father, too. I don't know if it's gonna happen on this trip," he said, "but I want to meet him."

I stepped on the starter. The motor caught. "Right," I said. If he heard me, I don't think he picked up on my irony. "I wish I had more room." Then I thought to add, in case he wanted to stay for a while, "I do have a sofa."

He looked at me and didn't say anything, just nodded. As I backed out and prepared to head out to the road, he looked out the window on his side. "Jeannie sleeps in your barn?"

"I guess she did last night."

"I don't know if it was my place to tell her you were my birth mother. I just figured she should know. It sucks to be the one who's left out of the loop."

My turn to nod. *Birth mother?* I let that rattle around in my head for a minute, not sure how to secure it. Finally I said, "Of course it was your place. It's your place to tell anyone you want. And it was thoughtful of you. I'm sure she appreciated it." It wasn't the conversation I most wanted to have at that particular moment, but after what he said about being out of the loop, I figured I owed it to him. So without going into detail, I told him about the storm last winter and how she got the scars on both arms. The bad ones.

He listened, then he said, "Yeah, she told me about it. She really wants that part to be included in your wall for some reason. I think that's why she added to it."

In town, I pulled in behind Wild Horses, watching in the rear view to make sure Paul followed. Before we got out, Ryan said, "I like the part she added. It kicks the whole thing up a notch."

My son, the art critic.

"If you want my opinion," he added.

"You do realize she's mentally ill?"

"She wouldn't be the first one."

"Can I give it some thought," I asked with my hand on the door handle, "about how to approach your father? There's no guarantee he's going to be thrilled."

"There was no guarantee you would be, either."

"Oh, I am! Are you kidding me?" I took his hand. "You have no idea!"

"Do you ever talk to him?"

"We don't really run in the same circles."

"It's weird to think he might run for President and, like, here I am and here you are."

"Yeah, pretty much." I wondered if there was still a chance of that happening. "What would that make us? The Second Family?" I touched my lower lip with my little finger, where he had his piercing. "What's this? A sapphire?"

"Aquamarine."

"I like it."

He squeezed my other hand. I let his go.

Jeannie stood by my door with her hands stuffed in her pockets, hunched against the wind, waiting for me to get out. When I did, she said, "Bonding?"

"I hope so."

"He's sweet."

I gave her a look, like, *don't even think about it*, but everybody else was there by then, ready to go in.

We got the corner booth at the front. When Ryan said to me, "I'll let you have the outside," Jeannie slipped around behind me and scooted in ahead of Joules so she could sit next to him on the other side. "Get the bison burger," she told him. "Trust me."

When we all had menus, Sheila said, "Is that what you're having, Ryan, the bison?"

"Yeah, sure."

"Oh, look, Joules. 'Wild caught salmon dressed in creamy dill on toasted sourdough.' That sounds good."

"You get that. I want the BLT and potato soup."

"Yep, okay. Vanessa, what do you like?"

This discussion of the menu in advance of one another's selections, strange to say, was unfamiliar territory for me. They seemed to operate on the assumption that no two people were allowed to order the same thing. Did they mean to set everything in the middle and dish it out family style? I didn't see how that would work with sandwiches.

"You get sweet potato fries, I'll get regular," Jeannie advised Ryan, leaning against him and running her finger down his menu. "You want the Jack Daniels sauce, but ask for it on the side. Forget ketchup."

Paul sat at the opposite end of the horseshoe-shaped booth from me. When the waitress came back, I said, "Why don't you start with him."

I ended up with the chicken club. It came with chips.

"So you're staying at your mom's?" I asked Sheila. "How long, do you think?"

"We're playing it by ear. Joules is the only one on a tight schedule."

"What kind of work do you do?" I asked Joules.

"I teach." She pulled her eyes away from Ryan and Jeannie. "Math and, uh, chemistry. As long as I'm back for Monday morning, Mom. We don't have to be in a hurry."

"What are your plans for Thanksgiving, Vanessa?"

I unrolled my utensils and fiddled with my napkin. "That's next week, isn't it?"

Jeannie answered for me. "Vanessa doesn't do Thanksgiving."

"Grandma never did," I reminded Sheila.

"And you've…kept that up?"

I turned to Ryan. "Your — let's see," I had to count back. "Your great-great-grandfather was a Crow medicine man named Alfred Thundering Bear. That makes you one-sixteenth Crow, with some Cherokee mixed in, maybe a teaspoon of Choctaw or Seminole. Grandma never divulged the whole genetic recipe. At least not to me; did she to you, Sheila? Anyway," (I used it as an excuse to touch his face) "that's where you get these high cheekbones."

Sheila seemed worried. It looked like maybe she reached for Paul's hand under the table.

"Anyway," I said to finish up and move on, "she took kind of a dim view of certain white traditions. Thanksgiving, Christmas, Easter.

She was an atheist, too, so that might've had something to do with it. Fourth of July."

"Columbus Day?"

"Ah, no."

"What does that leave, Labor Day?"

"She wasn't big on that, either."

"Maybe she just didn't like to celebrate."

I laughed. "That could be it." I liked the idea that he could make me laugh. It diluted the tension somewhat.

"I wish I had known her," Jeannie said. "People around here remember her. They still talk about her."

"What about?" Ryan wanted to know.

"So back to the question at hand," I said, quick as I could, "no. I don't have any big plans for Thanksgiving."

Sheila looked grateful. "Maybe you could come spend it with us."

"Oh." The invitation took me by surprise. I didn't know how well Jiminy would stand up to a thousand-mile round trip. I could ask Jarrod what he thought of the idea, but I knew he would advise against it. "I'd have to find a way to get there."

"Take the train," Jeannie said. Her tone said, *Duh!*

"Why don't you ride down with us and take the train back? There's a station right close to where you teach, isn't there, Joules?"

"I don't even know where a station is around here. I don't think Enid has one, do they?"

"Hold on." Joules was on it. She looked up from her cell phone. "Looks like Guthrie's the closest one. Guthrie or Oklahoma City. Nope, wait a minute. The one in Guthrie is closed. Let me check the one in Oklahoma City." She quoted me the price for one-way.

"I could do that. I'd just need to get someone to pick me up in the City."

Joules pouted at her phone. "The Friday's full," she said. "So is Saturday. Nope. Nope. You could come back on Tuesday."

"Tuesday after Thanksgiving?" While I wondered if I could afford to be gone that long so close to Christmas, the waitress arrived with our food. She knew who I was, because she called me by name as she set my plate down. I'd seen her around, of course — Keening's not a big place — but I couldn't think of her name or where I knew her.

Jeannie leaned forward to take her plate. "You worried about the shop, Vanessa?"

"I don't know what to expect this year. My inventory's so different from what it was in years past."

"You could trust me, you know."

"Oh, Jeannie."

"You could, though. I'm just saying."

"We'll talk," I said. In other words, not a chance in hell, but I needed to find a better way to put it, and not in front of my family, please.

She shrugged. "He's your son."

"Thank you!" Sheila said, taking her wild caught salmon on sourdough. "Well, whatever you decide. We plan on spending the day with Nana tomorrow. Ryan, what do you want to do?"

He looked at me. "I can stay on your sofa tonight, you said?"

"Of course you can," I said. "Yes!"

"What about Jeannie?"

"Oh, I'm good. Don't worry about me. Barn's actually pretty comfortable. I'm not allowed in the house." She took one of his fries and dipped it in his steak sauce. "Restraining order." She bit the sweet potato fry in two, smiling, crinkling her eyes at him. "I might chew on the furniture."

Ryan swiveled his head in my direction, then back at her. "You two have a complicated relationship, don't you?"

"We do, but your mama doesn't like to talk about it."

"Can we please?" I demanded.

# A TWEAK AND A HALF
# PAST NORMAL

Paul, Sheila and Joules headed back to Enid after lunch. The idea was to give Ryan and me a little more time, just the two of us, an evening and a morning to get acquainted before we all rode down to Austin together day after tomorrow. Sheila lingered with Ryan in the gravel parking lot behind Wild Horses, while Paul and Joules sat in the SUV. Jeannie waited with me in the cab of my truck.

"Seems like you did your sister kind of a huge favor."

I asked what she meant.

She shrugged. "Paul seems like a nice guy."

"I'm sure he is." I didn't see what that had to do with me. What I wanted to know: what was I going to do with her? "What's going on between you and your mother?" I asked. "Why aren't you living at home?"

She let out a blast of air, leaned against the door, not looking at me. "I told her."

"Told her...?"

"She's in denial. Her precious Billy would never do such a thing."

"What, the video?"

"While I was locked up, he went up in the attic and took the camera out. Why? Because me and my big mouth, that's why. I told Eugene I didn't care anymore what he did to me. When he came out to Fort Supply, I said, 'I've got nothing left for you. Nothing more to give you, nothing for you to take. Even my blood is not my own blood anymore. It's all donated by the Red Cross.' I should have quit while I was ahead, but I didn't. I told him if he ever showed his face to me again, I'd turn him in for what he did. There have got to be laws, right? He never had my consent. Even if he did, I was a minor. He could go to jail for what he did. They both could."

"Do you have any evidence?" I asked her.

"Exactly. I knew he had to be scared or he wouldn't have come. That's why he came out to your place, that day in February. He found out I worked for you. He must have been shitting his pants, worrying what I might say to someone like you."

"What does that mean? Someone like me?"

"You have a reputation. He's scared of you."

"He is not. He was on a field trip, Jeannie. For the yearbook. Spider brings two or three kids out to see me every year. For pictures."

She shook her head. "Anytime I start to get close to someone, he finds out about it. He can sniff it out. He thought he had me back up against a wall, didn't he? Out at Fort Supply? But this time I knew better. He was the one in a corner. This time, he was afraid of what I might say to a therapist. A therapist would have to report it. If I said something to one of them, it would trigger an investigation. That's why he got Billy to cover their tracks.

"Uh, huh."

"When I got home, I showed my mom where he'd patched the hole in the ceiling in his room."

"She didn't buy it?"

"She admitted he'd gone up in the attic, but she covered for him. She said he was 'just looking for things he left behind when he moved out.' Four years ago, mind you. And suddenly he misses what? His tennis racket?"

"Why did you stay in his room? Why didn't you move back into your old room?"

"I did. As soon as I found out what they were doing. I got the ladder and searched every inch of the ceiling in my old room, in case they'd installed a camera there. I went up in the attic, too, and pulled up all the insulation just to make sure. It was too late to matter, though. They already had the video by then."

"Didn't you take the camera out?"

"Out of Billy's ceiling?" She checked me with her eyes. "I wanted to. But I had to go in his room to cut. Eugene had to see me do it. He said he'd show the video to Jarrod if I ever stopped. Said he'd leak it to everyone at school."

"If you stopped cutting?"

"That's where he drew his strength. Not his strength but..." She scanned the windshield, looking for the right word. "His vitality. *My* vitality. I flushed my blood down the drain, he soaked it up."

I sighed.

"I know you don't believe that, but it's true."

I didn't say anything. I watched my sister and Ryan having their mother-and-son conversation before she turned him over to me for a day and a half. I could only imagine what she was telling him. *Text me if you need us to come get you. You promise? You don't have to stay if you don't want to. If it's uncomfortable in any way.*

"Do you know Catholics believe Communion wine turns into the actual blood of Jesus Christ before they drink it?"

"I think I heard that somewhere."

"You go to church with people who believe they can speak in other languages without bothering to learn them."

"Angel languages. Yeah, I know."

"Angel languages? Is that what they say?"

"I don't know. I'm no expert."

"Fucking demon languages if you ask me. So tell me again how delusional I am?"

"Off the scale." I watched Sheila tuck a stray hair behind Ryan's ear and kiss him on the forehead. "I never said you were the only one."

"But whatever *you* believe: that, by definition, is sane."

"I didn't say that."

"It's what you think, though."

"I don't know any other way to think. If I don't believe something, I don't believe it. Why would I believe something I know to be insane?"

"You think I do? Look at me." She reached over and pushed my shoulder. "Look at me."

I looked at her. Her eyes matched her hair, still damp at the roots, a bedraggled color impossible to pin down. I tried to imagine what she saw through those eyes, how the mind at the other end of the optic nerve actually worked.

"All I ask of you—all I have ever asked of you—is to stop expecting me to think the way you do. I can't. Or actually, I do think the way you do. Because what's different about us isn't so much the way we think, it's the way you filter the in-coming information. I wish you'd stop expecting me to believe what other people tell me instead of what I know to be true. I know what I know from my own experience, and in that I'm just like you." She said it again. "Just like you."

I scanned her eyes. She made her position seem almost reasonable.

"Just allow me the same benefit of the doubt you would a Christian. Or a Muslim or a Buddhist or anybody else in the world. A scientist. I bet you believe all kinds of shit based on science you've never done for yourself. But you have a filter in your head that says, 'Oh, if it's science, it must be true.' A Christian has a Bible filter, and you have one, too. It just filters different kinds of information in or out."

True enough, in its way. But Ryan and Sheila said goodbye. He was coming over.

"Jeannie, I need some time alone with my son. Can I drop you at your house? Just for tonight?"

"You can drop me anywhere you like. I'm a resourceful girl."

"Shit." I couldn't let her stay in the barn. Not tonight. By the same token, I couldn't know she was sleeping outdoors somewhere else. "All right. You're sleeping with me, then. *Sleeping*," I emphasized. "But you have to give me some time alone with Ryan, and I don't mean five minutes. You can hang out in the shop if you want."

"I'll stay out of the way." She pushed the door open for him and scooted over next to me, wrapping my arm in hers. "So, Ryan. I'm on my best behavior. I get to sleep with your mother tonight. Tell me, do you find that sexy?"

I rested my forehead on the steering wheel, eyes closed. Ryan got in and closed the door. "Uh, she's my mother. So no."

"Not even a little?"

I suggested, with as much calm as I could muster, that her definition of "best behavior" and mine were not in one hundred percent alignment. Then I snaked my arm free of hers, stopped banging my head on the wheel, opened my eyes, and commenced to drive.

True to her word, she spent the afternoon in the shop. She kept it open for business, while in the house I made Ryan a cup of tea and me a cup of coffee and told him everything I could about his father, about the circumstances of his birth and about his disappearance from the hospital. I answered his questions as best I could.

"Marshall Caleb Anatoly," he said.

"I kept my identity a secret for as long as I could," I told him. "I didn't want to get your father in trouble. I don't know if it was the right thing to do or not. I had no reason to think he had anything to do with stealing you. I still don't think he did. I can't imagine how he could've known anything about you."

"So he didn't abandon me or anything?"

"No. That's what I'm saying. He abandoned me, not you. He didn't know you existed."

"What did you do? After that. Where did you go?"

"Well, where I went was—I went a little crazy." I didn't tell him I tried to kill myself. That would come out eventually, of course. I didn't want to overload him. "I spent a few weeks in the local psych ward. Not because I was really crazy. I was more of a behavior problem than anything. The authorities decided, based on what the hospital had told them, that I was not as old as I said I was. I guess they can tell from a person's physiology. The State put me in foster care. I bounced around a lot in the beginning. Nobody really knew how to handle me, and I didn't care about whatever their problem with me was. I wanted you back, that's all I cared about. It's all I thought about. They didn't have any solution to my number one problem, so they just wanted to put me in school and wash their hands of me. They expected me to act my age, you know, but I was completely screwed up about what age I was supposed to be. Kids in school, kids my biological age, they were children. I'd been living as an adult, whether I was one or not. So I wasn't exactly adoption material. I wound up, finally, on a farm with seven other kids, some older than me, some younger. Most of them were into drugs, or they had been. We learned a lot of different things. At least, I did. How to take care of animals and plants, how to shear a sheep, how to build stuff, make stuff work. The farm was run by a couple who were into natural remedies and alternative energy. They were more honest with me than anyone ever had been. Max and Doreen were their names. They took in animals that had been abused and abandoned and tried to get them to trust again. Everything from dogs and cats to goats, llamas, pigs and humans. That's what they did with us, too. They tried, anyway. They weren't always successful. In fact, they would tell you there's no such thing as success. They weren't about defining success for us or for anybody else. What's success to a pit bull that's been used to bait other, meaner pit bulls? You know what I mean? Their goal, I think, was to get us to figure it out for ourselves. If they could stop an animal from being abused, or a kid, that in itself was a step in the right direction. In my case, it meant I had to stop abusing myself, in a way. Stop blaming myself for not being able to find you and protect you. Not that it worked, but they taught me to do something in the meantime, how to mix cob while I worried about you and build with it while I felt like a failure for not knowing where you were, how to extend the useful life of a piece of trash by finding a new purpose for it. In a sense they taught me how to repurpose myself."

"That's where the name of your store came from?"

"Repurpose Farm? I never thought of it that way until just now, but I guess so. It was really about repurposing stuff, not myself."

"What made you come back here?"

"My grandma's attorney found me. When I turned twenty-two, according to her will, I inherited her house and her land. Before it could be sold off, he hired a private investigator, who apparently had no problem locating me. I wasn't the first runaway to end up on Max and Doreen's farm. I was afraid. I thought I was in big trouble, but it turned out I'd never actually been charged with any crime. The authorities had assumed I was the victim of a crime, not the perpetrator." I shrugged. "I came back because I could."

Ryan's eyes were the thing about him that most reminded me of his father. Even looking at a photograph of Patterson in a magazine, I could never call to mind the face of the young man I once knew. For one thing, the one he wore in the papers and on TV — not that he was plastered everywhere, but I did see him occasionally — was a public face, a political face. He hadn't had one of those when I knew him, or if he did he never showed it to me. When he looked at me, he looked at me. I said before that I couldn't recall his actual face, and that's true as far as it goes, but I never forgot the feeling I got from looking at him, from seeing him and from being seen by him. It felt like total absorption, like being soaked right up inside him like water to a sponge. And vice versa, like my heart was a sponge soaking him up. My son looked at me that way now. When I said I came back because I could, he looked at me with the dark, soaking eyes of his father and said, "I'm glad you did."

"Stay right here." I went to find my phone. "I want to take a picture of you. Then let's go take a look at your great grandfather's land."

"The medicine man?"

"No, that was on Grandma's side. This land belonged to my grandfather Cavendish when she married him. He was a white man. If I'm not mistaken, it's been in the Cavendish side of the family since the Cherokee Strip opened in eighteen ninety-whatever-it-was."

"He left it to you?"

"Grandma did. He died, I think before I was born. I don't remember him, anyway."

"She's the one who raised you? Your grandmother?"

"Till I was eleven."

"You ran away when you were eleven?"

"No, I lived with Sheila and Leon after she died, for three years."

"So fourteen?"

"Fourteen," I said.

"That makes you thirty-six."

"Close." I found my cell phone on the bench by the fireplace. "I had you when I was fifteen."

He shook his head in slow motion. I'd seen the look a hundred times.

"You can say it."

"It's young, that's all. You didn't get to be a kid very long."

"True. But not because I had you. I was old a long time before that."

"It's hard to imagine, though."

"What? Me being fifteen?" I took two head shots of him, then we posed for a selfie together, arm in arm on the couch. "So I can prove to myself later this wasn't just a dream," I said. "Grab your jacket and come on. You know how to drive a stick?" I handed him my keys.

On our way through the shop to let her know we were leaving, I had Jeannie snap a couple more pictures of us. "How's it going?" I asked. "You need anything?"

"Been pretty steady. I don't remember it being this busy."

As we pulled out of the driveway, two cars waited to pull in.

"Turn left." I sent him south to the section line, then west up the slow rise in that direction, churning a red cloud of dust behind us. He ground the gears the first couple of times he shifted, but he and Jiminy soon fell into a rhythm. "This section over on my side is our land. Used to be two sections, but I had to sell some of it off to stay afloat when I first come back and started building. When it was leased out, it pulled in about twenty grand a year. I ought to try and find somebody to rent it to again, but I haven't yet. You can see it's getting a little overgrown. There's a stand of blackjack over in the far corner, if you take the next right. That's where I get most of my firewood, there and from the woodlot in front of the shop. The bulk of what I take out is dead fall. This up here's a prettier spot but too far off the blacktop for business." When we got to it, I directed him to pull in at the cattle guard. A track cut through the grass and circled around the knoll to the other side of the blackjack stand. "Why don't we get out and stretch our legs," I suggested. I hadn't walked the land in a good while. It felt good to show it off. We climbed the gentle slope into the trees where the sun wove its way through the branches. If it was summertime, we'd be in the shade, but today the sun felt good and the brush slowed the wind some. I found my favorite tree, one with a saddle in the trunk, low to the ground. It offered a seat with a view across the pasture. "I used to walk up here from the house a couple times a week, just to sit and ponder."

"Be a nice place to build a house," he said.

"You could if you wanted to, you know."

"Why don't you raise sheep here? You said you know how."

"Think that's what I should do?"

"Sure."

"Would you want to take it over when I'm old and feeble?"

"Maybe. You'd have to teach me how to shear them."

"Want me to repurpose you? Sit there," I pointed to the saddle in the trunk of the tree. He humored me. I swept my arm in a wide arc. "Survey your domain, Ryan Marshall Caleb Gray Anatoly Cavendish."

He grinned at me, then looked across the waist-high grasses bowing and scraping before him. "It's a lot of land."

"Twelve hundred and eighty acres, all told. Most of it going to rack and ruin."

After a while, he said, "You might want to talk to my mom about it." He caught himself, but too late. "My other mom."

"Because?"

"You might want to, that's all."

I could see how Sheila might feel like she got the short end of the stick where Grandma's will was concerned. Did she feel like she had a stake in what I did with the land?

Maybe.

Probably.

"I will," I promised Ryan. "If you think I should, I will."

He reached out to me. I gave him my hand, he pulled himself up and pointed behind us up the little hill. "If it was up to me, I'd build a tiny house right up there. Right in the middle of the trees."

"It is up to you. And if you keep talking like that, I'm liable to take you seriously."

He squinted at me with one eye closed. "I'm not *not* serious."

"Grandma always said my daddy wanted to plant a vineyard here, but he never did. Here and on the other side. Come on, I'll show you the rest."

We finished our circuit of the west section, driving past the windrow along the north boundary and back out onto Keening Canyon Road. "This section over here, where the house and the shop sit, has anywhere from another hundred fifty to two hundred acres of pasture right here fronting the road, plus a long strip that runs alongside the canyon behind the house. The few acres along the road in front of the shop are wooded. The rest, back behind the pasture, is canyon. Not much grows down there, but it's pretty. If you like desert."

We pulled in past the shop. Another car in the lot, another customer to keep Jeannie occupied. I had Ryan park Jiminy in the barn and walk with me along the old path through the back pasture to the canyon. I didn't say anything about Grandma, though she weighed on my mind anytime I visited the canyon. I was sure he knew the story from Sheila, about the way she died. But he hadn't known her. I wanted him to see the land for itself, let it speak to him in its own way. Unfiltered by me and my tragedies.

By the time we got to it, the sun had stepped behind a cloud and the wind sailed out of the north, whipping at our coat sleeves and singing through the canyon. "You hear it? I imagine that's why they named it Keening Canyon. Lot of Scotch and Irish settled around here back in the day."

"Must've reminded them of bagpipes?"

"I guess so. I never thought of it like that."

He stood facing me with his back to the wind, blocking it for me. I stepped in close and rested my head against him. "I've missed you my entire life," I said. "I hope you know that."

He said, "I've missed you, too," and hugged me. Even if he didn't mean it, even if I wasn't what he expected or if he felt obligated to respond that way, I appreciated it. It boded well that he would make the effort.

Jeannie came in the house around 6 pm and handed me the cash drawer from the register. "I like the new flag out front," she said. "It's a lot easier to bring in than the old wooden sign. Why does it say Tangible Angels? Is that about the wall?"

"Not entirely. I decided to rename the shop. I haven't got around to repainting the name on the door. Did you turn the Closed sign around? People still drive up sometimes."

"Yep. Doors are locked, lights are out, thermostat's turned down, all the hatches are battened."

"Thanks." I sat at the kitchen table to count the money and subtract the bank I keep in the drawer for making change. "Wow. You have been busy. Three hundred and twenty-seven? Not bad for an afternoon."

"That's just the cash receipts. You haven't seen the credit."

She handed me the slip from the register. "Jesus!" I said when I looked at the total.

"Seemed like a lot of early Christmas shoppers. The ones I had a chance to ask said they'd heard about the wall. Saw it on YouTube or read about it on your website."

"Seriously?"

She sat across from me. "I told them I was the one who vandalized it. When I said you hired me back and agreed to collaborate with me on the wall, they just couldn't seem to get out the door without buying something. Other people responded better to the mother-and-child reunion story. I told them that one hadn't made the blog yet; they were the first to know. I laid it on kinda thick."

"Oh," I said. I would have preferred telling that story myself, my own way and in my own good time. "So now we're collaborating?"

"You're welcome."

Ryan laughed, joining us at the table. The two of them exchanged a look.

I counted out her wages for the afternoon, plus the hour-and-a-half she'd worked before we went to lunch.

"I had to stay open till almost 6. Still had customers."

I handed her another eight dollars. She fanned her cash out on the table.

"You should be on commission," Ryan said.

"My agent says I should be on salary plus commission."

"Yeah?" I said, writing in the ledger I keep in the back of the drawer. "Tell your agent you're still on probation."

"Seriously, Vanessa, you need me to keep the shop open while you're away. Black Friday, weekend after Thanksgiving, people traveling back through the woods and over the river from Grandmother's house? Not a good time to be closed."

"Have you thought about who else might be traveling this time of year? I expect Eugene will want to pay me a visit while he's home from college. Angela, too."

"Not if you email him and let him know you're in Texas. You have big news to share. Anyway, I don't care if he does show up."

"Who are you?" I wondered. "And what did you do with Jeannie Ivory?"

She combed her hair back with her fingers. "I'm trying to remember who she was."

"Moody goth girl used to sit behind the counter and chew her mittens," I said, trying to be helpful. "Allergic to people, pissed off at the world."

She rolled her eyes. "I mean who I was before Sewer Boy emerged. I don't think you knew that version of me. You know what?" She hesitated. "No, maybe you don't." Then she resumed. "Killing myself was the best thing I've ever done. Buddhists teach that, you know. Even Christians. They say you have to die daily in order to live. It's pretty much lip service, coming from them, but there's some truth to it."

"It's the daily part I worry about, Jeannie. Once was enough for me."

She stacked her bills and leaned back to stuff them in her pocket. "It's like—there are two ways to look at it, though. I was killing myself a little bit every day. Making an offering of myself. But that was an attempt to protect myself, wasn't it? I'd give a little bit and then a little bit more and a little more. Fooled myself into thinking I was safer that way. But safe from what? Annihilation? I thought once the video got out, the last shred of—not just dignity, but of anything worthwhile about me, would be gone. Like in a sense I *would* be annihilated. But it didn't matter, after all, did it? I'm still here. What do I give a fuck if people watch me having a good time, just because they're fucked up? The only thing I had left was to give in completely, give up, let him take what was left. All of it, all at once. So…" she turned her forearms up and pushed back the layers of sleeve, "no half measures. Right, Vanessa?"

This was why I hadn't wanted her in the house with us, why I'd sent her to run the shop. Her need to talk scared me. Her need to reveal herself. She had no filter at all. What I thought of as her delusions were, to her, simple matters of fact.

"You don't want to take credit for it. I get that. But I learned it from you. Just like you learned from your grandmother."

"You never knew her. You don't know anything about her." I didn't want her to freak Ryan out. After the day we'd had? I was afraid he might see her as an extension of me and wish he'd never come, never met me, never found me. I'd lose him again before I had a chance to know him, or him me. She was the reason Sheila had invited me to Austin with them. They'd planned to stay longer, but Sheila had changed her mind. She knew. She'd picked up on the fact that, for the life of me, I couldn't shake Jeannie off.

What did that say about me?

But that wasn't the half of it. I worried even more that she would *not* freak Ryan out, that she'd lock onto him the way she had me, that she'd fuck with his head, make him wonder if maybe the world could actually work—sometimes, in some places, or for some people—just a tweak and a half past normal on the dial.

She looked up, her eyes like a pair of wrens taking wing. They flew not to me but to him. I watched, helpless, as his eyes rose to meet her.

*You can't fall in love with her!* I wanted to scream. *She's not real! Nothing she tells you is real!* "Jeannie," I said instead, desperate to make a point. "Jeannie, did I tell you I met Amy Frye?"

She gave me a pitying look. "No. When?"

"A few weeks ago. At her house."

She let her eyes glide back to Ryan, a swooping, diving maneuver. "Neighbor lady when I was a kid," she explained. "She's dead." Then she told me, "You saw a ghost."

"Of course I did." I got up and opened the fridge. "Let's see what we've got for dinner."

"What?" Ryan said. "You saw a ghost, let's have dinner?"

"Welcome to Repurpose Farm," Jeannie said. "Oh, wait. I mean, Tangible Angels, don't I?"

# BREAKFAST FOR DINNER

I made us breakfast for dinner. Home fries, eggs scrambled with roasted red peppers and purple onions, a little salsa for kick and a dollop of sour cream to cool it down, everything folded up together in a fat warm flour tortilla spread with butter and refried beans. Mexican rice on the side. I kept it simple. I didn't want to show off, but I did want Ryan to know his mother could cook.

He devoured his burrito. I made him another one.

When I turned back from the stove with his plate in hand, I caught Jeannie leaning on the table with her chin on her fist, her eyes practically glued to the side of his face. She probably meant for me to see it, I can't be sure. It's a wonder she didn't take the skin off his cheek, she ripped her eyes away so fast. He reached for the plate, grinning as if he only had eyes for my burrito. I didn't buy his clueless act, either.

Was I jealous?

I was afraid.

I was so afraid.

I'd seen the way he looked at her. He made it less obvious than she did, but I saw what was happening. Ryan had his father's eyes. Not the poll-tested public gaze but the private one-on-one inquisitive look that paid attention to one person at a time and one person alone. It scared me shitless to think that if his eyes lingered on hers for too long, if I left him alone with her for more than a minute, he might—I don't know what—take her septic condition up into his bloodstream? Break out in schizophrenia?

*I made out with your nephew.*

Bad enough when he *was* my nephew.

Worse, she might absorb him. She would more than monopolize him, she would colonize him. I knew what it was like to get caught up in her, in a gaze so cold it burned, a mind so foreign it made itself familiar, a kiss so dirty it stripped you clean.

I had five minutes and a day's worth of experience being a mother. Were my feelings typical? rational? normal? I don't know that it mattered, they were mine and they were having their way with me.

I needed air.

"Jeannie," I said, veering past the table. I hoisted my jacket from the back of her chair and pushed it at her until she stood and started putting it on. "Would you give me a hand?" I grabbed my other jacket from the back of the door. "You stay and eat, Ryan. I'll be right back."

I led her in the direction of the barn, fuming through the dark like a locomotive. "What the fuck, Jeannie?" I said, turning on her halfway there. "What the fuck are you doing?"

She played dumb.

I pointed. "That is my son in there."

"Yeah, I got the memo."

*I want him to myself!* I did not say. But I did. I wanted to take him to my breast, wanted to change his diaper, wanted to witness his first true grin, his gurgling laughter, watch him discover his toes, my chin, each startling fact of his existence. I wanted his first word, his first steps, his first birthday. I wanted him back, all the years of him gone I wanted back. He was mine. He was stolen from me and he was mine and I wanted him back.

I settled on, "I don't want to share him with you right now."

"I get that."

I sought her eyes in the dark, tried to make out what she was thinking, but the sky was all stars and no moon.

"I didn't want to share Jarrod with you," she said.

"Jarrod?"

"But I did, didn't I?"

"I'm not talking a—"

"I'm done giving, Vanessa."

"I'm not *asking* you for anything!" I pleaded.

"You think your son just magically reappeared, don't you? You think everything that happens is just a chain of coincidences randomly linked together. No cause and effect. Nothing has anything to do with me, right? So why don't you just sit and say nothing, Jeannie? Why don't you pretend to be invisible? Be grateful for the scraps I toss you and stay out of the way, because I have my son back, and you can go fuck yourself."

"I never said—"

"You never said thank you."

I stepped away from her, mystified.

"I gave you everything I had. I gave you my life. I gave you your life back. You don't see the way things are connected, because you're blind to the way Sewer Boy works. I misjudged you, and that's on me. I own that. I thought you had an ounce of fucking courage in you, but I was mistaken. You heard your sister. She wanted her husband dead. I should have known better than to put my faith in rumors. Rumors have power, I know that, but they also have the power to deceive. So my bad."

"Goddammit!" I said, more to myself than to her. "I should've called the Sheriff the minute I saw you."

"Go ahead. That'll make an impression."

She was right, of course. If I called and had her arrested now, for no reason that would be in any way apparent to Ryan, I would look like the crazy one. I couldn't even change my mind about the sleeping arrangements, send her back to the barn. (For all I had the power to manage or to predict, unless I slept with one eye open, the two of them would end up in the barn together, anyway.)

"Jeannie," but my plea came crumpled from my throat, "Jeannie, he's my son."

She stepped up to me and tugged at my elbows. "You think I don't know what it means? You think I don't know how it hurts?"

"I don't know what you know!" I complained. "I don't know how your mind works. Or your heart. I can't—I can't fathom you, Jeannie."

"That's right." She pulled my arms around her, slid hers inside my jacket and encircled me, linking us in an embrace I did not want but had no energy to refuse. "I know," she murmured, "I know."

"I think your heart is damaged," I managed.

"You think?" She soothed me, her hands on my back, rubbing, rubbing in small circles, pressing me against her frame of sticks, her ribs jammed into mine. "Badly, badly damaged, yes, my heart. My sweet sick heart." She rested her head on my chest as if listening for mine. "It stopped, you know. It shut down. Pumped itself dry and shut the fuck down. But I am a miracle of modern compassion, Vanessa. I am flush with the blood of Middle America, homogenized, pasteurized, sweet as communion wine and foul as common sin. They stitched my pieces back together and jolted me with the juice of Frankenstein, and here I stand, full of lust and love and therapy and need and faith and pain and the itch that comes with healing. It's true, you can't fathom me. Problem is, you can't fathom yourself. I overwhelm you, don't I? And guess what? I will overwhelm your son, if he lets me. He might not have a choice. He'll be thinking about me the whole time you're with him in Texas, you know. That's what scares you. You think I'm infectious? Maybe. Maybe I am. I just wish you hadn't gone and immunized yourself against me. Not that I blame you for that, either. Not really. That was his doing. Sewer Boy and his Christian Fan Club. All that angel bullshit gratitude you spread."

"You think that immunizes me?" I asked her. I could not have been more serious. "If it did, I'd slather myself with it. I'd make myself a pot of gratitude tea and drink it every day if it would keep you away from me." But I was sick with her. It was too late for remedies.

Her lips found mine in the dark. Or mine hers, I don't even know.

"Not even a little," she whispered deep in her throat. Her hand materialized inside my shirt, up under my bra.

I pushed her shoulders away. "I can't. No!" I said. "I don't want this."

"Liar."

"Even if I did," I said, sliding my hands down her forearms, pushing her hands down, freeing them of my shirt, "I can't."

She gave a soft snort and withdrew. "Then I guess it's Ryan." She turned back to the house, her silhouette swaying in the light of the window.

"Come back," I said with too little force.

She merged with the dark again, until the door opened and she stood in the light, a skeleton, looking back at me.

"I need your help with —"

She stepped inside and closed the door.

I'd meant to have her help me drape the sewn-together sheets over the wall, my excuse for having dragged her out with me in the first place. Not that it mattered.

Not that it mattered.

# BRIDAL TRAIN

The reason I did what I did I can't explain. Where the notion come from, for the life of me, I don't know.

For several minutes I stood ankle-deep in the shallow end of a long pool of light overflowing the front window of my house, thinking, thinking.

Not really thinking, no. Seeing. Apprehending. Fitting puzzle pieces together.

My son had come home to me. My adult son, a stranger to me. I saw in him the fleeting face of his father. I watched him in my mind's eye like a piece of origami unfolding out of the unknown and into existence. Into my existence, anyway, whatever the nature of his existence had been over the past two, nearly two and a half decades. My lost boy.

In my memory, I felt Jeannie straddle me in the dark of night while a soft white storm raged in silence beyond my walls, sealing me in with her. I relived a dream that was not a dream, a vision in which she sipped my tears and spoke to me in the grawking language of the crow. *File ngitsalerveh vah tub shirep ton llash mih ni thevieleb ervehosooh tath nus nttogeeb ylno sih vage ee tath dlerw eth dvull ohs dog orf.* She spoke of my son's return, spoke as if she imagined him aloud to me. Whether she foretold his coming, or called him forth, or wished, or just supposed, it made no difference to me. He was my son. He had come to me.

She said I wouldn't recognize him, and at first I didn't.

*But I will know him,* she said. *Mih own lliw Ai.* In the language of the dream, if it was a dream, her knowledge reigned absolute, a claiming kind of knowledge, biblical in its certainty, prophetic.

I sat with Jarrod in my shop. I heard him say of his brother's fall from the tree house in Keening Creek, "She took a lot of shit for the things she said. If she hadn't said it, it wouldn't have happened. She commanded Dietz to step through that hole."

I turned and walked away from the house. In the dark of the barn I found, without having to look for it, a bucket I knew was there.

I'd put it there. In it I had collected Jeannie's blood, now nine months old, diluted in the thawed snow of February with a skin of decaying leaves, mosquitoes, beetles, flies. I picked it up by the handle and carried it from the barn along a path my feet knew well, through the back pasture to the canyon, taking care not to let the dark water slosh over the sides. The tall grass shushed to and fro in the starlight, hissed against my jeans as I passed through it and thinned away behind me as I picked my way down a runnel that fanned out into the canyon now, the seasons having eroded it in drastic new patterns since the days of my grandmother. I stopped to swap the bucket over to my left hand before I descended the long main spur. I didn't follow it to the end as my grandma had done, but two-thirds of the way along the ridge, I put the bucket down, sat, and slid a shorter way down to a secondary spur coming off the main one at an acute angle, then I reached and lifted the bucket down after me, taking the utmost care with Jeannie's blood, because it mattered where I spilled it. Don't ask me why. I followed the bidding of a power and a knowledge older than myself, a medicine older than my grandma. The shorter spur ended in a blunt face above a rock overhung by an ancient cedar tree. Sheltered from the wind, the tree had grown three times its girth and twice its height since the night Grandma sat in its shadow and lied to me. There, without thought or hesitation, I poured out the bucket. The long stream spattered the roots of the cedar and plunged into the darkness where once, as a child, I had buried my grandma's bread knife. I heard the liquid gurgle at the bottom, slaking the dry earth's thirst, a deep and dirty kind of laughter.

"Grandma," I said, "forgive me. I don't know what else to do."

I had the moon with me as I climbed back from the canyon, a horned shape disentangling itself from the naked wood by the road in front of my shop. I flung the bucket from me and dug my cell phone out of my pocket. When I entered my house by the back door, I surprised the two of them on my sofa.

I spoke with a certain volume, my ferocity not entirely bridled, "I don't care where you sleep tonight, my bed or the barn, but get off my son!"

I watched her stand and straighten herself in her undershirt, her nipples pronounced, her arms like two barked twigs, both vined in scar tissue. I did not look at him, afraid my eyes might singe him. He was a child compared to her, culpable but lacking in calculation.

Then I did look at him. Regaining most of my composure, I said, "This does not happen under my roof." And to her I said, "We have more to talk about, you and me."

She seemed pleased, interested. A little worried, maybe. She finished tucking her undershirt into her jeans. My borrowed sweatshirt lay on the floor, a casualty of my absence.

I rounded the sofa and took her by the arm. "If you'll excuse us, Ryan." I led her to my room and closed the door.

Her face changed and changed again as I told her what I'd done, doubt giving way before anger, anger condensing to scorn, and scorn succumbing to fear. "In a bucket? A goddamn plastic bucket? All this time?"

"That's right."

"He never knew you had it?"

I cradled my phone in my hands, texting with my thumbs. "He will here in a minute."

"You fucking bitch," she said without enthusiasm. "Don't, please."

"I can't imagine why I wouldn't."

Her eyes went slick with tears. "I'm begging you, don't do this to me again!"

"I'm having trouble seeing any other way this can work. I mean, you're right. I'm flying blind here. I don't know how any of it works, really. What did you think would happen if your blood soaked into the ground outside my window?"

"I didn't care what happened! Not then! I just wanted to die. You never told me you saved it. You saved my blood? Why?"

"Keep your voice down."

"Why? Why did you do that?"

"I don't know, Jeannie. Why did I? I didn't want it soaking into my yard, maybe? I didn't want it staining my house? I didn't want to be reminded all the time, every time I looked out my window. It was your blood, Jeannie. What if you died? What was I supposed to do then, with your blood in my ground?"

"All this time, it was you."

"Me, what?"

"Keeping him at bay. Keeping him from—he had no power over me. He couldn't take anything from me anymore. I thought—I thought it was because I died. I thought my death somehow—I don't know—canceled everything."

"You didn't die."

"I did die. I saw what my death is."

"You said you had nothing left to lose. Maybe that's what's kept you safe, don't you think? I think you just decided not to be afraid of him anymore."

She sniffed. "You really don't know anything, do you?"

"I know this: I know I've decided not to be afraid of you anymore. I didn't have to die to figure it out."

"Why would you? I'm the least of your worries."

"Just tell me, what is this thing you're doing with Ryan? What's that about? Payback for Jarrod? Seriously?"

She hugged her shoulders, looked aside and downward. "He was a gift. You didn't appreciate him."

My mouth worked at forming words, my mind at forming a thought. *I don't appreciate him?* But I stopped myself. It wasn't important anymore that sanity prevail. I brought my mind, my argument, to a grinding halt, stopped trying to out-think her, to work some kind of mental judo on her. Instead, I listened.

Her shoulders hitched, her face crumpled. "I gave you everything!"

I waited. I watched her control her tears and did not intervene. When it seemed like she had no more to add, I said, "I thought everything came from Eugene."

She balled her fists, uncrossed her arms. *"We're the same!"* The words exploded from her like a cork, unstopping her tears, her rapid speech. "That's what I never wanted to admit. I never wanted anyone to know. Least of all you." She stopped herself talking, her cheeks puffed up with air, with more violent tears. "You can't love me, Vanessa, can you? You can't, because I'm his replacement! Oh, shit!" she wailed. "Oh, shit, shit shit! I thought I could turn it on him, I thought I could send him back. Him, not me. But you fucked that up, didn't you? Now he gets everything! All of me, all at once! You gave it to him! You just gave it to him!"

I deleted my text, slipped my phone in my pocket. I hadn't been going to actually send it, anyway. And say what?

*Hi Eugene. FYI just dumped JI's blood from last winter into the canyon for you. Come pick it up whenever. Smileyface.*

I took a step and wrapped my arms around her. Her bones shuddered against me with fear, or cold, or both. She mashed her face into my shoulder. Hot tears soaked my shirt.

I turned with her at the sound of the bedroom door, not letting go. Ryan's face appeared. He kept his voice soft. "Hey."

I expelled a sigh that set Jeannie's hair aflutter. "Come on in."

"Well, um, listen. You two, I mean, clearly have something to work out, and I just—maybe I should go."

"We do," I said. "And that's thoughtful of you. But I don't think this is going to work itself out whether you're here or not. And I don't want you to go."

Jeannie sucked back her tears. "I'm the one that has to go."

When she pulled away and looked at me, I saw, I think for the first time, the actual color of her eyes, like the cast-off core of the earth, the color of dead stars, of iron beaten and folded a hundred times, and quenched. Still hot with her tears, they locked on me like magnets and let me go.

She kissed Ryan on the cheek and said in passing, "You listen to your mother."

"About what?"

She paid him no attention and went to the barn, but not to sleep.

As I stood at the kitchen sink, scrubbing the plates from supper, I saw her by the three-quarter light of the moon, one end of the stitched-together flat sheets from my wall of gratitude gathered around her like a gown, the rest of it trailing after her like a bridal train some thirty, forty feet long, bending the grass in her wake as she crossed the back pasture.

# A Permanent and
# Loving Family

I called Jarrod at work. I didn't know who else to ask. "I need a favor," I said. "I have to go to Austin. It's a long story, I'll tell you all about it. My sister is in town and I'm going to ride down with her, but I need to take the train back to Oklahoma City. I wondered if you wouldn't mind picking me up at the station next Tuesday?"

"It's nice to hear your voice," he said. I hadn't seen him since the day I met his mother. That was in what? August? September? Come to think of it, I hadn't actually seen him that day, either. I was supposed to meet him at his house, but I left before he got there.

"I know, I know, I know." I sounded pathetic, I'm sure. "I'm sorry, Jarrod, I just—" I wanted to say how busy I'd been, how crazy things had got between the shop and the wall and trying to keep up with everything on my own ever since Angela and Eugene had gone off to college, but my excuses were too flimsy to put into words. Truth was, before I met his mother, I felt like we had more in common, like we needed each other more than we actually did. Except now I did need him, at least, and I felt shittier than ever about asking him for a favor.

He said, "When are you leaving?"

"First thing in the morning." I told him when I'd be coming back, what time and where.

"Can I see you before you go?"

"I've got my family here. From Texas. My—" I looked at Ryan. "There're things I haven't told you, Jarrod. This is so important, and completely unexpected. Please do this for me. I'll make it up to you."

He didn't say anything.

"Please?"

"Be happy to."

"You don't sound it."

"No, I'd be happy to do that for you, Ms. Cavendish. You bet."

I swiped my phone off. "Shit," I said. "He's pissed." He said he'd do it, though.

The other matter I needed to attend to was to get in touch with Patterson Price. I Googled the United States Senate and called his office number in Washington, D. C. I left my name and number with the young-sounding man who answered the phone. I added, "The Senator might remember me as Anastasia Anatoly. Write that down for him, would you? You'll make sure he sees it? Good. Tell him I expect to hear back from him personally. And while you're at it, would you tell him for me that I applaud his support of Senate Resolution 580 and for recognizing that every child should have a permanent and loving family? Thank you so much!"

I turned to Ryan. "We'll see what comes of it. If I don't hear back, I still have the name of that attorney who came asking all kinds of questions, that Andrew Blake."

"What's Senate Resolution 580?"

"Oh," I said, "they resolved to celebrate children and families involved in adoption. Isn't that nice? Just in time for Thanksgiving. It's a way for politicians to feel good about themselves. I figured it wouldn't hurt to mention it."

It impressed my son, I could tell, that I would be clued in to that particular piece of Senatorial trivia. Truth to tell, I wouldn't have known the first thing about it if I hadn't gone surfing for Patterson's phone number and then tried to find out whether he'd be in Washington or back in Oklahoma for Thanksgiving.

We took a ride around to the other side of the canyon and paid a visit to Leigh Ann Sprague–used to be Carlisle and, before that, Bittle–my frenemy from junior high school. Leigh Ann didn't answer the door, but we heard machinery rumbling from the back yard and ventured around the side of the house. She was back there roto-tilling in what was left of a vegetable garden, turning her stalks and vines back into the soil, from the look of it, in a pair of those three-quarter length carpenter jeans and sneakers that made her calves look fat. I called out to her and waved.

She shut the roto-tiller down and came over. Her smile, the only part of her face not shaded by the bill of her baseball cap, darkened when she saw who it was.

"Got something I need to talk to you about," I said.

"What's that?"

"I don't believe you ever knew I had a son. This is Ryan."

She came closer, held out her hand, still not smiling. "No, I don't believe I did." In addition to the cap, she wore a pair of dark glasses. She and Ryan shook hands. She looked at me like, this is what you drove over here to tell me?

"It's about Mark."

She pursed her lips and pulled off her sunglasses to get a better look at me. "Do you know where he is?"

"I wish I did, so I could give him a hug." I told her who Ryan's father was and what Sheila told me about the note she'd found pinned to Ryan's blanket. "Signed 'M. B.'," I said. "As to how and why he come to have Ryan with him in the first place—whether he was told to leave him with Sheila like that or he acted on his own—I am completely in the dark. I know it's not much to go on, but I thought it might shed some light on things."

A vague look came over her. "Momma always said it had something to do with you. She always said that."

"I thought you would know, better than me, the best way to talk to your folks about it."

She nodded.

I explained that I would be away for the next several days, but if she needed me to sit with her folks when I got back and tell them what I knew, I would.

She pursed her lips again and puffed up her cheeks. "Maybe," she said. "I'll keep it in mind. You're not Momma's favorite person, you know."

"I know. That's why I come to you first."

"Tell me this. Do you think Patterson Price had Mark steal your baby?"

"No." I told her about the nursing assistant, Ellen Haddick, who probably did, then about my conversation with Andrew Blake, about the timing of Mark's and Marshall Caleb's—Ryan's—disappearances. "It doesn't prove a thing," I said, "but the fact that someone else put two and two together and come asking questions about me and Patterson makes it seem like it might be more than mere coincidence."

She told me Andrew Blake had visited her and her folks, too, which I knew. Then she said, "Of course, we didn't know your part in it at the time."

I let that slide. "If nothing else comes of it," I said, "I hope it might bring you and your folks some comfort to know that Mark tried to do the right thing."

"You want me to be happy for you, don't you?" She slid her shades back in place, still glaring at me. "For all I know, that might be what got my brother in trouble. Seems to be a pattern of bad things happening to people who try to help you."

That was the end of our conversation. Evidently, she had roto-tilling left to do.

I felt like Ryan deserved the entire story, so on the way to Austin I told him and Paul and Sheila and Joules everything I could remember about Jeannie Ivory and the Sewer Boy, including her accusation that Eugene and her brother had concealed a video camera and videotaped her masturbating in her bedroom, then used the video to blackmail her.

"I have no earthly idea where the truth ends and psychosis enters the picture," I warned them. "I remember Eugene showing me the code behind the slideshow header for my website, how he made one image so it fades out and the next one fades in. When your connection's good, the transition is so smooth you don't even notice it. When it's not so good, it kind of lurches from one image to the next, and you go, 'What the fuck?' That's how it is with Jeannie and her stories. When she's inside my head—when the connection between us is real good—her version of reality and mine kind of overlap. You know what I mean? One fades in as the other fades out? If I didn't have my head screwed on straight, I swear she could make me believe almost anything."

Most of the way I rode behind Paul, with Ryan next to me and Joules on the other side of him.

"What if your head *is* screwed on straight?" Ryan asked me. "What if the two versions really do overlap?"

I didn't know how to answer.

"Look at it this way: The validity of the code behind a website doesn't depend on your internet connection, even though your browser's ability to show it to you does. What if our ability to perceive one another's realities depends on our faith in each other—our connection, as you put it—but the validity of a particular point of view—in this case, Jeannie's reality—is independent of your ability to perceive it or comprehend it? Yours, mine, anybody's."

Sheila, from the front seat, hummed the theme from *The Twilight Zone.*

"No, wait. What if Eugene's connection to this world, our world of air and sunlight and human kindness, depends on Jeannie? What if her blood is the connection between them, and he needs it in order to function fully in our world?"

"Her blood or her pain?" I offered.

He agreed. "Her blood as evidence of her pain."

I saw Paul lift up his head as if he might be looking in the rear view. "Cut the shit, Ryan," he said.

"Yeah," Joules put in, "he's just fucking with you, Aunt Vanessa."

"No, I'm not. Right now, in this car, we have five different versions of reality all operating simultaneously. None of us share a hundred percent of our experience with any of the rest of us, but we share just enough to be able to understand each other reasonably well. We all agree that we're traveling south on I-35 in North Texas, so if Joules looks out her window and sees an oil well, and you look out on your side and see a farmhouse, there's no real argument to be had, right? You share enough relevant information that you don't doubt her experience, and she doesn't question yours, even though you have different sets of direct evidence. But!" He held up an index finger, like the professor on Gilligan's Island. "There are aspects of reality that we don't have any direct evidence for at all. Because we share so much of the world in common, we've come to accept certain things as true based on nothing but the reports of other people."

"For example?"

"Like near-death experiences or the existence of polar bears or the speed of light."

"We have evidence of polar bears and the speed of light," Joules said.

"We, the human species, maybe; but not we, the five of us in this car."

"I do, because I can look it up on my phone."

"Right, because you are connected to received information in two ways: by radio frequencies and by your faith in the authority of your source. But you've never seen a polar bear, have you? And you've never measured the speed of light yourself. You can also look up near-death experiences on your phone, by the way, so as far as what you know directly, the only difference between them and polar bears is the perceived authority of your sources. Same thing applies to Jeannie's so-called psychosis. For all we know—and I mean the five of us, here and now—the only difference between the belief in polar bears and her assertion that she created the Sewer Boy is the fact that we share a collective faith in the one but not in the other."

Joules pulled a set of wires out of her bag and plugged one end into her phone. "That and the fact that one is true and the other one's crazy."

"To the extent that you rigidly adhere to that belief, dear sister, you limit yourself to a sadly conformist view of reality."

"The sad reality," Joules said, slipping into the world inside her earbuds, "is you think she's skanky-hot and you want to get in her pants, so you're willing to believe whatever it takes."

Ryan sighed and propped his feet on the back of the console between Paul and Sheila. "I did feel a certain connection." He laced his fingers across his chest. "Which I think only goes to support my contention."

Over the next several days, while I was in Austin, Sheila and I agreed to split the section of land across the road from the shop between Joules and Ryan. I wanted Ryan to have the north half, where most of the blackjack stood, in case he ever wanted to come build a house there and help me raise sheep for real. In the meantime, they could each determine whether they wanted to rent their acreage out as income property or sell it. Until that time, I had access to the dead fall on Ryan's side, if that was okay with him, but I would not cut down any live timber of his. To make the idea seem more plausible and more palatable to all concerned, I pointed out that if he ever did decide to move to Keening, he could still work for Paul and Sheila remotely.

Sheila seemed pleased with the arrangement as far as dividing up the land was concerned. I think it was important to Ryan how she felt about it. "I'll get the paperwork drawn up as soon as I get back," I said.

Not much else happened during my visit except that my heart like to busted at the seams, I was so happy. It was bound to deflate again some. I mean, that's life, isn't it? You can only sustain a high like that for so long. The instant I set foot on the train back to OKC, all my helium turned to lead.

I had to face two things when I got back. First, I did not want to find out what had become of Jeannie Ivory. And second, I had a lot of explaining to do with Jarrod.

He picked me up around 6:30 in the evening and took me to a brewery around the corner from the train station. I had no appetite, but I drank a beer. In fact, since he was driving, I had two. He wanted to hear all about me and Ryan while he ate. "Well, first of all," I said, "he's three years older than you are."

He chewed and swallowed a bite of his Kitchen Sink Burger. "That's not news, though, Vanessa. You were fourteen when you had him."

"Fifteen." I didn't want to fight. I didn't know what I'd find when I got home. Jeannie dead? Or camping out in my barn? My wall demolished? The shop ransacked? All of the above? An image of Eugene hunkered down in the canyon, digging in the dirt where I'd poured out that bucket of bloody water, played in a loop in the back of my head. I wanted Jarrod to stay over. I wanted him to stay away. "The fact remains," I said.

He picked a crumb from his lip and studied it. "What fact remains?"

"I don't know. I don't even know what a fact is anymore."

"Facts are over-rated."

"My son is a fact." Everything I said came out wrong, as if I meant to contradict him. "Your mother is a fact."

"My mother?"

"I meant to tell you. I met her."

He set his burger down on his plate, wiped his lip with his thumb. "When was this?"

"I forget. A few months ago."

He laughed, not very hard. "Not my mom. My mom died when I was a kid. I thought you knew that. We talked about it, remember?"

"I went to your house, Jarrod. She was there. We talked."

He got a funny look in his eye.

"That wasn't your mom?" I said. "She said she was your mom."

He shook his head the way you do to get the cobwebs out, then commenced to take another bite of his hamburger.

"You told me you lived at home, Jarrod. And a long time ago, you said your father was dead. Now you tell me your mother's dead, too? So what do you mean when you say you still live at home? With who?"

"My step-dad. And my step-brother."

"Then who was that woman I talked to?"

"No idea," he said, chewing.

I fell asleep on the way home. We pulled in sometime around 9:30, 10 o'clock. It felt like the wee hours of the morning.

"You don't have to go, do you?" I pouted.

"I have to work in the morning."

I did not want to be alone. "You can get there from here, you know. I'll make you breakfast in the morning."

He seemed to be doing some kind of calculation in his head. I wasn't privy to his sums.

"Come on, Pat—Ry—Jarrod!" I said. I was so tired, still groggy from my long nap on the road. I slipped out of my seatbelt and rested my forehead on his shoulder, cringing.

He let me squirm for a minute, then he wanted to know. "Who's Pat?"

I rocked my head against him in denial. "Nobody you ever have to worry about."

"I can tell."

"The father of my son," I confessed, wincing in the dark. "Patterson Price."

"Why do I know that name?"

I told him who Patterson Price was. It didn't help matters. "He wasn't a Senator when he got me pregnant," I pointed out. But the damage was done. I'd wounded his pride, undermined his footing with me, which was none too secure to begin with, I'm sure. "It was so long ago," I complained. "You can't hold it against me. You can't!"

"I don't," he said. Then he unloaded on me. "I'm seeing somebody."

"Oh," I said, "shit." But in secret, I was relieved. "Anybody I know?"

He didn't answer.

"It's all right. I appreciate the ride," I told his shoulder.

I got out without looking at him, pulled my suitcase from the back seat and stood holding it, watching his headlights back away and turn around.

In the dark, the barn loomed beside me, a shadow leaning in the direction of the prevailing wind. My house huddled in silence behind me with no light in the window and no moon in the sky to show me the path to my door.

# CANYON GIRL

I didn't look at my wall for another week. When I did, I still didn't see right away what she'd done.

From the ground, the most notable difference was in the appearance of my eyes, which were nothing now but two black circles. I took out the ladder and climbed up to get a closer look. Then I saw what else was different. She had set a camera lens in place of Eugene's left eye and one in place of Billy's right eye, both angled downward so they pointed at the upside-down angel, whose fingers, I now saw, were interlaced and covering her crotch, to hide it.

The black circles over my eyes were the two lens caps.

I left the changes she'd made. Over the course of the next several months, all through the spring and summer, every minute I could spare, and quite a few that I couldn't, I spent setting shards of broken glass and china, mirror, metal, marbles, colored plastic — whatever I could scrounge that worked — to cover every square inch of my wall in a shimmery mosaic. For the smaller feathers in the wings of the angels, all but one, I overlapped old CDs. They shone silver in the sun. For Jeannie's upside-down wings, I used old vinyl: forty-fives for the smaller, overlapping feathers and LPs, cut to fit, for the longer ones, the flight feathers spread out to left and right along the base of the wall. They caught the light, too, and reflected it in their own way, iridescent as an oil slick or a crow's wings. The only blackness anywhere except for my two blind eyes, her wings and hair and body drew down the light — all that shimmer of mirrored sunlight, the silver of the other angels' wings, the shine of their porcelain faces — and extinguished it. Drank it.

For my hair and for the rays of the sun I used terra cotta. To the sky, I added a cloud made of broken-up off-white dinner plates, an ivory thunderhead, and from that cloud there fell a drenching rain in shattered ruby and cranberry glass. It fell on everyone, on angels and sinners alike, and soaked into the outstretched wings of my darkest angel, my blood sister, the deepest mystery and most persistent regret of my life.

I have never seen her again. I dream sometimes that I go chasing after her down into Keening Canyon, pleading with her not to go, telling her I have something for her, something I have neglected to give her. Sometimes it is my baby I am supposed to give her, sometimes it is something else, a picture of my grandmother or a child's storybook.

In my waking life, nobody ever asks me about her or speaks of her to me. Her mother moved to Tulsa some time ago. Her brother travels with a gospel band called Light Meter that Eugene Lamb manages.

Todd Lamb ran for Mayor of Keening and won. No one has run against him since. I have not darkened the door of First Assembly in many a year, though Ryan and Angela have been after me to go with them when they come back to visit. They live out in the sticks in North Carolina, where she studies glass-blowing and metalwork up at Penland School of Crafts. He still tells me I ought to raise sheep on his and Joules's land and sell the wool. Whenever he brings it up, I tell him talk is cheap.

They met that following summer, after Jeannie's disappearance, while Angela was on break from Kansas City and teaching classes out of my shop again. Ryan drove up on a motorcycle he and Paul had picked up for next to nothing and stayed with me for a weekend that turned into a month and a half. The rest of the year, I got to see him when he stopped over on his way to and from Kansas City. They've been together now for, let's see, a little more than five years. They intend to marry when she finishes at Penland.

I finally completed my Wall of Gratitude. Trowel in hand, a bucket of lime grout hooked to my extension ladder, sweat dripping from my brow and from the tip of my nose and running down my flanks as I added the last touches, I could hear two little girls talking down below me, commenting on the scene, on the black-winged angel in particular.

One said, "She's not a *good* angel. That's why she's upside-down."

The other one said, "She's a real person, though."

"No, she's not. She can't be."

"Yes, she is, and she lives all alone in the canyon."

"No way."

"She eats rattlesnakes and drinks their venom. Only dead ones, because she's part crow, and they only eat dead things like dead rats and other birds and things. And she can't find her way out, because the walls are too steep, so she just wanders around down there all the time."

"She could get out if she went way down that way by the bridge, where the road is."

"Yeah, but she doesn't know how to get there. You wouldn't want her to get out, anyway, because that would be a horrific calamity if she ever did. It would be like the start of the zombie apocalypse. For real."

"What's her name?" asked the one who wasn't so sure.

The other one, the more authoritative one, said, "At day camp they call her the canyon girl."

# Many Thanks

To Deborah Brown, Adrian Dunn, Peter Kahrmann, and Sarah Sutro for their patient readings, discussions, questions and suggestions. It is a hard thing to point someone back to the path when you don't know where he's going. You have managed that, each in your own way, with grace and wisdom.

To the hundreds of Facebook users and group members who have provided generous feedback, encouragement, insight, knowledge and expertise. My journey would be lonelier and less fruitful without ART-SPEAK: Artists Networking in the Berkshires and Beyond, Belinda Subraman's Gypsy Art Show, Indie Writers Unite!, the Insterstitial Arts Foundation, Fantasy & Science Fiction Writers in America, Fantasy Writers, the Speculative Fiction Cooperative, Writers' Asylum, and Writers' Feedback Cafe, to name only a few.

To Al Siebert and Learning Strategies Corporation for providing an intriguing new understanding of the mind and of the nature of psychiatric diagnosis.

To Harvey Lacey for his big, innovative heart and the development of Ubuntu Blox.

And not least to Jay and Annie at Blue Rock Station, who taught me how to pound sand, sling mud, love goats and repurpose with a passion.

I owe you all a Wall of Gratitude.

## ABOUT THE AUTHOR

An artist and an educator by training and a seeker by inclination, Ien Nivens grew up on the pentecostal plains of Oklahoma and moved to New England at the age of 23. He lives with his wife Michelle and a cat named Barnaby in a renovated textile mill in the Berkshire Mountains of Western Massachusetts, where he works as a web and graphic design consultant for artists, writers and musicians. His reviews of fiction, art, music and performance appear online at berkshirefinearts.com and artslashlife.com.

Mr. Nivens is the author of *The American Book of Changes: The Classic Divination System of the East Reinterpreted and Reinvigorated for the Western Seeker*. He is currently working on a fantasy novel about a disfigured princess and her portraitist. *Tangible Angels* is his first novel.

Connect with Ien on Facebook, Twitter and Goodreads and on his blog at iennivens.com or hang out with him and his writer peeps at specufiction.com. You might also enjoy the digital art available at tangibleangels.com.

www.ingramcontent.com/pod-product-compliance
Lightning Source LLC
Chambersburg PA
CBHW021130260626
47169CB00005B/1535